To Sharon
With love,
Betty Annand

THE LADY FROM
New York

Betty Annand

FriesenPress

Suite 300 - 990 Fort St
Victoria, BC, V8V 3K2
Canada

www.friesenpress.com

ISBN
978-1-5255-4198-8 (Hardcover)
978-1-5255-4199-5 (Paperback)
978-1-5255-4200-8 (eBook)

1. Fiction, Historical

Distributed to the trade by The Ingram Book Company

Dedicated to all those readers gracious enough to ask for more.

"He has never been known to use a word that might send a reader to the dictionary."

> —William Faulkner (about Ernest Hemingway).

Chapter 1

The SS Delaney left England May the 17th, 1861, and arrived in New York ten days later. It was a record time for the vessel, and Bob Nicholson, the captain, was smiling as he began piloting his ship up the East River to her slip. However, when he noticed all the soldiers around the forts, his mood changed. "By heavens, they really are at war," he remarked to his first mate.

After docking, he hurried to say goodbye to two of his passengers, Gladys Matthews and her six-year-old son, Eddy. He knew he would miss their company on the return to England and promised to visit them while he was in port. Gladys and her husband were part owners in a restaurant close to the pier, and because their cook was an old friend of Bob's, he looked forward to the visit even more.

Once they bid the captain goodbye, Gladys and Eddy were eager to get ashore, hoping Angelo would be there to greet them. Gladys was worried that the mail might have been delayed because of the war and Angelo wouldn't be expecting them. They were standing with their bags looking around the pier when she saw a soldier waving and walking toward them. "Oh, please. God, no!" she, silently, cried.

Eddy saw him at the same time, and pointing at the soldier, he said, "Mother, is that Father?" Gladys was so upset she couldn't answer and just nodded her head. Delighted, Eddie ran to Angelo and threw his arms around him.

"Dad, you look just like one of those toy soldiers you bought me for Christmas.

Are you really an honest to goodness soldier?"

"Yes, Eddy, I am a real honest to goodness soldier," Angelo replied, looking at Gladys as he said it. The look conveyed more than his words; it begged for forgiveness and understanding, but Gladys offered neither. Nevertheless, he gave her a quick hug and a peck on the cheek. Then, after hiring a boy with a cart to follow them with their trunks, they walked the short distance to their flat.

Angelo had cleaned the apartment, and there was a vase of flowers sitting on the kitchen table, but Gladys didn't say a word. She busied herself unpacking their clothing while Eddy chatted away to his father about his sisters, Eliza and Dolly, and how he had galloped on the big horse, Ali, while he was in England. When he finally wound down, he wanted to know if his twin cousins, Paulo and Louis, were downstairs in the restaurant. Angelo said he was sure they would be there as soon as they were out of school, and because it was almost that time, he let Eddy go and wait for them.

After he left, Angelo went into the bedroom, took hold of the gown Gladys was about to hang up, laid it back in the trunk, and, gently, sat her down on the bed. Then he sat down beside her.

"I know this is a shock, Gladdy, but I think you'll understand after I tell you what it's been like here lately." Gladys remained silent, so he continued, "Uncle Victor and Lottie have been impossible to work with, and then one day Uncle went too far. You know I wrote and told you that Ike Murphy, Uncle Vic's friend who owns the building attached to ours, had joined the army. And you remember how Uncle and I planned to buy his building as soon as we could afford to?"

Gladys just kept her eyes straight ahead and didn't answer. "Well, I happened to overhear Uncle telling a customer that, because Ike has no living relatives, he made out a will leaving the building to him. I was as mad as hell, and when I asked him why he didn't tell me about it instead of the customer, he made up some stupid excuse. Then he said that he prayed nothing would happen to Ike, but if it did, he didn't know if he would renovate the building, or sell it.

"I asked him about our plans to buy the building, so we could expand. Then I reminded him that was why we had been working so hard and why I couldn't go to England with you. All he had to say to that was that he and Lottie were sick to death of working night and day while you were off enjoying yourself in England. I couldn't believe it!

"I told him that I had been working every bit as hard as they had, but he just shrugged his shoulders. That's when I lost my temper and almost struck him, but I didn't. Instead, I said he could keep the goddamn restaurant and without stopping to think, I went and joined the army. I know, I should have waited and talked it over with you, Glad, but I was so damned angry, I didn't realize what I was doing.

"When Uncle Victor found out what I had done, he realized that he had driven me to it, and apologized. He and Lottie are constantly arguing, and I think he's almost ready to join the army, too. Lottie is driving him mad. One day, she's her normal self, and the next day she's like a screaming fish wife—throwing things and cursing. Even Sandy threatened to quit. I persuaded him to stay, but I think he's having second thoughts. I wouldn't be surprised if he joins up, too, and I don't think the restaurant could survive without him there to do the cooking.

"I am so sorry, love. I wouldn't blame you if you turned around and went right back to England, but I hope to God you don't. I need you now more than ever. Please, Gladys, forgive me."

A sensation of numbness had enveloped Gladys' entire body when she saw Angelo in uniform. It had given her such a shock that her mind shut down. She sat beside him in such a stupor that he may as well have been talking to the wall. When he put his arm around her and asked for forgiveness, she didn't even realize she had nodded her head.

Angelo said that Sandy was cooking a special welcome-home dinner for her and Eddy, so she followed him docilely downstairs without changing her clothes. If she noticed the change in the restaurant, she didn't say. Angelo sat her at one of the tables in what used to be the storeroom but was now part of the restaurant. Then he left to tell Sandy they were there. Sandy, a little hurt that Gladys hadn't come into the kitchen to say hello, came out to see her.

"Ah, Gladys, my girl, thank goodness you're back," he said, while bending down to kiss her cheek. Those were almost the exact words that her friend Percy had used when she arrived at Four Oaks just over two months ago, and it brought back memories of her daughter, Dolly, as she lay in bed almost dead with fever. She had been needed then, and Sandy's words, telling her that she was needed now, brought her back to her senses.

"It's good to see you, too, Sandy. How is everything in the kitchen?"

"Don't you worry about the kitchen today, my dear; we'll talk tomorrow. Now, I have a nice leg of mutton cooked just the way you like it. I'm just happy you're here," he said again before patting her on the shoulder and returning to the kitchen.

Gladys looked at Angelo. "I do not think I shall ever forgive you," she said, but before he could reply, Lottie, followed by Eddy, brought them each a bowl of soup. Without of word of greeting, Lottie put the bowls on the table and turned to leave. Gladys caught her arm and said, "Lottie, I missed you so much. Please don't bother waiting on us."

Lottie looked flustered, her face turned red, and although she wanted to say something, she couldn't. Lifting up her pinafore to hide her face, she ran into the kitchen crying.

"You and Eddy have your dinner, and don't come upstairs until Lottie and I come down," Gladys told Angelo. Then she found Lottie, put her arm around her, and took her upstairs.

Five days later, on June 2, 1861, Angelo, Ike Murphy, and 893 other soldiers of the 79th Highlanders, marched down Broadway to the sound of a pipe band on their way to Washington. The International Restaurant closed its doors, and the entire staff along with Angelo's uncle, Victor, his wife, Lottie, their twin boys, Paulo and Louis, Angelo's grandmother, Isabella, and Lottie's aunt, Theresa, and uncle, Peter Rutten, all stood with Gladys and Eddy, waiting to wave goodbye.

The day was doubly hard for Gladys because it brought back memories of a day sixteen years earlier. That day she had stood on the quay in Dover with her father-in-law as they watched her first husband, Tom Pickwick, his friend, Keith, and the rest of the HM 62nd Foot regiment march past them and onto a ship destined for India. Neither Tom nor his friend, Keith, survived that war, and Gladys had an ominous feeling that Angelo would suffer the same fate. She would never forgive him for joining the army, but she loved him enough to tell him she did.

"Here he comes, Mother! I see him! I see him!" Eddy shouted, as he jumped up and down. Then turning to the other spectators, he pointed to Angelo and added, "Look, that's my dad. He's going off to win the war!"

As Angelo marched past, he managed to glance at them and smile. Gladys smiled back and blew him some kisses, but her heart was breaking.

Not everyone watching the soldiers that day were supportive. In fact, a good percentage of the onlookers were there to discourage the men, as they were against abolishing slavery. Manufacturing cotton was a lucrative business and had made as many as 150 New Yorkers millionaires.

After the last soldier was out of sight, Gladys, and the rest of her group returned to the restaurant and had a quick cup of tea and a bite to eat. Then Lottie's aunt, Theresa, asked Victor if she could leave her husband, Peter, there while she attended a meeting. Peter Rutten had been the victim of a stroke and was in a wheelchair, but he owned the building and restaurant that Victor and Angelo were buying and enjoyed visiting it now and again.

Theresa said, "The volunteer Sanitary Commission is having a meeting to establish activities for local groups, and I intend to join The Women's Central Association of Relief to help provide clothing and other supplies when needed. You can come with me if you like, Isabella," she said to Victor's mother. "Then you'll be able to tell your friends about it. We don't know how long this beastly war is going to last, but I know they'll need as many volunteers as they can find."

Isabella was thrilled to be asked, and Victor said he would be happy to have Peter spend time at the restaurant. "We may even put you to work on the front desk, uncle. I wouldn't be surprised if some of your old customers show up."

The twins went off to school, and Gladys found some light chores to keep Eddy busy. Then she sent a note to his tutor telling him he could begin the following day. They were ready to open the restaurant by lunch time, and Gladys was happy to be working again, hoping it would take her mind off the war.

Lottie's temperament changed for the better after Gladys returned. As soon as Gladys saw her, she knew she was suffering with menopausal symptoms. Many years before, Millie, an elderly seamstress, who had befriended Gladys on her first day in Dover, was suffering with the same thing. Millie made a point of warning Gladys what to expect when she reached a certain age—having no idea that Gladys, having just run away from the slums in London known as Old Nichol, knew more about life than most grown women, even though she was only twelve years old.

Gladys insisted Lottie seek out a treatment to help her through the worse days, but Lottie was afraid any medication would prove to be addictive, so Gladys persuaded her to try a variety of Native American remedies, such as, henbane, sweetgrass, and black cohosh. Lottie found the black cohosh most effective if she took it with a little cannabis. This helped her mood swings, but she still suffered with hot flashes.

Another thing Gladys tried to do was explain to Victor why his wife's personality had changed without sounding too personal. He did his best to understand, and from then on, he showed Lottie more consideration and complained less. One day, while they were having a tea break, Lottie complained to Gladys, "God must know that I always have cold feet. So why didn't he give them hot flashes? No one would notice if they turned red and perspiration ran down between my toes, instead of down my face. It's so embarrassing. Sorry, I shouldn't complain, because things were a lot worse before you had a talk with Victor." Gladys looked surprised. "Don't look so innocent, Gladys, I know you talked to him."

"I'm sorry, Lottie. I had no right interfering."

"Oh, don't apologize. It's just too bad you can't lecture more husbands on the subject."

"That should be a job for our doctors, but I suppose that won't happen in our time. If some men had their way, we would still not be allowed to stay in the same house as them, when we have our menses."

"Yes, I heard about that. I suppose we should be thankful to them for that."

"You are joking, aren't you, Lottie?"

"I don't know. We're a lot better off now than the women were back then, aren't we?"

"If we are, it's because of women like Lucretia Mott and Elizabeth Stanton, not men. Your aunt, Theresa, told me about the Seneca Falls Convention held here in the 1840s, and how those two ladies stood up and said that according to the Declaration of Independence, where it states that men and women were created equal, women should be allowed to have the same legal and social rights as men."

"They also believed women should be allowed to vote, and although we still don't have that privilege, it made a lot of women stop and think. One of these days it is going to happen, mark my words." Gladys picked up her tea cup, and added, "To you, Elizabeth and Lucretia. Oh, yes, and let us not forget Amelia Bloomer, another great lady."

"And what will we be thanking Amelia Bloomer for?"

"Ah, I think she deserves the most gratitude. She, my dear Lottie, not only invented bloomers—I do not know how in heaven's name we ever managed without them—but she proclaimed that tight clothing for women is unhealthy, especially boned corsets."

"Pour me another cup, dearie, that lady deserves a much bigger toast," Lottie exclaimed, laughing.

For over a month, the Highlanders served in the defences of the capitol, and Angelo was allowed to send and receive letters, but because he wasn't allowed to disclose any military news, he mostly wrote about the good friends he had met since joining the army. He said that most of them called him, Matt, because his last name was Matthews. Aware that Angelo had almost fallen out with his uncle Victor over his friend, Ike Murphy, Gladys was surprised that Ike was the friend Angelo talked about the most. It seemed they had a lot in common. Angelo wrote that Ike had survived a life in Ireland even more dreadful than the one he and Gladys had experienced while growing up in Old Nichol. Gladys wrote back and said she found that hard to believe.

Angelo and Ike bunked beside each other, and because they spent their free time together, it wasn't long before they felt they could confide in one another. Angelo was the first person Ike had shared his memories with since arriving in New York. He told Angelo how he watched his parents die of starvation and sickness in Ireland before he, his wife, and their three-year-old daughter, were able to acquire passage to America aboard one of the "coffin" boats.

He explained that the ships were called "coffin boats" because only about two-thirds of the passengers survived the journey. Ike said it took over twenty horrific days to get to America, and the only food they had was what they managed to scrounge to take with them. Because they had set sail in the winter, they were plagued with stormy weather. Angelo asked him what the ship was like, and Ike said he didn't know if he could describe it—not because he couldn't find the words—but because he had tried to wipe the memory from his mind.

Angelo apologized for asking, but Ike kept talking anyway. "We only had one bunk about six feet by six feet, with a little straw for a mattress. We were lucky in that we had a top bunk. Many suffered with seasickness and dysentery, and those poor buggers in the bottom bunks had to put up with puke and shit dripping through the straw and slats above them. Maggie and Katie were so very brave. I know they could have put up with it if they hadn't come down with the ship fever an' died the third week we were at sea."

"Do you mean seasickness?" Angelo asked.

"No, it's a damn sight worse than that. If you get ship fever you get every horrid ailment you can imagine. Your head and all your joints ache and swell up so big they look like they could burst open. You get so sick, you can't even drink water, and then red spots start breaking out all over your body, and when the spots start turning into big, ugly, open sores, you know there's no hope." Ike didn't realize he was crying until Angelo put his hand on his shoulder.

"I am so sorry, Ike, I shouldn't have asked you about it."

"You know what was even worse? It was having them thrown overboard with the others who died. I know I should have watched, but I couldn't. Do you think they'll forgive me?"

"I don't believe it was your wife and daughter the sailors threw overboard, Ike. They left their bodies the second they died, and they're still with you, right here in your heart." Angelo said, as he put his hand on Ike's chest. Having lost his first wife and unborn child at sea, Angelo could understand what Ike had gone through.

Ike was over six feet tall and broad shouldered, but when he landed in New York, he weighed little more than a hundred pounds. Jobs were difficult to find, even if you were in good health, but for someone as weak as Ike, it was almost impossible to find work. He spent six months working for food as wages. He scrubbed pans in a baker's shop, washed dishes in a café, and every night he cleaned blood and fat off the equipment and floor of a butcher's shop. In return, they supplied him with meals. A friendly blacksmith allowed him to sleep in his barn for the few hours he wasn't working, and, eventually, he gained back his strength.

"For all that time I'd walk by that bar on the corner of Pearl and Fulton smelling the beer fumes, and never having the price of a drink," he said. "Once I'd had my fill of food, all I could think of was a big tankard of ale, but jobs were still as scarce as angels, and that's when I got mixed up with that bunch of crooks at Tammany Hall.

"They were always looking for big dumb men like me to do their dirty work, and since I didn't have anyone, including me own self, who cared whether I lived or died, I would tackle any job they gave me.

"I'm not proud of it now, but I was pretty bad, and I even learned to handle a deck o' cards, if you know what I mean. That's how come I got that building next to yours. I won it in a poker game.

"The fellow that lost it to me isn't around anymore, and even if he was, I'd not give it back. He was a bad one, and I don't feel any guilt in cheating him. Then one day I overheard my boss laughing when one of his friends was bragging about what he did to a young girl.

"You know, Angie, as I stood and watched them, I saw Maggie standing there looking at me just as clear as I see you now. I felt so ashamed, I cried out loud, 'I'm so sorry, Maggie.' Those two buggers looked at me as though I was crazy, and Maggie disappeared as quickly as she had come, but I knew what she wanted me to do. First, I knocked that blighter on the ground, then I told my boss I was quitting and that I would do the same to him if he tried to stop me. I thought about selling the building to you and your uncle and heading out west, but the more I thought about it, the more I knew Maggie would have wanted me to stay and fight for what she believed in, so I joined the army and here I am."

Angelo told Ike that he, too, had slept in a barn from the time he was five until he was in his teens, but he didn't mention that he was with his parents when they died a horrible death of starvation and other sicknesses. He told Ike how he and Gladys were both raised in one of the worst slum districts in London's East End. "So it seems we have a lot in common, doesn't it?"

Ike smiled and replied, "Well, at least we won't be grumbling about the grub like some of these poor lads who've never known what it's like to go hungry."

Chapter 2

After she received the first two letters from Angelo, Gladys began to worry less, thinking he would probably remain in Washington as a guard for the duration of the war. Although she and Eddy missed him, they didn't have time to dwell on it. The restaurant was so close to the docks that many of their customers were sailors, and now that the war had begun, there were soldiers, too. Before long, they needed more waiters, dishwashers, and cooks.

Sandy was a top-rate cook, earning the restaurant an excellent reputation. However, one cook, no matter how efficient, could not keep up with the influx of hungry customers. Fortunately, Sandy was acquainted with most of the cooks on the ships that docked in New York, and that is how he found Shorty, a young man who had worked as an apprentice cook aboard a ship for two years. Shorty was happy to find a job ashore, because his fiancée told him that she wouldn't wait for him if he went to sea again. Although Shorty's culinary skills were improving, he wasn't capable of cooking for a crowd on his own, so both he and Sandy had to work seven days a week.

Shorty's fiancée wasn't any happier with that arrangement than she had been when he was away at sea, so when he threatened to quit, Victor put a notice in the window saying they were looking for two more cooks with experience. They had quite a few applicants, but most had never even boiled water. Four were familiar with a frying pan and a kettle and Sandy gave them a chance. It only took a few hours to tell they weren't efficient or hygienic enough to fill the job.

One day, Victor was at the front desk checking over some reservations when a well-dressed man, carrying an umbrella and a carpet bag, entered. He was bent over laying his bag down when Victor looked up from his ledger. By the expensive clothing the gentleman wore, Victor took him for a well-to-do Englishman who had just arrived in town. "How do you do, sir; might I help you?" Victor asked.

The gentleman looked up, and said, "I certainly hope so."

Victor was shocked to see that the gentleman was Chinese. He wore a stylish moustache, and when he took off his top hat, it was obvious that his hair had been styled by a European barber. There were only about two hundred Chinese living in New York, and they looked nothing like this fellow. For a second, Victor didn't realize he had been staring instead of listening, and he had to beg his pardon.

"I am here about the advertisement you have in your window," the man repeated.

"What advertisement, sir?"

"There was only one that I could see."

"The one about two cooks?"

"Right you are. The one about two cooks. Although, as you might have noticed, I am quite alone," the man answered, with more than a hint of exasperation.

Victor could hardly believe his ears. "You mean you are applying for the job?"

"Yes, my good man, I am applying for the job. Do you have any ethnic objections?"

"No, no, not a bit, but it's my cook that you will have to see. I'll fetch him, if you don't mind waiting for a minute. Have a seat; I won't be long." He didn't say anything to Sandy about the man being Chinese, thinking it would be fun to see Sandy's reaction. Surprisingly, as soon as Sandy saw the fellow, he rushed up to him and grabbed him in a bear hug.

"Damn you, Norm, if you don't look like a right dandy!" Sandy said when he finally let the poor fellow go. "What in hell are you doing here? The last I heard, you owned a fancy restaurant in London. Don't tell me you got up to your old tricks and gambled it all away?"

"That, and a few other things, Sandy, and now here I am looking for a job again."

"Well you have come to the right place. Victor, this is an old friend of mine. Norman O'Rourke, meet my boss, Victor Rossini." The two shook hands, and Sandy went on to explain. "Norman was born in England, and he went to sea when he was just a young lad. When I first met him, he had worked his way up to chief cook aboard one of the ships that came to Dover. In fact, you cooked on quite a few ships from different countries until you bought that restaurant in London, didn't you?"

"That's right. That I did."

"Well, it sounds like we have a new cook," Victor said. "Welcome to our restaurant, Norman. Why don't you get him something to eat and drink, and then show him around, Sandy?"

Sandy took Norman into the kitchen, and after he poured them each a drink of whiskey, he said, "Are you going to stay in New York now, Norm?"

"I think so, Sandy. Are there many Chinese here?"

"Not a great number, but there are a lot of Irishmen. Most live around a district we call Five Points. It's a pretty poor district."

"Ha! Being both Irish and English on my father's side, and having a Chinese mother, I should fit right in."

"What do you have in mind, if you don't mind me asking?"

"I am not at liberty to say at the present, but I hear New York is a good place for a hard-working entrepreneur. Don't look so worried, old boy; I shan't let you down. Now, when do I start?"

"You can start tomorrow, and I'll set up another bed in my apartment that you can use for as long as you like, but we are going to need one more cook to work with you."

"How would it be if you left that up to me? I shall have someone here in a few days—that is, if you think your boss shan't object."

Sandy said he was sure Victor would have no objections and Norman started work the next day. He proved to be as proficient at his job as Sandy, and, true to his word, in three days he had found another cook—a Chinese man who said his name was Sammy. Sammy's English was a little hard to comprehend, but he was so jovial that no one minded.

During the next two months, it was necessary to hire three more dishwashers, two waiters, and two cleaning women. Norman seemed to have no trouble finding reliable help, although he had only been in the country for two months. That meant they now had a total of thirteen employees.

One afternoon, Sandy laughed and said to Victor, "We sure named this restaurant right, boss. You don't have to go any further than our kitchen to find a mixture of people from all different countries. I'm not sure what nationality I can add to the mixture, but there's no doubt this is, indeed, an International establishment."

"That's right. So far, they all get along, and everything seems to be working. Mind you, you don't see them walking home together."

Angelo's last letter home was written on July 12, 1861. He wrote that his regiment had been attached to Sherman's Brigade. The First Battle of Bull Run began on July 21st. Sherman, obeying orders, first sent the 2nd Wisconsin to capture Henry House Hill. They were shot to pieces on both sides and forced to fall back.

The 79th, led by their colonel, James Cameron, was then ordered forward, where they made three charges over the dead and wounded of the 2nd Wisconsin. Unfortunately, in all the smoke of the battle, they mistook the enemy flag for their own. Ready to rally, they stopped firing and were hit with a surprise attack, causing them to retreat. Their Colonel Cameron was killed in the second volley.

They left the plateau and waited behind the brow while other regiments carried on with the fight. They were also unsuccessful. This was Angelo's first encounter with the enemy, and although he had been told that as a soldier you had to kill or be killed, he hadn't fully realized it was true. He was shaking so badly after he killed his first victim that he had trouble hanging onto his rifle. "You'll get used to it, Angie," Ike promised, as he patted him on the back.

"I hope I never do," was Angelo's reply. When they were all driven from the plateau by Confederate reinforcements, the 29th acted as rear guard on their way to Washington. They had taken part in some of the fiercest fighting at First Bull Run and suffered some of the highest Union casualties. With fatalities, wounded, and those captured, the 79th had lost twenty-two percent of its strength.

Gladys' only news of Angelo's whereabouts was what she read in the newspapers. After the First Battle of Bull Run, the names of the wounded and the killed were periodically posted. It was all Gladys could do to make herself read the list, and there were times when she asked Lottie to do it for her, but even then, waiting to see the expression on Lottie's face proved to be just as nerve-racking.

After returning to Washington, Angelo's regiment was put to work building defences around the capitol and digging trenches with picks and shovels. Many of the men found the work so back breaking that on August 14th, 1861, they mutinied along with the 13th and the 14th regiments. They felt cheated when the three-month volunteers were allowed to return to New York while they, the three-year volunteers, were not.

They were equally upset that they were not permitted to leave the army, while their officers were. They also objected when Colonel Isaac Ingalls Stevens was appointed to replace Colonel Cameron; an understandable objection as they should have been allowed to pick their new Commander, as was the usual custom in the military.

Finally, Maj. Gen. McClellan, blaming the officers for allowing the unrest, appointed a regular army officer, giving him orders to mow the mutineers down if they didn't surrender. Ike and Angelo didn't want to mutiny, but they had no choice. Now, as they waited to see if the instigators were going to stand their ground or surrender, they felt as though they were facing another enemy. "What do you think, Angie?" Ike said, for no particular reason.

"I think it's a hell of poor way to get out of the army," Angelo replied.

"Let's get as far back as we can, and when the shooting starts, run like hell for one of those trenches we been digging," Ike suggested as he took Angelo's arm and inched him back.

Luckily, they didn't have to run; the mutineers, whose arms were stacked, realized they couldn't reach them in time to defend themselves. Therefore, not having a choice, they surrendered. Twenty-one were considered ring-leaders and sent to prison, and the 79th regimental colours were taken away and kept in McClellan's headquarters.

When *Harpers Weekly* printed the news of the surrender it reported that twenty-one soldiers were going to prison, Gladys, afraid Angelo might be one of them, thought of nothing else until the names were released.

Angelo was able to write letters once he was back in Washington, but his letters were much shorter, and he never mentioned the war or the mutiny. Gladys could sense the sadness in them. There were some New Yorkers who supported the Union Army but were critical over the mutiny. One day, while waiting on some of the customers, Gladys overheard one fellow say, "Those yellow-bellied mutineers are an embarrassment to our city. I'd shoot the whole lot of 'em, if I had my way." The next time Gladys walked passed him she accidently tripped and spilled a bowl of hot barley soup over his lap.

Dolly wrote often, wanting to know if Gladys and Eddy were out of harm's way. She said she wished they would come back to England and stay until the war was over. James wrote, saying he agreed with Dolly, but he knew she wouldn't leave until Angelo came home. Another person who often wrote to Gladys was Mary Baker, a rich socialite who had been a friend of Gladys when she was mistress of Four Oaks in England. Mary wrote and wanted to know when Gladys could send her some more American souvenirs and other craft items.

Gladys had taken some novelty items back to England the last time she visited there, and her English friends were very taken with them. She had also brought home a lot of items in return: beautiful Sandwich glassware, hand-knit articles, and pretty little ornamental tins she had filled with English tea. She put all the items in a display case, set up in the front of the restaurant, and everything had sold within a month. By chance, Gladys had begun her very own import/export business.

Norman, who always had an eye out for a business opportunity, was very impressed. He was already reaping in percentages with his business of finding employment for the needy. He hadn't wasted any time becoming acquainted with the poor folks who lived at Five Points, along with other needy folks in the city. After approaching Victor, and offering to find more reliable workers, he had no trouble finding good help. At first, Victor was a little suspicious when he learned that Norman insisted on handling their finances, but they were all so happy with the arrangement, he thought he better not interfere.

When Sandy heard that Norman had also found jobs in the city for other unfortunates, he knew they must have signed contracts allowing his friend a portion of their wages. This bothered him, and one day he confronted his friend, "So this is the plan you couldn't talk about. It sounds pretty shady to me."

"I deserve a little something for my services, "Norman relied. "I think I am being quite fair. I look out for these people, Sandy, and I see that their employers are fair with them as well. Besides, old cock, they do not need to hire me, if they choose not to. Don't worry, Sandy, love; so far I have managed to stay on the right side of the law, and I have no intention of crossing over."

"Well, I hope you don't have your clients pedalling that fellow, Ah Ken's, horrible cigars around town. He's got little stands all over the place."

"Good Lord, no! I dare say he shan't be in business for long. But maybe a good cigar stand would be an idea. I shall have to think about it." Sandy laughed and shook his head. Norman had lost his restaurant in London, but he had saved a little money. He didn't say anything to Gladys about it, but the idea of an import/export business intrigued him, and he thought Gladys would make an excellent partner in the future.

Now that the restaurant had four cooks, they could each work in shifts and have more free time. Victor, Lottie, and Gladys had seldom taken a day off, but because they had hired more help, they didn't have to work such long hours either, and the atmosphere in the restaurant was far less tense.

Gladys could tell Eddy was missing his father. Before Eddy and Gladys went to England, Angelo had begun playing baseball with him in the alley, and twice he had taken him and his cousins to see his favourite ball team, The Brooklyn Atlantics play against the

Brooklyn Eckfords. Knowing Eddy loved baseball, Gladys was going to take him to a game, but now that Victor had more free time, he offered to take him and the twins. Gladys was surprised when Eddy said he didn't want to go.

Eddy, a very perceptive young lad, could sense how much his mother missed his father, even if she tried not to show it. In fact, he had taken on the job of being the man of the house so seriously that it was getting on Gladys' nerves. He had to know exactly where she was going at all times, and if she wasn't going to the restaurant or to visit his grandmother, he insisted on keeping her company.

"Honestly, he is driving me bonkers, Lottie, but I don't want to hurt his feelings. Besides, I know there are other things he would rather be doing," Gladys complained.

Lottie didn't reply, but, the next time she was alone with Eddy, she confronted him, "Eddy, do you remember how difficult it was when you first came here, and your mother treated you like a baby? Remember, she wouldn't let you out of her sight?"

"Sure, but I was just little then."

"That's right, and now that you are older she sometimes allows you go out and play by yourself, doesn't she?" Eddy nodded, then, after looking pensive for a second, he guessed what his aunt was about to say. "Well, I know you are trying to take your father's place, and you are doing a splendid job, but maybe your mother wants to go and play by herself. You see shopping and visiting are grownups' way of playing. Do you understand what I mean?" Eddy said he understood, but he wondered why grown-ups had to use so many words every time they wanted to tell you something.

Chapter 3

For the next eleven months, the 79th took part in many skirmishes. Angelo seldom had a chance to write home, and when he did, his letters were brief. Nevertheless, it was still a relief for Gladys to receive them. The only letter he sent that had any news was one where he mentioned that the regiment had acquired three pets: two dogs and an alligator. He didn't say how they managed to get the alligator, but he did say that one of the dogs was called "Tip" and he only had three legs.

Most of Gladys' letters to Angelo were delivered infrequently and in bundles, but he didn't mind. She only wrote positive news about different humorous happenings at the restaurant. Because he shared the letters with Ike, they spent their free time talking about them, and it provided a respite from the battlefield. As time went on, Angelo realized it was going to take a lot longer to win the war than he had thought, so he began urging Gladys to take Eddy and stay in England until he returned. But she had no intention of leaving until he was safely home.

The newspapers were doing a fairly good job of keeping track of the fighting, and the 29th was reported as being one of the outstanding regiments taking part. In January 1862, they took part in the expedition to Port Royal Ferry, and in April, Gladys read they had become part of the 2nd Brigade of the 2nd Division of the Department of the South. Then, in May they saw action at Pocotaligo, South Carolina.

Gladys purchased a map, and she and Eddy marked all the places Angelo's regiment went, which made them feel a little more like they were with him. In June, the 29th regiment was part of the expedition to James Island and the battle of Secessionville—a battle so foolhardy and bloody that Angelo prayed Gladys wouldn't read about it in the newspapers.

The area was surrounded by a swamp and defended by rifle pits. The first attack was made by the 8th Michigan. The two regiments shared a mutual respect and had often traded hats and played pranks on each other. In fact, they were often referred to as the "Highlanders" and the "Michilanders."

The 8th Michigan's assault was cut down by murderous fire before they reached the enemy line, and the 79th fared no better when they advanced to support them. Trapped, without reinforcements, the Highlanders were forced to retreat across open ground. They lost 110 men out of the 474 engaged, but their bravery was recognized by the newspaper, *The Confederate Charleston Mercury*, which stated, "Thank God Lincoln had only one 79th regiment." Brigadier General Benham, the man who ordered the assault, was relieved of command, arrested for disobedience of orders, and his appointment revoked by Lincoln.

In the middle of July, the regiment arrived in Newport News, Virginia, to become part of the 9th Army Corps, Army of the Potomac. In August 1862, one year after Colonel Cameron's death at Bull Run, the 29th regiment was sent back to fight on the same battlefield in North Virginia, in Pope's Campaign. Unfortunately, once more it proved to be a failure. Then on September 1, 1862, when they were nearing the crossroads of the Warrenton and Little

River turnpikes, the Union forces collided with Stonewall Jackson's men, who were formed in a line in front of Ox Hill facing southeast near Chantilly Mansion.

In the ensuing battle, Cameron's successor, Brig. Gen. Stevens, led his regiment for one last time. He organized the 79th into three lines and led them into attack. As they advanced over the blood-soaked battlefield, Stevens ran past the body of his own son, who lay critically wounded. Stevens was later shot through the head after he had taken the flag from the hand of the sixth colour bearer to fall. He died amid the cheers of victory, with the colour staff gripped firmly in his hand.

The 79th's primary opposing regiment during that battle was the 6th Louisiana Volunteer Infantry of the famed Louisiana Tigers led by Irish-born Major William Monaghan. It was the most thoroughly Irish of all the Tiger regiments. The battle took place mostly during a thunderstorm and devolved into hand-to-hand combat. Angelo and Ike fought side by side, and when it was over, they had to step over bodies of both Union and Confederate soldiers to get back to camp.

Angelo hadn't gone far when one of the bodies he was stepping over called out, "Help me, please, help me." Angelo could see that the man's legs were in bad shape, so he called out, "Ike, over here." They both called for a stretcher, but none were in sight, and they could see that the poor fellow wouldn't live long if he didn't get to a doctor quickly. He was a large man, and the only way they could move him, was for each of them to put an arm under his armpits and drag him.

As soon as they moved him, he cried out in pain then, mercifully, passed out. They had him just about off the battlefield when one of the wounded enemy soldiers managed to fire his gun one last time. "Jesus, the bastard got me," Angelo cried, but he kept on walking. They made it back to camp before he fainted. A surgeon saved the soldier's life, but in doing so, he had to amputate both of his legs.

As for Angelo, he was hit just below his elbow on his right arm. When he regained consciousness, his arm was bandaged and in a sling, so he figured the surgeon had removed the bullet. Later, when someone asked Ike how he felt fighting against his own countrymen, he replied, "They could have been women and I wouldn't have noticed. I was fighting the uniform, not the person."

The 29th Highlanders sustained heavy losses in that battle, with 17 missing, nine killed and 79 wounded. Angelo had been heavily sedated, and as he lay recovering on a cot, he wasn't sure if he had imagined it or if it had really happened, but he remembered General Sherman bending over him and asking him how he was. When none of the other wounded men in the field hospital mentioned seeing the general, he decided it must have been a dream. Later he was told that the general said he had never seen regular troops that equalled the Highlanders in soldierly bearing and appearance.

Up until a month before Angelo was shot, there were no military ambulances. They were all privately owned—commandeered by the army and driven by civilians. Then Jonathan Letterman organized an ambulance corps under the leadership of General McClellan, and from then on, only the ambulance corps was allowed to pick up the wounded from the battlefield. Angelo and Ike knew this, but they also knew that the man they dragged off the battlefield would not have survived if they had left him to wait for an ambulance, thus they hoped no one saw them in the act.

Ike was more upset than Angelo over his injury, and as soon as he was able to, he went to visit him. Angelo was up and wearing his trousers when Ike found him. He had his arm in a sling and didn't look to be in much pain. "You don't look bad at all, Angie. You'll do anything to get back to that pretty colleen, won't you?"

"Don't you worry, partner, I'm not about to leave you to fight the war on your own. Somebody's got to look after you. This little scratch will be healed in a day or two, and I'll be able to hold my gun again, but I wish they hadn't wrapped it so tightly; I can't even feel or move my fingers."

"Do you want me to write to Gladys for you?"

"No, I should be able to do it myself by tomorrow. I think the doc will be in later today and I'll get him to loosen the bandage."

"How is that fellow we brought in doing?"

"I went to see him yesterday. His name is Otto Goebel and he's from New York, too. The poor bugger has lost both his legs, and yet all he can think of is how lucky he is. I think he knows that he's not got long to live, but he's determined to get home and see his wife and kids before he dies. He thanked me and said to thank you, too. He said he wouldn't be alive if we hadn't found him. I think he must have injured his head, too, because he thinks we deserve a medal!"

"I hope you told him that if he says anything like that to the doctor, we'll more than likely get thrown out of the army, or maybe even get a bullet through our heads instead of a medal on our chests."

"I explained that to him, and I'm sure he won't say anything. As soon as he's well enough, they're going to send him home."

"I hope for his sake that's soon! This stinking place would kill anyone if they had to stay here very long."

"I know. It's worse than Old Nichol. The food's pretty bad, and Gladys would have a fit if she saw how filthy the bedding and the men are, but everyone's doing the best they can."

They talked for a few minutes more, than Ike said, "Well, I have to go, but I'll be back as soon as I can."

"Don't go fighting the war without me now, you hear?"

Ike was on his way out of the tent when the surgeon who operated on Otto came in. While half awake, Otto had unknowingly told him about Ike and Angelo saving his life. The surgeon stopped Ike and said, "Are you one of the soldiers who brought Otto here?" Ike didn't know what to say, and when he hesitated, the doctor spoke up and said, "Don't worry, I'm not about to report you, you see I need a strong man, or two, to work with me; someone who can lift a man or hold him down when needed. I also need someone who shows empathy for the wounded. I have the authority to choose the men I want, so what do you say?"

"It would be an honour, sir, and I'd like to recommend my buddy, Angie, there," he pointed over to Angelo. "It was him that found Otto and got me to help drag him to safety. He got shot doing it."

"Just the sort of soldier I want. You tell him to come and see me as soon as his arm has healed. My name is Doctor Aldridge. Now, you come along with me and I'll give you a paper to take to your sergeant."

Before he left, Ike came back to tell Angelo what happened. He was excited about it and said, "He wants me to start tomorrow, Angie, and he wants you, too, as soon as your arm is healed." Angelo said he would do it, but after listening to the orderlies talk about all the workers who had become infected with diseases after working on the wounded, he knew the job would be almost as dangerous as being on the battlefield.

Food was scarce at the front, and what little there was, wasn't fit to eat. There were no fruits or fresh vegetables, and with the lack of vitamin C, many suffered with scurvy. The only time things improved was when Carla Barton, a very kind lady the soldiers called the "Angel of the Battlefield" came to distribute supplies that she collected.

Ike managed to return to report to Dr. Aldridge two days later, but he was working in one of the other field hospitals and wasn't able to visit Angelo for a week, then when he did, he was struck speechless.

"The buggers cut it off!" Angelo cried, as soon as he saw Ike, and tears rolled down his cheeks.

"Oh God, I am so sorry Angie, so very sorry," Ike said, as he sat down beside his cot, took hold of his left hand in both of his and held it. "Well, at least you're still alive, and you still have one good arm and both your legs, which is better than Otto and a lot of the other poor soldiers I've seen this past week. You'll be going home now, so I won't be able to be with you, but as soon as I get out of this army, I'll be there for you. I've got quite a bit of money saved, and I own that building next to yours and a house. Whatever I have is half yours, so you don't need to worry about finances."

Angelo pulled his hand away and snapped back. "I don't want your God damned charity. If I can't earn a living on my own, I'll send Gladys back to England and jump in the bloody ocean."

"Okay, okay, cool down. If that's how you feel, forget it. I'm sorry." Ike couldn't hide his disappointment as he confessed, "I guess I was mistaken. Just because I thought we had become as close as family doesn't mean you felt the same. I miss my family and I guess I wanted to try to replace them with yours, but if you'd rather I mind my own business, I understand." He got up and started to leave, but Angelo called him back.

"Sorry, Ike, it's just that I feel like I'm half the man I used to be, and I guess I took my anger out on you. I think of you as more of a brother than a friend. I've never had a brother, but I always wanted one. Too bad he has to be a dumb Irishman, though," he added, trying to sound less cranky. "But if you insist on being my brother, you may have to put up with me crying on your shoulder every now and again."

"I'll always be there for you, Angie. I've got some ideas I want you and your uncle to hear when we get back home, but we'll talk about that later." Angelo nodded, then he asked Ike how he liked his new job. "At times it's horrible, but at other times it's rewarding. I don't know how the doc keeps going. He only gets about two hours sleep every night. There are more of us assistants than doctors, so thank God we don't have to work such long hours. Anyway, I'm going to write a letter to your uncle and send it home with you, so I'd better go and do it." Ike only managed to visit one more time before Angelo was sent home.

When Gladys saw Angelo's name on the list of the wounded, she felt like someone hit her in the stomach with a club. There was no mention of how severely any of the soldiers were injured, and she knew that he could be dying, or already dead. As soon as she was able to function, she went directly to Army Headquarters and asked for the whereabouts of her husband. The officer in charge was sympathetic but didn't know much more than she did.

By the time she got back to the restaurant, she had made up her mind what she was going to do. "I'm sorry, Lottie, but I cannot sit by and wait while Angelo might be dying. I have to find him. I know it means leaving you with extra work, but I have to go. The sergeant told me that he might still be in a field hospital, or in Washington. I'm not going to wait around to find out. I am going to Washington."

"Don't you worry, Glad, you just go, and Eddy can stay with us."

"Oh, my heavens! Eddy! I have to tell Eddy."

"Are you sure? Maybe you should leave it until you get back."

"No, knowing Eddy; he would want to know, and I think he should, too, just in case—" Gladys' voice broke with the last few words and Lottie hugged her.

"Well, whatever you think is best. Do you want Victor or me to go with you?"

"Thanks, Lottie, but you are both needed here. Besides, I shall probably need your help when we get back. You know when Eddy and I returned from England, and I saw Angelo standing on the pier in that uniform, I was convinced I would lose him, just like I lost my first husband, Tom. I even talked myself into believing that if he was killed it wouldn't be as devastating, because I had gone through it once before. Now I realize how wrong I was. I don't think I shall be able to cope if Angelo doesn't survive"

Because she had heard there were Confederate sympathizers called "guerrillas" who had derailed some Union trains, Gladys decided not to take Eddy with her, but he was as determined to see Angelo as she was and cried so hard that she changed her mind. She warned him that his father's injuries might be fatal in order to prepare him for the worst. Unable to talk about it, Eddy showed he understood by squeezing her hand.

Fortunately, they were allowed to take a troop train, or they would have had to wait two more days for a passenger coach. Because his father had already fought the enemy, a feeling of pride crept over Eddy once he was seated in the car amid all the soldiers. The train they were on had just returned from Washington with a group of soldiers, and as they got off on the left side of the train, Gladys, Eddy, and more soldiers boarded on the right side. The conductor found them a seat and said they would be leaving shortly.

Eddy was sitting by the window, and all of a sudden, he realized that most of the soldiers who had just left the train were wounded and were accompanied by medical personal who wore red crosses on their sleeves. Watching them made him feel sad, and he was just about to turn to his mother and suggest they move to the other side of the train, when he caught sight of Angelo. "Dad!" he shouted.

"Where, Eddy? Where is he?" Gladys jumped up and looked out the window.

"He's right there beside that man on the second stretcher nearest to us. Do you see him, Mother? Come on, we have to get off." By this time all the soldiers were looking out the window.

"What's the trouble here, mum?" the conductor asked.

"We have to get off. One of those soldiers is my husband. He's not dead; he's walking; oh quick, please help us get off the train," Gladys cried.

One of the soldiers spoke up and said, "Which one is he? I'll jump off and hold him there, while you and the lad collect your belongings.

Gladys pointed in Angelo's direction and said, "He's that man standing by the second stretcher." Just then, Angelo turned around, and her voice dropped as she added, "He's that man, the one with one arm!" She looked down at Eddy at the same time he looked up at her. They didn't need words to convey how their hearts went out to the man they both loved with all their hearts.

When Angelo discovered he was being sent home on the same train as Otto, he sat beside him for the whole trip and helped look after him. Otto's operations hadn't been as successful as the surgeon would have liked, and he knew he might be coming home to spend his last days in the New York Hospital where his wife and their five children could visit him every day.

Except for the times when the pain was unbearable, Otto was amazingly sanguine and his optimism lessened Angelo's depression. For a time, Angelo had dreaded coming home, and felt so sorry for himself that he even contemplated suicide. Then Otto convinced him that things could always be worse. "You know, Angelo, I could have died out there on the battlefield like my friend Gus and all those other poor souls. Then I would never have gotten to see my wife and kiddies again. I'm damn lucky, you know that?"

Other times, after the medics had given him a dose of morphine, Otto would grin and say, "We are sure lucky, Angelo; there was a time they didn't have drugs like this and then you bloody well had to put up with the pain. How's that for luck, hey?" The fact that Otto had laid out on the battlefield in the rain for two days before Angelo heard him cry out, didn't seem to embitter him in the least.

The ambulances arrived to take the casualties to the hospital, and Angelo was telling Otto he would be going with him, because he had to check in with the doctors there, too, when suddenly he heard Eddy call, "Dad!" As much as Angelo longed to see Gladys and Eddy, he had been so worried about their reaction when they saw he had lost his right arm, that he hadn't look forward to the reunion, but now when he saw them coming toward him, he almost forgot he was handicapped.

"You've come home!" Gladys cried.

"Yes, I've come home, at least most of me has."

"Did you win the war, Dad?"

"I did my best, son."

Gladys was disappointed that Angelo didn't kiss her hello, but when she kissed his cheek she could feel the bones in his face against her lips and realized that he had lost a lot of weight and needed nourishment and rest. She suggested they take a cab home as soon as possible, but he explained that he had to go to the hospital with the other men to be checked over by a doctor. "I don't know how long I will have to stay there, Gladys, but I was told we had to see the doc before we could have visitors.

"You shouldn't be with me now. Any of us could be contaminated. There were all sorts of diseases going around in the field hospitals." As he was talking, he could see his sergeant coming toward them and the man didn't look pleased. "You had better leave right now or I will be in trouble. No, don't hug me, just go. If I don't come home tonight, come to the hospital tomorrow, New York Hospital," Angelo said as he turned and walked over to Otto.

Eddy was about to run after him, but Gladys, having noticed the sergeant as well, curtailed him and explained what was happening. It was heart-breaking for them to walk away, but she and Eddy were forced to return home alone while Angelo went with Otto in the ambulance.

Chapter 4

Everyone at the restaurant was disappointed when Gladys and Eddy returned without Angelo. When they learned that he had lost most of his arm, they were shocked. Victor did his best to assure Gladys that the army was supplying veterans with some wonderful new artificial limbs, and he was certain Angelo would be fitted with an arm.

It took two days before the doctors at the hospital managed to isolate all the wounded who might have been a threat to the public. Gladys and Eddy were waiting at the entrance on the day they opened the doors to the soldiers' wards. They went through two wards looking for Angelo—wards filled with sights that shocked and sickened them both. Most of the patients were missing limbs, but the ones with the facial wounds were the most pitiful.

Some looked to be teenaged boys who would be disfigured for the rest of their lives. Gladys couldn't help but recall some of the words to the song poor Quasimodo sang to Esmeralda, the gypsy in *The Hunchback of Notre-Dame*—a book written by Victor Hugo and given to her by her first husband, Tom Pickwick, before he left for Italy. It was the first book Gladys ever owned, and she had memorized every word. Now the first words of Quasimodo's song seemed that much more poignant, *Oh, look not on the face, young maid, look on the heart.*

Gladys couldn't help but think that the ones who had lost their sight along with their injuries might be the most fortunate. They would never have to see the shock on the faces of their loved ones. A lot of the men were moaning, and when one soldier cried out for his mother, Gladys couldn't ignore him. She knew Angelo would be waiting, but she told Eddy that she would only stay with the boy for a second. Eddy nodded his assent and even stood beside her as she took hold of the boy's hand.

His head was totally wrapped in bandages except for slits for his nose and mouth, so when Gladys took his hand and talked to him, he must have thought she was his mother because he heaved a sigh of relief. However, when she went to leave, he cried out in anguish once more, and she felt compelled to promise to come back the following day.

When they found Angelo, he was dressed in his uniform, with his right sleeve pinned up, and standing beside another patient's bed. "Here they are now, Otto," he said as he held out his hand. He gave Gladys a quick hug, then reached down and picked up Eddy with his left arm, saying, "And how's my boy? You know what? I'm going home with you today." Both Gladys and Eddy clapped their hands.

"First, I want you to meet a friend of mine. Gladys and Eddy, this is Otto Goebel. Otto, this is my wife, Gladys, and my son, Eddy." Gladys was immediately attracted to the man. He was dark and hairy. The hair on his head, although receding, was course and curly, and he had a dark complexion. His eyes had a twinkle causing Gladys to see a likeness to her own father—that is, before her father succumbed to alcohol. She could even picture Otto, like her da, swinging a woman off her feet to the lively tune of an Irish jig. Then she noticed that Otto hadn't any legs.

Otto saw the look of shock on her face but didn't let on. "You are even prettier than this man of yours said you were. And you, my boy, are the picture of your father. I've looked forward to meeting both of you," he said, offering his hand. His handshake didn't disappoint Gladys. He had a strong and sincere grip, and she meant it when she said she was happy to meet him, too. Then Otto told them about his wife, Iris, and their five children.

"Our two oldest boys, Robert and Rudy, are twins, and I'm afraid they will be off to join the army before long." Then, without a hint of self-pity, he laughed and added, "Though, maybe when they see me, they'll change their minds." Gladys didn't know what to say, so she changed the subject and said that she looked forward to meeting them and that she and Angelo would come back and see him soon.

Just before they took their leave, Otto reached for Gladys' hand, and said, "This man of yours has been a godsend to me." Then looking at Eddy, he added, "He's a hero, you know. You should be very proud of your father, Eddy. I wouldn't be here if he, and that Irish buddy of his, hadn't dragged me off the battlefield. That's why he got hit, you know."

"That's enough of that; you will have them thinking I am something I'm not. Otto here is the real hero, Eddy, but I think we've tired him out. We must be going, but we will be over to see you shortly. Then we will see about getting one of those fancy new wheelchairs, so we can push you down to our restaurant for a good plate of schnitzel, you and your family, too. What do you say, Gladys?"

"Oh, yes, indeed."

Otto didn't think it would happen, but he smiled and said, "Nice meeting you, Eddy. And, Gladys, if you ever need a good hug, come and see me. Now, that's something I can do better that this one-armed cripple of yours." Angelo punched him on his shoulder and laughed. He couldn't explain it if he tried, but Otto's words made him feel less like a cripple than any show of sympathy.

When they arrived at the restaurant, everyone gave Angelo a hero's welcome and they all circled around him and sang *When Johnny Comes Marching Home*, only instead of Johnny, they changed the name to Angelo. Victor was especially happy to learn that his nephew only had to go to the hospital once every two weeks to see the doctor. Although no one mentioned it, they all thought he looked extremely weak and tired.

"I don't know how much I can do here with one arm, Uncle Vic, especially as it's my left arm, but I'm sure I can do something. I'll start work tomorrow, if that is all right," Angelo declared.

"You'll not be starting work until I say you can. Now, come sit down and have a bowl of Sandy's good soup, then you get up those stairs and rest." Victor winked and added, "Perhaps Gladys had better stay down here."

Gladys told Lottie about the wounded soldiers she and Eddie had seen as they were going through the wards looking for Angelo. She also mentioned that one of them had his entire head wrapped in bandages and was crying for his mother. "I suppose it was wrong of me, but I felt so sorry for him that I took hold of his hand. Then when he mistook me for his mother, I didn't have the heart to deny it. In fact, I promised I would go back and see him tomorrow. Do you think I made a mistake?"

"I really have no idea. What is the boy's name?"

"The chart on the end of his cot said Harry McLeod, and he is just eighteen years old."

"Well, I think you should keep your promise."

"I think so, too. I'll go after work tomorrow. Perhaps I'll sing him a song. What do you think?"

"That's a splendid idea, and if the rest of the men enjoy it, perhaps I'll go with you sometime and we can sing together."

"Oh, Lottie, that would be wonderful." Then Gladys told Lottie about Angelo's friend, Otto. "Angelo is going to try to find a wheelchair so he can push him down here for a meal. He has a wife and five children and Angelo invited them all to come." Lottie said they would have to make it into a special occasion and cook a complete German meal.

When Sandy heard about Otto, he made a batch of donuts using a recipe he had been given by one of his German friends, then put them in a basket for Angelo and Gladys to take to the hospital the following evening with the advice that, "If his family don't want them, hand them out to the other patients."

Otto's wife and all five children were with him when Gladys and Angelo arrived the next evening, and the donuts were all gone an hour later. Otto was so happy to have his family with him that it had put colour back in his cheeks, and he appeared well and healthy. Gladys expected Iris Goebel to look like she had envisioned a typical German woman would look: fair skinned and buxom, with blond hair worn braided and twisted into a bun at the back of her head.

She also thought she would have a serious no-nonsense personality, but Iris was nothing like that. Although she was fair-haired and wore her tresses in braids, she had them arranged in a beautiful coronet on the top of her head. She was a petite woman, with an enviable trim and agile figure, especially for someone who had given birth to such a large and robust brood. Although both her and her children's attire were well worn, they were stylish and of good quality. She also had a warm smile and insisted on giving Gladys, Angelo, and Eddy a hug instead of a handshake. Gladys felt as though she had found another good friend.

When she told Iris she was going to visit a young soldier who had his head bandaged and maybe sing him a song, Iris offered to bring her flute the next time she came to the hospital and play while Gladys sang. "Maybe we can entertain all the soldiers one or two nights a week, Gladys. If you give me a list of the songs you sing, I'll see if I know any of them," Iris suggested.

"That would be lovely, and I have a relative who has offered to come and sing as well. I'm really looking forward to hearing you play, Iris. I play the piano, and my friend's uncle has offered to teach me to play the accordion, but I don't know if I shall ever find time." Then Gladys told Iris about the restaurant.

"My boys will be happy to help you anytime you need it. They are good workers, and it would give them a chance to do something for your Angelo for saving their father. Do you have children?"

"Yes, we have a little boy, Edward, who is six and a half, but he seems much older, and I have two daughters, Dolly and Eliza, who are in England."

Gladys thought Iris might ask why the girls weren't with her, but the woman was polite enough not to and instead said, "My Emma, the youngest, is just seven, but Greta is twelve and Friedl is fourteen. They could help, too, if you need someone to clean. All three girls are good workers and good students as well. Greta is determined to be a doctor one day, and I think she will be one, if we can afford to send her to university when the time comes."

"Thank you for the offer, Iris, but I know Angelo doesn't think you owe him a thing. Otto would have done the same for him. If we can use your boys, or the girls, we shall insist they receive payment for their services. You know, I have started a little import/export business and I'm sure the girls could make something that would sell in England. I shall have a talk with a very talented woman I met who does excellent beadwork. Her name is Ruth, and she is an American Indian. She makes lovely jewellery and beaded leather work, and I am certain she would show the girls how to make something they could sell."

Iris said she would appreciate it, then Gladys said she had better visit the young soldier. She told Angelo where he could find her when he was ready to go home, promised Iris she would bring a list of the songs, then said goodbye to the rest of the Goebels, and left.

The soldier named Harry was quiet when she entered the ward, but the man in the next cot said he had been crying most of the day and that the nurse had given him a strong sedative a few hours before.

Gladys sat down beside him and took hold of his hand. He didn't respond, and she leaned closer to hear him breath. The other soldier saw her and said, "Don't worry, he'll know you're there; he told me his mother was coming."

"I'm not his mother. I let him think I was, so he would rest easier. Do you know if they have sent for his real mother?"

"I doubt that, Missus. You see his mother lives in Scotland. He's gonna be upset when he finds out you was lyin', though."

"I didn't mean to hurt him. I was just trying to help. Perhaps if I sing a few Scottish songs he might forgive me."

"We just might all forgive you," one of the soldiers, who had his leg in a sling, replied, grinning.

"I wouldn't want to disturb anyone, though. Perhaps I should have permission from the head nurse."

"If you can find her. Those poor ladies are run off their feet, but we could all use a bit of music to take our minds off our troubles, right fellas?" All the men who were awake agreed, so Gladys began singing Robbie Burn's song, "Sweet Afton." She sang it as softly as she could, and while she was singing, Harry surprised her and squeezed her hand. When she was finished singing, he whispered, "Thank you."

Gladys asked if he would like another song and he nodded his head, so she sang "Bluebells of Scotland." All the men in the ward clapped and clapped then asked for more. She sang a few more, then she noticed Angelo standing by the door listening. She bent over and said, "I have to go now but I shall come back soon, Harry. Is that all right?"

When he nodded, she decided she had to be honest with him, so she confessed that she wasn't his mother. Once more he squeezed her hand then he reached for her face, pulled it close to him, and whispered, "I know, missus. My dear mother, bless her heart, sings like a frog."

The next time Gladys came to see Harry, he had had his bandages removed, and although one side of his face was scared, he was only partially blind in one eye. He had a handsome profile and a good head of red curls, so Gladys assured him he would have no trouble finding a wife when he returned to Scotland. Word had gotten around about Gladys' singing, and soon Lottie and Iris joined her, and they played at the hospital twice a week. Iris taught Gladys and Lottie a few German songs, and they even managed to learn the German lyrics as well. Gladys' favourite was "Abendsegen."

Otto always joined in whenever they sang his old country favourites, such as, "Kein schöner Land" and "Der Mond ist aufgegangen." They also sang Irish, Scottish, English, and Dutch songs, and some soldiers took part by playing their mouth organs or singing along.

Many of the soldiers requested their favourite hymns, and the most popular one was "Amazing Grace," a most fitting hymn as the author, John Newton, had been a slave trader himself before he became an ordained minister and wrote the song. The other most popular hymns were "Rock of Ages," "Faith of our Fathers," and "Oh God our Help in Ages Past"—songs the patients remembered singing when they were children.

Angelo's return home wasn't as fulfilling as Gladys had anticipated. He was always respectful toward her but didn't show any interest in renewing their passion. At first, he seemed happy to be home. He seldom complained and was content having Gladys help him with his personal grooming, but gradually he grew tired of being dependent. Strangely, Eddy seemed to understand his father's need to do things for himself more than Gladys. Whenever his awkwardness resulted in an accident, Gladys would rush to clean it up. Whereas Eddy waited patiently for his father to ask for help, and if he didn't, Eddy let him clean up his own spills.

Eddy even handled Angelo's angry outbursts better than Gladys. There were times when Angelo's struggle to become self-reliant became so frustrating that he would curse whatever he had in his hand and throw it down on the floor or across the room. Knowing Gladys didn't like him using profanity in front of Eddy, he only used words such as, damn and bloody, but they seemed to help.

Angelo had warned Gladys that he suffered with nightmares, but his doctor had told him that it was a common complaint with veterans and would probably stop a few months after he returned to civilian life. Gladys could tell the nightmares were horrific because Angelo dreaded going to bed every night, and until they stopped, she knew he would never be able to relax and be happy.

It had been a year and a half since Gladys and Eddy were in England, and Gladys missed the girls. Lately, Dolly's letters were much shorter, and she had stopped asking when they were coming to England. This worried Gladys because she was afraid Dolly had ceased to care. Gladys hadn't written to tell her about Angelo's injury, how dire the racial problem in New York was becoming, or how much worse it might be if President Lincoln were to bring in the Emancipation Act, because she didn't want to worry her.

"Do you think Dolly might understand why I can't leave if I write and tell her about your injury and how unpredictable the situation is here now?" Gladys asked Angelo one day.

Angelo both surprised and upset her when he replied, "I don't know, but I think you should take Eddy and go to England as soon as you can."

"Don't be silly! I am not leaving you. The next time I go to England, the three of us will be going."

"Gladys, I wish you'd think about it. Things are not that safe here anymore, and I would feel a great deal better if I knew you and Eddy were out of harm's way. At least go for a month or two, perhaps the war will be over by then," Angelo said, but he didn't believe it.

"No, I have thought about it a great deal, and I have decided I am not leaving, so if Dolly and Eliza feel I have let them down, they shall just have to put up with it. When the war is over, your arm has healed, and we have this place paid for, then the three of us shall go back together. I love them both very dearly, but they are safe and well looked after, while we have a job to do here. Now, how are you making out with your writing?"

"Not bad, and I managed to shave this morning with only one cut."

"Angelo, I told you I don't mind shaving you. Why didn't you wait for me?"

"Because I want to do it myself," he replied in a gruff voice.

A few days later on September 22, 1862, President Lincoln issued the preliminary Emancipation Proclamation and warned the southern rebellious states that if they didn't cease their rebellion by Jan 1, 1863, he would issue the final one. Up until then, the war had been to preserve the union, but now the legitimate war aim was freedom of the slaves.

Although the weather in November turned bitterly cold, it did little to cool the tempers of New York's very poor, who were nearly starving to death, and some of the city's very rich, who were afraid their fortunes might dwindle if the Union won the war. Different opinions as to what would happen if Lincoln's warning was ignored were offered around the tables at the restaurant, but as most of their clientele were of the same political persuasion, there were few heated arguments.

As Christmas approached, Gladys did her best, for Eddy's benefit, to appear enthusiastic over the preparations. This would be the second Christmas she would spend away from her girls, and not only did she miss them, but a strong feeling of guilt kept nagging at her. She would have liked to cook her own Christmas dinner and have it alone with just Angelo and Eddy, but as Angelo's moods were unpredictable, and she wanted to assure Eddy have a happy time, she agreed to accept the Ruttens' invitation, knowing that Victor, Lottie, and their twins would be there.

Sandy was invited, too, but he had made many friends since coming to New York and was having Christmas dinner with some of them. Gladys expected Bob Nicholson to come to the restaurant to wish everyone a Merry Christmas and was disappointed when he didn't. She often received compliments on her appearance and had never thought anything of it, but she could tell that Bob thought she was sexually attractive, and she couldn't help being flattered.

Angelo was behaving so coolly toward her lately that she found herself longing for the occasional intimate glance or smile. Not that she had any designs on Bob. Gladys was only in love with Angelo, but having an ardent admirer did a lot for her self-esteem. She was working in the restaurant kitchen with Sandy one morning and asked him if he had seen the captain. Sandy told her that he was just about to deliver a pot of chicken soup to him.

"I just heard that the poor fellow's been down with influenza for the past week and a half, or I would have taken him some sooner."

"Tell him I will try to come to see him in the next couple of days, Sandy. We are going to the Ruttens for Christmas dinner, but we must make sure Bob has a good meal and a gift, too. It may be on Boxing Day, but tell him we haven't deserted him."

It was impossible not to enjoy Christmas at the Ruttens. This year, the Ruttens' son, Mitchell, was home for Christmas, which made it even more exciting for his parents. Lottie had told Gladys that although Mitchell had earned a reputation as a brilliant engineer and had designed bridges in many foreign countries, he had also earned a reputation as a Casanova. It was rumoured that, there were so many irate fathers threatening his life if he ever set foot in their country again, that he was running out of places to work.

Chapter 5

As soon as Gladys met Mitchell, she could tell the rumours were true. He wasn't what she considered handsome. He was four inches short of six feet and quite slim, but when he looked at a woman, his eyes said all the things she longed to hear. He was one of the most charming men Gladys had ever met. Too charming to suit her, and having once worked as a barmaid, Gladys had met quite a few men like Mitchell. Surprisingly, she felt more empathy toward him than dislike, thinking he would probably end up a lonely old man.

Gladys had brought some cosaques, and she placed one beside each plate on the table. No one at the dinner, other than Gladys and Eddy, had ever seen them before, although they had been popular in England for around twelve years. Theresa, quite taken with them, remarked, "They are lovely, Gladys, but what are they?"

"They are cosaques, Aunt Theresa, but nowadays most people call them crackers."

"I've never seen them, but I imagine we must have them in some of our stores. Where did you find these?"

"I found them at a little shop a block from the hospital. These were made by Tom Smith himself. Mr. Smith lives in England and it was he who invented them," Gladys explained. Then she showed them how to make them snap when two people pulled them apart. Inside each cracker was a piece of paper with a fortune written on it along with a little silver ornament. Some of the ornaments were surprisingly suitable for the person who received them. Eddy had a little silver ship inside his, Gladys had a silver thimble, and Peter's contained a little silver accordion.

Some traded theirs for ones they preferred, and it started their Christmas celebration off with lots of chatter and laughter. Christmas dinner was as fine a meal as anyone could wish for, complete with a stuffed turkey, a roast of beef, vegetables, cranberry sauce, and all the extras, including hot mincemeat pie made with tender veal, apples, raisons, and suet.

After dinner, they adjourned to the living room and opened the presents that were piled up under the tree. The Ruttens spoiled them all, giving each of the three boys a game and a sled. The men received leather gloves, and the ladies were given wool scarves. Gladys made pretty nightgowns for all the ladies and knit stockings for the men, and Lottie surprised the other ladies with dainty little framed pen-and-ink sketches she had made. Gladys had had no idea she had such a commendable artistic talent.

There was enough snow on the ground for the boys to go out and use their sleds on a nearby hill, and while they were gone, Gladys played the piano and the adults sang Christmas carols. Peter even played a few songs on his accordion. Although he fumbled over some of the chords, no one let on they noticed. Mitchell sang bass, and it added a great deal to every song. Gladys had to admit she enjoyed his company.

When the boys came in all rosy-cheeked and happy, Lottie said they should be getting home, but they didn't want to leave, so everyone joined in playing a game of charades for another hour. Peter had his coachman take them home with the wagon so they could sing carols on the way. Gladys had missed the girls, but she had to admit, it was a lovely day.

The president kept his word. On January 1, 1863, he issued the final Emancipation Proclamation declaring all slaves within the rebel states must be freed. Although there were many who opposed this action, Angelo and Gladys never saw any signs of rioting as they went back and forth to the hospital to visit Otto and entertain the wounded soldiers.

Angelo's moods were so upsetting that at times Gladys felt she was living with a stranger. Unfortunately, his bouts of despondency were becoming more and more frequent as time went on. Another thing that worried Gladys, and the rest of the family, was his health. Although he had gained a little weight, his face was still pale, and he had dark circles around his eyes. He kept his arm stub bandaged and wouldn't allow Gladys to go with him into the doctor's office each time he had it dressed, so she usually went with Iris and Lottie into the wards to sing while he saw the doctor and visited with Otto. Later, he would find them, and they would walk home or take a cab if the weather wasn't favourable.

One evening, they were at the hospital and had finished singing, but Angelo hadn't come by to join them. They waited for a few minutes then Iris said, "Otto must be telling Angelo another of his long-winded stories about one of his treks through the Alps. He loves telling about all his adventures, but I fear poor Angelo must be bored. Come along, ladies, shall we go and rescue him?"

They were on their way when Angelo's doctor met them. "Ah, Mrs. Mathews, I was looking for you. Could you come into my office for a minute?" Gladys followed him, and he offered her a seat then sat down across from her. "I'm afraid I shall have to keep your husband here for a time."

"It is nothing serious, is it?" Gladys asked, afraid to hear his reply. As soon as she heard the word gangrene, a feeling of complete defeat overtook her, and she scarcely heard another word as the doctor went on to explain.

"Probably due to a Streptococcal infection . . . dissect the dead tissue . . . inject bromine . . . anaesthesia . . . pack with bromide-soaked dressing . . . Mrs. Matthews—" Gladys realized he was addressing her and she looked up. "Mrs. Matthews, I realize this is a lot for you to take in right now, but I want to assure you that we will do everything we can for him, and we have had a great deal of success with this procedure, so don't give up hope."

"Can I see him now?"

"Yes, I think you can have a short visit, but we start his treatment tomorrow morning, and then he will be in isolation until there is an improvement. Now, my dear, I've heard how you and your friends have brightened up the wards with your lovely songs, but now you must be brave and put on a good face for that husband of yours. If he sees you are upset, it will make it even more difficult for him."

Gladys didn't know if she could do what the doctor asked, but she thanked him and went to find Angelo. She had heard how some nurses, who looked after the patients in isolation, developed ery-sipelas and became very sick, even though they washed their hands in chlorinated soda between changing dressings, so she had an idea how toxic the treatment was going to be. When she found Angelo, she was surprised to see that he was sitting on the bed of another patient, talking as though nothing had changed.

"Oh, hello, Gladys," he greeted her. "Did you see the doctor?" Gladys said she had. Then Angelo wanted to know if Lottie was waiting to walk home with her. When Gladys said she didn't know, he insisted on walking out with her to find out. Lottie was in the waiting room and she suggested they take a cab home. Angelo was going to say goodbye then, but Gladys wanted time alone with him.

"I shall walk back to your room with you, Angelo, and Lottie will wait here for me, won't you, Lottie?" It was clear to Gladys that

Angelo didn't want to discuss his treatment. She knew he was afraid he would break down, but she couldn't let him go through it without telling him how much she loved him, and fearing this might be their last time together, she was not going to walk away without holding him close once more.

The following day, the doctor sent for her and she rushed over to the hospital expecting to find Angelo clinging to life, but when she walked into the doctor's office, he was sitting in a chair, looking no worse than when she left him the night before. The doctor, realizing she was about to collapse with worry, ordered her to sit.

When they were all seated, he began, "This morning we were fortunate to have Dr. Fielding and Dr. Spratt come to visit our hospital. These men are both expert surgeons, so I decided to hold off your treatment, Angelo, until they had a look at your stub. Now I don't know what you will think of this, but both of them thought you would be far better off to have the rest of your arm removed."

Angelo didn't want to lose his stub. He had become accustomed to using it to hold things still while he worked with his left hand. He knew that if he lost the rest of his arm it would cripple him even more. "I thought the treatment you were going to give me would kill the gangrene, doctor," he said.

"It only has about a forty percent chance, Angelo, and if it comes back, it may not be curable. If we remove the arm completely, there is a good chance you won't have any more trouble, and it will certainly eliminate all that pain you've been having."

Gladys had no idea he had been suffering, and she suddenly realized why he had been so short-tempered. She had been so busy working and entertaining other soldiers, she hadn't realized just what he was going through. Now she felt sick with guilt. She could hardly wait until they were alone to tell him how sorry she felt. Angelo interrupted her thoughts. "What do you think, Gladys?" he asked.

"I can't make that decision for you, darling."

"But I want to know how you feel about it. It will mean putting up with a man who is even more of a cripple."

"Angelo, you know I don't care if you have one, or no arms; I just want you with me for the rest of my life."

"Then, doctor, I think we had better get on with it."

Dolly was thoroughly annoyed with her mother. It had been far too long since she had come to see them. Eliza was excited to receive the gifts Gladys sent, but Dolly could tell she seldom thought about her mother. When Dolly asked her if she remembered Gladys and Eddy, Eliza said, "I should say so! Eddy gave me his pony, and she's the lady who sends me presents." Dolly was tempted to write Gladys and tell her, thinking it just might make her realize what she was losing by abandoning them, but she thought it too cruel an act.

A week later, when she received Gladys letters and heard about Angelo losing an arm in the war and how poor his health was, she began to understand a little more of what her mother was coping with. Gladys' letters also explained how heart-wrenching it was to visit the young soldiers whose wounds were so horrific that most of them had little desire to live. Then, as she read how her mother thought that her and Lottie's singing, along with Iris' flute playing, seemed to give them a certain peace and strength to carry on, Dolly recalled how much happiness her mother's voice had always brought to their home. For the first time, she realized that Gladys was needed in New York as much, if not more than, as she was in England.

Once again, she began taking an interest in her mother's life in America.

Not long after, Gladys wrote saying that Angelo had the rest of his arm amputated but was slow in recovering. Dolly talked to James about it and they both began writing letters hoping to persuade Gladys to bring him to Four Oaks to recuperate, feeling that the country air might be far better for him than the city.

James knew Angelo's presence in the house might cause a great deal of unfavourable gossip, seeing as Gladys was his ex-wife, but since he and Percy had renewed their friendship, he cared little about what people thought. Of course, James and Percy were forced to be discreet with their relationship—not because they worried about their reputations, but to avoid going to prison.

When Gladys received James' invitation for Angelo to come to Four Oaks with her and Eddy, she felt relieved and grateful.

However, Angelo would have to wait until his doctor decided it was safe for him to travel. Even though his operation was a success, losing the rest of his arm seemed to be the proverbial straw that robbed him of his purpose and resilience. He wasn't bitter. In fact, Gladys found his attitude a little too placid. He seemed far too content with letting others help him with his menial daily chores. This wouldn't have bothered Gladys so much if she knew he was happy, but she could tell that he wasn't.

What bothered her most was that ever since Angelo returned from the war, he no longer seemed interested in their sexual relationship. He avoided touching her or hugging her, and whenever she hugged him, she could tell he didn't like it. She felt abandoned. She tried her best to be patient, knowing the memories of what he had been through were haunting him. Periodically, he had such severe and dreadful nightmares that he would wake up dripping with sweat and suffering with anxiety attacks. Finally, Gladys talked to Lottie about it, and Lottie told Victor.

They both confronted Gladys one afternoon with an idea they thought might help.

"I hear that your ex-husband, James, has invited Angelo to visit his estate with you and Eddy, Gladys. Is that right?" Victor asked.

"Yes, he has, and I think it might do him some good, but I know he won't want us to go and leave you with all the work again."

"I don't know if Angelo told you, but Ike gave him a letter for me, and I think when Angelo hears what it says, he may feel differently. If you both stay a little after work today, I'll read it to you."

After the restaurant closed, the four of them sat down at one of the tables and Victor read Ike's letter.

Dear Victor:

Find enclosed a new will I have recently made. It states that in the event of my passing, my entire estate is to be equally divided between you and your nephew, Angelo. My friendship with Angelo has grown and I've come to regard both of you as my family. I consider your nephew a hero, and until I return, I trust I can count on you to see he has everything he needs.

If you and Angelo take the enclosed papers to my bank, they will give you both power of attorney and you shall have access to an account of mine. You will find it is a substantial amount, and also there are titles to the building adjoining yours, and a home in Gramercy Park. I have kept a separate, private account for my personal needs.

If you both agree to make me an equal partner in whatever business you have, or plan to have in the future, I will share these assets with you. If you agree, you both should sign the document I have enclosed with my will. I hope this will ease your workload as you will no longer need to worry about money.

Now, I would like you to take whatever you need out of the bank as soon as possible and pay your mortgage.

The padre here at the field hospital is writing this for me and he has seen that the papers I am sending are legal and in order. I pray you will agree to my terms.

Yours Sincerely,

"It is signed, Ike P. Murphy. I'm sorry I haven't read this to you all before now, but I couldn't make up my mind how I felt about it myself."

"My goodness, Vic, how could you keep something as important as this from us?" Lottie said, accusingly.

"I don't know. I suppose I felt a little nervous about it. I mean, we are a family, and as much as I like Ike, I can't help feeling that he might be trying to buy our loyalty. Can you understand what I mean?"

"Yes, I think I can, but it was you, Angelo, who has been with him the most and know him so well. What do you think?" Gladys asked.

Angelo didn't answer for a second, then, he stood up and began telling them Ike's story about coming to New York on the coffin boat. He didn't spare any of the gory details and told them how his wife and daughter had died at sea and were cast overboard. There were tears in his eyes as he talked, and when he finished, he sat down and said nothing more.

All were quiet for a time, then Victor got up, went into the kitchen, and came back with a bottle of wine and four glasses. He poured them each a drink, held up his glass, and said, "Here's to the partnership of Ike Murphy, Angelo Matthews, and Victor Rossini." It was the first time Angelo had smiled since he had the rest of his arm amputated. "Now, my dear nephew, I think it is high time you took this little lady of yours to visit her girls, don't you?" Victor suggested.

Angelo looked at Gladys, "I've been trying to convince her to go for a time now. Isn't that so, Gladys?"

Gladys didn't answer, but the hurt in her eyes when he said her, instead of us, wasn't missed by Lottie and Victor, and Lottie couldn't help but say, "I think you should go with her, Angelo. Gladys has waited almost two years for this, and I don't think you are being fair if you disappoint her now."

Angelo got up, and giving Lottie a scornful look, he snapped, "Well, it is not up to you, Lottie. It has nothing to do with you. This is strictly between Gladys and me. Now, if you don't mind, I am tired and will say good night."

Victor had begun to protest when Gladys put her hand on his arm to silence him, saying, "I think we have a lot to think about and we are all tired, so we shall talk tomorrow. I'll send the twins down, Lottie." She hugged them both and followed Angelo up the stairs.

Gladys was normally a warm and loving wife, but she felt the need to be loved in return. She also believed that if a marriage made a person miserable, it wasn't worth having. That night she decided she had been patient long enough. After Eddy was asleep and they were getting ready for bed, she took her time undressing then stood naked in front of Angelo instead of putting on her nightgown.

Angelo had taken off his shirt and dropped it on the floor. He pulled on his nightshirt before taking off his trousers, which he also dropped on the floor, while all the time keeping his eyes averted so as to not look in her direction before climbing into bed.

"Toughie," she deliberately used his old name, "look at me."

"I am tired, Gladdy. Come to bed." He replied with his eyes closed.

"Damn you, Toughie. Look at me!"

"I'm sorry, Glad, I can't."

Gladys thought of James and Percy, and it hit her like a bolt of lightning. "Oh, my lands! You and Ike. You were more than just good friends!"

"Ike and me? Do you know what you are saying? How could you think such a thing? You know damn well I'm not like that."

"How do I know? You haven't made love to me since you came home from the war. You haven't even touched me like you used to. It's as though you don't love me anymore."

"Gladdy, I love you even more, if possible, than I ever did." Then, he couldn't stop the tears. Gladys held him, and when he was done sobbing, he confessed that he didn't think she could love him now that he wasn't the man he used to be. He also admitted that the reason he hadn't tried to make love to her was because he was afraid he couldn't.

"Well, we shall just have to work on that now, shan't we?" Gladys said as she got into bed without her nightgown.

Angelo apologized to Lottie the next day, then he told Victor that he had thought it over and decided he might take James Hornsby up on his offer. "However, I think we should talk more about Ike's ideas before I make up my mind. He won't be home for over a year yet, and I don't think we should do much until then."

"He wanted us to take out enough money to pay off our debt to uncle Peter though."

"I know he wrote that, but somehow it just doesn't feel right using his money when he's not here. Let's go to the bank on Monday and talk to the bank manager. I think it would help if we had a better idea of how much money he is talking about."

Victor was pleased to see that Angelo was finally taking an interest in their affairs, and he readily agreed. The bank manager, who was well acquainted with Ike, looked through all the papers he had sent along with his will, then he sent them to a lawyer to have the documents signed and witnessed. After that was done, Angelo and Victor went back to the bank.

Ike wasn't exaggerating when he said he had saved a lot of money. "I guess everybody who has had dealings with that bunch of hoodlums at Tammany Hall has this kind of money cashed away," Angelo said, and as much as he liked Ike, he couldn't help but feel a little disappointed.

Victor noticed his look of displeasure and said, "He's no longer the same man, and he's certainly paying for what he did back then. You know, Angelo, I think that's one of the reasons he wants us to use the money. He wants to put it to good use, and he knows we hire a lot of folks who can't find work anywhere else. I think we should honour his wishes and do what he asks. Do you see what I mean?"

"Yes, I think I do, and paying off the mortgage won't put much of a dent in his bank account. Let's have the Ruttens in for a meal and surprise them with a cheque."

Chapter 6

Later that week, after they had closed for the night, Victor, Lottie, the twins, Gladys, Eddy, and Angelo went to see Ike's house in Gramercy Park. They knew, by its prime location, it would have to be a large and decent place, but they were expecting it to be vacant and somewhat neglected, so they were surprised to find that it was one of the fanciest houses on the street and the grounds were immaculate. However, they were surprised to see a light in a window on the third floor.

"Oh, someone must be living here," Gladys exclaimed. "Are you sure Ike has no relatives?"

"Not unless he didn't tell me the truth." Angelo replied. He checked the address again and saw it was the right place. "Well, we're here, so we may as well find out what is going on." They went up to the door, and Angelo made use of the knocker. "I wonder if they will be able to hear this?" he said, looking up at the light.

Before he had time to knock again, a middle-aged black man, wearing an intricate hand-knitted wool sweater over a shirt and tie, opened the door. "Yes, suh? Can I help you?" he asked cautiously.

"I am looking for the home of Ike Murphy," was all Angelo could think of to say.

"Are you his friend, Angie?" Angelo nodded. "Ah been waiting for you to come, Mistah Angie. Mistah Murphy, he left my wife and me to look after this place till he gets back. I got a letter from him a ways back, an' I ast the posts mans to read it to me. Mistah Murphy says you probly wouldn't mind if me and Liza stays in the servants' quarters. You sees, we keeps the yard done nice and the house clean."

"We won't mind at all, Mr.—?"

"I's just Simon, sir."

"Well, how do you do, Simon?" Angelo held out his hand, then introduced everyone. "May we come in?"

"Forgive me, Mistah Angie. Ah'm not used to callers. Come in and make yerself to home. Ah'll show you around if you likes." Angelo said they would like that, and Simon said that first he would run upstairs and let Liza know they had company. When they had completed the tour, Simon's wife had hot drinks and cookies waiting for them in the sitting room. The house proved to be a mansion, with enough crystal chandeliers, gold ornamentations, and rich drapery to render them all speechless.

About half way home on the tram, Victor said, "Wow!" and everyone but Angelo broke out laughing. Ever since they made love, Angelo was more like his old self, but the war had robbed him of his sense of humour.

A week later, Lottie's uncle Peter and aunt Theresa were invited to the restaurant for a special meal. When they finished their repast, Victor rose, held up his glass, and gave a toast to them both, saying how generous they had been to allow him and Angelo to purchase the building with such a minimal down payment. He went on to say more favourable things about them before presenting them with a cheque for the balance of their loan.

Theresa was noticeably impressed, but Peter was more puzzled than pleased. Victor and Angelo explained how their friend Ike had sent papers allotting them each a third of most of his fortune in exchange for an equal partnership in their business. Instead of congratulating them, Peter said he would strongly advise against such a move and warned them, "As the old saying goes, be wary of Greeks bearing gifts. Now I know this friend of yours is not Greek, but neither is he family.

"I've had dealings with the Irish before, and like any nationality, there's good and there is bad, but I've found the Irish to be very temperamental. In my opinion, they are also quite volatile and fond of the drink."

Angelo appreciated everything that Peter Rutten had done for him, but his loyalty to his best friend was too strong to put up with Peter's derogatory remarks. He stood up and declared, "I'm sorry, sir, but I would, and have, trusted Ike O'Rourke with my life. He is a man of his word, and I feel as close to him as I would to a brother, so in my eyes he is family."

"Angelo you are fairly new to this country and yet you have given so much more than many who were born here. I admire you for that, and I take your word that this friend is as honourable as you say, but I would like to make a suggestion, if you will allow me to." Angelo and Victor agreed to listen.

"You say he will be out of the army in just over a year? Well, I would suggest that you leave his money in the bank until he returns." Victor started to object, and Peter stopped him. "Wait, hear me out. Now you have been making double payments since you took over the place and I know how difficult that has been for you all. I am sure you know that your aunt and I are quite well off and we don't need your money.

"What I want to propose is that, as you are certain you will be paying off the rest of your debt to me when your friend returns, it wouldn't inconvenience me one bit if you ceased your monthly payments until then. That way you should be able to hire enough help so you four can come out to visit us more often. Your aunt and

I miss having you, and how we miss the sing-a-longs! How does that sound?"

"That is far too generous, Uncle Peter, but it is tempting. It's a lot to think about. Do you mind if we let you know in a day or two?" Victor replied. Peter said that would be fine and then he wanted to know what their plans were with the other half of the building. They talked about different ideas, and asked his advice, which they could tell pleased him.

Angelo and Victor decided not to use any of Ike's savings, instead they accepted Peter Rutten's offer, which would allow both Victor and Lottie some free time to spend with the twins, while Angelo and Gladys were in England. Gladys and Angelo began making plans for the voyage, and after Angelo saw the doctor, Gladys sent off letters to both Dolly and James, telling them that they should be able to leave for England sometime in March. She also mentioned that they hoped it wouldn't be an imposition if they were to spend up to three months at Four Oaks.

After she had seen Ike's house on Gramercy Park, Gladys couldn't wait to invite Dolly and Eliza to New York. She wrote and said that as soon as the war was over, they had to come because she now had room, for not only Dolly and Eliza but also Eliza's nanny and Dolly's companion, Blossom, too. What she didn't write was that she hoped they would want to remain in America. She knew James and Percy would be travelling quite a bit, and she hoped James wouldn't mind if the girls lived with her.

As much as Angelo wanted to bring Otto and his family to the restaurant for a meal, he began to see that, even with a wheelchair, the ride would be too hard on him. Most of the streets were paved and wouldn't be near as bumpy as cobblestones, but still the ride was sure to jar Otto and may cause him to suffer more pain, so he had given up on the idea. One day, as he was entering the hospital, an ambulance arrived with more wounded. As the attendants lifted a soldier on a stretcher out of the back of the wagon, Angelo had an idea.

"Otto do you remember when they brought you from the train to the hospital in the ambulance?" he asked as soon as he was at his friend's bedside.

"Of course, I do. Why?"

"Was it very uncomfortable?"

"Not that I recall. They just lifted the stretcher into the ambulance and then out of it. I think the stretcher sits on some brackets so it's not on the hard floor, and it didn't shake me up much at all. Now, what are you thinking? You're not still trying to get me out of here, are you?"

"Could be, Otto, could be," was all Angelo would say, but the next day he waited for Otto's doctor outside the hospital entrance and asked him if he could spare a minute. Knowing how close Otto and Angelo were, the doctor invited him into his office, where Angelo explained that all he wanted was to borrow a stretcher.

"You see, we have our own wagon, and I'm sure we can rig it up with brackets that will keep the stretcher suspended just like an ambulance. Then I shall have some of my strongest employees set him in his wheelchair when we get to the restaurant, and we can do the same to bring him back at the hospital. Do you think we could borrow a stretcher?"

"No, I am sorry, but it's out of the question."

Angelo's face fell. Then he had another idea, "Maybe my uncle and I can make our own stretcher. If we did that, do you think it would be all right to move him?"

"You are determined to take the poor fellow out, aren't you?"

"Yes, sir, I am."

"Look, I am going to be frank with you. Otto has an infection in his wounds that we can't seem to cure, even though it isn't gangrene. His health is becoming worse, and I don't think he will be with us for long. Now, it's Angelo, right?" Angelo nodded. "Well, Angelo, the reason I said you can't borrow a stretcher is because I think what you need is an ambulance, too, and the attendants to go with it. I agree with you; Otto deserves not only that special dinner but also a day at home.

"In two days, there is a hospital board meeting, at which time I shall ask for the use of an ambulance and two attendants for, not one day, but two, because I think he deserves both. How does that sound?"

"It sounds just fine, sir. And you and your wife are invited to join us for the meal, if you have time. We have a most talented chef, and I am certain you will not be disappointed."

A week later, an ambulance pulled up in front of the restaurant and two brawny attendants lifted Otto out on a stretcher and carried him into the restaurant. Otto's family, the Ruttens, and the entire restaurant staff were waiting for him inside, and as the hospital attendants carried him in, they all clapped and called out, "Willkommen," which Iris had told Gladys, meant "Welcome."

Otto was beaming, and tears of happiness were running down his cheeks. His doctor, who arrived shortly after, hadn't yet received written permission to use the ambulance, but he was as anxious as Angelo to see that Otto have a treat before it was too late. He also wanted to make sure his patient arrived back at the hospital no worse off than when he had left. Besides, he had heard rumours of Sandy's culinary talents and wanted to sample them himself.

Because they didn't want the guest of honour to tire, the beer and the meal were served shortly after his arrival, and what a feast it proved to be! As Teresa Rutten put it, "One didn't need a German palate to appreciate every delectable morsel."

The meal began with Leberknödelsuppe (liver dumpling soup) and continued with a selection of side dishes, including, head cheese, a boiled sausage called Regensburger Wurst—a fluffy yeast dough dumpling, filled with spiced plum jam and served with melted butter and a mixture of sugar and poppy seeds that Otto called Germknödel—red cabbage, sauerkraut,Obatzda—a soft cow's milk cheese with butter, onions, and spices—and a huge roast of pork with potato Knödel.

After the main course, everyone said they were too full to appreciate the tasty desserts Sandy had prepared, so they just visited for a time. Victor wheeled Otto around to show him the entire restaurant and explain what they intended to do when Ike returned. Otto and Iris were very taken with the murals of scenes from different countries on the restaurant walls, and they were especially pleased that one of them was of Germany.

When the doctor told Angelo that he thought Otto should get back to the hospital soon, Angelo had Sandy bring out the desserts. There was Apfelstrudel (apple strudel) with whipped cream and Topfenstrudel (cheese strudel) with vanilla custard. Otto had to have a piece of each one, and when he was done, he made a little speech, thanking everyone, especially Sandy, for cooking the best meal he had ever eaten. Sandy said it was a pleasure, and he hoped it took Otto back to the days when he was a boy in Germany.

"I'm sorry, Sandy, but only the wealthiest Germans could afford to eat like we did tonight. We were mere peasants and were lucky to see a bit of meat once a month. Now, Iris might remember enjoying three-course meals—her folks were far better off than mine. Isn't that right, Iris?" Otto asked.

"Yes, that's quite true, but it has been such a very long time since then, and I don't recall any of those dishes tasting as wonderful as they did tonight. I think you must have added some of your own ideas with the recipes, Sandy, but whatever you did, that was the best German fare I have ever eaten, and I would appreciate some of those recipes, if you would be so kind as to share them with me."

Sandy said he would be pleased to write them out and give them to her. Then he insisted that both she and the doctor take a basket of leftovers with them. Otto had tears in his eyes when he thanked Angelo, "I don't know what I did to deserve such a good friend as you, Angelo, for you not only saved my life but also you've made it so much more enjoyable ever since I've been back home." He then addressed the rest of the group, "This man is a hero, folks, and we are all lucky to have him."

Angelo shook his head, gave Otto a hug, then motioned for the hospital attendants, who had enjoyed the meal as much as everyone else, to put him back on the stretcher, and take him back to the hospital.

It took Otto a few days after his trip to the restaurant before he was rested enough to go home for a day. This time, the event had the sanction from the board of directors and secrecy wasn't necessary. He spent the entire day with his family and friends, but when it was time for him to go back to the hospital, he broke down and wept. He knew he wouldn't be home again, and it was the first time since coming home from the war that he allowed himself any self-pity.

Angelo had asked Gladys, Victor, and Lottie to send letters and parcels to Ike and they all wrote to him. Lottie and Gladys knit him socks, sweaters, and vests, and Sandy made shortbread cookies, promising they would only get better with time, and he packed them carefully layered in a tin box. He also sent fruitcake done up the same way.

Ike received more mail than any of the other soldiers in his company, and it gave him not only bragging rights but also a gratifying sense of belonging to someone. He would show off his sweaters and stockings and pass the baking around, proudly saying, "These are from my family."

Gladys was anxiously waiting to hear from James before finding out if Bob was sailing anytime in March. She and Angelo had taken him some Christmas pudding and cake when he was sick, and he said he would be going to England around then. She also began collecting gifts for everyone at Four Oaks, and was looking for something special for James and Percy because they had been so kind and generous, but she had no idea what to get them. Her problem was solved when the owner of a nearby livery stable came in for dinner one evening and mentioned he had a Western saddle for sale. It seemed that one of his customers had left his horse and saddle with him and never came back.

"I had no idea where to get in touch with him and was just about to go to the authorities when I received a letter from his daughter in Montana. It seems the poor man up and died, and his daughter wrote to ask me to sell both the horse and saddle for whatever I could get for them. She told me to take out what he owed me and give the rest to a charity.

"I reckon she doesn't need the money. I should have no trouble getting rid of his horse—it's a good one—but I don't know anyone right now who is looking for a saddle. It's a nice lookin' one, with lots of fancy hand-tooled leather, and there's some pretty nice silver trimmings."

Gladys' eyes lit up. "How much would you want for it?"

"Is it for yourself, Gladys?"

"Not exactly; it's for a dear friend in England. I don't think he has ever seen a Western saddle, and I know he would love to own one, but I can't afford to spend too much."

"Well, I think we can come up with a price to suit us both. And I suppose you want to give him everything he left with it. There's a blanket, a bridle, spurs, some rawhide rope, and chaps. Some of it is pretty fancy stuff. I reckon your friend will get a kick out of pretending to be a regular American cowboy, so you better take him the works."

It was a far more expensive gift than Gladys had planned on giving, but because they were staying with James for three months, Angelo insisted she buy it, so they had it crated and ready to take with them.

James and Dolly's letters arrived on the eighth of April, and both letters were full of plans for the upcoming visit. Dolly said she could hardly believe they were going to be together again after such a long separation. She said even Eliza, who wasn't quite sure why, was caught up in the excitement. Dolly said she would see that the manor was thoroughly cleaned, from top to bottom, so they could spend all the time they had together without interruption.

"I shall have to write and tell her that I am no longer the same pernickety woman I once was, and that she doesn't need to fuss over me," Gladys said to Angelo and Eddy when she was reading the letter to them. She read James' letter out loud as well so that Angelo would know he was as welcome to Four Oaks as she and Eddy. "It seems that he is looking forward to meeting you, darling. Isn't that lovely?"

"I can't for the life of me understand why he feels that way, but I am looking forward to meeting those girls of yours. Do you suppose they will think me a cripple, or worse, a freak?"

Eddy went over to Angelo and put his arms around him.

"They are going to think you are a hero, Dad, because that's what you are."

"Well, I guess we had better tell Bob we need a cabin," Angelo replied and gave his son one of his rare smiles.

The next day, Sandy told Gladys that Bob was going to England on March the 20th and she should let him know if she wanted to book a cabin. Gladys said she would see to it just as soon as they found out if the doctor thought it was safe for Angelo to leave New York by then.

Chapter 7

March began with a storm, and although the snow had almost disappeared, it was still very cold. Gladys came downstairs to work one morning just as Lottie and Victor arrived.

"You are so lucky not to have to go outside to get to work, Gladdy," Lottie said. "It's colder out there than a witch's bottom."

"How do you know how cold a witch's bottom is, Lottie?"

"Victor told me."

Victor laughed and, slapping Lottie on her backside, said, "That I did, and there's times when I truly believe you are a witch, my love, so I know all about witches' cold bottoms, and their cold feet, too. Where's Angelo this morning, Gladys?"

"He is helping Eddy with his sums before his tutor arrives," Gladys replied. Listening to Victor and Lottie joking about their personal habits had suddenly caused her to think how different her life in America had become compared to when she lived in England. In Sandwich, her closest companions were members of the aristocracy, and would never discuss their spouses' bottoms, even in the privacy of their own bedrooms.

She knew people like Mary and her other English friends would consider the slang she, Eddy, and Angelo had begun to use common and even vulgar, but she enjoyed its informal and relaxed tone. Those ladies could never understand why she preferred the life she was now living to the pampered one she had left behind, but she found it far more relaxing and it suited her personality. *They shall just have to accept us the way we are*, she thought.

The news that Gladys would be away for three months was upsetting for the patients in the veteran's hospital, but Lottie and Iris managed to recruit another lady who sang a little off key, but so boisterously no one minded, and a veteran who had lost both his legs from the knees down.

The poor fellow was suffering with depression when one of the other soldiers learned that he used to play the accordion but no longer owned one. Everyone in the hospital, including the doctors, gave what they could, and soon they presented him with a shiny new one. When Iris asked if he would join their little group, he was thrilled. Being part of something so worthwhile gave him a reason to live, and he even played some on the evenings when the rest of the group weren't there.

Gladys couldn't afford a new wardrobe to wear when she went to England, and because she hadn't bought any new clothes since moving to New York, she spent quite a bit of time during the next few weeks remodelling some of her old frocks and suits. When she had them finished and ready to pack, she asked Lottie if she would like to see them. Lottie was surprised and a little jealous that Gladys had money to buy such elegant gowns, so she had little to say.

"Don't you like them, Lottie?"

"Anybody would like them, Gladys. I'm sure you'll have everyone over there drooling over them."

"What's wrong, Lottie? Did I detect a hint of sarcasm?"

"Do you know how long it's been since I've bought a new gown? I know this sounds petty, but I don't see how you can afford three elegant gowns like those when we've all been scraping by."

"Oh no," Gladys laughed, "These gowns aren't new, Lottie. They are my old ones made over. I've just added some different trims and other bits and pieces. You remember this one? It was all green with a brown-velvet vee down the front. I just took that off, added a collar of black fur, and put some on the sleeves. I had such a wonderful friend who taught me how to do these little makeovers. What do you think?"

"I think you are a genius. I thought they were all new. You've just given yourself a job as soon as you come back from England. I have about four old outfits in my wardrobe that I'd like you to have a look at. I'm sorry I was so rude. You know what a big mouth I have."

"Nonsense, there's nothing the matter with your mouth. Now I want to show you what I've made Eddy and Angelo."

During the last two weeks before they were to leave, Gladys was kept busy doing last-minute chores and working at the restaurant. She was still entertaining the soldiers and sewing so didn't notice the change in Angelo's behaviour. One day he took a baseball bat to work with him, and when Victor asked him why, he said, "They wouldn't let me keep my rifle." Knowing how bad his nephew's nerves were since he came back from the war, Victor didn't think it would help to question him further and let it go.

Then, two mornings before leaving for England, Angelo was working on the front desk when he heard shouting coming from the kitchen. Not stopping to think, he grabbed the bat and ran. The first thing he saw was Rory, one of the Irish waiters, armed with a large knife, threatening Joe, the dishwasher. Joe must have just arrived, taken off his shirt, and was about to put on the one he wore to wash dishes when Rory came at him.

Angelo didn't stop to ask who was to blame, and if Victor hadn't managed to grab hold of him before he reached the Irishman, the fellow might have had his head smashed in. Fortunately, Angelo wasn't strong enough to push Victor aside.

"All right now. It's all right," Victor said, trying to calm his nephew down. "They are just having an argument." Then he spoke to Rory, "You don't want to do anything you'll be sorry for, Rory. Put the knife down and let's talk about it."

Rory kept the knife pointed at Joe, but he didn't advance as he tried to explain, "He had no right taking my food last night, boss. You tell him, Sandy. You know those leftovers were supposed to be mine, and this black nigger stole them. Tell them it was my turn."

"Yes, it was your turn, but Joe here didn't take your basket, so put that knife down and behave yourself, you hot-headed Irish fool. It was my fault not Joe's. Joe and I left before you, and I meant to tell you, but I forgot. I had your leftovers ready early yesterday and they were in my way, so I put them out in the cooler. I'm sorry about that, but it's cold out there and I'm sure they'll still be good. Can he take time off to run them home, boss? He shares them with some of his neighbours who are practically starving."

"What do you think, Angelo?" Victor asked.

"It depends on if he apologizes to Joe here, and if I ever hear that word in this restaurant again, it'll take more than my uncle to hold me back," Angelo said while swinging the bat in the air. The incident left Victor more concerned over Angelo's mental problems than his physical health.

Victor, Lottie, the twins, and the Ruttens were all on the pier to wave goodbye as Gladys Eddy, Angelo, and his grandmother, Isabella, left New York aboard the SS Delaney. Isabella had decided to return to Sicily to visit her niece for the three months Angelo planned on being in Sandwich.

Once they could no longer see the pier, they found their cabins. Gladys shared one with Isabella, and Eddy and Angelo had an adjoining one. Later, when Gladys and Angelo had a moment alone on deck, he complained, "Well, here we are again. I guess it's another ten days apart. I certainly hope we get to share a bed in Sandwich."

"Oh, dear, didn't I tell you?" Gladys said, trying her best to keep from grinning, "James insists the women sleep in the East wing, while the men are housed in the West wing."

"You're joking, aren't you?" Angelo asked. Gladys managed to keep a straight face and didn't deny it. "I don't believe you, but if you're telling the truth, I am going to go with grandmother, and you can visit your friend alone. And, if Eddy wants to come with me, I'll take him along, too."

"But that's not fair. I want to go to Italy, too. You promised you would take me there some day, remember?" Eddy had overheard them talking when he came looking for them.

"Are we going with Nonna to Sicily, Dad?"

Angelo said that they might, and Gladys suddenly realized he was angry. She could hardly believe it, but then she recalled that he had lost his sense of humour. The war had cost him more than an arm.

"Oh, Angelo, you didn't really believe me, did you? I'm so sorry, I was just joking." Before he could answer, she assured Eddy, "No, dear, we three are going to Four Oaks, but another time we shall visit Italy, won't we, Angelo?" She reached up and kissed him on the cheek as she said it, and he repaid it with a slight smile.

Captain Bob Nicholson spent most of his off-duty time visiting with the Matthews during the voyage, and he mentioned that, now that both his boys had found careers and left home, he planned on bringing his wife with him to New York as soon as the war ended. Gladys was about to offer accommodations in Ike's home, but Bob said that Theresa Rutten had already said his wife was welcome to stay with them.

"It will probably only be for a week, because I expect there'll be a lot of people waiting to go back and forth as soon as the war is over, and I will have plenty of passengers. I imagine your girls will be among them, too, Gladys."

"That's true, and I can hardly wait," Gladys replied.

They only suffered with rough sea for a day, and then it started to rain and kept raining for four days. "I think we are following the rain, Mother. Maybe captain Bob should stop the ship for a day and allow the rain to go on by," Eddy said jokingly.

When they arrived in London, Angelo's cousin, Ruth, was there to meet them. She had come to England a month earlier to visit her elderly in-laws and had stayed to travel back to Sicily with Isabella. They all spent the night in a little inn near the dock, and the following day, Angelo, Gladys, and Eddy stood on the wharf and waved goodbye to Isabella and Ruth when they left for Sicily.

Eddy had waited three years to take his father on the train that he rode on when he came from Sandwich to London to meet Angelo for the first time. Now as they boarded the train, he was so excited he could hardly wait for Angelo to sit down so he could start explaining how the train ran. But he wasn't five anymore, he was eight and was determined to behave accordingly. As quietly as he could, he described how the engine was powered with steam and how the fire box had to be stoked with coal to make the steam.

"The conductor will be in presently, Dad, to get our tickets. He's a good egg and will help us if we need something, so don't be nervous," Eddy assured him.

"You forget that your father rode home from the war on a train, Eddy," Gladys interrupted, thinking that Eddy was talking too much.

Angelo frowned at Gladys as he replied, "Yes, that's right, but I never had a chance to learn anything about it. We were all crammed into one coach and didn't see anything. I'm very interested in what Eddy has to tell me, Gladys. Go on, son, tell me more."

Gladys was sorry she had said anything, and for the rest of the trip, she left them to entertain each other while she enjoyed the scenery. She had bought along a book written by Nathaniel Hawthorne entitled *The Scarlett Letter*. Like many of Hawthorne's stories, this one was set in England where the heroine was forced by the cruel and self-righteous aristocracy to live in shame and poverty. The same fate that Gladys would have had to endure, after she found she was going to have an illegitimate child, if James hadn't saved her with a proposal of marriage.

It was far too sad and poignant a story for Gladys' taste. She had been on both ends of the stick, so to speak, and disliked each of them equally, so she decided to leave the book on the train. The train was nearing Sandwich and Gladys couldn't hide her excitement as she saw the familiar countryside roll past.

"You are happy to be back here, aren't you?" Angelo asked.

"Yes. We're almost there. See that road?" she asked, pointing to a road they were just passing. "We'll be taking that road to Four Oaks in a very short time."

"I wish I was as happy about it as you and Eddy."

"Don't worry, darling. You are going to love it here."

Although they had sent word saying which train they would be on, Gladys didn't expect anyone but the second footman, Abdul, at the station to meet them, so when she saw Dolly and Eliza standing on the platform, she was thrilled. "There they are, Eddy," she cried out. "See, Angelo, there are my darling girls."

As soon as she stepped off the train, she ran and threw her arms around them both. "Oh, my darlings, I've missed you so much." She didn't want to ever let them go, but Eliza wanted to know where Eddy was and wiggled away.

"I guess he went with his father to look for our luggage, darling, but let me look at you both. My goodness, Eliza, you've grown so much I hardly recognize you, and, Dolly, I believe you are taller than I am. I don't know if you have grown that much since I saw you last or I have shrunk, but you look wonderful. Oh, it's so good to be with you again."

Gladys said Dolly looked wonderful, but in truth, she was shocked by her appearance. She was dressed very stylish, but her outfit was far too matronly for an eighteen-year-old, and her beautiful red curls were pulled back and rolled up in such a tight bun that not even a single ringlet could escape. A stranger would have thought she was Eliza's nanny and not her sister. As for Eliza, Gladys thought she was even prettier than she remembered.

"Welcome home, Mother," Dolly said after she gave Gladys a kiss. "Eliza, aren't you going to give Mother a kiss?"

It sounded more like an order than a question to Eliza, so she tipped her head back to receive a kiss before mumbling, "Hello, Mother."

"Well now, let us go and see why that brother of yours is taking such a long time. I guess they haven't finished unloading the luggage and boxes. I'm afraid we have too much for Abdul to load onto the buggy. He may have to come back with a wagon to get it all."

"James thought you would have quite a lot, Mother, so he had Ruby come along too with the wagon. There he is, loading the wagon at the end of the platform. Oh, and there's Eddy. Doesn't he look handsome?" Dolly exclaimed.

"May I go and see him, Dolly, please, please?" Eliza begged.

"Of course, dear, run ahead and we shall follow."

That Eliza hadn't asked for her approval, instead of Dolly's, really upset Gladys, even though she understood why. I guess I'm going to have to earn that privilege again, she thought, but she knew that each time she left and didn't return for a long period of time, added another block to the barrier. It was sad, but even sadder was the thought that Dolly must feel the same way.

Eliza, dodging between the suitcases and passengers, ran across the platform and threw her arms around her brother, almost knocking him down. He was both embarrassed and pleased. Taking no time for hellos, she blurted out, "Eddy, I have a dog. She's a girl dog, and guess what I named her?"

"I haven't the slightest idea."

"I call her Sidder. Can you guess why?"

"That's what I used to call you when you were little."

"I know. That is why I called my dog Sidder."

"Thanks, but now that you're older, I think I'll call you Sis, okey-dokey?"

"Okey-dokey, Eddy." Eliza loved to imitate Eddy when he used, what she called, American words. Every time Eddy attempted to walk away, Eliza would tug on his sleeve and tell him something she had planned for them to do while he was at Four Oaks.

As they were making their way across the platform, Dolly had a good view of Angelo. She had harboured a feeling of resentment toward him ever since he took her mother and Eddy away, and she was prepared to dislike him. But now, looking at him standing beside Eddy, her sentiments leaned more towards empathy than antipathy. Besides, she reasoned, he wasn't just any ordinary man, he was a soldier like her father was, and because he and Eddy looked so much alike, she almost felt as though she already knew him. Although Dolly was aware she wasn't pretty like her sister, she had always been proud whenever someone said that she resembled her father, so she could understand why Eddy was so fond of Angelo. Now, as she approached them, she had a feeling she and this man were going to be friends.

Gladys waited for Dolly to hug Eddy before she introduced both the girls to Angelo. They were both grateful when he just offered a handshake instead of an embrace. Angelo was amazed at the difference in the girls' appearances. Eliza was an exceptionally beautiful little girl, whereas Dolly's features were quite plain. Nevertheless, it was Dolly he felt drawn to. He liked the way she looked directly into his eyes with interest and not pity.

He had heard of people meeting someone for the first time and feeling as though they had always known them, but until now, it had never happened to him. "I've heard so much about you, Dolly," and then he remembered to include Eliza, "that I feel I already know you both," he said.

"I think I know what you mean," Dolly replied. "Now, I expect you are all a bit weary and anxious to arrive home and have something to eat. Do we have everything?" Angelo said he thought everything was on the wagon. "Then I guess you have already met our second footman, Abdul, and our stableman, Ruby."

"Yes, they introduced themselves. Shall I ride with them?"

"Heavens no! We have plenty of room in the buggy. James would be terribly annoyed with me if I allowed such a thing."

"Well I certainly don't want to cause any trouble. Abdul said the carriage is around the corner. So, ladies, shall we go?"

Gladys worried that Dolly wouldn't like Angelo, and she could hardly blame her if she didn't. If it wasn't for Angelo, Gladys would never have left Four Oaks, nor would Dolly have learned her mother was an imposter. Now as she watched them talking, she could tell that they were going to be friends. It was such a relief that she laughed, and said, "Yes, let's go, my duckies. I can hardly wait to see everyone."

Eliza kept Eddy busy answering questions all the way to Four Oaks, but when they came to the gate, Eddy ignored her and turned his attention toward Angelo. "Look, Dad, we have a gateman, and he makes sure no unwanted guests get in." Angelo was impressed, but not nearly as impressed as he was when he saw the mansion.

Gladys had never mentioned what James looked like, and because of the manor's grandeur, Angelo pictured him as being a very large and formidable looking character, but when the huge front doors of the manor opened, and James came out smiling, Angelo was pleasantly surprised.

James had a slight build and didn't appear to be the least bit formidable as he ran down the stairs and gave Gladys a big hug. Then he gave Eddy a vigorous handshake before addressing Angelo. "And,

I would wager that, you, sir, are this lad's father, Angelo. I am James, and I am very glad to meet you at last."

His handshake was firm and sincere, causing Angelo to feel truly welcome. "And I am pleased to meet you, James," Angelo replied.

"Gladys!" The voice was week, but its owner, who was standing in the doorway, was still recognizable.

"Aunt Jean," Gladys cried as she ran to give the elderly woman a hug. "I've missed you so much." A look of confusion crossed Jean's face, but then she smiled, and said, "Are we going to have tea now?"

Dolly had caught up to Gladys by then and answered, "Yes, Auntie, but I think we had better let these poor folks get cleaned up and out of their coats first." Dolly's efficiency never ceased to amaze Gladys. Later, when she found out that she had hired a housekeeper and was now the official mistress of the mansion in every sense of the word except as a wife, she admired her even more.

As proud as Gladys was of her oldest daughter, her independence made her sad. She doubted Dolly would ever come to her for advice in the future, and in a way, it was like she had lost two daughters. If she had her way, Eliza and Dolly would be spending more time with her than with James after the war ended, but she had to admit that even if that happened, Eliza had become so accustomed to being nurtured by Dolly, she doubted she would ever look to Gladys as a mentor.

She was so preoccupied with these thoughts that she hadn't asked Angelo what he thought of Four Oaks, James, or the girls. Now, as they were getting settled in one of the apartments in the west wing, she asked him what he thought.

"When you said you and Eddy lived in a fancy home with servants to wait on you, I had no idea just how fancy you meant. My God, Gladys, what an understatement! Both James and Dolly gave me a warm welcome, but I doubt I'll fit in. You should have realized that, Gladys, and come alone."

"Nonsense, I can tell that Dolly already likes you, and I know James will, too. They aren't the least bit snobbish. You haven't even given them a chance, Angelo, so please don't make assumptions until you've been here for a while."

He agreed but he didn't believe her, and they went down to have tea. Freda made a delicious meal, and after they ate, Gladys took Angelo into the kitchen to meet her and the other girls. Eddy insisted on going with them and making the introductions. Angelo had to admit that he couldn't have been made more welcome.

Both James and Dolly thought Angelo didn't look well, and they were determined to do everything they could to cure him, so they asked Freda to cook whatever he preferred. After their dinner, they retired to the sitting room. Gladys had brought presents for all the family, and after they had opened them, she asked James and Dolly if they would mind if she invited the staff to come to the parlour so she could give them their gifts as well. Neither approved, but they remembered how Gladys believed the help should be treated as equals and agreed. It was great fun to see them open the gifts, but as soon as they had thanked Gladys, they looked at Dolly, who dispelled them with just a slight nod.

"Ah, Dolly, my dear, you truly are what I could never be," Gladys remarked

"I think you had your own method of handling things, Mother, and it was every bit, if not more, successful than mine. I remember you saying that you were never happy being an aristocrat. I didn't really believe it then, but I do now."

"I was born an aristocrat, and I must admit that there are times when I regret it," James remarked.

"That's a sweet thing to say, James." Gladys said, "I don't think Angelo will ever strive to be one, but we both would like to own a nice home some day. Isn't that right, darling?"

"A person doesn't need to be born in aristocracy to be successful in America, which is fortunate for someone like me," he replied

"And that is the way it should be here as well," James added.

If James was trying to make Angelo feel at home, he was succeeding. Angelo was beginning to realize that although James was wealthy, he had lot in common with Gladys and him, and for the first time since leaving New York, he began to relax.

Gladys asked James when Percy would be coming for a visit. "We didn't have time to see him when we were in London."

"He is looking forward to seeing you again, so I'm sure he will show up before long."

Gladys laughed, and said, "I couldn't help but notice you're look of disappointment when I had a present for everyone but you."

"I must admit, I do feel a little neglected."

"I'm sorry, but I brought something I think both you and Percy can enjoy together. It's out in the tack room in a crate and you mustn't open it until Percy is here to help you."

"Then I shall pray he arrives tomorrow. Now, if you and Angelo are not too tired, I would love to hear you play the piano and sing us a few songs. What do you say?"

"I am sure Gladys will be happy to, James, but if you will excuse me, I think I will retire. I am rather tired," Angelo replied. Gladys was about to say she would go up with him, but Angelo spoke first, "Eddy, perhaps you had better come with me. I'm not sure I have my bearings yet. You stay and play, Gladys."

Gladys knew better than to argue, so she told Eddy that he could come back down for a short time before he went to bed.

Chapter 8

James looked forward to showing Angelo his property, but it began raining that night, and it was still raining in the morning. Percy arrived midday and James insisted they all don raincoats and umbrellas and go out to the stable to see the mystery present Gladys had brought for Percy and him. James had, secretly, been out to look at the crate and confessed, "Thank God you arrived when you did, Percy, or I would have gone mad guessing what is in it."

"I didn't know that it was for me too, or I would have been here yesterday. Well, let's not stand around guessing. By the size of the crate, I don't think we could figure what it is if we were to guess all week. Ruby, have you something we could use to open this?"

Ruby picked up a tool, "I think this will do, Master Percy. If you like, I'll open it."

"You'll probably do it a lot easier than James or I would, so have a go at it, then."

When they saw the saddle and all the other pieces of cowboy paraphernalia, both men were speechless and stood staring at it with open mouths. Finally, Gladys asked them, "Don't you like it?"

"It is absolutely fantastic," James said.

"So this is the kind of saddle and outfit the American cowboys use. My heavens, Gladys, it is simply beautiful," Percy remarked. "Here, gather around. I want to give the three of you a hug."

"Not all Western saddles are this fancy, but otherwise they are much the same," Gladys told them. "The first nice day you shall have to try it out on one of your horses."

"Have you used one, Gladys?"

"No, I've never used one. We haven't any horses of our own, right now, so we mostly use cabs or walk." Then, knowing Angelo would be embarrassed if James were to ask him the same question, she added, "I don't think Angelo has used one of those saddles either, have you, Angelo? You see Angelo and I both grew up where no one could afford a horse, except for Mr. O, who had a faithful old horse he called 'Old Knickers.' Old Knickers must have been about thirty years old, but he was still able to pull Mr. O's wagon. Then when I lived in Dover, my first husband's father owned an estate, and he gave me my horse, Tig, but Angelo never lived in the country, so he never did learn to ride."

Angelo, expecting to receive looks of pity from the men, was upset with Gladys for saying what she did, but when no one seemed to consider it unusual, he relaxed.

"Well, we have just the horse for you to learn on, Angelo, and Ruby is the one to teach you. Isn't that right, Ruby?" James asked.

"I will do my best, sir," Ruby replied.

"Ruby is one of the best horse trainers in England, and you may be assured that any horse he has handled can be trusted, so I hope you shall take him up on his offer. It would mean a great deal to me, because I have looked forward to taking you riding and showing you my lake and the rest of the estate while you are here," James said.

James' invitation was given in such a forthright and friendly manner, Angelo felt he couldn't refuse. "You may have quite a job on your hands, Ruby. I am not yet as proficient with my left hand as I hope to be."

"Don't you worry, sir, you shall be riding in no time. Mandrake, that Cob there," he pointed to a horse in a stall at the end of the stable, "he's a good one to begin on, and then we have Chester, he's quiet, but adequate. He's a Cleveland Bay and should do just fine. Before you know it, you'll be asking for a Courser."

"I have no idea what a Courser is."

"A Courser is the horse you would ride if you went on a fox hunt, Dad. Isn't that right, Uncle Percy?" Eddy spoke up, surprising them all.

"That's right, Eddy. It seems Ruby has taught you well, but I have never taken part in the sport, and I don't recall you hosting one on your estate, James, at least as long as I have known you."

"No, and you shan't. I dislike the sport immensely, but then I dislike hunting of any sort. Now, we had better decide where we are going to with this magnificent saddle."

"I guess the sensible place would be with the others in the tack room. That is if you plan on making use of it, or were you thinking of having it mounted in the house as a trophy?" Percy asked, jokingly.

"I don't know about you, but I can hardly wait to try it out, and as soon as the weather is favourable, I think we should saddle up and corral some of those wild steers out on the range." Percy joked back.

"I bought a book in a saddle shop at home. That should help you put it on correctly," Gladys suggested.

"If you'll pardon me, missus, I have used one before at an exhibition an American brought to London. I was fortunate to be invited to join them, and I must say, I enjoyed it thoroughly, but I couldn't, as one of the wranglers put it, rope a steer any better'n a blind nun," Ruby said, blushing over his attempt at American humour.

"Well, Ruby, someday you must come and visit us and we'll all take the train out west. Gladys and I have been longing to see the prairies ourselves," Angelo said.

Ruby's face lit up. It was something he had always dreamed about, but never thought it would happen. Now that the missus was married to such an amiable man, and they were living in America, his dreams might actually come true. "I would appreciate that, sir, I most certainly would," he said with a grin.

Gladys was pleased to see Angelo so relaxed, but she could see that James wasn't amused. *Here we go again*, she thought, *the same upper-class thing.* James had never accepted the close friendships she had developed with members of the staff when she was mistress of the manor, and as much as he admired Ruby, he resented any familiarity between any of his servants and his guests. He had changed a lot since Percy had come back into his life, but Gladys knew that some of his stuffy old habits and ideas were still with him.

To get his mind off Angelo and Ruby, she suggested, "How about we leave the saddle for Ruby to look after and bring the rest into the house. We have nothing to do this afternoon, and it's far too wet a day to spend outdoors, so perhaps we can have a fashion show and you both can dress up as cowboys?"

"I am game if you are, Percy," James said. Not waiting for an answer, he continued, "If we look like authentic cowboys, I think I shall go into town in a day or two and have Roland Pearsall—you remember him, Percy, he was on our cricket team—come and take our pictures. He is doing quite well since he went into that business."

Angelo asked if they minded if he stayed in the stable for little while longer instead of returning to the house. "I want to get acquainted with the horse Ruby is going to let me ride. I'll be along shortly. Gladys, you and Eddy go ahead and help them sort out that gear." Angelo was more excited than he let on, but he was also nervous. He wondered if his handicap would interfere with his balance and he wanted to ask Ruby what he thought when no one else was around.

Ruby showed him the horse he would be using, and he was pleased when Angelo asked if he could brush him. He could tell Angelo was self-conscious over his handicap, but instead of ignoring it, he said, "As you only have one hand, you shall have to handle the reins a little differently than most, but it won't make any difference to the horse, so you needn't worry about that." Then he picked up some reins, and said, "You see, sir, you just take the reins and put one between your thumb and the next finger and the other rein between your little finger and the finger next to that. Then you can rein to this side just by moving your hand like this, and to the other side like this. Here, you try it."

Angelo took hold of the reins but dropped them on his first attempt. Frustrated, he swore, "Damn me to hell!"

"Take your time, sir, take your time. It will come, don't you worry. Now try again."

"I'm sorry, Ruby. Sometimes I don't seem able to control my temper. You go along and do what you have to do, and I'll practice for a while and, Ruby, please call me Angelo. I'm just a working man like you, so it bothers me when you call me, sir."

"Thank you, but I think the master would not approve."

"Surely he won't object to us being friends. I can't see how it is any skin off his nose."

"You are not in America now, sir. James Hornsby was raised as an aristocrat, and there are rules the gentry abide by. He is one of the kindest and fairest employers I have known, but he expects his employees to honour his wishes, so if you don't mind, I shall continue to refer to you as, sir." Angelo said he understood.

By the time Ruby finished his chores and returned, he was pleased to see that Angelo was able to pick up the reins and place them between his fingers almost as fast as anyone with two hands. "Good lad," he said as he slapped him on the back.

Gladys had been worried when Angelo took so long to come to the house, so she came looking for him. She was just entering the stable when she heard Ruby congratulating him, and although she hadn't any idea what was going on, she was delighted to see a slight smile on her husband's face.

"What have you two been doing all this time?"

"Your man here has already learned how to handle reins with one hand, so it isn't going to take him long before he will be riding."

"I hope it's nice tomorrow, and if you feel like it, darling, you can begin. I bet Eddy will be thrilled to have you ride with him, but now Freda has dinner ready, and, Ruby, Nora probably has yours ready, too."

After dinner, James and Percy decided it was time to dress up in their cowboy clothes. Gladys had found two pairs of second-hand trousers and two second-hand shirts, all similar to the ones in the picture of a cowboy that was on the front cover of the book she had bought for them. The hats and boots were the two things Gladys had worried about the most, because she had to guess the proper sizes. Most second-hand hats and boots were too well worn, and Gladys couldn't afford to buy new ones, but with Lottie, Iris, and Aunt Theresa's help, she had found what she was looking for.

She was surprised to find that some cowboys wore bandanas around their necks made of silk and patterned in calico. She was also surprised that most of them were over thirty inches square. She ended up buying one each for the men and two for herself—one to use as a shawl, and the other for a table cloth.

James took the book that Gladys brought them up to his room, so he and Percy could use the picture on the front cover as a guide. It took about three quarters of an hour before they had everything on and in the right place. When they were ready, they came to the door of the parlour, and in a loud voice, Percy announced, "Just tie your horse here, partner, and we'll go in this here saloon and have us a drink."

James answered, "An' maybe play a little poker. Let's go, Pard." They strode in together and James called out, "How do, all you city folk!"

Percy kept the charade going by adding, "We're the toughest, roughest gang in the west an' thar's only one man we're a feared of. That's that sure-shooter, Sheriff Eddy Matthews. Have any of you cowboys seen him?"

Eddy, playing right along with them, answered, "Here I am, you robbing, thieving bank robbers. You better draw your guns, because I'm going to shoot you dead."

James threw up his arms, "It's no use, Pardner, we may as well surrender. We left our guns back in New York." They both held up their hands and everyone clapped and laughed.

"I am sorry about that," Gladys said, "But I wouldn't know what kind of guns to buy, even if I could find them. I guess you will have to get those yourselves when you come to visit us. But even without your weapons, you both look smashing. Where did you learn to talk like cowboys?"

"We are both fans of James Fenimore Cooper and have read all five of his *Leatherstocking Tales*. Can you remember them all, Percy?" James asked.

"I think so. Let's see, the first one was *The Pioneers*, the second was *The Last of the Mohicans*, but I'm not sure if *The Pathfinder* was the third or fourth."

"It was the forth. The third was *The Prairie* and the last one was *The Deerslayer*. I think you mentioned that was your favourite, Dolly. Have you read any of them, Eddy?"

When Eddy said he hadn't, James said, "I think you would enjoy them. The protagonist in them all is a woodsman named Natty Bumppo. I have all Cooper's books in the library, so maybe you can read one while you are here. If not, I'm sure your tutor will have it for you. I think you would enjoy *The Last of the Mohicans* the most. Eddy said he would like to look at them, but he still felt a little nervous about entering James' library. He wasn't afraid of James anymore, but memories of that awful day when James had shaken him, and called him a bastard, hadn't completely faded.

Gladys asked James if he had told his friends, Mary Baker, and Tina and Bob Rudyard, that they were coming. They had been good friends of Gladys when she lived at Four Oaks. "You are going to have to put a show on for them as well, you know."

"I told them you were coming, but not the exact date. I think I shall wait until Percy and I are comfortable using the Western saddle before I invite them. Then we shall meet them out at the corral. That should be even more fun."

Before the men left to change, Gladys begged James to go into the kitchen, so the help could see what a cowboy looked like. At first, he refused, but when Percy said they should, he gave in. Jenkins wasn't as pleased as the rest of the staff. Although he would never say it, he thought the outfit far too demeaning for a man of his master's station. The rest of the staff laughed and clapped their hands causing James a little embarrassment at first, but he was soon answering their questions with as much enthusiasm as Percy.

The questions they asked were the same ones he and Percy had asked Gladys earlier that day, so they were able to answer with a certain amount of pride and confidence. All in all, it was an exciting day, and for a time, even Angelo forgot the war.

The weather didn't improve during the following two days, but Angelo was so determined to learn to ride that he spent most of his time in the barn. He had Mandrake saddled and ready, and as soon as the rain stopped for a few minutes, he would lead the horse out to the corral, and using the mounting block to get on, he would ride slowly around talking to the horse until Ruby had time to give him a lesson. Having a goal to work towards helped Angelo from becoming too depressed, but during the nights, his nightmares persisted, and he begged Gladys to move into another room, so she could get a good night's sleep.

Knowing her presence helped calm him, she refused. Some nights, after a nightmare, he would sit on the edge of the bed crying and insisting that he was letting Ike down. "I feel I should go back to New York. At least I'd be closer to him there. We vowed to look after each other, and now I'm over here, thousands of miles away and I feel like I've let him down."

Gladys assured him that their letters would help cheer him up. "He'll be waiting to hear how you are making out with your riding lessons. I bet he never had a horse, either, and if you learn to ride, you can each buy a horse when he comes home, and you can teach him." From then on, Gladys made sure they took time to sit down and write to Ike every day, which helped ease Angelo's conscience, even though he had no reason to feel guilty.

Gladys had brought some beaded leather goods and other souvenirs for Mary's friends, so one day she borrowed one of James' buggies and went into Sandwich to deliver them. She knew Angelo and Eddy wouldn't mind if she was gone for the day. Angelo was spending most of his time in the stable, or the corral, learning to ride, and Eddy was having a good time playing with Eliza.

Mary said she was happy to see her, but Gladys could sense there was something amiss. Mary had paused a little too long before she reached out to hug her. Nevertheless, a half-hour later they were chatting away as friendly as ever, and she decided it must have been her imagination. After they enjoyed a tasty repast of dainty cheese and watercress sandwiches and some delicious cakes, Mary had her footmen bring in the trunk of crafts that Gladys had brought with her.

She was amazed at the amount of goods Gladys had. "They are absolutely beautiful," she said, "but I hope you will understand,

Gladys, I simply cannot carry on with this arrangement. If you remember, I only asked you to bring me things from America because my friends wanted me to. And it was they who gave me the names of the women who make articles for you take back with you. Now strangers are knocking at my door wanting to buy American souvenirs."

"Isn't that a good thing, Mary?"

"No, Gladys, that's not a good thing. I have not the least desire, or the need, to run a business."

"But you wrote and said you wanted more."

"I only did it because my friends begged me to, and at first it was a novelty. Now it has gotten out of hand, but I do not expect you to take these lovely things back with you. I did some inquiring and I found a woman who said she would be delighted to work with you.

"Her name is Claudia Cowan. She runs a little gift shop here in Sandwich, and she asked me before if I knew where she could buy items like the ones you brought before. She is a most pleasant creature and has a lot of spunk. She reminds me a little of you. I have discussed it with her, and she was quite excited about the idea. We can take this lot to her today if you like."

"Of course, I understand, Mary, and if you give me the address of her shop, I shall drop in to see her. You needn't come with me, my dear. It might take us a while to come to an agreement. I must go now, but I was wondering when you and the Rudyards are going to come out to Four Oaks to visit us. Percy is here now, and I want you to meet my husband."

When Gladys returned to Four Oaks, she related to James and Percy how Mary had behaved when she asked her to come to Four Oaks. "First, she looked embarrassed, and then she wrung her hands. I've always wondered if people actually did that, but I certainly didn't expect to see Mary do it.

"Poor Mary, I know she didn't want to hurt my feelings, but she finally had to confess what was bothering her. It seems she had heard a rumour that some folks in town are saying Four Oaks has become a den of iniquity, and she is worried that a visit might damage her reputation. She said she thought the Rudyards might feel the same."

"What did you say to her?" James asked.

"I told her that I understood, but I hoped we could still be friends. We bid each other goodbye and I left to visit the lady she told me about. I was quite impressed with her little shop, and she appeared to be quite intelligent and honest, so I gave her the trunk of crafts, and she promised to have a shipment of knitting and Sandwich Glassware ready for me to take back to New York. I was just leaving her shop when Mary arrived in her little shay.

"She said she was happy that I was still in town, because just after I left her house, Tina and Bob Rudyard came to see her. She told them I was here, and she also suggested that it might hurt their reputations if they were to visit us. Then she admitted that Bob scoffed at the idea and said to the devil with the gossips. He also said he and Tina were coming to visit us even if Tina didn't.

"The next thing I knew Mary was hugging me and apologizing for being so silly. They will all be here on Saturday."

"I never thought I would ever be involved in a sex scandal," James said, winking at Percy.

Chapter 9

Ever since Gladys' friend, Mary Baker, had been a young girl, she had been admired for her beauty and poise. She knew it was often said that she was the epitome of a proper lady, and she had always been proud of it. That is until she met Gladys. Mary had a trim and shapely figure, but after seeing the love and attention Gladys received from people she met, she began to realize that the regal posture she had strived to maintain caused her to appear untouchable. Children never offered a voluntary hug, and although men looked at her with admiration, it was never with desire. Her life had been devoid of compassion.

Mary didn't marry until she was thirty. At this point, she chose a husband carefully from the list of the town's most eligible bachelors—men with the most wealth and a prestigious background. This qualified Reginald Baker the third, a man eighteen years Mary's senior. Reggie, as Mary called him, certainly had a fair share of esteem and fortune, but, unfortunately, he lacked sensitivity and passion. When Reggie died of a heart attack one year after they were wed, Mary, who was fond of her husband, missed his presence everywhere but in the bedroom.

After Bob Rudyard said that he intended to visit Four Oaks, with or without his wife, Tina, and Mary, both women had agreed to go with him. In the days that followed, Mary thought a lot about Gladys and the rest of James' guests. She remembered the good times they used to have together before Angelo came back into Gladys' life. They all rode together and spent countless evenings playing games or singing while Gladys played the piano. She missed those enjoyable outings and evenings and had begun to realize just how alone she was. She worried about her future. She didn't want to be an old maid, and she longed to be loved.

By the time Bob and Tina came by in their buggy to take her to Four Oaks, Mary had decided she was going to be more like Gladys, hoping that someone might eventually seduce her. The Rudyards were shocked when she greeted each of them with a hearty hug and a big smile. This was so unlike their friend, and that, along with the casual way she had her hair styled, caused them to wonder what was going on with their friend.

Angelo was also surprised and confused when he was introduced to Mary. Gladys had made a point of warning him, saying, "Mary is a very elegant lady and she's very formal with everyone she meets, darling, so don't feel she doesn't like you, when she greets you with just a weak handshake," but Mary had refused his hand and instead given him a hug that wasn't the least bit weak.

She had also changed her hairstyle to resemble Gladys' and it lent a different ambience to her character. Angelo had expected to meet a woman who appeared cold and frigid, but Mary wasn't at all like that. He was impressed by how attractive she was, and told her so: "Gladys told me how beautiful you are, and now I can see she wasn't exaggerating. I am very pleased to finally meet you, Mary."

Mary almost swooned. Here was this handsome man looking and talking to her as though she was just a pretty woman instead of statue on a pedestal. It was the most exhilarating feeling she had ever experienced. "You flatter me, kind sir, pray, do not stop," she answered back, coyly, then she couldn't suppress a giggle—something else she had never done before.

The cowboy outfits were a hit, and the afternoon and evening went by too quickly. Gladys tried to convince Angelo to have a rest for a little while, but although he would have liked to have a nap, he refused, afraid he might have a nightmare. Gladys managed to warn everyone not to talk about the war, so they only inquired about the restaurant and New York and kept the things they were most anxious to learn until they were alone with Gladys.

Angelo was surprised how relaxed he felt among them, and later that night he told Gladys he thought they were all good people. "I'm glad I met them, and I think we should have Mary over for a visit after Ike comes home. I think she is just right for him."

"Ike and Mary? They couldn't be more unsuitable. She is an aristocrat through and through, while he is just a poor Irishman. I guess I can't say that, can I? He's probably as wealthy as she is. What made you think they would like each other?"

"I don't rightly know. It was just something about her that made me think she needed a man like Ike. She's not the least like you said she was."

"Well, Mr. Matchmaker, I wish you luck, but I doubt it will ever happen, and I don't know what was going on tonight, but that was not the Mary I know."

It had only taken a week for Angelo to be able to handle a horse well enough to go riding with Gladys and Eddy and he thoroughly enjoyed it. He would have ridden every day but didn't want to take advantage of James' generosity. James had said he wanted to show his whole estate to Angelo personally, so a few days after Mary and the

Rudyard's visit, he asked Hilda to make a picnic lunch for Angelo and himself.

They had only ridden a short distance when James congratulated Angelo on his equestrian skills, and Angelo replied, "I had a good teacher, James, and you have some very patient horses." Around noon, they stopped at the lake to enjoy their lunch, sat on some chairs at a little table James had had his handyman build, and were eating when a doe and two spotted fawns came out of the trees not far from where they were sitting.

Angelo had never seen a live deer before, and he couldn't take his eyes off them. After a minute or two, the doe spotted the men, and for a moment, she appeared frozen. Then, when James reached for the picnic basket, she turned, and with two huge leaps, she disappeared into the woods with the two fawns close behind. "Beautiful, aren't they?" James remarked. "Now you can see why I don't allow hunting on my property."

"I would feel the same way if it was mine. Being out here is another thing that makes me realize how much Gladys and Eddy had to give up. I hope I can make up for it some day. My uncle and I have a good friend who is going to be our partner as soon as he leaves the army, and we have some plans that I hope will be successful. If we are, I intend to buy some acreage and build a home. The kind of home Gladys and Eddy deserve. I don't imagine it will be as grand as Four Oaks, but I intend to have our own stable and horses. I only wish I could give them what you have given them."

"Angelo, what you have given them is far more precious than all this. I can assure you they would not change places if they had the chance. It is not the material things in life that make you happy, dear boy, it is being with someone you love and who loves you. Speaking of love, I suppose Gladys has told you about Percy and me?"

"She told me how much you and Percy care for each other and how happy she was when she heard that you had stopped denying it.

I have to confess, your kind of relationship was difficult for me to accept, and when Gladys first told me about it, I didn't look forward to meeting either of you. Then I met Percy and was surprised that he was as manly as any of my friends. I'd like to be friends with you both, if you will allow me to."

"I consider it my pleasure," James said, while offering his hand.

"I also want to thank you for all you have done for us. I know I haven't been the best of company, but I haven't felt that well lately, physically or mentally."

"Because of your injury?"

"No, I don't think it has anything to do with the loss of my arm. I have a friend who lost both his legs and he doesn't suffer with depression. There are lots of soldiers far worse off than I. No, it's not that."

"Could it be what you went through in the war?" James asked. Angelo just shrugged his shoulders causing James' curiosity to get the better of him. "I imagine it must have been ghastly."

"I don't imagine it was any worse than hell, but it had to be every bit as bad," Angelo said. Then he got up and walked down to the lake.

James realized he had made a mistake by bringing up the subject, so he followed him, put an arm around his shoulders, and apologized. When Angelo didn't respond, James thought that maybe his gesture was taken to be more than an act of friendship, and he quickly withdrew his arm. Angelo turned to face him, and the look in his eyes portrayed such pain and anguish that James took hold of his arm and led him back to a chair.

Looking at James beseechingly, Angelo began to talk as though James was a priest and he the confessant. "I can still see the dead soldiers lying on the battlefield and imagine their bones breaking under my feet as I was forced to run over them. I can't help but wonder how many of those poor men were only wounded and not dead. I wonder if they felt anything when we trod on them.

"After I heard Otto cry out and Ike and I dragged him to safety, it was then that I began to wonder how many more out there were still alive and waiting to be saved. There are times when I even imagine I hear them calling, "Help me, help me!" And sometimes, in my nightmares, it's me lying there wounded and soldiers are running over me. I try to call, but my mouth is missing, along with half of my face!"

Angelo's voice became lower and lower until it was almost a whisper and James had to strain to hear what he was saying. "We were ordered to retreat, and the guns were firing. I should have tried to help them, but there was no time. There were so many bloody bodies, and I had to run over them to find cover. The ground was so slippery with blood that I slid and fell. Oh God, I fell, and one hand fell on a face. It was only half there." Angelo covered his face with his hands and moaned, "There are times when I think I shall go mad."

James had been standing while Angelo was talking, but when he began describing the battlefield, he allowed his imagination to picture the scenes too clearly, and he soon began to feel ill and so weak in the knees he had to sit down. It took a few minutes after Angelo finished for James to stop shaking enough to get up and pour two glasses of the wine Hilda had put in their basket. "Here, drink this," he ordered.

Angelo did as he was told. Then the realization of what he had done dawned on him. "My God, James, I am sorry. I had no intention of breaking down and bothering you with my troubles."

"You have nothing to apologize for. I should never have asked you about the war. It was an unforgivable thing to do. It is I who should do the apologizing. How do you feel? Would you like to go back to the house and have a rest?"

Angelo rose and took a deep breath. Then he smiled. "Actually, James, I feel pretty good. You know this is the first time I've been able to tell anyone about my nightmares. Gladys knows I have them, of course, but I've never told her what they are about. It's not something I think she should hear. Thank you, James. I hope it didn't upset you too much."

"Well, it certainly made me realize how fortunate I have been, but if those nightmares, and this business of blaming yourself for something that was not your fault, continue to plague you, I shall insist we take a trip to London very soon. Percy had a dear friend who was one of London's most respected doctors, and I know he introduced Percy to many of the finest specialists in England, so we shall have no trouble finding help for you."

Angelo thanked him but said he would wait to see his army doctor when he went home. Guessing why Angelo was hesitant to visit any of the specialists in London, James said, "Your army doctor is not a specialist, Angelo, and if it is the fee you are worried about, I promise there shan't be one. There are many doctors and politicians that are in our—er—group, and we all do favours for one another. You should take advantage of it while you are here, even if it's just for a consultation." Angelo said he appreciated the offer and would think about it, but he didn't intend to see any doctor but his own.

Gladys could tell the difference in Angelo after he had spent the day with James. For a time, he didn't suffer with nightmares and he even laughed out loud once when he was watching Eddy play with Eliza. Regrettably, it only lasted for a week before the nightmares returned, and because Angelo thought he was rid of them, they depressed him even more, and his personality changed. He didn't want anyone around him, even Eddy, but preferred to borrow one of James' horses and go riding by himself.

One day he had been away longer than usual, and when it was getting close to tea time, James had a talk with Percy and Gladys. He confessed that Angelo had told him about his nightmares and that he had suggested Angelo allow Percy to find him psychiatric help.

"I am afraid we've not taken his illness serious enough, his mental illness that is, and there's no telling what a person in his state of mind might do.

"I am sorry, Gladys, I did not want to alarm you, but it shan't be long before dark, and I am worried. I think Percy and I should go and look for him. What do you think, Percy?"

Gladys spoke up before Percy could answer, and said, "I'm coming too. If he has had an accident, I want to be there with him. Let's not wait any longer." Eddy had been listening, and he asked to go along, but Gladys suggested he stay and wait at the house in case Angelo came back and needed someone. She knew Eddy was the one Angelo listened to the most.

They all rode out on trails going in different directions. Percy took the south trail, down the gulley and up on the rise, where he could get a good view of the lowlands, and James took the lake trail. Gladys went to all the tenants' houses to ask if they had seen anything of Angelo before she took a path that circled around and met the trail to the lake.

As soon as James came to the lake he saw Angelo. He was sitting on the far bank with old Lockhart, the poacher. Angelo had Lockhart's rod in his hand and neither he, nor the old man, noticed that they were being watched. Suddenly, Angelo jumped up, "I've got him! This time I'm not going to let you get off, you rascal," he shouted.

"Atta boy!" Lockhart shouted. "Now, reel 'im in slowly. I think you got yerself, old Foxy. I been tryin' to catch that bugger fer ten years. There you go, easy now. 'Ere you, that's it right into my net with you. By Jesus, son, we got 'im. Yippee!" Lockhart said as he performed a little dance. Then he spotted James. "Oh, damnation, if you'll pardon me, sir. I'm not supposed to let anyone else fish 'ere. I have to go, and I better take the fish so's 'e won't know you been fishin'." Quickly, he dropped the trout into his basket, grabbed the rod out of Angelo's hand, and took off running.

When James got to Angelo, he said, "Thank, heavens you are all right."

Surprised to see him, Angelo smiled, and said, "I don't know what happened to the old fellow who was here with me, James, but he seemed worried that you would be mad if you knew I was fishing in your lake, and he just took off running. He took my fish with him, too. He showed me how to fish and let me use his rod. I caught a huge fish, but the son of a gun took it with him. I would have really liked to show it to Eddy. I tell you, James, it was one of the most relaxing things I've ever done." Angelo was so excited about catching a fish that he hadn't stopped talking until James' words finally hit him.

Looking up, he noted the concern on James' face, and a foreboding feeling crept over him. "What is it, James?"

"Do you realize what time it is? When you didn't come home for tea, we were worried that you had an accident. Percy and Gladys and I have been looking for you."

Angelo felt sorry for causing everyone to worry, but he was so relieved James hadn't come to tell him some bad news, that his apology wasn't as sincere as it should have been. "I'm so sorry, James. I was sitting by the water when I noticed the old fellow fishing. When I approached him, he seemed nervous, but when I said I had never fished before, he was kind enough to show me how it was done. It's really something special when you feel that first nibble on your line, isn't it? Anyway, we sat and talked and waited for the fish to bite, and time just went by. I didn't realize how late it was. I am really sorry."

"I can remember how I felt the first time I had a fish on my line, and I understand how you feel, but we had better find Gladys and Percy and get along home, or Eddy and Ruby will be out looking for the four of us."

They were about half way home when they met Gladys and Percy. Gladys rode up to Angelo, jumped off her horse, and hugged his leg, "You are all right! What happened? Did you fall? Oh, thank goodness, you are safe."

"Of course, I'm safe, darling, now let go of my leg so I can get down and show you how sorry I am."

The rest of the way back to the stable, Angelo never stopped explaining to Gladys how one should hold a rod and how to properly reel in a fish. He said he was determined to find a place in New York where he could take Eddy fishing. When they arrived at the stable, Gladys ran to the house to tell Eddy his father was safe while the men took care of the horses. Angelo told Percy what James had said about seeing a London specialist and then he said he had thought it over and decided he would like to see one if it could be arranged.

"It's funny but sitting on the bank fishing made me realize how wonderful life is, and I thought about the things I still want to do with my son. I shan't be able to do any of them if I'm locked up in an asylum. So I would really appreciate it if you would see what you can do for me." Percy said he would leave the next day and do whatever he could.

Chapter 10

Knowing that he might have professional help did a lot to lift Angelo's spirits, and Gladys was tempted to write and tell Lottie and Victor how much happier he seemed but decided to wait until they heard from Percy. One thing that still worried Angelo was that it had been weeks since he had heard form Ike. Finally, he couldn't stand the wait any longer.

"I am sorry, Glad, I know it is hard for you to understand, but if I don't hear from Ike by the end of the week, I want to go back to New York. I don't want you and Eddy to come. You owe it to the girls to stay longer, but I have this gut feeling that Ike needs me closer. It's silly, I know, but I can't help it."

"Very well, darling, but let's wait until Saturday. That will give Percy five more days to find someone. If he doesn't by then, you can go back without us. I can't say I agree with what you are doing, but I don't think anyone could understand how you feel unless they had been in the war." There was such a sincere show of love and gratitude in Angelo's eyes that Gladys knew she had made the right decision.

Two days later, there were two new happenings that changed Angelo's plans. In the morning, the mailman brought a bundle of Ike's letters that Victor had forwarded to them, and in the afternoon,

Percy arrived with good news. He had found a psychiatrist who was renowned for his success working with soldiers suffering with post-war mental problems. "His name is Andre Beaulieu, Angelo, and he has agreed to come and see you here," Percy said.

"Will he be coming alone?" Gladys asked.

"Yes. He had a very close friend who died recently, and he felt it would do him good to get away for a few days. I should have asked you first, James, before I invited him, but I didn't want to waste time. I was also afraid that he might receive another patient who he might not be able to refuse."

"Well, I am certainly glad you didn't wait. Now, Angelo, let us pray this man is as good as his reputation, shall we?"

"I will be indebted to you both for the rest of my life if he can help me, James. It's really quite remarkable the way things have turned out, isn't it?"

James grinned, and said, "I don't think I have ever read a book that had such an unbelievable story, even a fictional novel. I think we all agree that wherever Gladys is, there is sure to be something unusual happening."

"I can't argue with that," Percy remarked. "Life would be very boring without our Gladys around to brighten life's dull moments. What on earth would we do without her?"

"I'm sure your lives would be far more peaceful, but I'm afraid you're stuck with me, so you just have to grin and bear it."

Ike's letters were just what Angelo needed to put his mind at rest. Ike managed to write as though he was working in an ordinary hospital, instead of a makeshift tent beside the battlefield where he could hear the constant noise of gunfire. It was as though he had become so accustomed to the sounds, he could ignore them. However, Angelo knew Ike and could imagine him holding a dying soldier's hand and shedding tears of sorrow when the poor man died, even if he never wrote about such things.

His letters were full of plans for the future and how he could hardly wait to get home. He was happy to learn that Angelo had learned to ride, but he said that he wouldn't need lessons, as he had been given a horse to carry him from one field hospital to another, when needed. "We'll buy some good horses when I get home, Angie, and we'll take some long rides. I can hardly wait for that," he wrote.

Ike added short letters for Gladys and Eddy along with Angelo's and thanked them for sending him parcels. "Sure, and all the hospital staff are that jealous," he wrote. "They are always saying I have the best family of anyone here. If that doesn't make me want to come home, I don't know what would."

Gladys had tears in her eyes when she read that, but she was even more touched when Ike said he was pleased she liked his house, and he hoped she and Angelo would think of it as their own. "I hope we feel as close to him when he comes home, as we do when we read his letters," she told Angelo.

Dr. Andre Beaulieu was a very likeable man. Although he was small in stature, he had an ambience of strength and knowledge similar to Percy's late German doctor friend, Helmut. Like Helmut, Andre also had enough humbleness to his character to allow his patients to feel at ease in his presence. He arrived on Saturday as planned, and after insisting everyone call him Andre, he immediately began treating Angelo.

Andre stayed at Four Oaks for a week, and he seemed to enjoy himself. Most of his time was spent with his patient, taking long walks, riding, and fishing together. At first, Angelo said very little, but by the last day, he had told the doctor every little detail of his life including the time he spent in the army. Before he left to return to London, Andre gave Angelo some medication to take if he suffered with bouts of depression. That week with the doctor made quite a difference in Angelo. He was more like he was before he went into the army, and although he still suffered with nightmares, they weren't as vivid and horrific as they had been and were far fewer.

The doctor also had a long talk with Gladys before taking his leave. "Angelo's problem is far from unique, Gladys. War causes more mental wounds than physical ones. The trouble with the mental wounds is that most men are afraid to admit they have them. They have this ridiculous idea that it makes them less manly if they admit they were afraid, and they keep their demons to themselves until they end up in an asylum. As it is now, most army doctors don't understand the problem, or how to treat it, but thank heavens, more and more are beginning to refer their patients to specialists.

"I think a lot of Angelo's problems began when he was a child and witnessed his father and mother's tragic deaths. Without real-izing it, he felt he had deserted his mother when he ran and left her body in that basement where they lived, even though she had made him promise to do it." Angelo had blocked that memory from his mind, and even Gladys didn't know about it until the doctor told her. "He's carried that guilt around for all those years without knowing it. Then, when he had to leave those soldiers on the battlefield, it added to that guilt.

"On top of all that, it seems that he and his good friend, Ike, made a pledge to look after each other while they were in the army, and once again, he had to leave him behind in the thick of things while he was sent home to safety. The poor man is unconsciously fraught with guilt. I have done what I could to convince him that none of these things were his fault, and I think if you keep encourag-ing him to talk about his past, and his nightmares, he will come to realize it himself. I would like to see him again in two weeks, and if I can't get away to come to Four Oaks, I would like you to bring him to London."

When it was time for the doctor to leave, Angelo was reluctant to see him go. "I wish you could stay longer, doctor. Your presence gives me confidence."

"I understand, Angelo, but if you find yourself feeling depressed, I want you to talk to Gladys or James about it. I've had a talk with them both, and your lad as well. I think they will be able to help you, now that they know more about your problem," Andre said as he put his arm around Angelo's shoulders. "It will take time, my boy, but I am confident that you are going to be fine." Then he rubbed his hand over Angelo's shoulder blades. "You could use a little more meat on these bones, though."

Except for one or two nightmares, Angelo enjoyed the rest of their holiday. When the weather was favourable, he went fishing with James, Percy, and Eddy, they all took turns riding the Velocipedes that Gladys' father-in law had bought at the World's Fair in London, and they played croquet. On rainy days, they played indoor games or just sat and visited. Hilda went out of her way to make tempting meals hoping Angelo would gain weight, so by the time their visit was over, he had put on a few pounds and looked much healthier. Andre managed to visit one more time but just for the weekend. James invited him to return any time, which was what the doctor had hoped for.

When it came time to return to New York, Angelo was almost as reluctant to leave as Gladys and Eddy. Although, he felt much improved, he decided to make an appointment with Andre the day before they were to sail, so they left Four Oaks two days early. Claudia Cowan had kept her word, and Gladys had a trunk of exquisite glassware all made in Sandwich to take home.

Freda cooked a special dinner the night before they left, and they all stayed up late not wanting the evening to end. "I think the war shall be over very soon, my loves," Gladys told Dolly and Eliza. "Then you shall be able to come to New York. We'll go to Coney

Island, swim in the ocean, and do all sorts of nice things together. And you both shall love the voyage on the ship. We'll book your passage the minute the war ends.

"I don't ever want to be apart from you for such a long time again. You know, I really appreciate how nice you've both been to Angelo. He's been here for less than three months, but he says he's going to miss you both very much."

Dolly said they would miss him, too, then she felt the need to ask, "Is he anything like Father, Mother?"

"Oh, yes, Dolly. He's very much like Tom. Maybe Angelo isn't as impetuous as your father, but he was just as kind and caring. I remember how excited he was when I told him that he was going to be a father. He would have loved you every bit as much as Angelo loves Eddy. Maybe someday you will think of Angelo as a father figure. He would like that." Dolly didn't answer, but she didn't object either.

Everyone came down to the train to see them off, and Eddy, hanging out the window of the train so far that Angelo had to hang onto the seat of his pants, waved until he could no longer see the station. When they arrived in London, Angelo went to see Andre and then they stayed overnight with Percy, who had come back a few days earlier to be ready for them.

Angelo and Percy sat up a little later than Gladys and Eddy to enjoy a brandy and have a visit. Percy was anxious to know what the doctor had to say, but was hesitant to ask, so he just said, "How was Andre, Angelo?"

"He said the time he spent at Four Oaks was just what he needed. I asked him what I owed him, and he said I didn't owe him anything. I hope you and James are not paying for his services, Percy. If either of you have done that, please tell me. I hope to be financially secure in a few years, and I will be able to reimburse you."

"You needn't worry about it. Andre refused to take a fee, and that is the truth. I think he actually gained as much help from his time in Sandwich as you."

"He has given me the name of a psychiatrist in New York, so if I ever feel I need help, I will have someone to I can go to."

They talked for a short time longer then Angelo said he had better get to bed before Gladys went to sleep so he wouldn't disturb her. When he said she was coming down with a cold, Percy insisted on putting the kettle and making a hot drink for Angelo to take to her.

Gladys wasn't sure if her stuffy nose or the wind pushing the rain against the bedroom window woke her before daylight. She had always loved the sound of a storm outside, and it made her bed feel even cosier, but when she tried to snuggle up to Angelo's back, a fit of sneezing overtook her. Rising, she groped around in the dark until she found the settee, which, fortunately, had a cushion and a warm knitted afghan on it. When the sneezing ceased, she managed to go back to sleep for an hour until daylight dawned and she could see enough to get dressed and take care of her toilet.

"Good morning," Percy, who already had a pot of coffee made, said, cheerily, when she entered the kitchen. "Oh dear, you do look dreadful, if you don't mind me saying."

Gladys said, "No, I don't mind, that is exactly how I feel," but it sounded more like, "Do, I don mine, dat dis sactly how I feel," and Percy laughed.

"Forgive me, Gladys, I couldn't help myself. You sounded so very funny. Here, sit down and drink this coffee. You don't have to be on board until eleven, so try to eat a piece of toast. I thought you and Angelo would rather have coffee than tea, but there is tea made as well."

Gladys and Angelo both preferred coffee in the mornings, but Percy hadn't the slightest idea how to make it. He always added salt and an egg, and it usually tasted like, what she imagined dishwater would, but she just said that would be lovely. She really couldn't taste anything with her cold anyway. A little while later, Angelo and Eddy came down and Percy served them breakfast while Gladys went upstairs to pack their nightshirts and toiletries.

Percy went to the pier with them, but he had an appointment and couldn't wait for the ship to sail, so they got settled in their cabin and then Gladys laid down while Angelo and Eddy went on deck to watch the workers load the supplies. Captain Bob had a quick visit with them then popped in to tell Gladys that if there was anything she needed to let him know. Gladys' eyes were bloodshot, and her nose was red and runny, so she didn't appreciate his visit.

Once they set sail, Angelo and Eddy insisted Gladys stay in her bunk while they brought her hot drinks, meals, and whatever else she required. Their cabin looked out on the deck, and with the door slightly ajar, no one could see her, but she could smell the salt air. She told Angelo that she could not have chosen a more suitable bed in which to recover. She had never been sick before when she didn't have to work at the same time, and with the constant attention, the soothing roll of the sea, and the rhythm of the ship's creaking timbers, she told Angelo that she had never felt so delightfully miserable.

After a few days of pampering, and hot toddies, she was feeling well enough to get up and about, but she was having such a lovely time she played the part of an invalid for another day. Then, her rest was over. The spoiling ceased, and she spent the rest of the trip waiting on her two favourite males.

They arrived in New York on the July 3rd. Victor and Lottie were pleased to see that Angelo not only looked healthier but also seemed to have regained his sense of humour. He had so much to tell them about his visit to Four Oaks that he insisted they get together after the restaurant closed the first night they were home. Both Angelo and Eddy had wonderful fish stories to tell, and the twins, Paulo and Louis, enjoyed the tales as much as the adults. "Eddy may look like his father, but he tells a lively story like his mother," Lottie remarked good-naturedly.

Angelo went on and on about the vast size of James' property, and how it took almost an entire day to ride around it all. "We shall all have to have a horse as soon as we can afford it, Uncle Vic. Paulo and Louis should have one now, and so should Eddy. You should see him ride!"

"Dad can ride with only one arm as well as anyone else at Uncle James' can with two," Eddy boasted. Angelo grinned and rubbed Eddy's head. Victor and Lottie were really impressed, not because Angelo could ride so well, but because he didn't mind Eddy mentioning his handicap. Before he went to England, no one had dared mention it.

When he finished talking about his holiday, Angelo said he intended to visit Otto in the morning and tell him about it, too, but then he saw the worried look on Victor and Lottie's faces and instinctively knew something was wrong. "He's not doing poorly, is he?" he asked.

"I'm sorry, Angelo, Otto passed away two weeks ago. Lottie and I went to see him when we heard he wasn't doing well. That was over a month ago, but he made us promise not to tell you. He said there was nothing you could do for him, and he didn't want you to come home just to watch him die. He said to wait until you came home then tell you that he loved you, and that you shouldn't feel sad. He died peacefully in his sleep one night with Iris sitting by his side."

"Did he have a funeral?"

"Yes. We were all there, and Karl, one of his boys, delivered the eulogy. He talked about how you saved Otto's life and allowed him to die in peace with his family by his side. You'll never know what a blessed act that was. Every time I went to visit him, he told me to tell you how much he loved you and Ike. He was a wonderful man, Angelo."

"How is Iris?" Gladys asked

"She's coping very well. She was so thankful he didn't have to suffer in the end. I know she'll be glad to see you, though. She would have liked you to have been there to sing "Amazing Grace," Gladys, but she asked me to do it, and she even played the flute as I sang. It was both heart-breaking and beautiful. She hasn't missed one of our music days at the hospital, in spite of her loss."

"I can believe that; she is special," Gladys replied.

"I would have liked to be with him at the end, Uncle, but I know you had to do what he asked," Angelo said. "Now we shall have to see that Iris and the children have enough income to survive."

"Oh, yes, I almost forgot to tell you, Karl, one of Otto's twins, enlisted in the merchant navy the day after Otto died, and the day after that the other twin joined the army. They were both here for the funeral, but they left soon after. Iris didn't try to stop them. I guess she knew they were going to do it for some time."

The next day, as soon as they had breakfast, Gladys and Angelo went to visit Iris. She had managed to get through the days following her husband's death, including the funeral, without shedding a tear, but as soon as she opened her door and saw Angelo and Gladys standing there, she broke down. Without realizing it, she had been waiting for them to come home to share in her grief. They stayed with her until dinner time, then Gladys told Angelo to return to their flat and to look after Eddy while she made Iris and her girls something to eat. She said she would stay the night and return home in the morning. By the time the two women were ready to retire, Iris was able to laugh again.

With encouragement from Gladys and Sandy, Iris spent Otto's pension on a little bakery shop close to her home, and her three girls helped her after school and on weekends. Gladys and Lottie missed

Iris' accompaniment on her flute when they sang for the soldiers twice a week, but she did most of her baking in the evenings and couldn't spare the time.

There was a lot more tension in the city by the time Gladys, Eddy, and Angelo returned from England than there was when they left. General Robert E. Lee had invaded the North through Virginia's Shenandoah Valley and thousands of Union troops had been sent to Pennsylvania to defend the Union. Many of those were volunteers from New York City, and as they hadn't heard from Ike for a while, Angelo figured he must have gone there, too.

New York City was in a state of fear. If the Confederate army was successful at Gettysburg, Pennsylvania, their troops might invade their city within days. Even after the Union forces drove the Confederate army back into the South, the tension remained, owing to the forthcoming enforcement of the National Conscription Act— an act that would make all single men aged twenty to forty-five and married men up to thirty-five subject to a draft lottery.

Angelo didn't agree with the act, which surprised Gladys and Victor. "I thought you of all people would see the necessity of conscription, Angelo. We have to end this war, and we need more men to fight it. I'm not just saying that because I am too old to enlist," Victor declared.

They were all sitting down in the kitchen enjoying a coffee break in between lunch and dinner. "I am not against conscription if it's necessary, Uncle, but I don't think it's right when a man, who can't find someone to take his place, is allowed to pay the government three hundred dollars and buy his way out of the draft. It's not a fair act, and I agree with those who oppose it."

"I didn't realize that. I had heard about it, but I thought it was only a rumour. If that is the case, then we should all protest."

Angelo's anger over it all worried Gladys, and she began to wish they had stayed in England until the war was over. "I think you both should keep out of it. You have done your bit, Angelo, so please don't get involved," she begged, but in the days that followed, she noticed quite a few strangers coming into the restaurant and talking to Angelo and Victor then leaving without ordering a meal.

When she mentioned it to Lottie, Lottie said, "They had better not be planning anything with that bunch from Five Points. I heard there is a lot of dissention going on there, and although I don't blame them, it's not our problem. None of those poor young men have the money needed to buy their way out of the draft, but we can't do anything about that. I think we should have a talk with our fellows right now before they let themselves in for something they can't get out of."

When Gladys and Lottie confronted Angelo and Victor they were shocked to learn that they were already committed to joining in on a march of protest to prevent the Army Draft from happening. Angelo did his best to put Gladys and Lottie's minds at rest as he explained, "It's just a peaceful protest. If enough of us march up to the draft office and form a barrier, we can stop anyone from getting in or out of the building. They will have to close it down, and with hope, it will start some negotiation. At least it will bring the injustice of the act out into the open.

"I didn't go to war to fight for a country that treats the downtrodden like animals. I'm sorry, ladies, but my conscience will not let me sit by while others fight for what I believe in. You feel the same, don't you, Uncle Vic?" Victor said he agreed.

"Well, if it is just a protest, then I think we should be there, too," Gladys declared, surprising then all, even Lottie, who looked very sceptical before she nodded her head in agreement.

"I should say not!" Victor demanded. "It may be a peaceful march, but you know there are always one or two hotheads among every crowd, and I don't want you anywhere near if things get ugly."

"Perhaps having some ladies there to protest will really make the authorities take notice," Gladys suggested.

"Huh, if you went, you would be the only 'ladies' there."

"That is a terrible thing to say, Vic. Any woman who stands up for what she believes deserves to be called a lady. I don't care who they are, or how poor they are," Lottie replied crossly.

"Angelo, will you ask those friends of yours if their wives will be joining in on the march?" Gladys asked. Angelo agreed, and they let the matter drop, hoping the government would abolish the draft before July 13th.

Chapter 11

Despite warnings from some of the Democratic politicians, the lottery was ready to begin on Monday, July 13, 1863. The morning began with what appeared to be a peaceful strike. Angelo, Gladys, Victor, and Lottie joined with some of the organizers, recruiting protesters, as they visited uptown factories and construction sites. It encouraged Gladys to see how many people volunteered to stand up for justice. There were fireman, artisans, groups of young people, and quite a few women among the protesters. However, they were shabbily clad, which made Gladys and Lottie feel a little conspicuous and nervous.

"Stay close, and don't let go of one another," Angelo warned as the crowd made its way toward the lottery offices pushing the four of them along, but as the numbers grew, so did the shouting. When the tone of the crowd became more and more boisterous and threatening, Angelo and Victor realized it was no longer a peaceful protest but more of a frenzied mob on the verge of a riot. Some of the latest to join the movement were carrying lethal looking sticks and clubs, and many appeared to be inebriated. Angelo nudged Victor and nodded his head to the side. Victor didn't need to ask what he meant.

Slowly the four of them inched their way to the outside of the pack. Gladys looked at Lottie and winked then she stumbled as though she was fainting. Angelo grabbed her with his one arm and motioned for Victor to pick her up and carry her down a side street where he lay her down. Worried, Angelo knelt down beside her. "Gladys, are you all right?"

Gladys looked up at him, smiled and said, "Yes, but I think we should pretend I'm not until we get home. That way we shan't look like we are deserters." Victor went to look for a cab and found one a few blocks away. The driver didn't want to take any fares, afraid he would be attacked by the rioters, but Victor promised him such a generous fare that he couldn't refuse. Gladys continued with the farce until they were all back at the restaurant.

Angelo had sensed the uncontrollable anger that was building up among the crowd and realized how close they had come to being involved in a riot. He insisted the restaurant be closed and the staff sent home. "When you do get home, be sure to lock your doors, and don't leave your house until this is over," he told them all, not knowing the riot would last for three more long and terrifying days.

The only authorities who were able to safely venture among the crowds that first night were priests, firemen, and Democratic politicians. Others sat in the dark, praying there would be no bricks thrown at their windows. Well-known abolitionists stayed home in the dark, with guns loaded ready to defend their families. Although Lottie's aunt Theresa and uncle Peter were active republican supporters, Victor assured Lottie that they lived far enough away from the rioting to be safe.

Having no firearms, Angelo and Victor decided to fight any intruders with food. They asked Sandy, Lottie, and Gladys to prepare a large amount of stew, thinking the smartest way to alleviate angry protestors was to offer them a hearty meal. They knew there were quite a few who had come out that morning with empty stomachs.

A few days before, they had put a sign in their window saying they were against the way in which the draft lottery was handled, so they hoped that might stop rioters from throwing bricks at their establishment. They also decided to leave the lamps lit.

There were no signs of rioters in the neighbourhood, but they could see flames and smoke in the distance, so Angelo didn't want Gladys to stay up in the apartment in case their building was set on fire. "There still could be trouble, because there are more jewellers here in Maiden Lane than anywhere else in the city, and some of the rioters may take advantage of the protest and break into one or two of the shops. I think you should go with Lottie and stay with the boys. Someone should be with them to make sure they stay in the house and don't come here."

Gladys had left Eddy with the twins when they left to march with the protesters that morning, and both she and Lottie were anxious to see if they were all right, but they were also reluctant to leave the men.

"I don't think there is anything in our neighbourhood that would interest the rioters, Lottie, so I'll walk home with you and Gladys. We'll go out the back way and hope no one sees us," Victor said. "I'll not be long, Angelo."

"Here, Uncle, take my bat with you," Angelo suggested, but Victor said he was afraid to carry a weapon in case the law mistook him for a rioter.

They had only been gone about fifteen minutes when five protesters—three men, a woman, and a young lad—hammered on the front door calling to be let in. As soon as Angelo opened the door, he could see they weren't armed, but they all appeared to be frightened.

One of the men had a nasty-looking gash on his head and his hair was matted with blood. Angelo said he should go into the kitchen and see if the cook could clean it for him, but the woman said she was his wife and would do it.

Sandy sat the other three at a table at the back of the restaurant where they couldn't be seen and gave each of them a big bowl of stew. Angelo found some clean bandages, and he helped the woman wrap one around her husband's head, then they came out to have something to eat as well. No one said a word until they had had their fill, then the man with the bandaged head told Angelo and Sandy what was happening.

"First, we were right with them when they reached the lottery offices. That's when our firemen stormed inside, smashed the selection wheel, and set the building on fire. Everybody hollered, 'Hooray' an' we thought that was all we had to do, but there were some who carried clubs and were dead set on usin' 'em. They tried to get everyone to go with them, but we wanted no part of it. We heard someone sayin' what they was goin' to do, and I tell you, mister, it was bloody murder. We tried to leave and get home, but then the cops came at us. They chased thousands of us down Broadway and caught up with us at Bleeker Street. Clubs were flying, and you couldn't hear anything but heads being hit and moaning and cursin'."

"That's when my Tom here got hit," the man's wife added. "Then we managed to get out of the crowd and we was running for our lives when we saw yer notice in the winder and figured you might let us in." She gave a little laugh and continued, "We didn't spect to get fed, though."

When the fugitives heard Victor come in the back door, they were ready to make a run for it until Angelo assured them it was only his uncle. During the night, more came looking for shelter, and by the time the sun came up, Sandy had run out of stew and was making pancakes and porridge. Most of the men, who came to the restaurant for shelter, had wives and children with them. They weren't carrying weapons and had only gone on the march intending to take part in a peaceful protest.

The law had no way of distinguishing between those who were looking for a fight and those who weren't, and if Angelo, Gladys, Victor, and Lottie had not left the crowd when they did, they too would have been looking for somewhere to hide.

During the first hours of the riot, the rioters managed to put a stop to the draft lottery for a short time, but that was the only goal they achieved. They did, however, manage to do a lot of damage before they finished fighting.

Soldiers were called in, and house-to-house battles went on in the East 20s, with artillery bombardments and cavalry charges, causing the crowds to become more desperate and vicious. Policemen seemed to be far more affective, and they were finally able to protect New York's African Americans. Rioters retreated to tenement basements, and by Friday the riot was over.

Some newspapers reported that there were over a hundred people killed and Protestant missionaries, Republican draft officials, war production workers, wealthy businessmen, and African Americans suffered the worst of the crowds' wrath during the fateful four days. Native-born New Yorkers were inclined to blame all the Irish Catholics for the riot, even though only a very small amount of those people took part in it.

Gladys and Eddy were happy to be back in their apartment once more, and Angelo was relieved to have them safe and sound. The staff returned to work, and once more the restaurant was open for business. Everyone did their best to behave as though the riot hadn't happened, but it was a difficult task when one saw the properties that were burnt and damaged, not to mention the folks walking around with bandaged heads and limbs.

Except for the short delay owing to their office being trashed, the uprising didn't stop the draft lottery, but only about eight percent of the Union Army was made up of conscripted soldiers, the rest were all volunteers. Nevertheless, owing to the northern war effort, and the re-legalization of the cotton trade with the rebel states, the city's economy bounced back, creating more jobs for the poor.

Gladys' first task after she and Eddy returned to the apartment was to write and assure Dolly and James that they were all fine and that the rioting was over. The second thing she hastened to do was to visit Iris. Since her boys had left, she had no one to protect her if the rioters had broken into her home, so Gladys was anxious to see her. When she arrived at the Goebels' residence she was dismayed to see that one of the windows in the front of Iris' house had been smashed and there was a newspaper stuck to the inside of it. Gladys couldn't help but think that although it might keep bugs out, it wouldn't stop thugs from getting in. Anxiously, she knocked on the door.

She hardly recognized Iris when she opened the door and she cried, "Oh Iris, you poor thing, what have they done to you?" Iris had two black eyes and a very swollen nose.

"I'm fine, Glad, I'm really fine even if I don't look or sound it. I just can't breathe through by nose." Iris was having trouble pronouncing her m's.

"Are you well enough to tell me what happened?"

"Of course. Come on in and I'll bake us a cup of tea."

"Here, let me do that. You sit while I get the tea."

"If you insist, Bossy Bessy," Iris replied, laughing.

When they had their tea, Gladys said. "I saw your broken window. Did those thugs break into your house? Did they hurt the girls?"

"No, it wasn't the rioters who broke my window, although they did come up this street, and they were carrying bricks, but they didn't break by nose."

"Then who on earth was it?"

"It was stupid be! I broke by own nose, and the window. When I saw them cobing up the street, I was afraid for the girls, so I grabbed the only weapon I could find. It was a stupid crutch I had when I sprained my ankle. Then I told the girls to stay inside while I went on the porch to wait for the troublebakers. When one of theb came up to be, I took that crutch and swung it with all by bight. Fortunately, I didn't hit the ban, but I did knock that silly betal crow I had hanging frob a bracket, right into by face. At the sabe tibe I lost by grip on the crutch and it went sailing through the air and through the window.

"The poor ban had seen be with the crutch and thought I needed help. Instead of running, he was kind enough to take the tibe to help me indoors where the girls looked after be." Gladys was bent over, and at first Iris thought she was sick but then she realized she was bent over with laugher. "You can stop laughing any tibe now, Gladys, it's not that huborous."

"Forgive me, Iris, but it really is. You sound just like I did when I had that cold coming home from England. Maybe if you could have pronounced your m's it wouldn't have been so funny." Gladys wiped the tears from her eyes then added, "Oh, my, I haven't laughed like that since this whole mess began."

"Well, anytibe you need another laugh, you can bloobing well go and find sobeone else to break their nose."

Gladys apologized, then she told Iris all about the happenings at the restaurant during the week. Iris said that she and the girls were going to open the bakeshop again in a day or two. "I can do the baking and the girls can look after the front of the shop until I look a bit bore respectable." When she saw that Gladys was still having trouble keeping a straight face, she added, "You can go hobe now, Gladys Mathews. I can banage very well without your sybpathy."

Once again Gladys apologized, then she hugged her friend and said she would be back soon. Iris was waving goodbye as Gladys walked down the street, but she closed the door with a bang when Gladys called back, "I shall let everyone at the restaurant know what happened. They'll be relieved to hear you weren't attacked, at least not by any rioters."

The next day, Gladys decided she had gone a little too far with her teasing, and she had Sandy cook a big pan of schnitzel for Iris and her girls. She also took her one of the necklaces she had bought in England. Iris was pleased with both gifts, and, during their visit together, Gladys managed to stifle every laugh and giggle, no matter how many m's Iris mispronounced.

Two months after Gladys arrived home, she had a letter and a cheque from Claudia Cowan in Sandwich. Claudia said she sold every article that Gladys had left with her inside of one month and could Gladys please send double the amount of goods as soon as possible. It seemed her little shop had never been so busy. Gladys had no idea how she was going to supply the woman with that amount of goods. Luckily, Norman O'Rourke, their cook, came to her rescue.

Norman was an entrepreneur at heart, and he had taken an interest in Gladys' little import/export business, but he knew she would have to be registered if she was to expand, and he had made it his business to find out all the legal steps one had to take to start such a business. He had also made inquiries as to where he could lay his hands on some unique and foreign goods that no one else had thought to import. When he heard Gladys was looking for more goods, he approached her and made her an offer.

At first Gladys said she really didn't want a partner, but when Norman pointed out that if she wanted to expand her business, or make any profits, she would definitely have to do it legally, and that would mean a lot of paperwork, which he could handle. Besides, she had no idea where she could buy enough goods wholesale to supply Claudia and eventually more English clients. Norman professed to have the answer to that problem, too.

"Actually, Angelo, I cannot understand why Norman wants me for a partner; he is the one who has all the connections, and he is clever enough to understand all the legal paraphernalia as well," Gladys said.

"Perhaps he needs your expertise as a buyer, or he might just need someone to share in financing the business. I have become very fond of Norman since he came to work for us, but Sandy has known him a lot longer, and I think you should talk to him before you sign any papers. How much is it going to cost to get the business started?"

"I don't know, darling, but I want to be able to pay for it myself. I have a little savings and I shall use that." Gladys didn't say that most of that savings would be whatever the pawnbroker would give her for a gold locket James had given her, so she talked to Sandy the following day.

"I want to know what you think I should do, Sandy."

"Well, my dear, I never was one to gamble, so I can't rightly say you should go ahead and do it. On the other hand, if there isn't too much money to invest, I'd say Norman, for all his faults, would be the sort of loyal friend you could rely on to keep his word. He has gambled a fortune away in the past, but that was all his money. I doubt he would gamble with a partner's money, but just to be safe, I would have your own lawyer look at the partnership agreement to make sure your half of the business is secure."

"Thanks, Sandy. I don't know why I didn't think of that. I have the best lawyer in the world, and if Percy thinks it's all right, then I shall go ahead with the partnership. Norman said it would probably go along a lot faster if I just used my initials instead of my name. As per usual, women are expected to remain home raising children and knitting instead of going into business."

One month later, Gladys heard from Percy telling her that he had written to a lawyer friend in New York and asked him to look after Gladys' interest. He also wrote that he thought it would be good for her to go into the business. He said he had investigated Norman's background and had found him to be a fascinating character. Gladys wasn't sure if that was a good thing or not, but Percy also wrote that Norman had never been in trouble with the law and seemed like a trustworthy individual. Then he wished her good luck and sent his love.

Gladys showed the letter to Angelo, Victor, and Lottie so they would feel less apprehensive about her idea. Victor suggested they all go in on it as a sideline, but Gladys felt that, because she had begun the business, she would like to run her half on her own. "I suppose it is selfish of me, Victor, but I really want to see if I can accomplish it by myself."

"You are hardly doing it by yourself, Gladys. From what you have told us, Norman will be doing most of the work," Victor said a little too sharply.

"I say, Uncle, that's rather a cruel thing to say. Gladys has worked exceedingly hard to get her sales built up, and I believe she deserves to prove she can carry on alone," Angelo retorted.

"I never said she didn't. I just thought since we were doing everything else as a team, she would want us in on it, that's all."

Lottie shook her head and said, "Now you are being silly. Don't pay any attention to him, Gladys. He's mad because he bet me a shilling on the game last night and lost." She ruffled Victor's hair and said, "Come on, Grumpy Boots, smile, and I'll give you a chance to win it back tomorrow. I'll even go to the game with you."

Victor couldn't help but grin, then he mumbled, "Sorry, Glad," and left.

Norman and Gladys applied for a licence to begin their export/import business, and after they were given some papers to read and sign, they took them to the lawyer Percy had recommended. He looked over the papers, said they were in order, then gave them each a contract to read and sign that he had composed.

Gladys smiled and said, "It seems you have heard from Percy."

"Yes, and he seems to think a great deal of you, Mrs. Matthews. He also gave me his thoughts about your partnership, and I added what I deemed necessary to protect not only your investment but also yours as well, Mr. O'Rourke."

The respect shown to him in the contract, and the personal respect the man showed him in his office, pleased Norman greatly. When he first learned that the lawyer had the contract waiting for them to sign, he began to feel as though Gladys' friends didn't trust him, but after he read it through, he could see that he had been mistaken. Another thing that impressed Norman was that the lawyer refused to take a fee, saying that if they wanted to retain his services once they were in operation, he would then begin charging them his usual rate. For the first time in Norman's life, he felt he had met a businessman he could trust indubitably.

Once they obtained the licence, Norman couldn't wait to find new sources of goods they could ship to dealers in England and was ready to start. They both knew that exporting cotton would have been the most lucrative business, but neither had enough money to invest in that.

Norman was extremely disappointed when he learned that Gladys only had one client in England and that that client just owned a small gift shop in Sandwich. This meant he was forced to curb his enthusiasm and be satisfied with making inquiries so as to be ready for when she could return to England and find more clients. They also had to decide where they were going to store the goods they imported. Fortunately, this problem was solved a few weeks later.

Chapter 12

Although Iris was busy with her bakery, she still managed to take one night a week off to play the flute as accompaniment for Lottie and Gladys. Thus they continued to entertain the hospitalized veterans. One night they were surprised when two Doctors, they had never seen in the hospital before, stood and listened to them for a few minutes. One of the doctors said something to the other and left, while the other one stayed to listen until they were finished singing.

Gladys had only seen Ike Murphy once or twice, and then it was when he was talking to Victor, and she hadn't paid much attention to him. Now, looking at the doctor more closely, she thought she saw a resemblance, but they had just heard form Ike and he was working in a field hospital. Curious, she went up to him and asked, "It can't be you, can it?" Then she realized how silly that sounded. "I am sorry, doctor, but for a minute I thought you might be our, 'er, I mean, Ike Murphy, a dear friend of ours."

Ike put his head back and laughed, "Tis none other than Ike Murphy yer lookin' at, Gladys, my girl. Now do you suppose you could give a dear friend a hug?"

"Ike!" Gladys screamed, and she held out her arms.

Iris heard the name Ike and she cried, "Otto's other angel!" She reached up, pulled his head down and kissed him on both cheeks.

Ike blushed and said, "Now I can understand why Otto wanted to come home so badly. Is he here, or are you managing to have him at home?"

Iris told him Otto had died, but that he had died happy, with all the family beside him. Then she told him they would talk later and said that she and the others would finish entertaining in the other ward and leave Gladys and Lottie to talk to him.

Lottie, who had stood back and was listening, waited for Iris to leave then said, "Can I have a hug, too? After all, I knit stockings and a sweater for you, too."

"Well now, you look like Carlotta, Victor's wife, but she would be much older than the likes of you!" Ike said, grinning. "Come here and give a lonely old soldier a hug."

"I though you would never ask, doctor!'

Ike explained that he was just an orderly not a doctor, and then Gladys wanted to know when he had arrived in New York, and why he hadn't been to see them.

Ike said he only came in with the doctor on a train of wounded the day before. "I haven't eaten or slept since I arrived, but I think we've caught up now. Doc just told me to take a day off and visit Angie. Are you about to go home?"

"We are now that you are here," Lottie said.

"I can't wait to see Angelo's face when you walk in," Gladys said grinning. Ike just took a minute to change, and they left. When they arrived at the restaurant, Angelo was at the front desk, and Gladys and Lottie just said hello and walked on by.

Ike held his head down, went up to the desk and said, "I'd like to reserve a table for eight."

The familiar tone of the voice caused Angelo to frown but he still didn't suspect anything. "Yes, sir. Will that be for tomorrow?"

"No, I would like it right now. You see there's this family I've not seen for a long time, and I can't wait to see them." Then he lifted his head and laughed, "Especially that old one-armed bugger named, Angie!"

"Ike!" Angelo reached over the desk, threw his one arm around Ike's neck and hung on while Ike pulled him over the desk and into his arms. Tears were running down both their cheeks and they held each other for a long time.

"God damn it, you're just as ugly as I remember," Ike joked, laughingly. Then he remembered there were ladies present and apologized. "Forgive me, I've not had time to become civilized again."

Gladys had never known what it felt like to be jealous, but when she saw how fervently Angelo greeted his friend, she couldn't help but compare it to the impassive manner in which he had greeted her when he got back from the war. She knew Angelo and Ike's relationship was nothing like Percy and James, but in a way, it was even stronger, and although it made her feel ashamed and guilty, she couldn't help but envy Ike. She realized that soldiers went through a lot together and that they were bound to feel close. On the other hand, she and Angelo had been through an experience just as traumatic when they were children in Old Nichol, and she thought that would have built just as strong a bond between them.

Victor was almost as pleased to see Ike as Angelo, and he suggested they all stay at the restaurant after dinner and have a drink. He had set aside some of their best scotch whiskey for this occasion and now that all three partners were together, he wanted them to sit around a table and toast the future.

"I won't be totally free until next year," Ike reminded them. "But Doc thinks we will be working at this hospital until then. He's a wonderful man, and I want you all to meet him soon. He's been supplying me with books to study. He seems to think I would make a good doctor, and if I stay in the Army, they'll pay for my schooling. Can you imagine this dumb Irishman being a doctor?"

Everyone congratulated him, but the look of disappointment on Angelo's face showed. "I suppose that means we won't have you as a partner after all, right?" he asked.

"I didn't say I've accepted the Army's offer, but if I did, nothing will change. We are still partners. I may have to be a silent partner for a few years, but I am looking forward to being part of your plans. I haven't slept for forty-eight hours, and if you don't mind, we'll have to wait to talk about them tomorrow. I haven't been to my house yet, but I know Simon always keeps a bed ready for me."

"Finish your drink, Ike, and I'll go out and flag down a cab for you," Victor offered.

The next morning, Ike was back at the restaurant before Angelo came down, so he sat in the kitchen and visited with Norman, since it was Sandy's day off. Norman explained how he and Gladys were in the process of starting an import/export business, and Ike said if they needed any monetary backing he would be glad to help out. When Angelo came down, Ike and he went for a walk along the docks.

"I see you've lost the rest of your arm, Angie. Was it gangrene?"

"No, but it was infected, and the specialist thought it would be better if he removed it."

"I think it was a smart thing to do. Other than that, how have you been?"

"I can't complain," Angelo answered, then he gave a quick laugh and added, "Although it's been rough on Gladys and the rest of the family."

"How's that?"

"I've not been very pleasant at times."

"I wish I could have been here for you, but now I am, and I think I can guess what you've been going through. I've seen a lot of sad cases, Angie, cases that the ordinary army doctors can't help.

Luckily, things have improved, and we do have a few specialists that are helping. If you like, I can find out the name of one you could see."

"Thanks, Ike, but thanks to Gladys' ex-husband, James, I saw a doctor while I was in London, who I think must be the best in his field. He gave me the name of a specialist here, if I need him. It was the horrific nightmares I was having that depressed me. I kept hearing more soldiers like Otto calling for help and I couldn't save them. Then I would dream it was you and I lying there, and soldiers were running over us. I really thought I would go mad."

"Thank God you were able to get help. What did the doctor do to help, if you don't mind me asking? You see, the doc has so many poor guys with similar complaints, so anything you can tell us just might save them from ending up in the insane asylum."

Angelo told him that he really didn't know what the doctor did to help except he had advised him not to keep it bottled up. "I think the smartest thing is to refer them to a specialist who knows how to handle cases like mine. The doc also gave me a pill to take if my anxiety attacks get the better of me, but ever since I returned from England, I haven't needed them. And believe me, Ike, things were pretty tense here when that riot was happening."

"If they agree, would you talk to some of the patients? I think it would help if they could talk to someone who has had the same problem."

"I don't know if I'm that well yet, but I suppose I could try to talk them into seeing a specialist, or maybe forming a support group."

Ike's health wasn't that good either, and it took him a month before he was able to relax enough to talk business with Victor and Angelo. He had lost a lot of weight, and his hair was more grey than black. Nevertheless, he was still a handsome man, and Gladys could see why Angelo thought he would make a good match for Mary, especially if he were to become a doctor. *My heavens,* she thought, *I'm thinking like an aristocrat and a proper snob!*

It didn't take long for Gladys to understand how right Doctor Andre Beaulieu, the London psychiatrist, had been when he said Angelo had felt guilty leaving Ike behind after he was sent home. Now that Ike was safely away from the battlefield, Angelo was far happier and a good deal more attentive to her and Eddy. Her jealousy soon waned, and she became genuinely fond of Ike.

Ike insisted on buying some riding horses for the family, and on his days off, he, Angelo, and Gladys often rode out to the country for a picnic, or they took the ferry over to Coney Island for the afternoon. Those outings gave Gladys an enjoyable feeling of nostalgia. They brought back many memories of the times she, her first husband, Tom, and their close friend, Keith, had spent during their free days riding or searching for treasure on Dover's beaches after a storm.

At first, Victor was content to let Ike take time off to enjoy himself, but when fall came, he insisted they make some plans. Ike was annoyed when he learned they hadn't done what he requested and paid off their mortgage, but now he insisted they make use of his bank account for whatever they decided to do. Victor wanted to knock down the wall that separated Ike's building and the restaurant so they could accommodate more customers. He also wanted to turn the top two floors of Ike's building into more apartments.

Ike thought they should sell both buildings, buy some prime property, and build something new and modern. Victor thought Ike meant a new restaurant and modern apartments, so he suggested they make a success out of what they already had first.

"Once we get all the new apartments built on your side and have them rented, then we can think about building more," he said.

"I wasn't talking about apartments, or restaurants, Vic. I was talking about a modern structure, uptown, for office rentals, like dentist offices, and that sort of clientele. You've all worked so hard, and now that we have the capital, I think it's time you became businessmen instead of labourers. I suppose it might be a gamble, but I think it'll be worth it. What do you think, Angie?"

"It's your money, Ike. We won't be risking that much, Uncle Vic, and if we lose our shirts, we can always rely on Shakespeare to give us a job."

Victor didn't laugh. "I don't know; it's a lot riskier than it sounds. I'm not as young as you two, so it's not all fun and games for me. What do you two think?" he asked Gladys and Lottie. "After all, you've both worked just as hard as we have. Are you willing to take the risk?"

"Ever since you said we are supposed to be a team, Victor, I have been doing a lot of thinking. If you men decide to become business-men, I want Lottie to come in with me as an equal partner on my half of Norman's and my import/export business. Maybe we will become as successful as businesswomen as you men. Will you do it, Lottie?"

"I'd love to, Glad. I always knew I was meant for something bigger than cook and dishwasher. In fact, boys, you have just rented out your first office. Of course, we shall demand a sign on our door."

"And what, would you like written on it, ladies?" Angelo asked.

"G. Matthews, L. Rossini, N. O'Rourke, Import/Export Experts, Inc."

Even Victor had to laugh. They all decided to think about it for a week before making any plans, and it was over a week before Ike had time to meet with everyone again. Victor was still not convinced that they should sell the restaurant. "This place meant a lot to Lottie's uncle. He sold it to us at a very low price for two reasons. One, because we are related and the other because he thought we would keep it in the family. I don't feel we have the right to sell it."

"I didn't know about that," Ike replied. "Look, forget my idea. I remember Lottie's aunt and uncle and I wouldn't hurt them for anything. We'll go ahead with your plans, Vic."

Gladys was standing up and she pat the top of his head, saying, "That's sweet of you, Ike, but may I make a suggestion?" Ike motioned with his hand for her to proceed. "Why can you not do both projects?" she asked. "I mean, you can spend a year or two fixing this place up, and if it turns out to be as profitable as you think it will, you can keep it in the family and hire someone to run it while you start the other building. Won't that work?"

"Personally, I think Gladys has a good idea. What say the rest of you?" Angelo asked. They talked it over for a little while longer, then all agreed.

While they were having a cup of coffee, Ike confessed that he had talked to a realtor who happened to be in the hospital visiting his brother, a veteran. "I asked him to keep a look out for some property in the city and he said there weren't many lots left. He was back yesterday and told me there was one lot on Henry Street, but it isn't very big, so I told him we wanted a double lot because we want to build a large building.

"He said he knew of a big one coming up on Leonard, just two blocks from the hospital, and, if I wanted it, I should make an offer before it hits the market. He also said that it'll probably be our last chance to find one. Now, I'd like to buy it now since he assured me it will be a great investment, even if we keep it for two years and then sell it."

"It is your money, Ike. If you want to buy it, you should," Victor stated.

Ike slammed his fist on the table, "I'll have no more of that from any of you, you hear? Didn't you do as I asked? If you didn't then I'll be bidding you goodbye right now."

"Not what in the devil brought that on?" Angelo asked him.

"I'll tell you what brought it on. You were supposed to put that account in our three names? I thought I was welcome as one of the family."

"You know damn well you are."

"Well what is this, 'It's your money' about then?"

"I'm sorry, Ike; I won't make that mistake again, and I agree with you. I think we should put an offer on that lot tomorrow, don't you, Angelo?"

"It sounds like we can't lose. You know the realtor, Ike, but will you be able to find time to do it?" Ike said he would take care of it. Then they began going over plans to remodel Ike's warehouse. Vic said he would get in touch with the City planner about knocking out some of the wall between the two buildings so they could expand the restaurant.

"What about us? Are we still going to be partners, Gladys?" Lottie asked.

"I would love to have you with me, if you still want to that is."

Lottie grinned, put out her hand, and said, "You bet."

The restaurant had to be closed for a month while the wall was being demolished. They were all sad to see Bruno's beautiful art work destroyed, but he had small drawings of all the pictures, and said he would be happy to do them again once they had the new wall cleaned and ready. The expansion would also give him a little more room to paint, and this pleased him almost as much as the fee he would receive.

Because Gladys lived in one of the older apartments, she had many good suggestions to give the men when they were planning the eight new ones, and she convinced them that they should make six larger units and ask that much more for the rent than they were getting for the older ones. "A couple with a family should have a bedroom of their own," she insisted. "And the rooms should be large enough to allow children to have their own beds. The stairway should be wider, so a person could have some decent-sized furniture brought up to their flat, and please make sure every flat has access to a fire-escape."

She also tried to convince them to install bathtubs and toilets, but Victor said that was going a little too far. Not many of the mansions in New York had that luxury. Norman was very adept at finding the most talented carpenters for the renovation. They were men who were overjoyed to find employment, especially as Angelo assured them that, if they proved their worth, they would be guaranteed a job whenever he and his company began construction on the new building.

Chapter 13

It was a busy time for them all. Gladys and Lottie did most of the cleaning up, besides visiting factories and wholesale dealers, looking for the most durable, but attractive, furnishings that were reasonably priced for the renovated restaurant. Gladys' expertise in materials helped. They still entertained at the hospital, and when they had the time, they collected items to send or take to Claudia's gift shop in Sandwich along with the samples Norman collected from Asian and other foreign dealers that he met on the docks. Having spent years aboard different ships, Norman had some very helpful and interesting connections.

The restaurant was ready to open one week later than scheduled, and Sandy was extremely pleased with all the improvements in the kitchen, which was now twice as large as before. Ike managed to buy the double lot he had mentioned, and they all went to look it over. It was deep enough to have some ornamental shrubs and a tree or two in the front of the building and large enough to build a four-storey structure. Ike said he thought they could have at least three floors of offices and maybe one or two deluxe apartments on the fourth floor.

"Who knows, we may even be able to install an elevator," he said, half-jokingly. There were hotels and business buildings in New York that had elevators, but they were extremely noisy, slow, and most would only accommodate one passenger at a time.

Because they weren't ready to start the new building, Ike decided that he would take the Army up on their offer and attend medical school. The Army doctor he worked for had taught him a lot, and he thought Ike could easily pass second-year exams if he was allowed to take them.

"I know the head administrator at the college here and I shall have a talk with him," the doctor said. "It's the Homeopathic Medical College on the corner of 20th Street and 3rd Avenue, and it's only been there for two-and-a-half years. I read about it in the last medical journal. It seems one of the civic leaders responsible for having the college built was William Cullen Bryant." When Ike said he had no idea who that was, the doctor replied, "He's a well-known poet."

"I've read a few of his poems. 'Thanatopsis' was one of them, and I was often tempted to quote some of it to the soldiers who were dying, but I wasn't sure if they would understand what Bryant meant. I have it somewhere among my belongings, and I'll find it and give it to you. That, and a short one he wrote called 'The African Chief,' makes us remember what we were fighting for in case we forget.

"Besides being the school's first president of the board of trustees, Bryant was also the editor of the *New York Evening Post,* and he may still be as far as I know. Anyway, one of the reasons he's so dedicated to the College is that he doesn't agree with some of the medical practices we have been using, such as bleedings, purges, and large doses of drugs."

"You have been complaining about those same things ever since I've been working for you," Ike said.

The doctor laughed and said, "I suppose I have. Good of you to put up with it, and not complain. Anyway, I hope they'll teach you some modern-day skills instead of the out-dated nonsense I was forced to take in college."

Ike did well in his exams, and along with the doctor's glowing testimony, he was able to eliminate two years off his studies.

Ike had his duties at the hospital, albeit a short shift, thanks to the doctor, and his studies took up the rest of his day. Because he had little time to spend in his Gramercy mansion, he suggested to Angelo and Victor that he move into Gladys and Angelo's old apartment and they move into the mansion. "You and Victor could both move into it," he told them one day. "After all, it is yours as much as mine. That way, Victor, you wouldn't have to rent the place you are in now."

"It makes sense, but I don't know what the ladies will think of the idea," Victor replied.

"I know Gladys has always wanted a big enough place to have her girls come and stay with us, so she might think it's a great idea. What do you think Lottie will say, Uncle?"

"I don't see how she could object," Victor answered with confidence.

He knew the two women got along well, because they worked together and planned on going into business together, so he thought there was no reason why they wouldn't want to live in the same house, but when he told that to Lottie, he soon found out he was wrong.

"Are you mad?" was the first thing she had to say when he told her. "I love Gladys like a sister, but I wouldn't want to share my kitchen or any other room of my house with her or a sister."

"Maria lived with us, and you didn't mind that."

"I had no choice then, but I do now. You can go right back and tell Ike that I will stay where I am, and Gladys may have the mansion. She'll need a larger place when her girls come to stay."

Lottie told Gladys what she had told Victor then apologized, "I hope you're not upset with me Gladys. If I had to live with anyone else, I would choose you, but I've been so accustomed to running my own household, and I'd really like to keep it that way."

Gladys said she understood, but she wished Lottie would move into the mansion and let her, Angelo, and Eddy move into one of the new apartments above the restaurant. "Ike can move into our old one," she explained. "I really do love living down by the water, and I'd rather live on Maiden Lane than anywhere else in New York."

"I don't think I would fit in up in Gramercy Park, Glad, and what about when the girls come to stay? You said you wanted a place big enough so they could bring someone with them."

"That would be Eliza's nanny, and Dolly's maid, Blossom, but the girls might not be able to come for a year or two anyway. At least not until this blessed war is over, and I hope, by that time, we shall have another big home built. If they come before, it will probably only be for a short visit, and perhaps you wouldn't mind moving into our apartment while they are here, and we could use the mansion. Does that make sense?"

"I wouldn't mind that at all, but like I said, I am afraid I'd feel out of place in Gramercy Park."

"We shall make sure you don't, then. It's about time I remodelled that wardrobe of yours, like I promised to do. A lot of people who live there came from poorer backgrounds than yours. Just imagine, as soon as we begin making a profit with our larger restaurant and new apartments, you shall be able join our City's aristocrats. You shall have your own fancy carriage to ride around Central Park in the evening processions."

"One time, I went to the park to see the parade, and I was disappointed to see that the only people I could see in most of the carriages were the driver and the footman. The passengers kept out of sight. They stay hidden in their covered carriages as though they are afraid we common spectators might contaminate them. I can't for the life of me see how they can enjoy the park that way. If I was them, I'd be riding in an open carriage and smile and wave at everyone as I rode by."

"And before long, the rest of them would be mimicking you. I think everyone wants to be like you, Gladys, but you can dress me up like the queen herself and I'll never look like a proper lady," Lottie insisted

"Nonsense, I am no more a lady than you, and it's the same with most of the women living in those fancy mansions. You just remember that when you move up there, and keep you head as high as the others."

The following month, Lottie, Victor, and the twins moved into Listla Cloone. Listla Cloone was the name of a castle that Ike remembered visiting when he was a little boy, so he named his mansion after it. Ike said he would do what he could to find employment for Simon and his wife, Liza, but in the meantime, Lottie said they could remain in the servants' quarters on the third floor.

The restaurant was enlarged and could seat almost twice the customers, so they had to hire more help. Paulo's art teacher, Bruno, had finished painting the new wall by the late fall. More and more Italians were coming to New York, and although Lottie had shared her recipes with all their cooks, she liked to be in the kitchen herself, now and again, just to be sure they were adding the right spices, and to see to it that the pasta was made the exact texture and thickness.

However, it didn't take long for her to realize that she could no longer spend time at the restaurant, take care of her family, and clean such a large home, so the next time Ike mentioned how difficult it was going to be to find employment and lodging for Simon and Liza, Lottie said she thought they would be much happier if they stayed and worked for her and Victor. Ike never let on that he hadn't bothered to look for a place for the couple, having no doubt Lottie would soon realize their worth.

The new apartment seemed like a mansion to Gladys, and she, Angelo, and Eddy were happier than they had ever been. She missed the girls, but she knew they would be coming to visit as soon as the war ended, and she thought that would be in the New Year.

When she, Eddy, and Angelo last visited Four Oaks, James had his friend come out to the estate to take pictures of Percy and him dressed like cowboys. Without telling Gladys, he also had the photographer take one of Eddy on Ali, the horse he was so proud to ride, and he sent it to Eddy for his eighth birthday. It was one of Eddy's favourite gifts. Another gift he appreciated was a pair of used ice skates from the twins. He could hardly wait for winter so he could go skating with his cousins on the lake in Central Park.

During the summer, they had all been so busy, they were only able to spend two Saturday afternoons in the park enjoying the concerts. When it first opened in 1859, there were many rules banning certain things, such as group picnics, tradesmen, and playing ball, and it was used mainly by the wealthiest New Yorkers. Then, when the rest of the people continued to complain, the officials were forced to change some of the rules. Now families of every class were allowed to have picnics there, and Gladys couldn't wait to spend a day with Dolly and Eliza in the park when they came to New York.

Eddy got his wish, and winter came early, but the lake didn't freeze enough to skate on it until mid-February. Lottie's uncle Peter, who was used to skating in Holland, had a small lake on his farm property, and before he had a stroke, he bought skates for Victor, Lottie, and the twins and taught them all how to skate. The first winter they were in New York, he also insisted Gladys, Angelo, and Eddy try it, using borrowed skates. Except for Eddy, who was quick to pick up any sport, they hadn't done very well.

Now, Eddy had his own skates, and he begged his parents to buy some, too. Neither wanted to, but they could tell how much it meant to him, so thinking they would just be doing it once or twice, they bought some from a second-hand store. They asked Ike to come with them, but he still had two months before he would be discharged and was too busy. Captain Bob Nicholson was in port and when he heard they were going skating, he offered to go along, saying that he was practically born with skis and skates on his feet.

Gladys and Angelo knew he wasn't just bragging when they saw how superbly he skated, but it made them feel that much more awkward, and they were ready to give up trying. Bob wouldn't hear of it, and taking hold of one on each side, he kept them going up and down the lake until they could make it on their own. Angelo wasn't having as much trouble keeping his balance as Gladys, and being more competitive than she would ever admit, this irked her

Therefore, when she fell on her backside, and they both laughed, she didn't think it was one bit funny, and complained, "You try skating while wearing this long, cumbersome skirt and heavy coat! You men don't realize what we women have to put up with. It's just like riding a horse. We have to do that wrapped in skirts, too. Wrap yourself in blankets and try it sometime." Nevertheless, she got back up, and with her head held high, she skated off, better than even she thought she could.

Spring came and the war continued. Gladys wanted to see the girls, and Norman was becoming impatient with her for not finding more connections in England, so she decided they should start making plans to go to Sandwich. Besides, Percy had written and said he might have a surprise for her the next time she came. She had no idea what the surprise could be, but she hoped it had something to do with the girls.

Angelo said he thought he and Eddy would stay home this time, since she would probably want to spend most of her time looking for dealers in London. For once, Gladys didn't argue with him. She knew she would feel guilty if they were with her and she left them alone in London. Besides, she had decided to take Lottie with her. When she suggested it to Lottie, she was shocked.

"Why on earth do you want me to go with you?" she asked.

"You are my partner, are you not?"

"Yes, but I don't know anything about the business."

"Neither do I, really, but I think it is time we learned, don't you?"

"Oh, my goodness, I have butterflies in my tummy just thinking about it. What do you suppose Victor will say?"

"Well, you shall just have to sell him on the idea. If you convince him you can do it, you shall have made your first sales. I figure we should go around the first of July. If we can start things moving, we should be all set up in time for Christmas. When did we plan on having Ike's surprise party?"

"I think he's discharged on the third of June, so we should have it that night, shouldn't we?"

"That's just two weeks away. Angelo will have to get a list of his friends from the hospital. The next thing we'll be celebrating is his graduation. It's going to be nice having a doctor in the family."

"He's not really family, though."

"As far as Angelo and Victor are concerned, he is, and I feel as though he's my brother, too." Lottie, having grown up with a sister, loving parents, and aunts and uncles, wasn't as anxious to adopt another relative as Gladys was so she just nodded.

It took very little persuasion to convince Victor that Lottie should accompany Gladys to England. He started to complain, but Lottie reminded him of the times she had remained home with the boys while he was away with the theatre group, and he knew he had no right to object. Norman had worked with Lottie in the restaurant and he knew she was a hard worker and reliable, therefore, he had no objection when Gladys told him she had given Lottie half of her share of the business.

Norman also had a list of places where Gladys and Lottie could buy items to take to England, but because some of the places were in such poor districts, he was obliged to accompany them. It seems he had let it be known that he would buy unusual items from exotic countries at a fair price and there were sailors, and even a few captains, who were happy to take advantage of the offer to make a little extra money.

Norman even agreed to change the name of the company to The International Import/Export Company, in keeping in line with the restaurant. He was also determined to stay on the right side of the law and declared all their transactions. As yet they had had no complaints from other businesses or the government, but he warned Gladys and Lottie that that would probably change if their business were to expand enough to threaten the big exporters in town.

The SS Delaney had to leave New York before Gladys and Lottie were ready to leave, so they had to book passage on another ship. Nevertheless, they made arrangements to return with Bob on the 14th of August.

When Ike walked in the restaurant on the evening of his army discharge, he had no idea there would be a party in his honour. Many of the hospital staff, including the doctor, had known about it and had managed to keep it a secret. The doctor had signed on for the duration of the war, and Ike felt he was letting him down by leaving, but he was finding it too difficult working all day and going to school every night. It was the doctor who had convinced Ike to carry on with his studies, since the war, when they were working at the front; there were times when Ike assisted him operating on patients who needed immediate surgery, so he had acquired a good amount of medical knowledge he wouldn't get in a classroom.

Not only did the doctor and some of the hospital staff come to Ike's party, but they told funny stories about him, and even made up a funny song. Ike was so touched, he couldn't stop the tears, and said thank you so many times that finally, Angelo, who had enjoyed a good many whiskeys, stood up on a box and banging on a cup with a spoon, quietened everyone down. Then he announced, "Ladies and Gentlemen, we have come together tonight to show our respect to the best Irishman in God's entire world."

Everyone clapped and hollered until Angelo held up his hand, then he continued, "Ike Murphy, you are more to me than a friend. You is—you are—my brother, and I love you, Ikey, ol' Ikey. We all love you, but if you don't quit saying "Thank You," we are going to throw you in—(he hiccupped) —the hoosegow! Now come on up here and say one last thank you, and then let's get drunk!" Then Angelo commenced to fall off the box and was caught by Ike and Victor before he hit the floor. Everyone laughed, and Ike stood on one of the chairs, and once more, thanked everyone.

The party was a great success, and Angelo cried with pride when Ike finished his forth pint of whiskey, borrowed Iris' flute, and played a lively tune while dancing around the room, singing his own rendition (off key and loud) of the "Irishman's Shanty":

> *Did you ever go into an Irishman's shanty*
> *Where fleas and bedbugs and mice were a-plenty,*
> *A three-legged stool and a table to match,*
> *And a hole on the floor for the chickens to scratch.*
>
> *Go into the house with the dirt to your knees,*
> *On the corner of the bed you see the fleas,*
> *The fleas are as big as kernels of corn,*
> *And this is the house where the Irishman's born.*

Ike left the restaurant, the same hour as they opened for business, and his last words as he was going out the door were, "Sure an' I loves them all!"

Chapter 14

Angelo, Eddy, Victor, Paulo, and Louis all insisted on waiting on the pier to wave goodbye to Gladys and Lottie, who had been instructed to board the boat two hours before it sailed. This made it that much more difficult for the ladies. Leaving Victor and Angelo was sad enough, but Lottie had never spent a night apart from her twins, and Gladys had only left Eddy a few short times when they lived in Four Oaks. For the first while, they both suffered with bouts of tears, but after one-and-half hours went by, they finally ran out of tears, and the men ran out of patience. When the ship finally pulled away from the dock, everyone was more relieved than sad.

The accommodation aboard the ship wasn't near as comfortable as it was on the SS Delaney, and the food not nearly as tasty, but Lottie didn't seem to mind. At first, it was hard for them both to relax. Having no one but themselves to be responsible for took a few days to become accustomed to, but once they did, they both felt a sense of freedom.

"I feel almost wicked," Lottie said, giggling, when she and Gladys were sitting outside on deck chairs. "I feel like a school girl, instead of a middle-aged old lady. Isn't that terrible?"

"No, but I think what you really feel is liberated," Gladys replied.

"What a delightful word. Liberated! I've heard that word before, but I never thought I would experience the feeling. Yes, that's exactly how I feel, so very, very liberated. Shall we go in for tea now, or shall we just stay here and take in the air?"

"I think we should pretend we are in London. Close your eyes and allow your imagination to take over. We have just entered—um—let me see—Potter's Gift and Souvenir Shop. The man behind the desk is a short, stout, formidable-looking character. He looks up from the paper he is reading and doesn't even ask us what we are selling. He just sees we are carrying cases, and frowns. Now, do you want to approach him, or shall I?"

"You, please. I'll watch and learn."

"Well, first I shall ask if he is Mr. Potter, and if he says he is, I shall compliment him on his shop and his fine assortment of merchandise. I think that should please him. Then I shall say we have just come from New York, and because we heard his merchandise was of good quality, and our company only handles the best, his is the first shop in England that we chose to visit. Now, being a gruff sort of chap, he will probably say, "Well let's see what ya got, lady. I don't have all day, so be quick about it." Of course, when he sees what we have, he will want to purchase it all, and will do his best to get it at the lowest price. That's why we have to price high, so we can bargain."

"Gladys, you are so good at it. I'll never be that good, I know. I think you should do all the talking and I'll handle the samples."

"We shall see. Although, I hope all our customers won't be like the Mr. Potter I made up. I'd really like to finish our business in London as quickly as possible, so we can spend more time at Four Oaks with the girls. James said we can use his flat while we are in London, and his flat is just a block away from Percy's. If Percy is home, he can give us some advice on how to approach our buyers."

"Has he had experience with this kind of sales?"

"Probably no more than we have, but he may have some good ideas."

They enjoyed the rest of the trip, reading, playing cribbage and writing letters. They arrived in London in the morning, but it was late in the afternoon before the boat docked and they could embark. It took a while to find a cab, and when they did, the driver complained over having to load their trunks on the back of the carriage. Besides the two trunks—one filled with their own belongings and the other with samples—Lottie and Gladys each carried a large satchel filled with more samples. They had to give the driver a large tip to help James' caretaker carry their trunks up the stairs and into the flat, but they were soon settled in and had the kettle boiling.

The caretaker's wife, who lived on the top floor of the building, thoughtfully brought them some ham sandwiches and pie before telling them that if they wanted to take their meals there, to let her know. "I am going to enjoy this, Gladys. No cooking, no cleaning, just living the life of an aristocrat."

"You wait until you see Four Oaks, then you will really feel like an aristocrat. I was a bit worried when I brought Angelo there, but he soon felt at home. In fact, Lottie, I think it saved his life."

"I hope I will fit in too, but I am so afraid I won't."

"Don't worry, they will all love you. Are you too tired to go for a short walk? I'd really like to see if Percy is home." Lottie said she would enjoy a little outing, and as luck would have it, not only was Percy there, but James, too. Gladys said she and Lottie would stay at a hotel if James wanted to use his flat, but he said he had intended to stay with Percy anyway. Lottie had met Percy before, and she found James to be just as pleasant.

"Since I last wrote you, Gladys, I've looked into this import/ export business a little more closely. You can go from shop to shop selling your products, but I understand you want to buy a selection of goods to sell in New York as well, is that right?" Percy asked.

"That's right."

"Well then, I think you should be dealing with wholesale dealers. Of course, they take a percentage of your profits, so it's not as profitable as the way you have been doing it, but if you are going to grow in this business, you will have to deal with a middle man, so to speak, understand?"

"Oh dear, when I began this business, I pictured myself dealing with little old men, or ladies, in friendly little gift shops, not big corporate businessmen in huge, cold, metal warehouses. I have a lady in Sandwich who owns a little gift shop, and she gathers English items, such as exquisite Sandwich glassware, and other handcrafted things for me, and I send her American souvenirs, but I guess if we are going to expand, Lottie, we might as well begin now. Lottie is my partner now, Percy, and I've told you about our other partner, Norman O'Rourke."

"Yes, I was really intrigued with his background: Irish, Chinese, and English. Quite a mixture! And you said he is also one of your cooks at the restaurant and has a number of other projects going as well. Quite an entrepreneur, I'd say."

"Well, Norman has cooked aboard many different ships, and he knows most of the captains who sail to exotic countries, so he has managed to import some wonderful things already. I guess we had better start visiting these dealers first thing tomorrow."

"I'm certain they have never had to deal with women before, and you may run into trouble. Would you like James and me to go with you?"

"No, but thank you, Percy. We might regret it, but we are determined to do this on our own. Have you got any addresses for us?"

Percy gave Gladys three names and addresses of companies he thought would suit her kind of merchandise. Then they had a cup of tea, and just before they left, Gladys asked Percy what he meant when he said he had some good news for her.

"Oh yes. I don't know how you are going to feel about this, but I had to go into Dover one day a month or so ago to see a lawyer for an old client of mine. The lawyer's name was Mansfield. Do you remember him?"

Gladys face turned pale, but she answered, "Randolph Mansfield?"

"That's him. Well, we got talking, and I mentioned I had a friend who used to live in Dover and that she had lost her inheritance through no fault of her own."

"You had no right to do that, Percy. That was a chapter in my life I wanted to forget."

"I'm sorry, Gladys, but I suppose being a lawyer, I cannot help but be interested in any unjust legal issue. Anyway, now I am glad that I did." He got up, went over to his briefcase, and took out a large envelope. "This belongs to you. Mansfield tried to get in touch with you, but he didn't know your name, or where you were living."

Gladys opened the envelope and there was a check for 864 pounds. "What's this," she said holding it up to Percy.

"That is twelve years of rent your husband's step brother, Peter, had collected from the house that belongs to you. Look at what else is in there."

Gladys pulled out a document and read it. "Why this is the house where Tom and I lived when Dolly was born. Why it is made out to me? It was Tom's father who owned it, not Tom."

"As you know, Peter inherited all of Tom's father's estate, but somehow a clause in the will was overlooked—a clause stating that Tom's father had transferred the deeds to that house over to Tom. Mansfield discovered it when Peter went bankrupt and lost all his property.

"It seems that both his step-father and he have a bad habit of gambling. They had to sell Oaken Arms to pay off their creditors, and that's when Mansfield found the mistake. You are a homeowner,

Gladys, and you needn't worry about Peter anymore. He and all his family have left the country."

"Well, even if I had known about it back then, I wouldn't have wanted to stay in the same town as those horrible people one day longer than I had to. You know, fate sometimes has a way of working things out. If all that hadn't happened to me, I may not have found Angelo again, or met all you wonderful people."

The next morning Gladys and Lottie were both awake early being too excited to sleep. "What shall we wear, Glad?" Lottie asked.

"I think a tailored, but stylish, suit would be the most suitable. And we don't want anything too tight around our legs, just in case we have to run."

"Please tell me you are joking. Surely you don't think there's a chance we'll be in any danger?"

"Of course not, but some of these places are situated in unsavoury areas of the city, and I always like to be prepared. Take your umbrella with that large glass ball of a handle, too."

"If you are trying to scare me, Gladys Matthews, you are doing a good job of it."

"I am sorry, my dear, but I grew up in a place where you had to be ready to defend your honour, and I certainly don't intend to lose mine at this late date. Take that umbrella, and make sure you can bring your knee up in a hurry."

"That's disgusting. I could never do that."

"As you like, but just for my sake, don't wear that tight skirt, all right?"

The first warehouse they visited was across from the pier, and, as they were used to living close to the water, it didn't seem too bad. The cab driver, noticing the heavy valises the ladies carried, thought they must be going to board a ship, so when they asked to be let out at the warehouse, he protested, "You don't want to git out 'ere, Yer

Ladyships. Tis not really safe fer ladies of yer station to be wallkin' bout unescorted here 'bouts."

"I am quite sure we shall be fine, but if you'll be kind enough to wait for a minute, we shall let you know if we need a ride back."

"Be glad to, Yer Ladyship. I'll be right over there across the street when yer needs me."

After coming in from outside, the entrance to the building seemed very dark, and it took the ladies a minute to distinguish the gentleman sitting inside a wire cage. He must have realized this, and in a slightly feminine sounding voice, he said, "It does appear much darker when you have been out in the sunlight. Good afternoon, ladies, are you looking for someone?"

Gladys could now see, and she noted the voice belonged to a most pleasant looking middle-age gentleman. He had a small, but rotund build, and his bald head had a fringe of hair around it that looked as though a white halo had slipped off the top of his head and got hung up on his ears. His face appeared to have been scrubbed and polished and shone pink and rosy.

"Are you Mr. Turnbull?" she asked.

"Good heavens, no! Mr. Turnbull has been dead for forty years. My brother and I have it now. I am Sidney Black and I do the book-keeping. Nicholas does—well—I guess he might say he does everything else. Did you want to see Nicholas?"

"Yes, please, if he is on the premises."

"I think he is in the back. Come along; follow me." He looked at his pocket watch and smiled, "It is just about tea time. I brought some of Hetty's biscuits to work this morning, if you'd care to join us for a cup of tea." Gladys said they would love some, but first she would have to run out and tell the cab driver not to wait.

Sidney kept talking as he led them into the warehouse, where there were plenty of windows and gas lights, giving the place a much cheerier look. Two men were being ordered to move crates around, and Sidney said that the fellow doing the ordering was his brother, which, because of the difference in stature, the ladies found difficult to believe.

They went through another door and into what was obviously a lunch room. Lottie leaned over and whispered to Gladys, "If all the warehouses in England are as spotless as this one, it will make our job much pleasanter." There wasn't a speck of dirt anywhere, and the workers had been wearing white smocks. A small coal fire was going in a little pot-belly stove, and Sidney opened the door and gave the coals a poke with a poker just as Nicholas entered the room.

He waved a hand across his face, "Phew, Sid, you have gone and opened that door too quickly. Now we shall have to dust again." Sidney didn't answer, but he nodded his head from side to side, then silently mouthed the same words, while winking at the ladies, before busying himself making the tea. If Nicholas noticed, he showed no sign of annoyance. "And who do we have here?" he asked, motioning to Gladys and Dolly.

"I, sir, am Gladys Matthews, and this is my partner, Carlotta Rossini. We are from New York, and we are in the business of importing and exporting beautiful hand-crafted souvenirs and gifts. May we show you some of our samples?"

The only characteristic Nicholas and Sidney had in common was they were both short, but unlike Sidney, Nicholas had a very slight frame, a full head of black curly hair, sideburns, and a heavy moustache. This made him appear far sterner and more unsociable than his brother. He also had a deeper voice. "I say, what is this world coming to, when men send ladies out to do their work?

"It is rather a shoddy act, I should say. That is what it is. Now you both appear to be respectable and well-bred ladies, so if you take my advice, you shall return to your employer, and tell him you intend to remain that way. Tell him we do not tolerate such behaviour here in England. We are still a civilized country, where women are revered.

Once people go to the Americas, they think they do not have to abide by any morals or rules. Poppycock, I say! You ladies should hasten to return to New York and stand up to the blighter. Refuse to do his work for him."

Sidney, in the meantime, had set out the tea, and trying to make light of Nicholas' diatribe, spoke up brightly, "Oh, Nicky, you do go on, but for now, let us enjoy our tea, and Hettie's biscuits." Surprisingly, Nicholas couldn't think of an apt response, so after seating the ladies, he tucked his napkin into his shirt and put cream into his cup so Sidney could pour his tea.

While they were enjoying tea, Sidney asked the ladies how they managed to be living in America. This gave Gladys the opportunity to tell how she had become interested in the import/export business. "I would hunt around town and find unique gifts to bring back to my friends (she didn't mention she had daughters) when I came to visit, and they were always so pleased with what I brought them that they begged me to buy them more. Thus I had the idea that I would like to do it in a grander and more profitable manner. I talked Carlotta into coming in with me, and here we are.

"You see, our husbands are partners in a restaurant and apartment building, so we thought we should have our own business as well. It is a different world over there, and it is going to be a lot more different as time goes by."

Lottie couldn't help but add her thoughts too, "It's a lot freer than here, and some of the other old countries."

That wasn't the wisest thing to say. Nicholas turned to her, and said, "What is that you say? Old country? Is that what they call us now? Let me tell you, young lady, according to the latest scientific studies, this country is no older than America, and we are far more advanced in all fields of technology."

"Forgive me, Mr. Black. I didn't mean that to sound derogatory. It is just that most people use that term when they talk about where they came from, but I certainly won't use it again." Lottie looked so upset when she apologized, Nicholas couldn't help but forgive her. When they finished the tea, Lottie went to get up to help Sidney clear the table, until she saw Gladys frown. Later, Gladys explained that "proper ladies" never offer to help with the dishes when someone serves them tea.

Gladys liked these two elderly men, and she wanted very much to do business with them, so after thanking Sidney for the tea, she decided to do her best to win them over. She addressed Nicholas, "Mr. Black, Lottie and I visited some warehouses and display rooms in New York, and may I say, they were a disgrace compared to your lovely place here. Before we leave, would you have the time to show us around?"

Lottie was watching her partner and learning. *Now she's turned on the charm, smiling and looking him in the eyes when she talks*, she thought, *and he's practically swooning.*

Lottie was right. Nicholas blushed with pride, and said, "I think you shall be even more impressed with our showroom, ladies— what, Sid?"

"I should say so!" Sidney answered beaming.

Nicholas started to take the ladies to the showroom when he noticed their valises. "Here allow me to carry those bags for you. My, they are heavy, are they not?"

"Yes, sir, but there is so much we wanted to bring with us, we just couldn't leave anything behind."

"Well, I shall put them out by the door here, and you may pick them up when you are ready to leave." It was apparent that as flattered as he was, Nicholas Black had no intention of buying their wares.

Most of the items in Black's inventory were large, such as teak furniture and fancy framed pictures, but he did have a few smaller items as well. The room smelled of exotic woods, and Gladys was reminded of the first time she was in Victoria Station and saw the venders' stalls. At that time, she had been in awe of the wood carvings and the scent they gave off. Now, as before, she longed to purchase some of them, only this time she could afford to.

"Oh, Mr. Black, these are simply wonderful. May we purchase some of them?"

"I am sorry, my dear, but as you know, we are wholesale dealers, and it would not be right to sell to you when our customers make their living by selling our merchandise."

"I did not mean to buy them for our own use, sir. I meant can our company purchase them? Most are made in the United Kingdom, right?"

"Well—I have never done business with a woman before."

"I can assure you, sir, I am as trustworthy as any of the men you deal with, but we do have another partner who is a man, and if you prefer, you could deal with him hereafter. Lottie and I visit England often, so that is why we decided to come this time."

"What sort of items would you like?"

"We would prefer smaller items to begin with, like this ornate dinner bell, items easier to ship, and as most of our customers are small, privately-owned gift shops and souvenir shops, smaller items would be more appropriate. Mind you, we have been approached by some of the large department stores in New York who have seen some of our gifts, and I am certain that we shall need larger pieces in the future. What items do you think would sell in New York, Lottie?"

Lottie pointed to different things that appealed to her. Ike had managed to get Gladys alone before she left for England, and he had insisted on giving her a generous sum of money, so she added up the cost of the items in her head as they went along until she had had reached the same amount as Ike gave her, then she said that would probably be enough. Sidney itemized it all, and when Gladys insisted she pay him with cash, Lottie had to sit down, or she would have fainted.

Nicholas promised to have it all crated and delivered to the SS Delaney the day before they were to sail for home, and just before they took their leave, Gladys turned to him, and asked, "Do you mind looking at what we have, Mr. Black? Perhaps you can advise me as to which dealer in London would best suit our merchandise?"

"Certainly, my dear, perhaps we had better take them up to the store room where we can see them more clearly."

An hour later, they left with empty cases, and enough money to pay off Ike's loan.

They also invited the brothers to have dinner with them in one of Percy's favourite dining establishments. Of course, Gladys intended to ask Percy to join them, and James, too, if he was still in town.

"I shall never doubt you again, oh wise one!" Lottie said as they rode back to James' flat in an exuberant mood.

"Just as long as you don't tell Angelo or Victor that I borrowed that money."

Chapter 15

As soon as they returned to the flat, Gladys left Lottie to rest while she walked over to see if Percy was home. Percy and James were both there, and they were trying to decide where they would dine. They were both pleased and happy to hear that the ladies had sold all their samples and received a large order for more.

"They were so darling, Percy, that we couldn't resist asking them to join us for dinner, I mean tea, at the Royal Guardian. I remember you saying it was one of your favourites, so I thought the food there must be exceptional. I hope it isn't too highly priced though, as I said it would be our treat. I guess I should have asked you about it first, but I had heard that it's customary to treat a new customer to a meal when they place a big order. Do you think I made a mistake?

Just as Gladys had hoped, James suggested Percy and he join them, and then he said they needn't worry about the cost. "This will be our treat to you both for your unbelievable audacity in entering our world, that is, a man's world."

Gladys was feeling guilty for tricking them into coming with her and Lottie, but she felt better when Percy spoke up and said, "I had more than one reason to give you their address. You see, I've always wanted to meet the Blacks, and, I hope, receive an invitation to get inside that old mansion they live in. I've heard it's full of priceless antiques and artwork."

Later, when they were getting dressed to go to dinner, Gladys said, "You know, Lottie, I'm becoming quite a proficient schemer."

"Yes, you certainly are. It's a side of you I haven't seen before."

"One I haven't seen before either, and although it certainly gets results, I don't feel very proud of myself. Do you know what I mean?"

"I think so, but I don't think we'd have gotten anywhere with the Blacks if you hadn't charmed them. It makes one have a little more understanding for the way our politicians make promises they don't keep, doesn't it?"

"I like to think Mr. Lincoln stuck to his principles, though, but he may have had to use a little false flattery at times, too. Still they wouldn't have named him "Honest Abe" if he wasn't. Anyway, I hope women won't always have to rely on guile and flattery to get what they want in this world."

The dinner was a huge success. James and Percy were as taken with the Blacks as Gladys and Lottie. They appreciated their little eccentricities and were excited to learn that they still lived in their great-grandparents stately home and hadn't disposed of any of the furnishings, except to replace outdated mattresses and appliances. They learned that Hettie was their housekeeper and that neither man had been married, although Nicholas was in a long-time court-ship with a lady named Regina Pinesap. Her surname required a good deal of self-control and good manners on Gladys and Lottie's part, but there wasn't so much as a snicker to be heard.

After the second bottle of champagne, Nicholas related that Regina looked after her elderly aunt and had vowed not to wed until the aunt's demise. Unfortunately, as the years went by, the aunt, with the aid of Regina's tender loving care, managed to retain excellent health, while Regina's was slowly declining. Nevertheless, the couple's courtship continued with a routine stroll around Regent's Park every Saturday afternoon from five until seven.

Percy and James could have kissed Gladys and Lottie when Sid—as they were told to call him—invited them for afternoon tea the following Sunday. When Gladys mentioned that they had a trunk full of saleable items they were taking to a lady who had a shop in Sandwich, Nicholas insisted they allow him to see the items so he could order more. He also said if she would sell to him exclusively, he would supply Claudia with whatever she needed.

"Sid and I close the warehouse for two days every six months and take samples, or pictures of them, to our customers. We have four customers in Dover and will be delighted to add your friend to our list. I have always wanted to visit Sandwich."

"That will be wonderful, Gladys; we won't have to bother looking up any more dealers," Lottie cried.

"Then we can leave for Four Oaks tomorrow." Gladys was overjoyed; she had thought they would have to spend at least two more days in London, and she wanted to see Dolly and Eliza so much that she hugged both of the Black brothers, causing even Nicholas to blush. Then, when James invited the brothers to come to Four Oaks for a visit whenever they were in his neighbourhood, they both raised their glasses and offered a toast to their new-found friends. Before they left the restaurant, Nicholas said he would be at the flat in the morning to see the samples.

He was there at six the next morning, ordered a dozen of everything the ladies had in their trunk, had a cup of American coffee, confessed that it wasn't half bad, and left before eight. Gladys and Lottie were able to get the morning train. They found an empty compartment, and the train was just about to leave, when someone said, "May we join you ladies?"

"James, Percy! You didn't tell us you were coming, too," Gladys said.

"We thought we would surprise you, but we shall have to come back next Sunday to have tea with the Black boys."

Percy replied, "I hope that's all right?"

"Of course, silly! Now give us a hug." There were hugs all around, and as they settled down, Gladys couldn't help but chuckle to herself. During the six years she and James were married, they never once hugged each other.

Lottie had never been anywhere in England except London, and she enjoyed the train ride so much, she was sorry to see it end. Gladys had told her a little bit about Four Oaks, but she didn't expect to find it so grand and in such a serene, park-like setting. James apologized when he had the coachman take them to the back entrance, saying that it was far easier for his footmen to carry their luggage to their rooms from there.

Once inside, Gladys took hold of Lottie's hand and, practically running, pulled her up the stairs. "Dolly, Eliza, I'm home," she called out as she hurried into the nursery, but there was no one there. "They must be in the observatory having tea. Come along, Lottie," she called, as she was running back downstairs.

"Wait for me, Glad! If I lose sight of you, I'm sure to get lost."

They weren't there either, so Gladys went to find Freda, the cook. After receiving a warm welcome, she was told that the girls had taken a picnic out to the lake and would be back in about an hour for their tea. Gladys showed Lottie to her room and said cook would send her up cup of tea and a biscuit if she didn't mind waiting while she rode out to the lake to see the girls. "I just can't wait, Lottie, sorry."

"Can I come with you?"

"Do you ride?"

"I used to when I was a young girl in Italy, and I don't suppose one ever forgets how." Gladys had bought along two riding skirts she had made intending to give Dolly one, but she knew Dolly probably wouldn't wear it, so she gave it to Lottie. They changed, said goodbye to James and Percy, and left. When they got to the lake, Gladys was surprised to see that there were other children playing there too. Eliza was in the water up to her knees and was shrieking loudly while splashing the other children as they splashed her.

Dolly had her skirt tied up and was standing up to her knees in the waters as well. She was holding a towel, ready to dry Eliza off. She, too, had been victimized and even her hair was wet. She had let it down to dry and Gladys thought she looked like an angel. "Come now, Eliza. That is enough. We must dry off now or we shall be late for our tea," Dolly, good-naturedly, ordered.

"Well, now, aren't you a sight for sore eyes," Gladys called out as she galloped her horse across the lake shore to them.

"Mother, you are early!"

"Yes, dear, isn't it wonderful?" Gladys said as she jumped off the horse and into the water.

Even Eliza laughed and ran over to hug her mother. When Gladys introduced the girls to Lottie, Lottie looked at Eliza and said, "What an angel." Then she looked at Dolly and declared, "And you, young lady, look just like your mother." Dolly fell in love with her right then.

Gladys dried off Eliza while Lottie towel-dried Dolly's beautiful red hair. When they were dry enough to ride back, Dolly began pinning her hair up in a tight bun and Lottie said, "Oh no, please, Dolly, don't hide those beautiful curls. They must look just like your grandmother's curls that your mother told us about. Here let me help." She wrapped some of Dolly's hair in a loose bun and let the rest hang down over her ears. "There now, Gladys, doesn't she look pretty?"

"She always looks pretty to me," Gladys said and kissed her daughter's cheek.

That night, Lottie tried to stay awake as long as she could and, every once in a while, she would get up and look out the window to make sure she wasn't dreaming. The sunlight streaming in the window the next morning woke her along with a cheery little voice saying, "Good morning, mum, here's your tea, mum. Breakfast is ready in the conservatory whenever you want it, mum." Little Ines had put a tea tray on a table beside Lottie's bed then opened the curtains.

"Thank you—a—what is your name?—if you don't mind me asking."

Ines giggled and answered, "No, mum, I don't mind. Mum says we should tell the guests our names so they can address us proper like, but sir doesn't like that much. Miss Dolly, well now, we calls her the missus; well, she's not fond of the idea neither, but seeing as you're with our other missus, we will probably go by her rules. Would that be all you be needing, mum?"

"Your name?"

"Oh," more giggles. "My name? I almost forgot. It's Ines, but they all calls me Little Ines."

"Well, Little Ines, thank you again, and I won't be needing anything else right now."

"I'll bring you up some warm water to wash with and leave it outside the door. That's what I do for the missus." With that she turned to leave while waving goodbye as she backed out the door. Lottie hadn't had her tea in bed since her honeymoon in Italy. She and Victor had stayed in a lovely guest cottage on the sea for two nights and they were served breakfast in bed both mornings. Now she lay back on the pillows and drank her tea thinking, *I could soon become accustomed to this.*

When she finally came down for her breakfast, Gladys was waiting for her in the conservatory. "Well, Lazy Bones, I thought you were going to sleep the day away. Here it is nine o'clock and you haven't had breakfast."

"Oh, Glad, I am so sorry. I didn't realize the time. I should have asked Little Ines, but she is such a talker that I didn't like to interrupt her."

"She is a little jewel, that one, but I fear I have spoiled her. Poor Dolly has such a time trying to restore the order that I managed to ruin when I ran this place, but never mind that, you need to eat. I'll send for some food. You'll love Freda's pancakes with bacon and golden treacle."

"Please, I don't want to be a bother."

"Believe me, you shall bother Freda more if you don't eat." Gladys rang for a maid, and when she came, she said, "Mrs. Rossini would like pancakes and bacon, Molly dear, and we would both like a pot of tea, please." Molly beamed; she hadn't been called Molly dear since Gladys left.

Dolly had made plans where they could spend all their days together and was obviously hurt when Gladys said they had to spend one day going into Sandwich to take Claudia the merchandise they had brought with them and to tell her about the Black brothers. "But you shall only be here a fortnight, Mother. It's just not fair!"

"Then why don't we all go into town? Lottie, you, Eliza and me? We can make a day of it, and even have our tea in a restaurant. And while we're there, we'll see if there is anything on at the theatre during the next two weeks. I think we should treat your aunt Lottie to an English performance, don't you?"

If Dolly wasn't so proper, she would have jumped with joy, but instead, she smiled and replied, "That sounds like a splendid idea, Mother."

"Then it is settled, and, Dolly, I have something I have to do in Dover while I'm here—something I would like the two of us to do together. Do you think we can do that?"

"We have never been back there, Mother, not since we went to say goodbye to Gamby at the graveyard, but if you have to go, yes, I shall go with you."

The next day, Gladys, Lottie, and the girls went into Sandwich for the day. First, they delivered Claudia's order to her. She was very happy with everything, especially the miniature covered wagons, but she didn't like the idea of dealing with anyone else. Gladys assured her that the Black brothers were both honourable men and that she would like them. She also promised to visit the store every time she was in England. The rest of the day in town was devoted to Dolly and Eliza.

They spent most of the day shopping, and besides buying some pretty dresses for the girls, they ate dinner in the dining room of a fancy hotel and didn't arrive home until the sun had gone down. Luckily, the moon was full and the horse familiar with the road, so they had no trouble.

A few days later, Gladys and Dolly caught the train into Dover. When Gladys asked Lottie if she would mind staying at Four Oaks without her, Lottie said, "Not at all. I'd love to spend time in James' library, if he doesn't mind, and Eliza has asked me to go riding with her. Ruby said she is quite capable of handling Chestnut, and we shan't go further than the creek and back. I had almost forgotten how much I loved riding. You two go and have a good day together."

The train arrived in Dover at ten in the morning, and as they were closer to the house that Gladys had inherited than to Randolph Mansfield's office, Gladys decided they should walk there first. As they neared the cottage, she was pleased to see that the occupants had kept the front garden in good repair. There was a pretty selection of asters and Zinnias mixed with wallflower, all the same kind of plants that Gladys had planted when she lived there. She waited until they were in front of the gate before turning to look at Dolly.

"It is our house, isn't it, Mother?"

"Yes, dear. I didn't know if you would remember."

"I remember. I remember when we planted flowers just like those. We were doing it one day when Gamby came, and he picked me up, put me on his shoulders and galloped around making noises like a horse. I felt like a princess, and then we went in and had hot chocolate." Tears were running down her cheeks. "Oh, Mother, why did you bring me here?"

"I brought you here because this house is now your house, or it shall be as soon as we see Gamby's lawyer, Mr. Randolph." Dolly said she didn't understand, so Gladys explained what had happened and how the deeds to the house were signed over to Tom before he left for India and were in the registry office in Dover.

"The house is yours now, Dolly, and I know your father would be pleased to know you have it. Your father and I were so happy here, and you were born in this very house."

"But what will I do with it?"

"I don't know. You can do whatever you like. You can even sell it, but I hope you don't. Or you can continue to rent it. By the looks of the garden, you have a very responsible tenant. That way, you can have a little income of your own. The house is in excellent repair and should last throughout your lifetime. What do you think?"

"I shall never sell it, Mother, but if the present tenants leave, I think I should like to keep it vacant so as to have a place to stay whenever Eliza and I come to Dover. What worries me the most, though, is what if that horrid man tries to take it away again?"

"That horrid man and his entire family have all left the country, so you needn't worry, love; no one is going to take it away from you, now or ever."

"Do you suppose we can go in? I would love to see the inside."

"Well, I think it would be a good idea to introduce ourselves, seeing as you are now their landlady. Shall we knock on the door?"

They were surprised when a young woman, with a small child perched contentedly on her bony hip, opened the door and asked, "Yes, mam?"

Dolly spoke up and said, "Is your mother at home, miss?"

"I am the lady of the house. What can I do for you?"

She looked far too young to have a child, so it took Dolly a few seconds to answer, "We are sorry to bother you, but my name is Dolly Pickwick, and this is my mother, Gladys."

"Pickwick? Gladys? Why you used to live in this house. Mr. Grimsby has told me about you, Mrs. Pickwick. He comes by once in a while to give me advice about the garden."

"Yes, he was the one who introduced me to gardening, too. However, I am no longer Mrs. Pickwick. I am Mrs. Matthews now, and Dolly is your landlady. We were in the neighbourhood and thought it would be nice to meet you. I hope we are not intruding Mrs—"

"Brooks. Mrs. Gordon Brooks. And this is our daughter, Marylee. Please come in. Can I get you a cup of tea?"

"If it's not too much trouble, you see this house meant so much to us and we were anxious to see it again," Gladys replied

"You're welcome to look wherever you like. The stairs are—oh—of course, you know where the stairs are," she smiled. "While you are looking, I shall put the kettle on."

The entire house was tidy and spotless but extremely bare. What little furnishings the Brooks had were old and well worn. Peter must have sold the furnishings Gladys left behind and bought some old second-hand pieces before he rented the place. He must have even taken down the pretty curtains Gladys had made and sold them. The curtains that were on the windows now were also homemade, but they were made out of flour sacks.

When they finished looking at the house, the girl had the tea made and set out on a box that she had covered with a cloth in the living room. Dolly noticed that she had prepared the tea and set it out without putting the child down. When she finally did put the little girl down on a blanket, the child was just as happy as she had been on her mother's hip, and Gladys was reminded of the many times she had put Dolly on the same floor with a toy while she made

Millie a cup of tea. She remarked how good-natured the child was and how it brought back memories of the time Dolly was the same age. For some reason, Dolly didn't appreciate the comparison.

Although the teacups were chipped, they were clean, and the young woman had put out a plate of homemade cookies. When Gladys noticed that Dolly didn't touch her tea and refused a cookie, she made a point of eating two cookies and having a second cup of tea, which pleased the young woman, who asked Gladys to please call her Edna.

They learned that Edna's husband had found employment in the Dover Brewery in the spring and how delighted they were when they found such a lovely house to rent. Although Edna was an amiable hostess, she seemed to be quite nervous, and it took a while for Gladys to realize that she might be afraid that Dolly had come to tell her she was going to raise the rent, or even to evict them. After Gladys assured her that wasn't the case, the young lady seemed to relax, and she chatted away about how much they loved living in the house.

"Well, Edna, if you keep the house and garden as tidy as you have been doing, I shouldn't be surprised if Dolly lowers your rent," Gladys said, receiving an unmistakable look of disapproval from Dolly. Nevertheless, Gladys didn't stop there. "Did you rent this place with the understanding it was furnished?"

"Yes, we did."

"Well, I should say your landlord had a very poor idea of what a furnished house should consist of, wouldn't you, Dolly?"

Dolly, obviously annoyed, rose and said, "Yes, well, I shall think about that. Now, Mother, we must be going. I will leave you my address in case there is anything you need, Mrs. Brooks, and because I do not live in Dover, I shall open a bank account here and you can deposit your rent in that."

"We shall have some decent furnishings sent to you today if we get time, my dear, and if not, we will see to it soon," Gladys promised as they were leaving.

Dolly never said a word as they walked downtown and found a nice place to have their lunch, but after they gave their order and were given a glass of wine, she looked at Gladys and said, "Now, Mother, I should like to know what gave you the right to tell my tenant that she is going to receive a reduction in her rent, and do you intend to buy her new furniture, because I certainly am not going to. James pays me well for looking after the house, but not that well."

"Dolly, I waited for you to say something and when you didn't, I had to. That young girl and her husband are taking such good care of your house, they deserve something. And you wouldn't want to live in a house without something comfortable to sit on in the evenings. They don't even have a table or enough chairs, and that divan, ick! It needs to be thrown out. How can you possibly treat people like Peter did, especially after the way he treated us? I have a cheque here for you. It is the rent Peter collected all those years illegally. It's a good amount, and I should think you could use a little of it to help that nice couple."

Dolly was pleased to hear about the money, and she knew her mother was right to promise the girl new furnishings, but she resented being treated like a child. "You didn't give me a chance. You just went ahead and made me look like I was an idiot and didn't know how to be a landlady."

"I'm sorry, dear. You are right. I should have waited and talked it over with you first. I'm really sorry. Sometimes I forget you are no longer my little girl."

"I am still your little girl, Mother, but you have to allow me to make my own decisions."

"You have always made your own decisions, Dolly, that's just one of the things I love about you."

After they ate, they went to look for the lawyer's office, and when they found it, they learned that another lawyer had taken it over and Randolph Mansfield, who was quite elderly, was only handling the odd client out of his home. The man in the office gave them Randolph's address. He also told them it was on the other side of town and advised them to take a cab. Randolph's wife had died five years earlier and the only cleaning done inside his house since that time was by his own hands or his sister's, who was in her late seventies, and only visited him once a month.

Nevertheless, there was a particular orderliness to the disarray of the room that he used as his office. The odour of all the leather-bound books blended with the smell of his pipe tobacco and gave off a warm and homey ambience that Gladys found enjoyable, but Dolly thought it just smelled unclean.

Dolly was a little disappointed, as she had looked forward to seeing Mr. Mansfield again, but the Mr. Mansfield she remembered was much younger and tidier than the man sitting before her now. Because Randolph no longer was obliged to go to his office, he neglected to visit his barber regularly and seldom put on a suit. Instead, he preferred comfortable corduroy trousers and old favourite sweaters.

As soon as he had them seated, he looked at Dolly then smiled and said, "Do you remember me, Dolly?"

His eyes and his smile were all it took. Dolly was no longer disappointed. "Yes, Mr. Mansfield, I certainly do. You brought me Gamby's little dove pin. I don't think I would have ever been able to accept his death if you hadn't brought me that pin."

"That is one thing he would not let go of, Dolly. It meant more to him than anything else he owned, because you gave it to him. Do you still have it?"

"I buried it beside his grave so he would have it close to him forever. We are going to go and visit his, and my father's, grave after we leave here."

"Are you going back today?"

"Yes, we have to. I have an American relative who I brought with me when I came to Four Oaks, and I think she will be looking for me to come back," Gladys answered.

"That is too bad; I would have liked to take you two lovely ladies out to dinner, but I suppose you won't have the time."

"We would have liked that, Mr. Mansfield. Perhaps you will take me out to dine the next time I am in Dover," Dolly replied.

Gladys had sent Randolph a note saying she didn't want Dolly to know that the house had been in her name, so when she was signing the deed over, Randolph took Dolly over to the window to show her the last blooms on his favourite rosebush. Before they left, Randolph gave Dolly the deeds, and she said she intended to put them in James' safe for a while, so she could take them out and look at them now and again.

The graveyard wasn't far from Mr. Mansfield's house, but because they still had to buy furniture, and get to the train on time, they kept the cab waiting while they visited the lawyer, so it didn't take long to arrive at the Grimsbys. Although the graveyard and the Grimsby cottage grounds were still tidy and colourful, with an assortment of fall flowers, there weren't near as many as Gladys remembered. When she saw Mr. Grimsby walking along inside the fence, she could see why. He was far more stooped than he used to be and walked with two poles.

"Oh, poor Mr. Grimsby," Gladys said to Dolly. "Do you remember him, Dolly?'

"Not really, but I do remember Mrs. Grimsby. She played me songs and sang to me and made gingerbread men. I really liked her."

"Stop the cab here, driver," Gladys ordered. "Please wait for us; we shan't be long." They got out and Gladys called out to Mr. Grimsby. "Hello there. I wonder if you can show me the difference between weeds and flowers?"

"If thee doesn't know by now, thee never will," he answered back, then chuckling, he came up to the fence. "Is it really you, Gladys?"

They hugged over the fence, then Gladys introduced him to Dolly. After he went on about how he knew it was her by her lovely red hair, Dolly said they were going to surprise Mrs. Grimsby and knock on her door.

"Ah, my dear, did thee not know? My dear missus has been gone three years now. Three long years! She talked about thee both a lot during the last few months she lived. I wish she could have seen thee once more. I have some things in the house that she wanted thee both to have. She said that if thee ever came back to give them to thee. Come along, we will go in and get them. Can thee stop for tea?"

Gladys wiped the tears from her eyes and said, "I wish we could, but we want to visit Tom and Andrew's graves, and we have to get back to town and do some things before we catch the train."

The gift Mrs. Grimsby had wrapped up and left for Gladys was a linen tablecloth she had embroidered, with pictures of all Gladys' favourite flowers. And the gift she had wrapped up and left for Dolly was a small pillow, with an embroidered angel, that she always gave Dolly to take to bed when Dolly stayed at her house. "She used to say, 'You can sleep now, darling, this angel will watch over you.' Now, the angel shall watch over me wherever I am," Dolly said with tears running down her cheeks.

Mr. Grimsby walked to the graves with them, and they laid the flowers they had brought with them on the ground, vowed to return every year, then said a goodbye prayer and left. Gladys took Dolly to a furniture store she remembered going to when they were building Oaken Arms and was pleased to see the same clerk there that was there when she lived in Dover.

He told them he had just bought a load of furniture from a customer who didn't need it anymore because he had inherited a fully furnished mansion. After they looked it over, Gladys and Dolly decided it would fit perfectly into Dolly's house. They bought it all, including beds and bedding, curtains, dishes, and cutlery.

"I wish we had time to see Edna's face when all this is delivered," Dolly said. Now she was as excited about it as Gladys. It was a special day they would both remember for the rest of their lives. They caught the late train home and never stopped talking until they were at the Sandwich station. Ruby was waiting for them.

Chapter 16

James invited Mary and the Rudyards for an evening of music and games, and when they heard Lottie sing, they embarrassed her with praise. Now that Dolly was a young lady, she could join the adults and that made eight, so they were able to have two tables of whist.

Lottie and Gladys missed the boys, but both felt guilty that they were having such a good time there were times when they didn't think about home. Eliza had been disappointed when Eddy hadn't come. She had been diligently working on her piano lessons hoping to impress him. Gladys and Lottie were both aware of her displeasure and they made such a fuss over her playing that it made up a little for Eddy's absence. One day, Gladys and Eliza secretly practiced together, and that evening, they surprised everyone with a piano duet. Eliza was closer to Gladys after that.

The weeks went by far too fast, but knowing they wouldn't be apart for long, Dolly and Eliza didn't complain when Gladys and Lottie had to leave. Everyone came down to the station to see them off, and Freda packed them a nice lunch to have on the train. Dolly hadn't changed the style of her hair since Lottie had styled it at the lake and she looked far younger than the last time Gladys had seen her.

When they boarded the SS Delaney, Lottie was amazed at the difference in their accommodation. She knew Captain Bob Nicholson from the many times he frequented the restaurant, but she didn't realize how fond of Gladys he was until she noticed the way he looked at her when they dined with him.

"You are going to have to watch that man, Gladys. He is frightfully handsome," she said the third day they were at sea.

"Bob is a good man, Lottie, and he has a wife and two boys he adores. Besides, he knows I love Angelo, and he is a man of honour, I assure you."

"You may love Angelo, and believe me, I no longer doubt that. No one would leave that paradise you lived in to live in a tiny flat in New York if they weren't crazy, or madly in love, but the way Bob looks at you, anyone could see that he is thoroughly smitten. You must be careful, my dear, not to break his heart."

Gladys knew Lottie was right. She just needed someone to tell her. She had to admit that she had enjoyed what she thought to be a harmless flirtation, but now she realized that there is no such thing. Angelo was just as loving lately as he had been before he went to war, and she made up her mind never to flirt again. However, it was a habit she would find difficult to break.

Because they had set a return date before they went to England, everyone was on the pier waiting for them when they arrived. After an abundance of hugs and kisses for everyone, Gladys and Lottie were happy to be home, but they were also a little sad their holiday was over. "I guess we'll be back at work tomorrow," Lottie said, "so I'll see you then."

"I think we had better have a meeting with our partner in the morning, if he's not working, and go back to work in the afternoon," Gladys suggested.

Eddy had been coaxing her to hurry and return to the flat, so she knew there was a surprise waiting for her.

They had cleaned and polished everything in the apartment and there was a bouquet of flowers and a cake on the table. "Don't you dare tell me you both have enlisted in the army?" she said, jokingly.

"Not this time, Gladys. This time we just missed you," Angelo said, and he and Eddy hugged her again.

Gladys could see Eddy eyeing the cake, so before she changed her clothes and unpacked, she made a pot of tea and cut the cake. Eddy wanted to know everything she did and if Eliza was riding Chestnut. When she told him they were playing in the lake, he clapped his hands and said that he was going to swim in it the next time he was at Four Oaks. Angelo wanted to know how Lottie liked Four Oaks and Gladys said she loved it and that before they left, both girls were calling her Auntie Lottie.

"She may be living in a big house now, but I don't think even it is big enough to hold all the people she has invited to come and visit her. She even invited the Black brothers!" Angelo and Eddy wanted to know who the Black brothers were, so Gladys related how they owned an import/export business in London and how darling they both were. Angelo was pleased that they had found a reliable dealer there and that they wouldn't have to look for another one.

"They bought all the samples we had and gave us a huge order, and wait until you see the things we bought back with us. Bob let us bring the crates back on the Delaney."

"I didn't see any crates."

"I told Bob we had to find a place to put them, and he said we didn't have to unload them until tomorrow or the next day. Angelo, do you think we could use the back of Ike's building for a warehouse until we can find one?"

"You'll have to speak to Victor and Ike about that. You'll be surprised at what we have done with the building since you've been gone, but there is still a little room left on the lower floor at the back.

Now, young man, do you think you and I could talk your mother into giving us another piece of that cake?"

The next morning, right after breakfast, Gladys and Lottie met at the restaurant and talked to Victor then they waited for Ike to come for lunch and asked him if they could use the room. Once they had everyone's consent, they talked Victor and Sandy into taking the wagon down to the boat and bringing the crates back.

Norman didn't show up until four days later, and by that time, Gladys and Lottie had the place scrubbed and painted. They made tables out of the crates and covered them with a rich blue material to better show off the merchandise. They had all the items out on display, and Norman was so delighted with what they had that he said he would have some clients up to see the display the following day.

Victor and Angelo had agreed to carry on in the restaurant without Gladys and Lottie's help while they were getting the showroom set up, but they didn't do it without grumbling.

"I thought all this was supposed to be just a hobby, Lottie, and you were still going to help with the cooking," Victor complained.

"We are as busy with the new apartments as you are with your business, but we still have to put time in at the restaurant or our business will suffer," Angelo told Gladys.

With her sleeves rolled up, and her hands on her hips, Lottie exclaimed, "You poor dears! And here we are having such fun scrubbing, painting, and making over a dirty old room into a lovely showroom. Maybe if we'd had some help here, we could have been back cooking and waiting on tables by now. What do you think about that?" There was no more said.

Gladys was so busy during the following months that she hardly had time to write to the girls. Lottie found it impossible to keep up with her and finally had to admit it was too much. They were unpacking crates one day and she said, "I'm not as young as you,

Gladys, and I just don't have the energy anymore. I'm afraid I have to either give up working at the restaurant or my share of our business."

"We won't always have to work this hard, Lottie. As soon as we have a few more customers, we can hire a man to work in our warehouse, and I don't see why Norman can't do some of this heavy work once in a while. In fact, I shall talk to him about it this afternoon. You don't need to work here; I can manage myself, and we can always pay our three boys to do some work. It would do them good to have a job, and they would probably like to make a little spending money. What do you think?"

"I know they don't like working at the restaurant but maybe they'll want to work here. I'll ask them tonight."

"If they say yes, I'll train them tomorrow and you can just work here with me when we're doing the ordering and bookkeeping, all right?"

"You are an angel, you know that, and I love you so much."

When Gladys told Norman they needed him to help work in the warehouse, he said he would do what he could. Norman had enjoyed cooking, but he was ready to give up manual work and spend the rest of his life as a businessman. As far as he was concerned, his future was in the entrepreneurial world, and he could always find someone to do the heavy work. The next time Gladys arrived at the warehouse, there was a very muscular man waiting to begin.

He proved to be a good worker and was very proficient at crating and un-crating goods. However, he was inclined to be clumsy, and after breaking a few items, Gladys decided to leave the handling of the delicate articles for the boys, who were happy to earn a little money. They also enjoyed handling all the different carvings, especially the intricate miniature sailing ships that the Black brothers sent over.

If Gladys didn't visit the hospital every week, she would have thought it was safe to have Dolly and Eliza come for a visit, but there were still trainloads of wounded soldiers coming into New York to remind her that they would never be safe until the war was over. Angelo, with Ike's help, had started a support group at the hospital, so he was there a few nights a week, and, no matter how busy they were, Gladys, Lottie, and Iris made time to entertain the soldiers.

Theresa Rutten was kept as busy as ever working for The Women's Central Association of Relief, and the restaurant was just as busy with soldiers and sailors. The racial situation seemed to be a little less prevalent, and the streets a little safer for all races, but unbeknownst to the average New Yorker was a plan by Confederate agents to do what they could to disrupt the election.

However, when they set fires to ten downtown hotels, the American Museum, Niblo's Theatre, and the Winter Garden on November the 25th, all the fires were quickly extinguished, and the culprits had to escape to Canada. Only one of them was captured and executed after returning to the United States and that was Robert Cobb Kennedy. For all those who had allowed themselves to feel detached from the fighting, it was a wakeup call.

December 22, 1864. The tree was a beautiful dark-green, nine-foot spruce. There was no snow, so Ruby had hitched up the wagon, put enough bales of straw in it to seat James, Dolly, Eliza, and Blossom, and taken them out for an afternoon to find a Christmas tree. Freda had packed a lovely picnic basket, and Dolly had seen that they were well stocked with quilts to keep them warm. They found the spruce on the far side of the lake, but James refused to let Ruby cut it down, saying that as he was master of the house, it was his job to fell the tree. When it was time to return home, they had three more trees in their wagon: one for the servants' quarters, and one each for Mary and the Rudyards, plus a bundle of greenery.

Although James did his best to cheer Dolly up by getting everyone to sing carols, she couldn't get over the fact that her mother hadn't made an effort to spend this Christmas with them. "She hasn't even written and said she would miss us," Dolly complained to Blossom earlier that week. "I really am upset with her. This time I shan't listen to any excuse she tries to give me."

When they arrived home, Eliza wanted to put the tree up right away, but James said they had to wait until Christmas Eve and then they could decorate it. Dolly and Eliza had wrapped Gladys, Eddy, and Angelo's presents and given them to James to mail weeks before, and they had made gifts for James, Percy, Aunt Jean, and Blossom and had them all wrapped in pretty paper and tied with red ribbons ready to go under the tree. Eliza could hardly wait to see what Father Christmas would put under the tree for her, although she knew there wasn't such a person. She had asked for the big baby doll she had seen in one of the store windows, and she knew her father would see that she had it.

Finally, the two days were up, and it was Christmas Eve. Right after breakfast, Eliza started chanting, "Christmas tree time, papa, Christmas tree time."

James took out his watch and looked at it. "I have decided that tree is too big for us to decorate, so I have sent to London to get some expert decorators. They should be here in two hours. In the meantime, we shall have Richard put the tree up so it will be ready. Now, Dolly, where would you like it?"

This was too much for Dolly, and she threw her arms in the air, and announced, "I really do not care. Let your experts place it anywhere they decide." With that she walked out of the room. Instead of looking upset, James just grinned.

James had the tree put up in the parlour, then they all had lunch and went to their rooms to rest for a while. At two o'clock, James knocked on Dolly's door and said, "Dolly, they will be here any minute. Now I want you to see that Eliza is downstairs ready to greet them."

Dolly answered without opening the door, "I'll send Blossom down with her."

James had never spoken sharply to Dolly before, but this time he gave her an order and she couldn't refuse. "You get your sister and come downstairs in ten minutes, do you hear?"

Dolly did as she was told, and a few minutes later, a coach pulled up to the front door. "Here are our experts now, my loves," James said. Then he laughed and gave the girls a little shove toward the steps.

"Merry Christmas," Gladys called when she saw Dolly and Eliza standing in the doorway.

"Merry Christmas," Eddy and Angelo called as they followed her out of the coach.

"Mama, oh, Mama, you didn't even let on you were coming," Dolly cried as she ran and hugged her.

"I knew you would come, Eddy," Eliza said as she hugged him.

"Doesn't anyone care that I'm here, too?" Angelo said as he got out of the coach, trying to handle an armload of gifts.

It was the most wonderful Christmas Gladys had ever had. She had all her loved ones with her. They decorated the tree using the precious ornaments they had used in Dover, along with the ones they made in Sandwich. When they finished decorating, it was dark outside and they lit the candles on the tree and shut off the other lamps. It was a glorious sight, and they all sang carols, drank hot toddies or hot chocolate, and ate Christmas cake until almost midnight. James was with his dear friend, Percy, his daughter, Eliza, and his best friends. His son, Horace, and family had sent their love, and he had never been so happy in his entire life.

Dolly was feeling sad because she had no presents to put under the tree for Gladys, Eddy, and Angelo, but then she saw that James hadn't mailed them to New York, after all, and they were all under the tree on Christmas morning. Santa brought Eliza her baby doll and Dolly gave her a doll buggy. Gladys brought her a pretty fan, a parasol, and a fur coat all made in China. She gave Dolly her beautiful pearl and tortoise-shell comb that the customers at Watt's Inn in Dover had given her when she left the inn to marry Dolly's father as Dolly had always admired it. "I hope you wear it, at your wedding, darling," Gladys told her.

Gladys had purchased presents for everyone from her own company, because she hadn't had the time to make any. They were unique gifts from all over the world: fur hats, muffs, and gloves all from Russia; carvings from the East Indies; brass ornaments from India; and leather goods from South America. All her gifts were very much appreciated. Although Aunt Jean couldn't remember what happened yesterday, she always knew Gladys when she saw her. Sometimes this proved to be an embarrassment, because she still thought Gladys was married to James.

Gladys was very fond of the elderly lady, and ever since Jean confessed that she had had a lover and lost him, Gladys didn't see her as a fussy old maid. She saw her as an attractive, but unfortunate, woman who was forced to give up her only love because of England's ludicrous class system.

It was kind of James to keep his aunt at Four Oaks instead of sending her to an asylum, but even with the excellent care she received, her health was rapidly failing, and knowing this was probably the last time they would be together, Gladys tried to spend as much time over the holidays with her as she could.

As usual, the time they were in England went far too quickly, and Gladys tried to talk Angelo into extending their visit, but he felt obliged to return. He also wanted to get back and take part in the renovations and do his share of work in the restaurant. James, Dolly, and Eliza had planned to go to London to see them off, but two nights before they left, it started to snow and then it froze. The roads were very slippery, and it was so cold, Gladys convinced them all to stay home and keep warm.

"Freda is cooking us a lovely dinner tonight, and after we have that, we shall sit around the fireplace and talk about all the things we've done while we were here and what we'll do when you come to New York. We can say our goodbyes here in the morning."

James agreed that it might be better if the young ones stayed home, but he thought he and Percy should go with them to lend a hand with their luggage. "We have a few things to attend to in London anyway," he said

They were at the station the next morning, waiting for the train, when Mary Baker arrived with a travelling trunk and two small cases. She rushed over to Gladys and hugged her, saying, "I am so glad I made it on time. I was afraid I would miss the boat if I didn't catch the same train you did."

Gladys was completely taken aback. "Miss the boat? What boat, Mary?"

"Why, the SS Delaney, of course. Oh my heavens! I never told you, did I?"

"Told me what?"

"You remember me saying I wish I was going back with you, and you said that would be nice? Well, I went into London the next day and found out that there was still room for one more passenger aboard the Delaney, so I booked it. That was only three days ago, and I have been so busy packing that I forgot to let you know. I hope you are not annoyed with me, Gladys. I can stay at a hotel if you cannot accommodate me."

She seemed to be sincerely upset and sorry, so Gladys felt she had to say she didn't mind, but in truth, Mary had been getting on Gladys' nerves ever since she went through a metamorphic change in her personality. Now she appeared to be mimicking all of Gladys' characteristics. Besides, Gladys didn't know how she would find time to entertain her at this time of year, and she didn't know if Lottie would agree to have her stay at Listla Cloone.

"I'm sure we can find some place for you to stay, Mary. I only wished I had known you were coming."

"Oh dear, perhaps I had better not go, if it is going to inconvenience you."

You know damn well it's going to inconvenience me, Gladys thought, but she said, "Of course, you won't inconvenience me, Mary, but I hope you realize that there is still a war going on and New York weather can get much colder than it does in England, so there isn't much we can do at this time of year." She almost added, *and you know very well that I told you not to come until spring, and until the war is over.*

Gladys had seen the sensual way Mary looked and touched Angelo, and she didn't appreciate it, now she thought, *if you have your eyes on my man, you had better watch yourself. You aren't dealing with Lady Gladys now. You're dealing with just plain Gladys Matthews and I intend to fight for what's mine.* Gladys would not admit it was jealousy that was bothering her, but there was something about the way Mary clung to Angelo every time she was near him that angered her, and she wasn't looking forward to the voyage home.

She needn't have worried, as soon as Mary saw Captain Bob Nicholson, she hadn't eyes for anyone else. Bob was flattered by her attention, but he missed having more time with Gladys, who seemed to be more devoted to her husband and son than ever.

Gladys didn't ask Lottie if Mary could stay with her, instead she asked the men if she could stay in one of the new apartments while she was in New York, thinking it might do her good to rough it. "It is not as grand as you are used to, Mary, but it's new and clean."

Mary, determined to be as adventurous as Gladys, replied, "That will suit me just fine, Gladys, dear, and you needn't worry about me. I have spent time at a resort in Brighton. Of course, I had Agnes, my maid, with me then. You don't suppose Lottie has a spare girl I could have while I am here?"

"Lottie and I do not have maids, Mary, but I do know a lovely young lady. Her name is Greta Goebel, and she might want to earn some money. She intends to be a doctor someday, so she needs all the help she can get. Mind you, Mary, this is not England, and here we treat our help as equals. I'll ask her if you like, but only as a companion. I know she will help you with your dress and your hair, though."

Mary was determined to show she had as much grit as Gladys, and said that would be fine. "Now, when shall I meet this charming fellow, Ike, that Angelo thinks is so special?"

"I shall arrange to have a party at Listla Cloone, and you can meet everyone there. Let's see, how about we have it this coming Saturday?"

"Wonderful! I would like to look at some of your best dress shops if I could. I brought a few gowns with me, but it's always nice to see what they have here. Could we please go shopping, one day this week, Gladys?"

"I'll see if Lottie will go with you. She had to work more than usual while I was away and a day off will be good for her." Lottie was delighted to spend a day shopping. Mary bought two dresses, and insisted on buying Lottie one that she had admired. It gave Gladys free time to catch up on their business, which had done exceedingly well over the holidays.

Because Gladys, Angelo, and Eddy missed having Christmas in New York, Lottie and Theresa Rutten were just as anxious to have a party as Gladys. Theresa offered to have it at her place, but Lottie and Gladys thought it was time they hosted the event at Listla Cloone. Like the Ruttens' home, it wasn't large enough to have a massive ballroom, but it did have a decent size one, and it was adjoining a large dining room, so the guests could spread out and mingle.

There was a piano in the room, and Iris brought her flute. The veteran who had lost his legs came and brought his accordion, and the lady who sang with Lottie and Gladys at the hospital was invited too, so they provided their own music. They hired caterers to make and serve the finger food and serve the champagne, so their own staff could come and enjoy the evening.

The Ruttens, Iris, and her girls, Ike's doctor friend and his wife, four of Ike's friends—two nurses and two medical students—Eddy's tutor, Paulo's art teacher, Captain Bob Nicholson, and all the restaurant staff and their spouses came, and altogether, there were over fifty guests.

Mary was under the impression that they were having it just for her, and although Gladys hadn't planned it that way, she had to admit that if Mary hadn't come for a visit, she probably would have had a much smaller gathering. The party was a huge success, and Mary was in her glory. There were enough single men at the party to pay her attention, but Gladys was so busy playing the piano and seeing that everyone was being served, she didn't have time to see if Ike was one of them.

Everyone seemed to like Mary, and she was invited to go ice skating in the park with Ike and his friends one afternoon, to go out to dine with Paulo's art teacher, and to spend a few days with the Ruttens. Mary said yes to all the invitations and asked Theresa if she would mind if she brought Greta with her when she came to visit her. She had grown fond of the girl, and Iris was afraid she was spoiling her.

"She keeps giving her clothes and jewellery," she complained to Gladys. "I am afraid she'll try to talk her into going back to England with her, and I am finding it difficult to manage at the bakery without her help." Gladys tried to assure Iris that Mary had her own maid at home and didn't need another one, but even she wasn't convinced. Gladys certainly couldn't complain about Mary infringing on her time while she was in New York, because the woman received plenty of invitations.

Angelo mentioned it to Gladys one evening when they were having their hot chocolate before going to bed. "Mary isn't at all like you described her, Gladdy. She's not the least bit snobbish, and in some ways, she reminds me of you." Gladys had all she could do not throw her cup at him.

Mary had only planned on staying in New York for a fortnight, but as the SS Delaney wasn't sailing until a week later, she stayed until then. Gladys didn't know whether to warn Bob or not, then she decided that if he was going to have an affair, there was nothing she could do about it.

She was helping Mary pack her trunk the day before she was to leave when Mary said, "It has been a most wonderful holiday, Gladys. I rather think I love America. The Ruttens have a lovely little place, and she has asked me to come and stay there next time, but perhaps you will be living in your new mansion by then. Living in one of these flats is not quite suitable for you, my dear. You deserve far better,"

Ah, thought Gladys, *That's the real Mary talking.*

"You know, I'm really quite fond of that girl, Greta. I think I shall ask her to come back with me. I always wanted a daughter, and I think I could make a proper young lady out of her. What do you think?"

"I think you had better leave her alone."

"What do you mean, Gladys?"

"I mean, she is a proper young lady now. A far more proper young lady than she would be if you dressed her all up in finery and taught her to think she is better than anyone else. She has ambition, Mary. Do you know what that is? She wants to become a doctor and heal people, and she wants to help her mother while she is doing it. If you take her away now, you will kill her spirit."

"Well, if that is what you think of me, I am sorry I came. If you disliked me so, why didn't you tell me before I left England?" Mary said as she started to cry.

"Oh, damn it, Mary. I don't dislike you. I am even a little jealous of you. You are enjoying the carefree life I once did when I had no responsibilities, and I envy that. But I wouldn't change my life for anything, and I meant what I said about Greta. Can you understand what I'm saying?"

"I think so. Well, not entirely, but I know what you meant when you said you were jealous. I've been jealous of you since I first met you. As for Greta, I shan't ask her to come with me if you think she is better off here. Can we still be friends, Gladys?"

"We are still friends, Mary, we truly are. You know, I think I'm suffering with the same complaint Lottie has been going through for a time now."

"Oh, that! I still have a little of that, too. You know, Gladys, I admire you more than anyone I've ever met, and I hope you never stop trying to make a decent human being out of me."

"I hope you will always be so sweet as to put up with my lectures. Now, give me a big hug and let's get you packed."

After Mary left, things settled down. With the holidays over, it was time to begin looking for Easter gifts for the showroom, have pamphlets printed, with pictures of their stock, and to send them to Sidney and Nicholas. They had written and said they had acquired sales in five more, smaller gift shops in London and would be requiring more goods.

"We are going to have to have more space, ladies," Norman said to Gladys and Lottie. "It's time we bought our own building. We should be branching out into bigger items. I can get my hands on some very ornate carved chests, some lined with aromatic camphor wood, and some top-quality brass beds, but we need to have room to display them. Then we have to contact the big department stores. We have to think big if we are going to be big, ladies."

"We have a fairly healthy bank account, Norman, but not enough to buy a decent building," Lottie replied.

"I won't borrow any more from Ike without asking the men this time, and I think until they rent out all their apartments, they will have used up most of their capital, so I doubt they have any to lend us. How much more would we need, Lottie?"

"I don't know how much it will cost to buy a building, or if there are any available, do you, Norm?"

"I do have one in mind. It's not far from here, but we would have to spend quite a bit of money on repairs and cleaning it up, like getting rid of the rats, etcetera. You see, it's on the waterfront and it used to be a cannery." Gladys and Lottie made arrangements with the realtor to look the building over, and they both thought it could do very well, except they were afraid they wouldn't be able to rid the place of the smell of fish. When they mentioned it to Norman, he said he could find some reasonably paid workers to tear out the old machinery, and then scrub and disinfect the entire building. "We can put down new floors, build walls, put up shelving, and paint the whole place. I'm sure that will take away the fish odour," he said.

When they found out how much the building cost, Norman told the realtor that it would cost so much to get rid of the smell that they could only give him two-thirds of his asking price. When the man agreed to accept, they still didn't have that much in the bank, so they agreed to ask Ike, Victor, and Angelo to see if they could borrow five thousand dollars while promising to pay it back in a year at three percent interest. The three men agreed, and after they bought the building, it only took a few months before the warehouse and show-room were ready. They were all delighted with the results.

"I am so glad we didn't allow anyone from the restaurant to see the building," Gladys said. "Now we shall have them all down for some champagne to christen our very own business establishment. When is the sign we ordered being put up, Lottie?"

"They promised they would put it up this weekend for sure."

"Wonderful, then let's have our party here on the ninth."

Gladys had no idea how joyful that celebration would be when she planned the party. On the same day, General Lee surrendered his army to General Grant, and the Civil War was officially over. It was late in the evening, and they were eating food that Sandy had brought with him and drinking champagne, when someone banged on the big doors and hollered, "The war is over. The war is over." When they went to see who it was, they could see the fellow running down the street knocking on all the doors and calling out, "Lee surrendered. The war is over."

Although many at the party were not believers, they all joined hands in a circle, closed their eyes, and said a prayer of thanks. Then they sang all the war songs they could think of. Angelo, Ike, and Victor were most impressed with the warehouse, and all predicted their business might even surpass their own endeavours. Gladys felt she had accomplished what she set out to do, but what really made her the happiest that night was to hear that the war was over and know that, finally, her girls could come to New York.

Chapter 17

Four days after Lee surrendered, Abraham Lincoln was assassinated by John Wilkes Booth, a popular young actor. Lincoln was enjoying a night out with his wife at the Ford Theatre—the same theatre Booth often starred in. The news of the president's death shocked and saddened not only Northerners and Southerners but also people around the world. Numerous governments declared periods of mourning on April 15th. On April 18th, mourners, some who had come from other cities, were lined up, seven abreast, for a mile to view Lincoln in his casket in the black-draped East Room of the White House.

On April 19th, hundreds of thousands watched the funeral procession, and millions more lined the seventeen hundred–mile train route that took Lincoln's body through New York to Springfield Illinois. Angelo and Victor closed the restaurant, and they all went to watch the train carrying the body of the president go by. People wept openly. Lincoln had been determined to unite the country as soon as the war ended, but sadly he wouldn't live to see it happen. The war cost America around six-hundred twenty thousand of her bravest. Many believed there would never again be such a loss, while others prayed they were right.

Now that they had their large showroom ready, Norman began ordering larger items, and he told Gladys and Lottie they would have to see about getting clients from the big New York furniture and department stores. Gladys suggested that he do it, because he was a man, but he insisted he had enough to do with his end of the business, besides, he was still cooking at the restaurant. He had mentioned to Victor that he intended to train two more cooks to take his place as soon as the import/export business showed enough profit, and it was close to doing that.

Gladys and Lottie set off one morning with their briefcases to visit the bigger stores. The first one they visited was a furniture store owned by a Mr. R. B. Dornan. As soon as they entered the store, they were met by a tall, pleasant-looking salesman who greeted them warmly and wanted to know how he could help them.

"Is Mr. Dorman in?" Gladys asked.

"Yes, I believe he is, but I am sure I can help you ladies. Were you looking for something in the latest styles or maybe some very lovely period pieces I could show you."

"We would rather see the owner, if we may."

His attitude changed and his smile disappeared as he replied, "Very well, ladies, if you wait there, I'll see if he's free." He left them standing.

"We may as well have a seat Lottie," Gladys said. "I wouldn't be surprised if he takes his time." She was right, and they sat for a while, then got up and started looking around.

"It's not very clean in here, Gladys. Do you think they do a good business?"

"I really don't know, but we have to start somewhere." Just then, the salesman came back and said, "Mr. Dornan can see you now," and he led them to the back of the store. Mr. Dornan's office was small, and yet the salesman insisted on coming in with them.

"Good day, ladies. I am sorry to keep you waiting," Mr. Dornan said as he rose to greet them, kissing each of their hands when they offered them.

Gladys immediately took a dislike to the man, and was thankful she was wearing gloves. He was far too gushy to suit her, but she knew that, when it came to business, every customer must be treated with respect.

"That's quite all right, Mr. Dornan."

"Call me Roy. Now, what can I do for you?"

As she thought respect doesn't have to mean familiarity, Gladys answered, "Here is our card, Mr. Dorman. We have just moved into a new building, and we have a new showroom. We would like to invite you around to see our wares. We have some very unique things in right now that I think you might like. Different-sized chests and exquisite beds."

Lottie gave him one of their cards with the address and said, "We are open in the evenings from seven until ten. Right now, we are having a grand opening special I think you would be interested in. Gladys or I will be happy to wait on you."

"We would be pleased to come to your show, but I didn't get your names."

"I am Lottie Rossini, and this is Gladys Matthews. Tomorrow night is our official opening, so we'll look forward to seeing you there."

"Wonderful, you can count on us."

Gladys and Lottie smiled, said goodbye, and left. As soon as they were outside, Lottie said, "That wasn't too difficult, Gladys."

"No, it wasn't, and you did beautifully, but I'm going to insist Angelo or Norman be with us tomorrow night. I just didn't like the looks of that fellow, Roy."

Gladys might not have liked his looks, but he certainly liked hers. As soon as she and Lottie left the premises, the salesman said, "Gee, boss, I've never seen a salesman who looked like that before."

"They aren't salesmen, stupid. They're whores. Didn't you get it? We have unique chests, in other words, they have whores with big tits from Asia and other exotic countries. Or we can have our pick between, who was it, Lottie or Gladys? That's it. This is our lucky day, Stan. We're gonna be there tomorrow right at seven and get some of that honey before it gets tainted!"

When the ladies left Dornan's store, they went to two large department stores and one more furniture store. It took a great deal of charm and time to convince the buyers of all three places that women were capable of running a business, but they arrived home tired and happy with two tentative buyers and one who said they would think about it.

The following evening, Roy Dornan and his salesman, dressed in their Sunday best, were at the warehouse door at seven sharp. Norman let them in, and as soon as Roy saw that Norman was Chinese, he nudged Stan and whispered. "What did I tell you, Oriental girls."

"Follow me, gentlemen, the showroom is this way," Norman said as he led them into the showroom where Gladys, Angelo, and Lottie were waiting.

Gladys held out her hand, "Ah, Mr. Dornan, how good of you to come. And don't you look nice, but you didn't have to dress; this is quite an informal grand opening. Lottie is serving champagne if you would care for a glass. This is my husband, Angelo. Angelo this is Mr. Dornan. He owns that lovely big furniture store on Beekman Street." Dornan looked confused as he shook Angelo's hand, and Gladys had to ask, "Mr. Dornan, your face looks quite red. Are you all right?" When he didn't answer, she added, "I don't believe I know your salesman's name."

"My salesman? Oh yes, yes, my salesman. It's Mr. Phillips."

"Mr. Phillips, this is my husband, Angelo." As the two men were shaking hands, Norman brought two more men into the room, and Gladys told Mr. Dornan to look around and if he wanted anything to leave his order with Lottie, then she went to greet the other gentlemen.

Phillips had his mouth open ready to say something, but Dornan glared at him and mumbled, "Say one word and you're fired!" They placed a small order, and left, the only disappointed customers. Although Gladys and Lottie had only gone to four stores, the news of the new showroom had gotten around town, and the grand opening was a huge success. In fact, all three partners were a little overwhelmed.

"It seems I shall have to train those cooks in a hurry, Gladys; this job is going to take all of my time by the look of things; but I promised Sandy I'd never let him down, so I cannot leave until he has all the help he needs," Norman remarked as they were finishing up the champagne.

"You know, I think Sandy is anxious to have a change, too. He's always talking about the wide-open spaces the ranchers brag about when they come to town, so I wouldn't be surprised if he takes a year or more off, too," Lottie replied.

"I don't blame him, and God knows he's earned it. I don't know what we would have done without him when we were starting up," Angelo remarked. "As soon as we have things under control, I'd like to take the train out west myself, wouldn't you, Gladdy?"

"I'd leave tomorrow, if I could," she answered, "but the way things are going, I doubt we will be free to go anywhere for a time yet. I sometimes wonder if we have what it takes to be truly successful in the business world. If it means we have to neglect our families, I would just as soon give up now."

The changes to New York after the war were extraordinary. The city grew at a phenomenal rate, with new machinery for the factories that had been built to accommodate the war. New people arrived to fill the place of those lost in the war. New York was becoming one of the greatest cities in the world.

Gladys wrote and asked James if the girls could come to New York, at least for the summer if not longer. He answered that he and Percy may bring them over, stay for a little while, then return without them. Gladys wrote back and said that would be fine, but in truth she would have rather had the girls to herself. They planned on coming in August, and Lottie agreed to change houses, so Gladys would have a suitable place to house them all. Blossom was invited to come, too, so that made five rooms to prepare. Gladys hired a few maids to help Liza with the meals and cleaning.

When they arrived, Gladys, Angelo, and Eddy were waiting for them at the dock. Dolly waved as soon as she saw them, but Eliza looked miserable. She had suffered with sea-sickness throughout the entire voyage, and although she insisted her nanny didn't need to come with them, she complained about her absence when she became sick. Gladys went to pick her up to comfort her, but she turned and held her arms out for James. "She will be happy if we can just get her to bed, Gladys," he said.

They were all so concerned over Eliza that their arrival wasn't the joyful occasion Gladys had looked forward to. No one seemed to be impressed with the grandness of Listla Cloone except Percy, and suddenly Gladys realized that, compared to Four Oaks, it was just an ordinary house, albeit grander than most. Eliza was feeling very sorry for herself, and her morose attitude toward her alien surroundings spread throughout the household that first day.

Gladys spent the next two days cooking little treats that she knew Eliza was fond of and sitting by her bedside reading to her. She only left her side when she was needed at the warehouse or when James or Dolly stayed home.

In the meantime, Angelo entertained James and Dolly by showing them around the city. On the fourth day, Gladys decided that her daughter was quite over her sickness but was enjoying the attention so much she didn't want it to end. In one way, this made Gladys feel needed, but she knew it had gone on long enough, and said, "Today, I think you are well enough to go for a ride, darling. What do you think about taking your father, Uncle Percy, Dolly, and Blossom for a picnic in the park? It's a lovely day, and we can go in our open carriage."

"I think that is a splendid idea, Mother. Can Eddy come, too?"

From that day on, the girls' visit was far more successful. They visited the Ruttens a few times, and, in the evenings, they sometimes attended Irish vaudeville shows in the Bowery. On two occasions, Gladys and Angelo took James and Percy to the opera house. They were having a warm summer, and Gladys wanted to go to the beach before James and Percy left, so she booked four rooms in an upper-class hotel on Coney Island for a week.

"I shall have to come back to work every second day, but I shall be here most of the time," she told them all. Gladys had gone to Coney Island once before and had rented a bathing dress. It was made entirely of wool, and when it became wet, it weighed over twelve pounds. She told Angelo that she feared Dolly, Blossom, and Eliza would drown if they went in the ocean wearing an outfit with that much added weight dragging them under.

"That's too much added weight, and even though they say that wool bathing dresses and suits are supposed to keep the body warm when wet, I found the opposite to be true. They take far too long to dry, and if you are sitting on the beach when you come out of the water, you get cold, not warm." Fortunately, there were others who felt the same and the manufactures had begun making swim wear out of flannel. Gladys purchased one for herself and one for each of the girls.

The dresses came down just below the knees and had long sleeves that gathered at the wrists. The pantaloons came down to the mid-calf, with ribbon ties and ruffles. There were places at the beach where the men could rent a bathing suit, and as they didn't consist of so much material, they only made them out of wool.

Although Dolly and Eliza thought the bathing dresses were pretty, it took a great deal of persuading to talk them into wearing them in public. Gladys finally convinced them that no one would notice them, because even the wealthiest guests wore them, so on the second day they made their way down the path from the hotel to the beach where it took even more persuading to coax them into the water. Gladys said they should at least go wading as they were dressed appropriately.

A safety rope ran from a piling out in the water to the shore, so a person could hang onto it and walk out without worrying about being swept away. Dolly had only agreed to wear a bathing dress, to please her mother, but she didn't do it without insisting, "Proper ladies do not wear bathing suits in England."

"Well, my dear daughter, over here we consider all ladies proper, and if they enjoy swimming, they swim," Gladys explained before she dashed out into the water and began to paddle around.

Dolly was both shocked and amazed, but Eliza was terrified. "Come back, Momma, come back!" she called out.

"She is all right, Eliza," Eddy assured her. "Look, watch me, I can duck under the water and I'm going to learn to swim, too. Mama says we are all going to take lessons." Eddy walked out into water until he was up to his waist then he ducked under.

Eliza screamed until his head bobbed up. "You frightened me, Eddy; please don't do it again."

"There's nothing to be afraid of, Eliza. Here, take my hand and wade out with me a little. Mother," he called, "come take Eliza's other hand."

"We will only walk out as far as you like, dear," Gladys promised.

By the end of the week, they were all enjoying the water, except Dolly, who preferred to sit under a beach umbrella and watch. James especially liked the water and he even learned the art of floating. It was a wonderful week. James and Percy had only planned on staying in New York for two weeks, but they were having such a good time, they were reluctant to leave and stayed an entire month. As James put it, "This is truly a 'New World.'"

Unfortunately, even though they had enjoyed being with Gladys and Eddy, the girls missed England, and Eliza insisted on returning home with her father. Dolly was just as anxious to leave. Gladys was extremely disappointed, and she tried to talk them into staying longer. "You haven't given yourselves time to become accustomed to it," she accused them.

"We shall come again, Mother, we promise. Eliza is still quite young, and this is the first time she has left home. I think she is a little homesick." Although Dolly was trying her best to spare Gladys' feelings, her words hurt more than they helped. Hearing Dolly say that Eliza was homesick made Gladys realize that her daughters would always think of England as their real home. All these years she had clung to an impossible dream, and now she had to face the truth. The only way she could have her girls with her permanently would be to go back to England and leave Angelo and Eddy. Gladys knew she would never do that. "My life from now on is going to be divided between here and England," she told Angelo, after the girls left with James and Percy.

The next time Dolly and Eliza came to New York was for Christmas, 1866. They came by themselves, now that Eliza was nine and far more mature. Fortunately, she no longer suffered with seasickness, so she didn't dread the voyage. The weather was cold, so they had two weeks when the lake in Central Park was frozen enough for skating, and both of girls enjoyed that. When it was time to leave, they actually seemed reluctant to go and promised they would spend a month in New York every summer.

Gladys began to enjoy their visits without feeling so guilty when they left. In the next few years, she and Angelo had many visitors who were looking forward to seeing America for the first time, like the Black brothers, who had never been outside England before. Six months prior to their visit, Nicholas' fiancée had suffered a heart attack and passed away, and Sidney was happy when their trip proved to be beneficial in easing his brother's sorrow.

Mary Baker surprised everyone when she unexpectedly arrived with a new husband, but what surprised everyone even more, was that her husband was none other than Theresa and Peter Rutten's son, Mitchell. Mary had reverted back to her original self and looked even more sophisticated and elegant than she had when Gladys first met her. She later confessed to Gladys that Mitchell preferred her that way.

Mitchell was obviously enjoying his new role as a gentleman and an aristocrat. Theresa and Peter Rutten were so overjoyed that their son had finally found someone to settle down with that they were content to overlook his newly acquired, pretentious mannerisms. They hosted a post-wedding dinner for the newlyweds at one of the best hotels in New York and invited Victor, Lottie, Gladys, and the boys.

Angelo was worried that Ike would be upset when he heard of the marriage, but when he confronted him, Ike wanted to know why it should make any difference to him who Mary married. Angelo confessed that he had thought Ike was interested in her.

"I don't know what gave you that idea, but I should have told you that I've been seeing someone and we're pretty serious about each other. I haven't brought her around to meet you because we've been too busy studying. You see, she's going to be a doctor, too, and she's studying at the Medical College and Hospital for Women here in New York. If all goes well, we'll both graduate next year at the same time.

"We're planning on getting married right after graduation and opening a practice together here. Don't worry, Angie, I won't get married without my best man. You will be my best man, won't you?"

"I'd never forgive you if I wasn't."

"Now that I've told you about her, I'll make sure we take the time and come to the restaurant for a meal. We have to eat anyway, but we can just come for about an hour. Okay?"

A few weeks later, Ike saw Gladys at the hospital, and told her that the name of his fiancée was Melissa Robertson and that he would bring her to meet them the following day. Sandy cooked a special meal for them, and Lottie made them an engagement cake. Gladys and Eddy hung up balloons and made a big sign to put up saying "Congratulations." When Ike and Melissa came in the door, everyone was waiting for them and clapped their hands.

Melissa had a look of kindness that added beauty to her rather plain features. She wasn't shy, but she didn't offer her opinion on any subject unless asked to do so. Gladys thought she would like to have her for a doctor and told her so.

"Very well, Gladys, I'll hold you to that, and you'll be my very first patient."

"Could I be your second patient?" Lottie, who had overheard the conversation, asked.

"My goodness, I'm going to make Ike jealous. We haven't even graduated and I already have two more patients than he has. However, don't be surprised if you are my only patients. People just don't accept the fact that we ladies have brains, but from what Ike has told me, you and Gladys are proof of that. I hope I can be as successful as you both are."

"Well, we'll certainly spread the word, and I think you can count on Theresa and Iris, too," Gladys said.

Another one of their unexpected visitors was Ruby, James' stableman, who came over with James and Percy. They all wanted to take the train out west together. Gladys was pleased to see that James was treating Ruby more as an equal than a servant and she joked with him, saying, "You know, James, if you keep visiting us, we're going to make a socialist out of you yet."

"Good Lord! I'd better not come so often then. I can't say I will ever want to talk like an American, although you seem to do it with a certain amount of dignity," was his answer.

During the next five years, both the International Import/Export Company and the International Enterprise Company (the name Ike, Angelo, and Victor chose for their new company) prospered. The restaurant had grown in size and had become one of the most popular eating establishments in the city. Their new four-storey building was finished, all the office spaces rented, and they were making plans to build another. Ike and Melissa both graduated, were married in St. Thomas More Church, and had a reception in the International Restaurant. They set up their practices on the bottom floor of their new building, but as Melissa suspected, people hadn't yet become accustomed to women doctors, and she only had a quarter of the number of patients that Ike had.

Although Gladys preferred to live near the waterfront, she knew she didn't have room for visitors in her apartment, and she couldn't ask Lottie to continue moving out of Listla Cloone every time the girls came to stay, so she agreed to have a suitable home built close to Gramercy Park.

Victor and Angelo were kept so busy with the new building and making plans for another, they didn't have time for the restaurant, so Louis, one of Victor and Lottie's twin boys, agreed to take it over so it would remain in the family. Gladys and Lottie no longer worked in the restaurant, therefore, they had more time to devote to their business. Gladys hired help to look after her new home, so it would always be in a state of readiness for her girls, or whoever else might come to visit.

Chapter 18

The news at the beginning of 1870 pleased many New Yorkers, but it made just as many angry. In February, Hiram Rhodes Revels, an African-American Republican from Mississippi, was sworn into office in the United States Congress and took his place in the Senate. Then, the following month, the 15th Amendment to the Constitution was declared ratified by the Secretary of State, giving the right to vote to African Americans.

Gladys was delighted that race would no longer be a reason for banning voting rights, but she thought gender shouldn't be either. "I wonder how long it will be before we are given that right?" she said to Lottie after she finished reading the news.

"There's not much we can do about it, Gladys, except try to convince our husbands. If all women did that, we may win. But then, if they're all as stubborn as my Victor, I doubt anyone can change their minds."

Gladys had noticed that Lottie was becoming quite forgetful, and it worried her. She mentioned it to Victor one day, but he just shrugged and said she was always that way. Lottie looked after the company's books, but Norman had been finding she made quite a few mistakes lately, so he suggested they hire a qualified bookkeeper.

This upset Lottie, so Gladys made up an excuse, saying that all businesses had to hire an official bookkeeper when they became as successful as theirs. The fact that Lottie believed her was another indication that she wasn't herself.

The next time Gladys planned on going to England, Lottie asked if she could go with her. Angelo hadn't planned on going, and Eddy said he had some important exams to attend to. What he didn't tell Gladys was that his teacher, Mr. Van Dyke, who had once tutored the son of a professor at the US Naval Academy in Annapolis, was so impressed with Eddy's knowledge of ships, he had written to the professor on Eddy's behalf. The professor hadn't promised anything, but he had sent Eddy an application form from the academy. Eddy didn't think there was a chance he would be accepted, but just in case he was, he wanted to be home when the notice came.

As she would be travelling alone, Gladys thought a change of scenery might be just the thing Lottie needed, and it would be nice to have the company. The voyage was going well, until, one night, when the water was calm, and Gladys and Lottie had their cabin door propped slightly open so they could enjoy the salt air. At about 2:00 a.m., Gladys was sound asleep in her bunk when she was wakened by a woman's screams. Sitting up, she said, "Lottie, did you hear that?" There was no answer, so she called out again, and then when Lottie still didn't reply, her heart missed a beat.

Jumping up, she looked in Lottie's bunk. It was empty. "Lottie, Lottie! Oh, God, Lottie!" she called as she ran outside. She was just going to wake the captain when Lottie ran into her arms.

Shaking and sobbing, she tried to explain, "Oh, Gladys, something terrible happened. I woke up in the wrong cabin. I was in a man's bed. Oh, Gladys! I hit him and hit him, then I ran. He—he—was naked!"

By this time, the poor elderly passenger had pulled on a pair of breeches and come out to join them. "I say! You broke my bloody nose," he said. His nose was indeed bloody; blood was running from his nose down his chin and into his hairy chest. "Is she mad?" he asked Gladys.

Gladys apologized and told him that Lottie was a sleepwalker and that she was sorry. "I shall just get her settled in bed and then come back and help you get cleaned up," she said.

The man said he could manage, then he winked at Gladys and said, "I understand perfectly. I had an aunt who walked in her sleep, too." Gladys was glad that Lottie was sobbing so noisily she hadn't heard.

It took the rest of the night, and a few drinks of gin from a flask she had brought along with her, to calm Lottie down. The following day, Lottie said she had no idea how she managed to get the cabins mixed up. She said she woke up and couldn't get back to sleep, so decided a stroll on the deck might help. "I guess when I went to come back to bed I must have gotten turned around, and for some reason, I thought Victor was with me, so I crawled in with him to get warm. Gladys, do you think I am losing my mind?"

"No, dear, but I do think your memory isn't as good as it used to be. I think you had better make an appointment with Melissa when we get back home."

A few days after they arrived at Four Oaks, James' aunt Jean suffered a stroke and passed away. Her death was a blessing, because she hadn't recognized anyone for some time and she was very confused and fearful. They all went into London where she was buried in the family plot. Gladys was glad she was home when it happened because Dolly took the old lady's passing quite hard.

James was upset as well, but he was thankful she was at peace. He was surprised to find that Jean had left him a good-size inheritance, not that he needed the money, but by the frugal way she lived her own life, he never thought she had that much.

Although neither Lottie nor Gladys were church-goers, they offered to attend Church with Dolly and Eliza, as both girls were now in the choir. Eliza at thirteen looked beautiful in her choir gown. There was one particular young man in the choir who Dolly seemed attracted to and later, when they were having their tea, Gladys mentioned it to her. "His name is Benjamin White," Dolly said, "and he is a few years younger than I, but, Mother, you should hear him sing. He has beautiful voice."

"He's quite handsome, don't you think?"

Dolly blushed, and said, "I suppose so, but he is popular with all the ladies, and I doubt he even knows my name."

It was nice to see Dolly so happy. She was twenty-five, and Gladys was beginning to worry that she was dedicating her entire life to Eliza, instead of socializing with young people her own age.

Lottie enjoyed the visit, but not as much as she had the first time she came to Four Oaks. The incident on the boat worried her, and she was afraid Melissa was going to tell her she was becoming senile. Gladys could tell it was on her mind and did her best to cheer her up. "I think you may find that a lot of women have the same trouble at your age," she suggested.

"I hope you're right, Gladys, but I'll be glad to get home and see Melissa. I'm so happy we have a woman doctor now and can talk freely about our personal problems."

The voyage home was uneventful, but Gladys locked the cabin door at night and kept the key under her pillow. On their arrival, Eddy and Angelo were waiting on the wharf for them, and, after they hugged Gladys and kissed her, Eddy said, "I'm sorry, Mother, but you are in for a bit of a shock, only this time, it is I who might have joined up."

"No, Eddy, you didn't?"

"Yes, Mother, I sent an application to the US Naval Academy in Annapolis and I just received a letter yesterday. It seems they won't take me until next year, when I am sixteen, but they want to interview me now in person. They have cut down on classes, and so I'll not likely get in, but I'd like to try. I have to be there in two months. Will you and Dad come with me?"

"I didn't even know you applied. You are still so young, darling, but I shan't stop you. You've wanted this all your life and you deserve it. I'm so very, very proud of you. Of course, we'll go with you, won't we Angelo?"

"Certainly, we wouldn't miss it for anything. I've always wanted to see the place anyway. It is quite a ways, though, even on the train."

Gladys was happy for Eddy, but the thought of him going away was heart-breaking. As long as she had him with her, she missed the girls a little less. Now they would all be apart. Everything had been going so well lately, but now she had an ominous feeling that things were about to change. She remembered her da saying, "You don't get berries without seeds, luv." *I don't know if I have the fortitude to take the seeds anymore,* she thought.

Lottie didn't tell Victor she was going to see the doctor, instead she asked Gladys to accompany her. Melissa's office was on the same floor as Ike's and they were identical. Both had a reception room, a change room, and an examining room. Melissa had a white coat on and looked very professional. When Lottie told her what she had done on the boat and how she was becoming forgetful, Melissa didn't say much until after she gave her a thorough examination.

"Well, you seem to be in good health, Lottie, so that's a good sign, but I want to do a few tests." She then gave Lottie four numbers to remember, talked about England for a few minutes, then asked her to repeat the numbers. Lottie could only remember two of them. Melissa asked her what year it was, the date of her birthday, and some other questions before she offered a diagnosis.

"Do I have dementia, Melissa? Will I lose my mind?"

"I don't think so, Lottie. You are suffering with some memory loss, but as we age, we suffer a lot of different losses: teeth, eyesight, hearing, and memory. There are a lot of new experiments going on all over the world, but so far, unlike the other losses, there's nothing we can prescribe for memory loss. Anyway, I don't think you have dementia, but I think you may be suffering with Bright's disease."

"What is that?"

"It's a disease named after a Doctor Bright, and it affects the kidneys and the arteries. I can't explain it simply, but I don't think you will ever have to worry about losing your mind." She didn't tell Lottie about all the other unpleasant symptoms that went with the disease. "I would like to see you once a month, though." Melissa told her to make the appointments with the girl in the reception room on her way out. When they were out of the office and in the buggy, Lottie began to cry. Gladys thought she was crying because she was sad, but Lottie said she was crying with relief. "I was sure I was going to be put in an asylum, Glad. I know Melissa was trying to spare my feelings, but I don't think I am that well."

"She didn't say that."

"Gladys, you know yourself that I'm right. The look on her face when she said I had that disease wasn't good. I've known I'm not well for a time now, but I can live with that. As long as I don't lose my senses, I can face whatever comes, but I don't want Victor or the boys to know."

"I shan't tell them." Then, without realizing she said it, she muttered, "More darn seeds."

"More what?"

"It's just something my da used to say. Whenever things went wrong, he'd say, 'You don't get berries without seeds.' You know that I love you, Lottie, and I shall always be here for you."

"One would never think we would feel this close to one another if they saw us that first day when you got off the boat!" Lottie said as she put an arm around Gladys' shoulder.

"Yes, if looks could kill, I'd be dead and buried long ago," Gladys said laughing.

That night, when Melissa and Ike finished with their patients, Melissa told Ike that she suspected Lottie had Bright's disease. "I know I shouldn't discuss my patients with you, darling, but I think Victor should know. It's likely to advance rather swiftly, and if I were him, I'd want to spend more time with her. What do you think?"

"I think you had better talk to Lottie about it first. I've known her for a long time, and I think she would want to know approximately how much time she has left. I'd also try to convince her that Victor and the boys have a right to know, as soon as possible."

The next time Lottie came to Melissa's office, Melissa told her the truth. Lottie wanted to know what she could expect to happen in the oncoming months, and Melissa said she could suffer with convulsions and blindness. Lottie didn't have to be convinced to tell Victor and the boys. She now knew that she had no choice. It was better if they knew what to expect and how to help when it did. Mellissa said that she and Ike could be with her when she broke the news. Lottie said she would like Gladys and Angelo to be there, too. "I'd like them all to know what to expect, so I may as well tell them all at the same time."

Paulo had gone to Washington with a group of artists, and they didn't know when he would return, so Lottie asked Victor, Louis, Gladys, and Angelo, along with Ike and Melissa, to come for tea one night, and then she had Melissa tell them all about her disease. At first, Victor showed little emotion and seemed to accept the news as though it was nothing more than a bad cold. In a matter of fact manner, he wanted to know what they could do if Lottie suffered with a convulsion or had a heart attack and how much rest she should have in a day. Melissa and Ike knew he was in shock, so they let him go on asking questions.

He had just asked about a cure, even though Melissa had already told him there wasn't one, when Paulo walked in. "Hi, everybody. Whose birthday is it?" he asked, jokingly, when he saw everyone was there. Then he saw the look on everyone's faces and he knew something bad had happened. "What's the matter, Dad?" he asked. That's all it took. Victor broke down, and crying, ran out of the room.

Lottie motioned for everyone to stay where they were, and she went after him. Melissa explained to Paulo what was wrong, and he and everyone else in the room cried too. Ike said that the best thing they could do was to leave so the boys could be alone with Lottie and Victor. They all gave the twins a hug and said that if there was anything they could do, to let them know, and then left.

The next time Gladys visited Lottie, Lottie said that she had to become angry with Victor in order to persuade him to leave her long enough to attend a meeting with the builders. "Honestly, Gladys, he is smothering me with kindness," she said, but she didn't look the least bit upset.

Now that there weren't many veterans in the hospital, Gladys and the rest of the entertainers only went to play and sing twice a month. Lottie insisted on coming with them as long as she could, but she was having more and more trouble remembering dates and so missed many of them. Gladys tried to spend as much time as she could with Lottie, not only for her own sake but for Victor's as well. When it was nearing time to go with Eddy to Annapolis in Maryland, Gladys convinced Victor that it might do Lottie and him good to come with them.

"Lottie would probably love the trip. You two haven't had a holiday together since I've known you, and I think it might do you good," she said.

Victor was afraid it might be too hard on Lottie, so he went to see Ike and asked him. Ike called Melissa into his office and they discussed it for a few minutes, then they decided that she could go. "Whatever gives you enjoyment, that's what you should do," he advised. Lottie was thrilled with the idea when she heard about it and began to make plans, but she confessed to Gladys that she couldn't make up her mind what to take, so Gladys packed a suitcase for her.

They all enjoyed the change of scenery, and then when they arrived, they were all impressed with the large and official looking buildings of the academy. "Oh look, Angelo, see, that's the figurehead from the ship the USS Delaware. I think it's known as Tecumseh. I read all about it when they were putting it there two years ago," Gladys said.

After Eddy checked in, they found out that the superintendent would not be able to interview him for another hour, so one of the officers offered to give them a tour through the dormitories. When Gladys saw how immaculate the beds were and how tidy all the buildings were kept, she was glad she had brought Eddy up the way she had. However, he had never had to make his own bed, and she made up her mind that, when they returned home, that would change.

Lottie didn't have the strength to walk the grounds, but she was able to go far enough to see the ships the cadets trained in. It amazed Gladys how unperturbed Eddy was when it came time for him to have his interview. "Aren't you nervous, darling?" she asked.

"Not really, Mother, I'd very much like to get in, but I heard they were cutting down on class sizes, and not many applying would be accepted next year. I am certain there are many who are better qualified than I am, so I shan't be too disappointed, and Captain Bob has promised me a job on his ship, so I have an alternate plan." He had just finished talking when an officer came to get him. The officer told the rest of them they could wait, and he would have some tea or coffee sent in for them.

Angelo, suspecting the interview would last for over an hour, suggested that Victor take Lottie back to the hotel where she could lie down and rest while he and Gladys waited. It was a good thing he did, because not only did Eddy have his interview, but he was taken on another tour as well, and it was over two hours before he came back to see them.

Gladys could hardly wait to find out how he made out, but she hadn't a chance to ask him before he told her that the superintendent had suggested he spend the night at the academy in order to see what it would be like if he were to be accepted. "They have a room where I can bunk, Mother, so you and Dad go back to the hotel and I shall come there after I'm through in the morning."

"But we want to know how it went. Do you think he was impressed?"

"I have no idea. I wasn't with him for long, and he never let on how I did. The rest of the time, I was with one of the professors. We toured some of the classrooms and the gym. I can tell you this, though, it looks like I'm going to have to work very hard if I ever want to graduate."

"You don't have to do it, Eddy. We won't be disappointed if you change your mind," Angelo said.

"Oh, I won't change my mind, Dad. I just hope I have what it takes to stick to it."

"How long do you think it will it take for you to graduate?"

"If I do well, I could graduate in four years. Now, I had better go and find the professor, so I know where I will be sleeping tonight." They kissed him goodbye and left.

The next morning, they had their breakfast and were waiting in the lobby of the hotel when he came in. His face was flushed, and Gladys thought he might be feverish, but he said that he had just been running. "After seeing how those fellows can run, I thought I'd better start getting used to it," he said.

On the way home, Eddy told them all that he had learned while there. "They have dress parade every evening except Sunday. The students are called cadets or sometimes cadet midshipmen and they do athletics. They have weekly dances, so you'll have to teach me to dance now, Mother. I talked to some of the students and one said the wags now call the academy 'Porter's Dancing Academy' after the superintendent. And we—I mean the cadets—get class rings. Isn't that swell?"

Gladys could tell he was already thinking he was one of them. "It all sounds wonderful, dear, but what about this hazing I've heard about?" Gladys asked.

"I saw a little of it last night when one of the students had to carry another's books and follow him around. It didn't look too bad, and I think it only lasts a short time."

Chapter 19

Gladys, Angelo, and Eddy were at Four Oaks for Christmas, and they stayed to welcome in the New Year. James, with Dolly's help, hosted a New Year's ball, and Gladys was surprised and pleased over the amount of young people who came. James and Percy invited the Blacks, along with some more of their London friends, and almost every room in the mansion was filled. A constant stream of people were either coming or going in the hallways, and they all stopped to say a few words with one another. Thus they became well acquainted before the ball. As Angelo said, it was like living in a train station— not that he minded. They all found it amusing.

Dolly had ensured that enough extra help was hired to allow Freda to sit back and give orders instead of doing all the cooking herself, so she was happy, especially when she received personal praises from the guests. Some out-of-town guests stayed at Four Oaks for four nights, one of which was the night of the ball. When the last one left, the noise was both missed and appreciated.

Before the ball, Gladys had asked Dolly if the young man named Benjamin who sang in the choir was coming. Dolly said that he had been invited, but he might not be in Sandwich then. "He is really making a name for himself, Mother. He already owns a construction company and is building houses all over the country. Right now, he is building a number of them in Hastings. He isn't home very often, so I don't see him that much, but I hope he arrives in time."

The ball was well on its way when the young man arrived. He made quite a dashing picture dressed in the latest style dress coat and a gold brocade vest. He had a good thick head of black hair, with just enough curl to give it body. His nose was slightly Roman shape, but the rest of his facial features were evenly formed. He had a lovely smile, and Gladys liked him as soon as they were introduced. She could tell he was fond of Dolly, but she couldn't discern how fond. He danced with other young ladies, but when he wasn't dancing, he stayed close to Dolly, James, and Eliza.

Eliza was the most popular girl at the dance. The young men wouldn't allow her to sit out a dance, but she preferred to dance with Eddy or Benjamin and kept pulling them up on the dance floor. Eddy did the usual brotherly complaining, but he was enjoying himself. Ever since he arrived at Four Oaks, he had been running, exercising, and going to bed and rising early. James wanted to know what was going on, but Eddy had asked his parents not to tell anyone about the academy in case he wasn't accepted, so Gladys just said that he just liked to be outside, even though she was bursting to tell the truth.

Gladys was worried about Lottie, yet she didn't want to leave the girls, but when she received a letter from Victor, she knew she had to. He wrote a very brief note saying that Lottie had had two convulsions and her eyesight was failing. He said she missed Gladys, but he didn't say they could manage without her and not to hurry back, so she knew it was a plea for help. She talked to Eliza and Dolly and tried her best to explain why she had to leave.

"I haven't told you, my dears, but Auntie Lottie is very sick. She hasn't long to live and could die any day. I just received a letter from Uncle Victor and he said she has failed a lot since I left. You know we are very close. I feel like she's my sister—a little like how you two feel for each other. Now, I don't want to leave you, but I feel I must be with her now. Can you understand that?"

"Why doesn't she come here?" Eliza wanted to know.

"Yes, Mother. We could look after her, and then we would all be together." Dolly added.

"I wish it were that simple, darlings, but Lottie's family are all there, and that is where she would want to be when the time comes."

"Of course, Mother. You have to do what your heart tells you to. You always have," Dolly said.

Gladys didn't know if Dolly meant it in a nice way or not, but she put her arms around them and said, "I'm sorry, my loves; Lottie really needs me right now. I just hope she lasts until I get there."

Dolly wasn't normally vindictive, but the disappointment she felt over the news of her mother leaving caused her to say, "And where would you like to die, Mother, when your time comes?"

"Dolly, that's not fair."

"I am sorry, Mother, but I cannot help but wonder. Would it be here with us, or over there with your friends?"

"Of course, it would be here with you two. You should know that," Gladys replied, but she felt she had just promised to tear herself in two. Then she looked at Dolly's face and saw the relief and was glad she said it.

They arrived home three weeks later, and Gladys went directly to Lottie's house. A maid answered the door and said that Lottie was resting and that Mr. Rossini had left instructions that she wasn't to be disturbed. Gladys asked to see Liza who was so glad to see her she cried. "Come in, Missus Matthews. She's in the sunroom. Mister had a bed put there so she could rest in the sun. She is goin' to be so happy to see you. You just go on right in and I'll bring you both a nice cup of tea."

Lottie was sleeping when Gladys entered the conservatory, so Gladys sat beside her and took hold of her hand. Lottie didn't wake up right away, but she seemed to know it was Gladys and squeezed her hand. When Liza came with the tea, it woke her, and she turned her head to look at Gladys. "I was having a lovely dream, Gladys. We were walking hand in hand along the beach at Coney Island, and here you are. What are you doing here? I thought you were in England."

"It wasn't as much fun without you, so I came home. How are you, Lottie?"

"Do you want the truth?"

"Yes. Don't spare me. I didn't come all this way to be lied to."

"Well, if you can imagine how you'd feel if you were hit by a train, then you'd know exactly how I feel. But now that you're here, I'm going to be a lot better. What do you recommend, Doctor Matthews?"

"First, a spot of tea and one of Liza's molasses cookies, then I shall decide what to do with you."

Lottie sat up and drank her tea but only took a few nibbles out of her cookie.

"Come on, you have to do better than that or Victor won't allow me to visit you anymore. Eat half of it and I shall finish the other half, then he'll never know." Gladys broke the cookie in half and Lottie managed to eat her half.

"I have no appetite, Glad. They won't let me do anything, so I don't get hungry; but you haven't told me, when did you get home?" When Gladys said she just arrived, Lottie insisted that she leave and go and unpack. "I'm sure you have to see how things are running down at the warehouse. I'm sorry, but I haven't been there for over a week. Ever since I took a convulsion, Victor won't let me out of his sight for more than an hour at a time. I want to get up and do something. I feel so useless, I may as well die now. I wouldn't say that to Victor, but I knew you would understand."

"I do, my darling, I do. And I shall talk to Melissa tomorrow and see if I can't take you with me to the storeroom once in a while. If we can't do that, perhaps we can visit your aunt Theresa or just go for a drive."

"God, it is good to have you back!"

Gladys was just about to leave when Victor came home. He looked worn out, and when he hugged Gladys, he whispered in her ear, "Thank heavens, you're home."

"Hey, you two, I am going blind, not deaf. Was I that much trouble?" Lottie called out.

"No, my darling, but I can see how much better you look now than when I left, so I think you were getting tired of my company. Gladys, I dropped in at the restaurant to see how Louis was doing and Angelo came in. He told me you only arrived two hours ago. You must want to unpack and get settled, so you should get on home. If you have time, come back tomorrow afternoon. We have a nurse come every night and every morning to see how she is doing, and she should be here any minute; so don't worry, we will see our girl is well looked after."

Angelo and Gladys arrived back home at the same time. He had been to see Ike, but when he saw that his waiting room was full of patients, he left and went to the restaurant where he found Victor talking to Louis about his mother. Angelo told them that Gladys had gone to see Lottie and wanted to know how she was.

"Sometimes I think she has just given up," Victor said. "She really missed Gladys, so thank goodness you're back. Oh, I almost forgot, Merry Christmas and Happy New Year," he added then gave Angelo a warm hug.

Angelo was fond of his uncle, however, he often felt like Victor considered him a burden; but now, although he knew his uncle wouldn't say it, Angelo could tell he was just as happy to see him as Lottie would be to see Gladys.

The next day, Gladys spent the morning with Norman going over the orders and admiring their latest imports. When she left, she went to Melissa's office and was pleased to see there were two women, one with a small child, waiting in the waiting room. The receptionist, a young woman, recognized Gladys, and as soon as the patient Melissa had in her office left, she told her to go in.

Melissa said that Lottie should get out more and enjoy the time she had left. "If she feels well enough, let her do whatever she wants, but, Gladys, be aware that she could suffer with an epileptic seizure at any time, or a heart attack." She then told Gladys what to do if Lottie did have a seizure. "Now, you and Victor must understand that this can happen if she is out for walk, or lying down resting at home, so don't feel guilty if it happens when you take her out," she said.

When Gladys arrived at Lottie's, she was up and dressed. "I knew you would be nagging me to get up when you came, so I thought I'd beat you to it," she said grinning.

"Good for you. Now, where would your Highness care to go? But I must warn you, it's colder than Santa's nose out there, so wrap up warmly."

"It's not Santa's nose, it's a witch's bum, remember? And the colder, the better. I would have married an Eskimo if Victor hadn't asked me first."

Gladys had a little shay, similar to the one she had in England, and she had brought along a big fur rug to put over their knees. First, she took Lottie to see the new items Norman had in the storehouse, then they went for a ride around the park before she took her back home. They were sitting in Lottie's parlour, having a cup of coffee, when Lottie said how much she had enjoyed working with Gladys in their business.

"It has been so much fun, Glad, but I know I can't work anymore, so I would like you to take my name off our contract. It was you who started the business, and you deserve to have all of your half in your own name."

"Not on your life. You're not getting out of it that easy, my dear. Norm and I count on your advice. Don't you remember telling us that those wooden stools we thought of buying were too flimsy? Well, Masons bought a load of them and I've heard that they lost a lot of money reimbursing the customers who bought them. And just today, you pointed out how that toy we were thinking of ordering wasn't safe for little children. We need you, Lottie."

"That's wonderful to hear, Gladys, but I know, and you know, too, that I'm not going to be around much longer; no, don't say that's not true, because we both know it is. At least I can talk to you about it, and you'll never know how good that feels. I want to get some things off my chest, and the business is just one of them. Now, I think in our contract it states that if anything happens to either of us, our quarter share goes to the other one, right?"

"I think so, but I don't think it should be like that. I think if you go before I do, I want to add both of our shares in with our men's business, with the agreement that I am made a shareholder. Remember Victor saying that we should keep everything all in the family? Well, I think he was right. Anyway, if you're not here to share it, I shan't enjoy it as much. What do you think?"

"Wow! I don't really know what to think." Lottie sipped her coffee and looked very thoughtful before she smiled and said, "I know how much the fight for women's rights means to you, and at first it sounded like you were giving up, but this way, you'll retain your equality. I think it is a brilliant idea. You never cease to amaze me."

Gladys would have liked to visit the girls once again before the summer, but she wouldn't leave Lottie for that long. Gladys, Angelo, and Victor took Lottie on the train to Niagara Falls and she had a wonderful time. Gladys enjoyed the falls, too, and decided to take the girls to see them when they came in the summer. Unfortunately, the excitement might have been too much for Lottie, because she collapsed on the trip home.

Theresa and Peter Rutten visited Lottie often, and when Lottie's eyesight became so dulled that she could no longer enjoy the scenery, they all went to visit the Ruttens for a musical evening, although Lottie's voice was becoming weaker. By the time Dolly and Eliza arrived that summer, she had failed so much that Dolly said she hardly recognized her.

Gladys wanted to show the girls a good time, but she didn't like to neglect Lottie. Fortunately, Iris and Theresa said they would take turns sitting with her while Gladys took the girls on the train to see Niagara Falls. The train went from New York to Kingston, Albany, Schenectady, Syracuse, Lyons, Rochester, Lockport, and lastly Niagara Falls, so they had a lot of interesting stops on the way.

They had a wonderful time and were only gone for five days. The rest of the time the girls were in New York, Eddy and Angelo helped entertain them. There was now a zoo in Central Park, and Eliza would have gone there every day if she was allowed to. Gladys wasn't able to take them to Coney Island, but the girls didn't seem to mind, as neither one was fond of swimming, and Dolly was happy not to have to wear a bathing dress in public again.

Gladys was pleased when Eliza began referring to the room Gladys gave her as "My room," and calling Dolly's room "Dolly's room."

"At least she feels a little more at home here," she told Lottie.

The girls stayed for most of the summer, and both spent quite a lot of time visiting with Lottie. Gladys was so proud of them. She asked Dolly about Benjamin, and if he had begun to court her.

"No, Mother, he is not home very often, but when he is, he always comes to visit us and brings chocolates and fruit. I think he is so busy making his fortune that he hasn't time for courting."

"If he comes out to see you every time he is home, that is courting in a way," Gladys said, grinning.

They were sitting down to their evening meal one night when the doorbell rang. Raymond, their butler, answered the door and brought a letter in for Eddy.

"It's from the academy. I don't think I can open it, Mother; will you open it for me?"

"Of course, dear, but whatever it says, I'm sure it will be for the best." She tore the envelope open, and read the letter while Eddy stared at her, eagerly watching her face to see her expression. When she finished, she looked up and kept Eddy waiting for a second before she smiled. Eddy jumped in the air and shouted, "Hooray, hooray! I can't believe it. Did they really accept me, Mom?"

"You've been accepted, Eddy. You're now a US Naval Academy cadet. Congratulations!"

"I think this deserves a celebration, and as you won't be here for your birthday, we should celebrate that, too, even if it is a month early. That way the girls will be here to join in. What say everyone?" Angelo asked. They were all in favour and Gladys said they would have a party a week later.

Because Gladys had to spend so much time with Lottie, she hadn't time to plan an extravagant party and only invited the immediate family, along with Ike, Melissa, Iris, her family, Norman, Sandy, and a few more from the restaurant who had worked there for a number of years. Angelo and Victor had become good friends with some of their business associates and wanted them invited too, and Eddy had some friends he wanted there as well, so it turned out to be quite a crowd.

Most came bearing gifts for Eddy—gifts they thought might be useful to a young man away from home for the first time. The gifts his young friends brought were mostly funny and some a little risqué, causing Eddy and the young girls to blush. It was a great party, but when it over and most of the guests had left, Gladys had time to look around the room. She felt like she had a weight pressing on her chest. The girls and Eddy were going through all his gifts, Lottie was watching them and having a last cup of tea before Victor took her home, and Gladys thought they all looked like angels. How she wished she could stop time and keep the scene from ever changing. *I don't want them to leave me, God,* she silently prayed, but she knew that, in a week's time, her children had to leave, and Lottie would be gone too.

Melissa had told Gladys that Lottie's heart was very weak and she hadn't long to live, so when it came time for Eddy to go, he knew his mother wanted to be with her best friend until the end, so he said there was no need for her or Angelo to travel back to school with him. "I shall have to begin training as soon as I arrive," he said. "So I wouldn't be able to spend time with you anyway."

Gladys agreed to stay home if Angelo went, and he said he intended to. They could tell that Eddy was pleased, and he and Angelo left a few days after the party. Two days later, it was time for the girls to go.

Even though their mother had spent most of the time they were in New York looking after Lottie, the girls seemed to enjoy their visit more than ever and were sorry to leave. When it came time for them to go, Lottie insisted on going with Gladys to see them off, and even though she couldn't make them out on the boat, she waved goodbye as enthusiastically as Gladys.

Gladys couldn't hold back the tears when they returned to Lottie's house and Lottie held her in her arms and said, "Don't cry, dear, they are out of sight, but they are in your heart with you, and they will be with you again before long." Gladys realized how selfish she must be to cry on her friend's shoulder when Lottie knew that when she said goodbye to her boys, it wouldn't be for just a few months.

"I'm so sorry, Lottie; I don't know what's wrong with me lately. I am not usually so weak. I can't seem to stop myself."

"And didn't I see you fanning yourself yesterday when we were having tea?"

"Yes. I hate to mention it, Lottie, but I think your butler is keeping your house too warm."

"It's not my house that is too warm, my dear; you are just beginning to have what you told me I had five years ago. Now, don't you go through it without telling Melissa. She's such a good doctor and probably knows of some new medicine that can help."

"You mean I'm going through menopause?" Lottie nodded. "Well then, you had better stick around. You promised me you would help me put up with it, remember?"

"I'll do my best, but I think you should talk to Iris, too. She has just finished hers and she's a good listener."

A week later, they had been to Theresa's for tea and Gladys was helping Lottie down form the carriage, with Simon's help, when she collapsed. Gladys told Simon to send one of the servants to fetch Melissa and one to find Victor, while she stayed with Lottie, who was unconscious but breathing shallowly. Her colour was deathly, and Gladys prayed the doctor would get there in time to revive her.

It seemed to Gladys that she was sitting on the curb holding Lottie in her arms for hours before both Melissa and Ike arrived. With Simon's help, they managed to carry her into the house and lay her down on a sofa. Melissa shook her head. "She's going," she whispered. Lottie kept breathing until Victor came and held her hand. She passed away peacefully a few minutes later.

Chapter 20

The year Lottie passed away, graves were being removed from many of the city's churchyards and relocated to Woodland Cemetery—a cemetery created during the Civil War. Victor purchased a family plot and had Lottie buried there. He wanted Angelo to purchase one too, but Gladys said they should think about it first. When they were alone in their house, she confessed, "I don't know what to do, Angelo; I have the girls to think of, and I am not sure if I want to be buried in America."

"But this is where our home is, Gladys. This is where we live and where we will die."

"Not necessarily. I've never said anything about it before, but if Eddy does become a captain, he will be at sea most of the time, and who knows when or where he will settle down. It may even be in England. When we retire, we could buy a lovely home by the water in England where I could be near the girls. They'll be getting married before long and start having babies. I want to be near my grandchildren, darling. I don't want to have to put up with just seeing them once a year like I've had to do with Dolly and Eliza."

"Well, this is all news to me. I thought you were happy here. I don't want to go back where people treat people who happen to be born poor like scum. We had enough of that growing up, and I don't want to live in that sort of environment again."

He said it angrily, and Gladys knew he was disappointed with her. "I'm sorry, Angelo, but things are changing over there. Besides, there are people like that here, too. There are lots of good people in England, and you don't have to associate with the ones who think they are superior."

"Well, your family may live in England, but mine are here in America, so it seems we will have to make a compromise and be buried at sea," he replied laughing.

"That's not funny. Both your parents and mine are buried in England, so you might say our roots are over there."

"Good God, Gladdy, we don't even know if our folks were buried. Why did you have to bring that up?"

Gladys remembered her promise to Dolly and she started to cry. She mumbled, "I don't know. Forget it; forget I said anything."

Angelo shook his head, picked up his coat, and left. He went as far as the corner then turned back. When he came in the house, Gladys was pouring herself a cup of tea. "Want a cup?" she asked as though nothing had been said.

"Sure," he replied. "Gladys, when I came home from the war, I know I was a royal pain in the ass, but you put up with me until I improved. Now, I suppose what you are going through with these hot flashes and mood changes is something like I went through, so I promise I'll try to be more tolerant in the future. I'll not walk out on you again. Forgive me?"

"Of course, but it wasn't my condition that made me say what I did; I've been thinking about it ever since Lottie died. We'll have to make up our mind one of these days." Angelo didn't believe her. She was having some depressing moments lately and he was sure that was what was making her get these crazy thoughts, so he just gave her a hug and drank his tea.

A month after Eddy left to attend school, Gladys went down to work at the warehouse and Norman told her that there had been a fire in San Francisco that had destroyed 17,450 buildings and killed 250 people. "I heard there were around ninety thousand left homeless, and I don't know if it's true or not, but Andy said he also heard that, on the same day, a fire started in Chicago and a one in Peshtigo, Wisconsin. He said that fire spread across six counties in one day, killing about two thousand people."

"My heavens, that's dreadful!" Gladys replied "I hope he's mistaken. I'll pick up a newspaper on my way home." Norman's friend was right, and a few days later, Lottie's aunt, Theresa, canvassed around the neighbourhood asking for donations of money and clothing to send to the victims.

Then, on October 27, all of New York's newspapers had the same front-page story announcing that Mayor Boss Tweed had been arrested.

Ike expressed how he felt about it, saying, "It's about bloody well time! I think Thomas Nast and his talent as a caricaturist had a lot to do with showing everyone what sort of rascal he was. Nast deserves a medal." Most people felt the same way, but there were a few of Tweed's friends who Ike said must be shaking in their boots hoping they weren't named.

Eddy wrote home and said that he was doing well with his classes and that he was fortunate to have a senior who wasn't too harsh with his hazing. "When it comes time for me to haze someone, I don't think I shall be as hard on my victim as some of these chaps. One went too far the other day, and the poor fellow ended up leaving the academy. I think some of the professors are against hazing, but I doubt they can stop it."

He went on to write that he would only be allowed one week off at Christmas and so would only be home for a short time. "If you want to go to England, Mother, I can stay here. There are quite a few cadets that won't have time to get home and back, so they will have to stay here, too. I shan't be alone."

Gladys couldn't bear the thought of leaving him in the dormitory over Christmas, so she wrote and asked Dolly if she and Eliza could come to New York. She added that she had plenty of room for James and Percy and that she didn't want to leave Victor and the twins on their own for their first Christmas without Lottie. Dolly wrote back that they would rather wait and have Gladys come for a visit in the New Year and that they could exchange gifts then.

Because the girls weren't going to be with them, Gladys, Angelo, and Eddy spent Christmas Day at the Ruttens, as did Victor and the twins. Mitchell and Mary were living in England, but they came home for the holiday. Everyone did their best to make it a jolly Christmas, but Lottie's absence was felt so profoundly that no one could ignore it. Eddy and Paulo helped by telling about their experiences: Eddy about the academy, and Paulo, who had been studying art in Paris, about France.

"The Metropolitan Museum of Art is opening here in late February, Paulo, and I hear they will be showing one hundred and seventy-four paintings by famous artists," Gladys said. "Your mother and I were going to go to the opening. Do you think you'll be here for it?"

"Bruno wrote and told me about it. He sounded very excited, so I decided I would stay and see it. I would love it if you were to come with me, Aunt Gladys."

"Nothing would please me more, and if Angelo and I are back from England in time, that's a date. I'll see if Iris wants to come too."

As soon as Eddy left to return to Annapolis, Gladys and Angelo left for England. Bob Nicholson had taken time off to spend with his family and wouldn't be bringing the SS Delaney to America again for four months, so they had to sail with another ship. It was a rough trip, and there were times when they were ready to man the lifeboats, but they arrived safely. However, they didn't look forward to their trip home.

Norman had complained about the lack of English merchandise they were receiving lately, so Gladys and Angelo dropped into see the Black brothers before they left London for Four Oaks. The brothers were especially happy to see them, because they wanted to break the news that they were thinking of retiring to Gladys in person.

"We are finding the work a little too exhausting of late. It seems to take much longer to get around to all our customers than it used to, Gladys, and for the last six months, we have been entertaining the idea of retiring," Nicholas confessed.

"I hate to see you leave, but I think it would be nice for you to be able to enjoy the rest of your lives doing whatever you want. Do you think you would have any trouble selling your business?" Gladys asked.

"Well, Nickerson, he and Fuller own the biggest import/export company around here, and one day he met Sidney at a horticultural show and asked him if we would consider selling. You see, Sidney and Nickerson are both fond of roses. Anyway, Sidney told him we had thought about it, and Nickerson said to let him know when we made up our minds."

"As long as they give you a fair price, Nicholas, it would mean you wouldn't have to wait to find a buyer. Is theirs a reputable business?"

"I have never heard anything to the contrary, my dear. However, I have only talked to them a few times, but they both appeared to be gentlemen. Now, Sidney and I have no intentions of selling to anyone who will not agree to take over our contract with you. Would you be able to meet with the chaps if I can arrange it?"

"What do you think, Angelo?" Gladys asked.

"We sail for home on the 20th of February, so we could leave James' a day early, and if they could meet with us here on the 18th of

February that would be fine." The brothers said they would arrange it, and Gladys and Angelo left for Four Oaks.

Because their Christmas tree had lost most of its needles, James was forced to throw it out, but he and the girls went out and cut down a little one to put in its place. The day Gladys and Angelo arrived, it snowed, and with the tree up and fresh greenery about, it felt like it was actually Christmas Day. Hilda cooked a big goose with all the trimmings, and Dolly made little cardboard Christmas tree name tags for each table setting. Gladys had missed Lottie so much that she really didn't enjoyed Christmas at the Ruttens, but now she couldn't help but be happy as she and Angelo sat at the table with her girls and held hands while Percy said grace.

Gladys knew that, although she might have other good friends in her lifetime, she would never be as close to them as she was to the two she had lost: Millie, the first friend she found when she escaped from the ghetto, and Lottie.

Angelo now enjoyed spending time with the girls, and James and Percy as Gladys, and if they didn't have businesses to attend to, they would have stayed at Four Oaks longer.

When they returned to London, the Black brothers took them to Nickerson and Fuller's showrooms to meet the two men and talk about their contract. Nickerson did most of the talking, but Fuller was the one who knew all the important figures and had to correct his partner more than a few times.

Nickerson appeared to be a man about town and he dressed accordingly. He was a large man, with an imposing figure for an elderly man. He had a ruddy complexion and could have appeared fearful if he didn't have such a warm smile and pleasant personality. Fuller was just the opposite, and although he wasn't rude, he said very little and never smiled.

Gladys was very impressed with the variety of items in their showroom, and she hoped they would continue dealing with her if they bought the Black brothers' business. Nickerson wanted to know who the owners of the International Import/Export company were, and Gladys explained how she and her partners owned half the company and Norman O'Rourke owned the other half. Nickerson then surprised her when he asked if this Norman O'Rourke happened to be part Chinese.

"Well, yes, but how on earth did you know that?" she asked.

"I remember Norman, if he is the same Norman who had a restaurant up town some years ago. The best food I have ever eaten. I always wondered what happened to him after he left. Seems he became a little too friendly with the wife of one of his customers, but that is probably just a rumour. He was a decent bloke as far as I could tell. Well, well, well, so Norman is now in the same business as I am. Tell you what, Mrs. Matthews, if these boys let me buy their business, I would be more than pleased to do business with you. Just tell Norman that he owes me a four-course dinner." For the first time, Fuller smiled and said, "Make it two dinners, and I shall agree."

Gladys and Angelo knew Norman would be pleased to hear that their new partner in England would soon be giving them three times more business than the old one.

They just arrived home in time for the grand opening of the Metropolitan Art Museum. Paulo had talked Victor and his aunt Theresa into joining them. Iris, and Ike and Melissa came too, so there were eight of them. Ike was pleased that Paulo had persuaded his father to join them. "The more he keeps busy, the easier it will be on him," he told Paulo. "Make sure you let him know he's needed. That helps more than anything."

All the ladies attending the affair were dressed in their finest and the men in top hats. The museum's president, John Taylor Johnston, and the museum's trustees were so thrilled with the visitors' favourable comments that they were beaming with pride the entire evening.

There was one very impressive Roman stone sarcophagus on display, and one of the directors said they were going to acquire many more ancient artefacts in the coming years. He even promised they would have a mummy to display before long.

Having Paulo and Bruno along to explain the different techniques of some of the painters made the exhibits that much more interesting. There were drawings and etchings by Dutch artists, such as, Rembrandt, Adriaen van Ostade, and Jacob van Ruisdael. And masterworks, such as, Jan van Goyan's "View of Haarlem and the Haarlemmer Meer." There were so many works by Dutch artists exhibited that Theresa said she would have to bring Peter the next time she came.

"Someday, we shall be coming here to look at your paintings, Paulo," Gladys overheard Bruno telling his former student.

"If that ever happens, it will probably be your grandchildren who'll be looking at them. Many of these artists have been dead for years," Paulo replied. They were there for most of the day and still didn't have a good look at all the exhibits. "We can come back again," Paulo suggested. "I think Auntie Theresa is getting tired."

"I must remember to take James and Percy to the museum if they come this summer," Gladys told Angelo, after she arrived home. "I remember the first time I was in James' library and how mesmerized I was with a painting he had hanging over his mantle by a Japanese artist. He is quite a collector and will enjoy seeing the ones at our museum immensely."

"I know he plans to go with us to Niagara Falls the next time he's here. I think we all should make that trip. I know you took the girls, but I'd like to see it again, and this time we shall go across the Suspension Bridge, so we can all say we've been to Canada," Angelo suggested.

"Oh, Angelo, that's a splendid idea!"

The following month another tragedy happened. Victor received a wire saying that Isabella, his mother, had passed away in Italy. Before she died, she told her niece that she wanted to be buried in Italy beside her husband's grave. Even though he was still grieving over Lottie, Victor felt he should attend the funeral, and Eddy, who was very fond of his great-grandmother, was given compassionate leave from the academy and offered to go with his great-uncle. Angelo wanted to go as well, but that would mean leaving Gladys in charge of the import/export business as Norman was away on a buying trip.

It took a lot of persuasion for Gladys to convince the men that she could handle it on her own. "After all," she declared, "I was doing it all on my own before any of you men joined the company."

"But it's a hundred times bigger now, love, and with Norman away, you will have to deal with a lot of men—some who I doubt you'd call gentlemen," Angelo protested.

"We've a good strong man in the warehouse, and I shouldn't have to go anywhere else to deal with customers until you get back. My goodness, Angelo, you will only be gone a few weeks."

Finally, she convinced the three of them she would be safe on her own and they left for Italy. Everything went well until she, foolishly, allowed a prospective buyer to talk her into meeting her at a hotel up town. Gladys knew she shouldn't have agreed to the meeting, but the man said he was just in town for the day and hadn't time to come to her warehouse. He said he had to be home the following day for his wedding anniversary.

That was all it took to assure her he was a happily married man, and besides, he sounded like he would be signing a very big contract. Gladys' ego couldn't resist making such a big deal on her own. She intended to show both Angelo and Victor that a woman could accomplish anything, and more, than a man in the business world.

When she arrived at the hotel, the desk clerk said that the client she was supposed to meet in the lobby had set up the meeting in his room with her, his secretary, and himself. Once more, Gladys ignored the warning signs, and she went up to the room. When she saw that there was no secretary there, she was told that the woman had a migraine and had retired to her own room. Gladys should have left then but the man seemed sincere, and she proceeded to negotiate with him.

The deal he offered was even better that she thought it would be, but after he signed the contract, he poured out two glasses of champagne and asked her what she was going do to show her appreciation. Although, she instinctively knew what he meant, she got up from her chair, ready to run, and asked what he meant.

"Come on, my dear, they wouldn't send a beautiful woman to negotiate unless there was a pay off." He rose and started toward her. "Now I really don't have much time, my lovely, so let's see what you got."

Just as she had instructed Lottie to do years before, Gladys used her knee, and when the client was bent over in pain, she tore the contract up then left the premises. Angelo and Victor never knew what happened.

James and Percy didn't come to New York with the girls that year. Instead, they went to France with the intentions of buying a cottage with a view of the ocean and enough grounds to allow them some privacy. Eddy managed to get home during the holidays and they were all impressed with how fit he looked. He said there were only twenty-five graduating that year, and eight of the graduates were going to make the navy a career.

When Gladys asked him what he intended to do, he said, "I don't really know, Mother, but I hope you won't be disappointed if I decide to go with Captain Bob for a time. I've never given up the idea of being a captain of my own ship and being free to do what I want with it."

"I'm afraid you will have to work a good many years before you can afford a ship as large as Bob's."

"Well, I doubt I'd ever be able to do it on what the navy pays, but you never know, I may become so fond of military life by the time I graduate that I won't leave."

Gladys wasn't sure what she would prefer Eddy do, but she knew she would support whatever career made him happy.

The girls seemed right at home now when they came, and everyone relaxed more. Gladys didn't insist they go to the beach or go swimming, and they were perfectly content just to attend the theatre, the art museum, and out to the Ruttens in the evenings. Eliza loved shopping, and although Dolly wasn't that fond of the latest fashions for herself, she enjoyed seeing the pleasure it gave her sister.

Gladys wished Dolly would think of herself more often, and it worried her to see how dedicated she was to ministering to her sister's wishes. If Eliza behaved like a spoiled child, she may have tried to put a stop to it, but the girl wasn't the least bit affected, and continued to display a kind and pleasing nature. Dolly said very little about Benjamin, except that he still visited Four Oaks every time he came home, which wasn't that often, so Gladys began to think Dolly would never wed.

James and Percy came with the girls the following summer, and that year, the museum moved into larger quarters in the Douglas Mansion on West 14th Street, so they had many more exhibits on display. James and Percy spent days looking at all them. At the same time, there was still a lot of news in the newspapers about Jesse James and the James and Younger Gang robbing a train out west. It was the first successful train robbery to take place, and people were anxious to know every detail.

James and Percy were quite intrigued with it all. James read it out loud as they were sitting at the breakfast table one morning: "On July 21, 1873, Jesse James, along with the James and Younger Gang, daringly held up and robbed the Rock Island Express at Adair, Iowa. The robbers absconded with three thousand dollars. The article goes on to give a little of this man Jesse's background. There are some who consider him tantamount to our Robin Hood. Here, Percy," he said as he handed the paper over. "I know this shall rouse your imagination. You must keep us informed, Gladys. For us, it is a story about the untamed prairies, and it has an aura of romance to it."

During their visit, Eddy was able to be home for three weeks, and they all went to Niagara Falls. They crossed the Niagara Falls Suspension Bridge by carriage on the lower of three decks, and Percy and Eddy said they intended to walk across it coming back so as to have a better view.

The two upper decks of the bridge were just used by trains. The bridge was the world's first working railway suspension bridge and spanned eight hundred and twenty-five feet. It was two-and-a-half miles downstream from the falls and connected Niagara Falls, New York, to Niagara Falls, Ontario. As soon as they got to the other side, James said, "Have a good look around, girls, you are now in Canada." They went by another carriage up to the Horseshoe Falls, and although they had no idea what was going to happen, they arrived just in time to see a phenomenal event.

A thirty-two-year-old Englishman, Henry Bellini, was about to attempt to tightrope walk across the falls. They were told by the announcer that the rope was fifteen hundred feet in length and two-and-a-half inches in diameter. It weighed twenty-five hundred pounds. Bellini was going to use a balancing pole that weighed forty-eight pounds and was twenty-two feet long.

When he started across the wire, Dolly couldn't watch and turned her back while the rest all held their breath in fear until the man was safely across and on the other side, but then they had no sooner relaxed when Bellini leapt over the falls and into the Niagara River below. Gladys didn't know if everyone else screamed or not, but she knew she did.

"Will he be all right, Papa?" Eliza asked.

"Yes, dear," James replied, but he was certain the man would be killed. "Now, I think we had better find that hotel I had booked." He was anxious to get the ladies away from the reporter, so they wouldn't hear the news if it was as tragic as he surmised.

Later, he heard that Bellini had survived the leap and was picked up by a waiting boat. He told the ladies, and said, "I also heard he plans on repeating the feat a few more times this year, but I shan't be here to see it. I don't think I could stand to watch it again." Percy and the girls agreed with him, but Eddy said he would come to see it if he had time.

Chapter 21

James and Percy stayed for the whole summer. They left on September the 10th, and eight days later, the New York stock market crashed and set off a financial panic that caused bank failures. The restaurant didn't see much change, and Louis managed to keep the same staff working, but the International Corporation, which now included the import/export business, suffered a big loss. Fortunately, the Black brothers had sold their business to Nickerson and Fuller, so they got out just in time.

"If I didn't know how honest the brothers were," Gladys told Norman, "I would have thought they had some inside information." She also told him how Nickerson had remembered him, but never mentioned anything the man had told her about Norman's alleged affair with a customer's wife. Gladys was relieved when Norman decided he would go over to visit Nickerson and tell him how the sales had dropped in New York and that they wouldn't be able to give them their usual large order until things improved with the stock market.

The following year, Gladys, Angelo, and Eddy spent Christmas at Four Oaks. Eddy had to leave right after Christmas Day, but

Gladys and Angelo stayed to celebrate New Year's. As it happened, it was fortunate that they did, because Gladys' help was needed.

Instead of having a big party, they all agreed to celebrate New Year's Eve quietly with just the family. They were sitting in front of the fireplace in the parlour enjoying a hot toddy when they heard someone knocking. They couldn't imagine who was calling and were all curiously listening when Jenkins answered the door. Hearing a man's voice, Dolly said, "Why, that sounds like Benjamin."

She was just going to get up to greet him, when Jenkins came in and announced that it was, indeed, Master Benjamin and that he had asked to have a word with Dolly in private. Dolly's face appeared flushed, but she looked at Gladys and gave her a slight smile and shoulder shrug. "If you will pardon me, everyone, I shall see what Ben wants and then invite him in," she said before leaving. It wasn't long before she returned, smiling. "I hope you shan't mind, James, but I had Jenkins show Ben into the library. I probably shouldn't say anything, but he said he has something to ask me."

"We shall be anxious to hear what the young man says, my dear." Gladys replied. Dolly blushed and left to see Ben.

"I was beginning to think it would never happen," Gladys confessed. At first, she was so pleased for Dolly that she didn't noticed the look of disappointment on Eliza's face, but when she turned and saw how sad she appeared, she realized that the childhood infatuation her youngest daughter had shown toward Benjamin might have developed into something more serious. It hurt her to think of Eliza being upset, but she knew how beautiful she was and how many more suitors she would have in the future, whereas Dolly's prospects were not that favourable.

They were all waiting to congratulate Dolly, but Jenkins returned alone with the message that James and Miss Eliza were now wanted in the library.

Gladys was a little hurt that Dolly would want to tell James and Eliza the good news before she told her own mother, but she was so happy for her, she rang for the maid to bring some glasses and a bottle of champagne in readiness for a toast. She, Angelo, and Percy waited for another thirty minutes while talking about when they thought the young couple would wed and where they would live. Percy said he didn't know Ben's family, but the lad seemed to have had a good upbringing.

When they heard footsteps approaching, they all stood ready to congratulate the happy couple. James was the first to enter and immediately Gladys saw that he wasn't smiling. Instead, he appeared to be confused. Ben and Eliza entered next. *Ah, at least they are smiling*, Gladys thought, but Dolly wasn't with them.

"Please sit down everyone, I have some rather surprising news to announce," James said in a serious tone of voice. "This young man has just asked me for my daughter's hand in marriage." Eliza couldn't wait, and she rushed to Gladys, threw her arms around her, and said, "Oh, Mother, isn't it wonderful? I'm going to be Mrs. Benjamin White!"

Gladys was shocked. She tried to sound happy when she replied, "Yes, dear, if you are sure that's what you want, but where is Dolly? And what does she think about it?"

"Dolly doesn't know yet, Mother; she wasn't feeling well, so she went to her room. I can hardly wait to tell her. I know she will be so happy for me; she has always liked Ben and he is very fond of her, but you must come and give Ben a hug and welcome him to our family."

"You are not married yet, Eliza. Are you engaged?"

"Not really, but we shall be soon," Dolly said defensively. "Mother, aren't you happy for me?"

"I want you to be happy, darling, but you have just turned seventeen, and I wonder if you know what you are doing. Are you sure you love Ben, Eliza? Think about it. It will mean having children and not being able to attend parties with the rest of your young friends." Gladys didn't say anything about Ben being nine years older than Eliza because James was almost twice as old as she was when she married him.

"I do not have to think about it, Mother. I love Ben. I have loved him since the first time I saw him." She went over to Ben and looked up into his eyes. "I love you, Benjamin White."

Gladys' heart was aching, but she hugged Ben, then she asked him, "Why did you want to speak to Dolly?"

"Dolly is my best friend," he replied. "I was afraid I was far too old to ask for Eliza's hand, and I knew Dolly would advise me what to do. I wanted to know if I should ask Mr. Hornsby before I asked Eliza. She said it would be a good idea and for me to wait for him in the library and she would send him in. I haven't seen her since. Where is she? I wanted her to be the first to know."

"I don't think she is feeling well this evening, but I had a feeling we would be celebrating, so I sent for some champagne. Percy will you see everyone has a glass? I shall be back in a few minutes. I just want to see if Dolly is feeling well enough to join us."

Oh, my poor darling, Dolly, Gladys thought as she ran up the stairs to Dolly's room. Dolly had her head over the wash bowl, and Gladys could see that she had been ill. Her face was white, and she was shaking. Gladys grabbed a throw and put it around her shoulders, then she wrapped her arms around her and held her close.

"Oh, Mama," Dolly hadn't called Gladys that since she was a little girl. "I am such a fool."

"No, my darling, you are not a fool. It was Benjamin's fault for not saying how he felt sooner."

Dolly was still sobbing and her voice broke as she replied, "I can't face them. I know if I look at him, I shall start to cry. Oh, how could

I have been so blind? I should have known he would never fall in love with me. I am so ugly, and Eliza is so beautiful."

"You are not ugly, Dolly. You are beautiful, and Ben is the stupid one not to have seen that. But he is very fond of you, and he says you are his best friend. I don't think he would have asked Eliza to marry him if you had told him not to. I know that doesn't help when you have a broken heart, but it will in time."

"Was Eliza happy, Mother?"

"Yes; she said she has always been in love with Ben, and I think she truly has. I noticed her expression when you went out to talk to him, and I could tell she was heart-broken thinking that he was going to ask you to marry him."

"I wish I could be happy for her."

"I think you will in time. She loves you so much that I don't think she would marry Ben if you asked her not to."

"I would never do that," Dolly said in between sobs. "You go down now. I shall be all right. Tell them I am still feeling ill and have gone to bed. Tell Eliza I am happy for her, but not to disturb me tonight."

When Gladys said she would return later, Dolly said not to worry, but Gladys knew she would be waiting for her. As she made her way back down to the parlour, she tried to look cheerful for Eliza's sake, but it was difficult, knowing what Dolly was experiencing. Gladys recalled how she felt when she heard that Tom had been killed in India, and although she and Angelo were happily married now, it still hurt to think of it.

She also knew that, in some respect, death was kinder. With a death, one didn't suffer the same humiliation and self-reproach. Gladys wondered what she would say to ease Dolly's suffering when she returned to her later that evening.

Eliza was so disappointed when she learned that Dolly wasn't feeling well enough to join them that she had tears in her eyes. She was determined to go up to see her and it took Gladys awhile to convince her that Dolly meant it when she said she just wanted to sleep. They had a few toasts and spent an hour talking about Ben's future plans. He said he had done very well for himself in the contracting business and that he intended to either buy an estate or find some property near Sandwich and build a home for Eliza. "I should like one about the same size as Four Oaks, but I doubt I can find a place with such a large amount of land. Times have changed, and there are not many pieces of property like this to be found."

They discussed the wedding, and James said he would like to have it at Four Oaks, if that would be agreeable to everyone. Eliza said she would have to see what Dolly thought. Every question they asked, Eliza gave the same response: "Let's wait and see what Dolly thinks." It was obvious that Eliza relied on Dolly to think for her in every situation, and Gladys wondered how that was going to work when she was married to Ben.

Ben's family had a farm not far from Sandwich, so James suggested they include his parents with the planning. Ben had four brothers: three were married and living outside the country, and there was one who lived with his parents and intended to take over the farm. Mr. and Mrs. White, senior, were both quite elderly and not in the best of health, but Ben said they would probably be thrilled to hear that he was marrying a local girl and planned to settle down nearby.

Gladys spent the night comforting Dolly. It was breaking daylight when she finally fell asleep, so Gladys was able to quietly creep out of the room and back to her own bed and Angelo. "How is she?" he wanted to know.

"I think the difficult time is ahead for her. Having to keep smiling in front of Eliza and Ben is going to take a lot of determination."

"That's something she has a lot of."

"Yes, but we are going to have to help by trying our best to cheer her up. Her self-esteem has been hurt as much as her heart. It just tears me apart to see her suffer like this."

Dolly slept most of that day and was able to come downstairs in the evening for a while. Eliza was so relieved that she fussed over her, fetching her a blanket and juice. However, when she began talking about wedding plans, Gladys knew Dolly was about to break down, so she quickly interrupted and said that Dolly was too tired to think and that she should get back to bed. "She can answer all those questions when she is feeling a little stronger, dear."

The next day, Dolly managed to join them all for breakfast, but she had her beautiful red curls pulled back and twisted into a tight bun on the top of her head in an old-maidish fashion once more. *She's reverted back to the way she was before Lottie talked her into letting her hair down,* Gladys thought, sadly. She was also afraid that she would remain that way for the rest of her life.

In the afternoon, Dolly found the strength to ask Eliza where Ben was. "Oh, he had to go back to Hastings. I think he has gone to buy me a ring. I wouldn't mind if he doesn't buy me one, because none of the girls I know who are betrothed wear one. He should be here tomorrow. Oh, Dolly, I am so glad you are better. I need you so much now. There are so many things to decide, and I simply cannot do it without you."

"It is your wedding, not mine, and it is you who must make the decisions," Dolly answered more sharply than she intended. Eliza was obviously hurt. Her sister had never talked to her in such a harsh tone of voice before. Her bottom lip quivered, and that was all it took. "I am sorry, Eliza dear; of course, I shall help you; I am still not feeling well that's all."

Dolly threw her arms around her and kissed her. "I am sorry, Dolly, I should not be bothering you with my troubles when you have been so sick. I shall not say one more word about the wedding until you want me to. Now, let me pour you another cup of tea."

Dolly looked over at Gladys as though to ask, "How can I not love her?"

Ben returned the next day, and Jenkins showed him into the parlour, where Eliza, Gladys, and Dolly were sitting around a table looking at pictures of wedding apparel. Ben would have like to have taken Eliza into his arms as soon as he saw her, but propriety prevented him from doing so, so he bowed to everyone and then presented Eliza with a lovely garnet birthstone ring while quoting a Georgian poem, "By her who in this month is born / No gem save garnets should be worn / They will ensure her constancy / True friendship and fidelity."

Everyone clapped. Eliza was thrilled that he went to the trouble of finding out her birthday was in January and said she was going to show it to her father, who was in the library. "Tell him to come and have tea, dear," Gladys said as she pulled the cord for a maid. Dolly hadn't said a word, and Ben looked perplexed, so to relieve the tension, Gladys asked him about his business. His reply was brief.

Ben wasn't a shy person, and at times his candour was embarrassing; after he finished telling Gladys about his work, he came right out and asked Dolly why she hadn't congratulated him. "When I spoke to you the other evening, you didn't object to me proposing. Have you changed your mind?"

Dolly felt as though her chest was naked, and Ben could see her broken heart. Her throat ached as she held back the tears, "I am sorry, Ben, I am still not feeling well. Congratulations, I know you will be happy together."

"That makes me feel much better. You know how much your consent means to us both. We both depend on you. The three of us have so much to do. I want you to help me find a home, or help me plan one that will be suitable for Eliza."

James and Eliza came in just in time to save Dolly from answering. "Well, that is quite a ring, Ben. I am afraid you are going to spoil our little girl," James said.

"I shall do my utmost to do just that, sir."

They had their tea, and Gladys asked Ben if he would like to stay for dinner. He said he had to get home, but that he was taking the next two weeks away from work, so they could make their plans while Gladys and Angelo were still at Four Oaks. Then he surprised them and announced, "I fear it shall not be possible for us to marry for a year or two. I have a few projects I must finish before I am ready to settle down." Eliza didn't seem to mind, and Gladys thought it would give Dolly a chance to become used to the idea. Nevertheless, James suggested that Ben bring his father, mother, and brother to dinner to meet Gladys before she and Angelo left.

Eliza could sense that Dolly and Gladys lacked enthusiasm when they talked of her wedding plans, and she began to think that neither of them approved of Ben. One morning, while Dolly was busy attending to the servants, Eliza looked for Gladys and found her reading in the library. "Mother, could I have a word with you?" she asked.

"Yes, dear, of course. Is anything the matter?"

"Do you and Dolly dislike Benjamin?"

"Not like Benjamin? What on earth made you think that?"

"Well, you do not seem very happy about the wedding, and neither does Dolly."

"I am very happy for you, darling, and I think Ben will be a kind and devoted husband. If I hadn't been so worried about Dolly's health, I would have been a lot more excited."

"What about Dolly? She does not seem the least bit happy for me."

"She is probably feeling sad because you will be leaving and moving into a home of your own."

"Oh my! I thought she would know that I would never leave her. Wherever I go, she shall go with me, or I shan't go."

Gladys had been afraid that Eliza would say that, so she tried to make her understand that Dolly had her own life to lead. "This has been Dolly's home for many years and she may want to stay here, or she may even want to come and live with Angelo and me. You shall be mistress of your own home soon, Eliza, and you shan't need Dolly anymore."

"Nonsense, Mother. I remember the day you left us; Dolly told me then that she would never leave me."

Eliza's words caused Gladys to feel sick with guilt, and she could hardly look at her as she tried to refute them. "How could you remember that? You were just three years old?"

"I remember, and I remember other things, too. Many times, I have asked Dolly to explain why the three of us all have different names, and she always tells me that I shall have to wait until I am grown up, and then ask you to explain it. Now that I am about to be married, I think I have grown up enough for you to tell me."

"Very well, you do have a right to know, but I warn you, Eliza, when I told Dolly my true story, she was very angry with me for a long time. Now, I pray you will be able to forgive me for all the mistakes I've made and still love me, because I intend on being at your wedding no matter how you feel. I think we should wait until this afternoon, though, and then we'll go up to my room where we won't be disturbed."

That afternoon, Gladys took Eliza up to her room and left orders that they were not to be disturbed, except by the maid with a pot of tea. Eliza had never been told anything about her maternal grand-parents, therefore, she didn't share the same feelings of betrayal that Dolly had felt when she learned that they lived in the slums called Old Nichol. And because Eliza knew Angelo, and had witnessed how much Gladys loved him, it helped her understand why her mother behaved in such a manner.

On the other hand, Eliza tended to have strict moral principles, so when Gladys told her about their passionate rendezvous in London, she was shocked, and if she hadn't been betrothed and extremely inquisitive about what to expect on her wedding night, she may have been more judgemental.

After Gladys finished her story, Eliza put her arms around her and said, "You are even more special to me now, Mother, than you were before."

Gladys smiled and answered, "And you, my darling, are absolutely wonderful."

Chapter 22

Benjamin, his brother, and his parents were invited to dinner a few days after he gave Eliza the ring. Jenkins showed them into the parlour, where James, Percy, Eliza, Gladys, and Angelo were waiting to welcome them. Ben's father, Mr. Rodney White, was quite stout and had a bushy beard and matching eyebrows. What little of his countenance was visible was wrinkle free and rosy. His eyes were a warm brown, and like Ben, he appeared to have an outgoing personality. Ben had said his father was quite elderly, but Gladys thought it wasn't apparent. Ben's brother Ernest inherited more of his mother's personality, but it was his father who he resembled.

Unlike her husband, Mrs. Ida White showed her age, and Gladys thought the poor woman looked quite tired. She was dressed neatly, but simply, and wore no jewellery. She wasn't unsociable, but had little to say, that is until Gladys mentioned gardening. Then her face lit up and she proudly announced that she grew a great showing of flowers, which she offered for the wedding, if it was to be held in the summer.

"It's the mister who likes to read and discuss political things," she said, "but I just like to putter in my garden when my chores are done."

Ernest had overheard them talking and explained, "Mother refuses to have any maids, and every time Father hires one, she indubitably ends up waiting on them. Is that not right, Mother?"

Ida White smiled and blushed beautifully. "Yes, my boy, and I fear I shall never be any more than what I am. You see, Gladys, my folks were hard-working farmers and as we had no servants, we were all brought up to do our chores. Now that I have my own home, I enjoy cleaning it and do not want any other woman interfering.

"Rodney, now, he gets all worked up and goes on and on about me still milking Nellie Girl, but she doesn't like anyone else to handle her, and I've always enjoyed tending to the chickens, so I keep telling him, if that's what I enjoy the most, why should I stop? He has lots of fellows doing his work for him, because he likes to be a proper gentleman and sit around down the town talking politics and that sort of thing."

Gladys thought she might like Rodney White, but she knew she was going to like his wife even more. It only took that one conversation to see the woman may be hard working but she was thoroughly content with her life. She had the strength of character to feel at ease no matter where she was. In fact, all the Whites seemed to be fortunate enough to have that same attribute.

During the evening, it was agreed that when the wedding did take place it should be held at Four Oaks, and Ida volunteered to make the wedding cake. Gladys was proud of Eliza when she said that would be wonderful. Eliza was pleased when Gladys offered to make her wedding gown, and Dolly didn't say no when Gladys said she would make her a dress for the occasion as well.

Eliza and Ben both belonged to the church's choir and the church's young people's group, so they wanted to invite them all. Although the wedding was still a year or more away, Eliza insisted they plan the menu while Gladys was there, just in case Benjamin finished his projects early.

The day before Gladys and Angelo were to leave, Dolly asked Gladys to take a short walk with her. The weather was cold, and a little frost was still visible in the shady spots of the garden. Gladys was the first to speak, "Do you think you'll be able to cope with all this planning, darling?"

Dolly, not wanting to worry her mother, was slow in responding. "I know I shall never love anyone but Ben, Mother, but I love Eliza too, therefore, I have made up my mind that I shall be content just to be near them both for the rest of my life. Now, I know you do not agree, but it is my life, and that is what I intend to do."

"I can't lie to you, Dolly, I think you are making a big mistake, but if that's what you've decided, I'll support you. I love Eliza and Eddy with all my heart, but I think you and I will always have something special together, something deeper than I can explain. Perhaps it's because you were there with me when we lost your father, your aunt Millie, your Gamby, and Lottie. We've been through so much together, and I want you to know that I shall always be there for you if you need me."

"I know, Mother. You are the only person I would ever tell about my feelings for Ben, and I also know you shall keep it a secret. I am going to miss you so very much, but I shall be all right, so please do not worry." Gladys knew Dolly meant what she said, and it made her departure that much easier.

As soon as Gladys arrived back in New York, she began looking for material to make the two gowns. She decided on a deep cream satin for Eliza's wedding gown, as she thought that white wouldn't show off the hue of her delicate skin. For Dolly's gown she chose light green velvet, which she thought would look lovely with her red hair.

Instead of a veil, Eliza said she would prefer a garland of flowers, because she had seen such a picture in a story book of a little fairy princess with one on her head. Luckily, Gladys friend Millie had been a seamstress and she had shown Gladys how to make dainty velvet and satin roses and daisies in different colours, so Gladys made enough small ones to go down each side of the centre panel on the wedding dress and a wreath for Eliza's hair.

During the next few months, Gladys and Angelo were both very busy with the import/export business and the construction of a new building. Eddy had written and said he had met his future bride; although they thought it was just a teenage crush, they wrote back saying they were happy for him. Then, when two weeks went by and they didn't receive any letters, they began worrying that he and the young girl had done something foolish. It was a relief when he arrived home unexpectedly.

However, when they learned why, they wished it had been because of a girl. Eddy had been expelled for fraudulent and mendacious behaviour. Both Gladys and Angelo were certain that there had to be some mistake, because neither one had ever heard their son tell an untruth. He had always been honest, and they were ready to leave the next day and go to the academy on his behalf, but Eddy begged them not to. Then he told them what had happened.

One of his classmates was the son of Admiral Benson, a port admiral in the English Navy, and the admiral had come to visit the academy in order to check on his son's progress. Eddy would probably not have been expelled if the admiral hadn't brought his daughter, Amelia, with him. Amelia was an exceptionally beautiful young lady, and at first sight of the fair damsel, Eddy, along with every other cadet at the school, was smitten.

A banquet and dance were held in the admiral's honour, and because Eddy was one of the top students, academically and socially, he was fortunate to be one of the five chosen to dance with the young lady. Eddy was as handsome as his father, and it only took once around the dance floor in his arms to Strauss' "The Blue Danube" to convince Amelia that she had met the man she was going to marry. Eddy's sentiments were much the same.

Amelia and her brother, Lionel, were very close, and when she accidently overheard her father threaten to take Lionel back to England if his marks didn't improve during the next six months, she was afraid she might never see Eddy again. After gaining her father's consent, she sent a message to Eddy asking him to have tea with her. They spent an hour together before agreeing that they must continue with their friendship, and it was then that Amelia told Eddy about her father's threat to take Lionel back to England.

"I fear that if that happens, Edward, we shall not have the opportunity to see each other again," she said

"Then we mustn't allow it to happen, then, must we?"

"But what can we do? Lionel is having such a struggle. You know, Edward, I do believe he would be happy to be back in England. He really does not care for the sea and would much rather work in an office or a bank. If only he could graduate, I think father would be so proud that he would allow him to do whatever he wants."

"Perhaps I can help. Do you think he will allow me to tutor him? We could keep it a secret."

"Oh, that would be wonderful. I shall ask him right away. Thank you, Edward."

"You're welcome, and most of my friends call me Eddy."

Before they left for England, Amelia told her father that she had met a young man she would like him to meet, so Eddy was invited to dine with them. The admiral and Eddy got along splendidly. Benson had been a ship's captain for many years, and when Eddy told him that's what he would like to be, the admiral said that if he were to join the British Navy, when he graduated, he would do what he could to ensure Eddy get his wish. Eddy was impressed.

The admiral also noticed that the two young people were smitten with each other and was pleased that Amelia was drawn to a lad who loved the sea. He had married and had his two children late in life. Then, after his wife passed away, he found the responsibility of raising two teenagers very difficult, and so might be overly anxious to see them settle down with a reliable spouse. Thus Eddy was allowed to spend a little time with Amelia before she left, and he even managed to kiss her as they were walking around the grounds.

Eddy didn't tell Gladys and Angelo everything that had taken place. He only said he was helping out a classmate with his work, but when it came time for exams, the fellow didn't feel he would pass. In desperation, he copied all of Eddy's answers. Unfortunately, he was found out, and the head accused Eddy of cheating, too, even though Lionel swore Eddy had nothing to do with it. Thus they were both expelled.

Gladys was furious, but Angelo told her that he had witnessed similar inequitable actions, and knew that the majority of times, it did little good to complain. Nonetheless, if Eddy had not asked her not to, she would have gone to the academy and given whoever was in charge a piece of her mind. He hadn't thought to ask her not to send a letter, though, so without telling anyone, she composed and mailed one that left no doubt how disappointed she was in the academy's poor judgement.

One month later, Eddy received a request to meet with the academy's head of education at his earliest convenience. This time, Angelo insisted that he and Gladys accompany him. Evidently, Lionel finally convinced the head that Eddy had nothing to do with his deviant behaviour, and Eddy received an apology and an invitation to return to his classes. He never found out that his mother's letter and one from Admiral Benson also had a lot to do with his reinstatement. Eddy had tried to let on he wasn't upset over his expulsion, but Gladys and Angelo could see how happy he was to have the chance to graduate. Lionel returned to England, found work in a bank, and was much happier.

The year 1870 was going to be very exciting for Gladys and Angelo. Eddy was hoping to graduate, and Eliza and Ben had set their wedding date for June, but they were still concerned over Victor. He missed Lottie so much that when they left to go to England for Christmas, he was still suffering with bouts of depression. However, when they returned, he seemed extremely happy to have them back and genuinely interested in all their news from Four Oaks.

When they asked how he had been, he said he had been keeping well and that Iris had been a big help to him. Although he didn't say any more, Gladys later told Angelo that she thought there just might be another wedding before the year was out. "Things are happening too fast," she said. "Eliza getting married, Eddy graduating and having to decide what he is going to do with his life; I just wish they would slow down a little."

"What do you hope Eddy decides to do, Glad?"

"I would love it if he just came home and worked with you, but I know that isn't what he wants. I feel we're going to see very little of our darling boy from now on, and it makes me very sad."

"I know what you mean. You know, darling, I've done a lot of thinking about what you said about not being able to see your grandchildren. I think it's time we started to look for some property in Sandwich."

"Really? Do you really mean it?"

"Yes, I think I do. Mind you, I think we should keep a place here, too, in case Eddy decides to settle down in New York. I want to be near my grandchildren, too. Anyway, let's not rush into anything. We have to see what these young ones are going to do first."

Gladys agreed with Angelo, but her mind had already begun a hunt for a home near Four Oaks. She could hardly wait to write and tell Dolly. Now that she had dresses to make and Eddy's graduation ceremony to look forward to, Gladys didn't spend much time with the business, and wanting to be fair to Norman, she decided she should hire someone to take her place in the storeroom, but as usual, Norman, already had someone in mind to replace her. "You never cease to surprise me, Norman. You always have these expert workers just waiting for you to call them."

"Ah, but this is not just anyone, dear Gladys. It is my own flesh and blood." With that he went into the office and brought back a beautiful young woman. "Gladys, this is my daughter, Elizabeth Mae O'Rourke. Elizabeth, this is the woman I told you about—the one who began this business."

Gladys was so taken with the young girl's appearance that for a few minutes she was speechless. Elizabeth looked to be about sixteen, and although her colouring differed from her father's, Gladys could see that she was, indeed, Norman's offspring.

Later, Gladys learned that Elizabeth was in her mid-twenties, had excelled in her studies, and was more than qualified to take over Gladys' responsibilities. Gladys was very impressed with the young woman and not knowing that Eddy had already chosen his future wife, she thought Elizabeth might be a good match for Eddy, in spite of the difference in ages.

Now that she no longer had to worry about the business, Gladys had time to spend on herself. She wrote to the girls and asked them to come for a visit in February, as that might be the last chance Eliza would have to come to New York without a husband. They agreed to come for the whole month, and Gladys intended to show them the best time they had ever had.

The first week was spent looking for Eliza's trousseau and the second week they spent just shopping. Gladys managed to buy a new gown to wear at Eddy's graduation ceremony, and with the help of the girls, she persuaded Angelo to buy a new suit with all the accessories, including a pair of soft Italian leather boots. While the girls were visiting, Captain Bob arrived along with his wife, Asta. Victor invited them to stay with him because Gladys and Angelo had the girls staying with them.

Asta spoke little English, but, with hand signals and facial expressions, she managed to share her views on most subjects. Although she always came to evening gatherings whenever Gladys invited her and Bob, she didn't appear to enjoy them. Bob had hoped she would like New York and perhaps want to live there, because he intended to retire in a year and would have liked to settle down in America. They were only in port for six days, but before they left, Bob came to see Gladys and Angelo by himself.

"I'm really disappointed with the way Asta has behaved while she's been here," he said. "You've all been so kind to her, but all she wants to do is return home. She didn't like the voyage coming here and won't even try to like New York."

"Bob, you can't really blame her. You have been at sea for most of your married life and she has been home bringing up the children. I imagine she has made a life for herself and likes it. Do you think she has been sitting at home all those years just waiting for you to come and say, *I'm all done with the sea now, and I want you to forget your family and friends and settle down in a strange land with people that you can't understand?* I know I would resent that if I were her. You should go home when you retire, Bob, and who knows, you might find what you are looking for there," Gladys advised him.

Bob looked doubtful and just shrugged his shoulders. Before he left, Angelo told him that Eddy would like him to come to his graduation if he was in port at that time. Bob said he would do his best to be there.

The weather had been cold enough through January to freeze the lake in the park and it was ideal for skating, but it started to warm up in February and danger signs were put up on certain areas of the lake where the ice was thinning. Gladys asked Angelo if he thought they should take the girls skating, but he said he didn't think it was a good idea. Then, when the girls appeared to be disappointed, he suggested that they all take their skates and go for a drive in the buggy. "If the lake is posted as safe when we get there, we can have a skate, but if not, we'll have had a nice outing," he suggested.

When they arrived at the lake, the sun was shining and the ice on the lake looked inviting, but there were only a few children skating, and a few signs were up in certain areas warning, "Don't skate beyond this sign."

"That's warning enough for me," Angelo said. "We can sit here and watch, but I don't want any of you on that ice. I think there's a stall over there selling hot chocolate. What do you all say?"

Gladys appreciated Angelo taking charge and grinned as they all called out "Yea!" Angelo jumped down and went to order the drinks. Then Gladys decided she should help him and got out of the buggy and ran after him.

Dolly and Eliza were watching two little girls trying to perform some new moves on the ice while their mothers sat on a bench and watched. When the oldest child spun around in a circle, Eliza clapped her hands. "She is so talented, Dolly, and look at that little girl, she is skating backwards. I could never do that."

The girl was skating backward rather swiftly, and she called to her mother, "Look, Mommy. Look how fast I can go." Her mother looked at her smiling, but the smile froze on her face as she noticed the danger sign. She started screaming, "Stop, Gloria, stop!" The little girl was wearing ear muffs and didn't hear. One minute she was laughing and the next minute the ice gave way under her and she sank under the water. Her mother tried to run after her, but the other women held her back. "The ice won't hold you," they insisted.

Gladys and Angelo were just about to the wagon with the mugs of hot chocolate. Angelo threw the mugs on the ground and shouted to Gladys, "Take the buggy and go for help." She started to protest, and he shouted at her again, "Gladys, take the buggy and go for help, now!" Gladys got into the buggy and did as she was told while crying, "No, Angelo! Oh god, no!" She had to go all the way to the entrance of the park before she found a park ranger to tell him what happened and before she could turn the buggy around and race back to the lake.

The mothers were huddled over someone when they got there, and Gladys jumped down from the buggy and ran over to them. "Angelo?" she cried, but there was just a little girl wrapped in a blanket. "Where is my husband?"

The women looked up at her and shook their heads. "Where is he? Where is my husband?" she demanded.

They continued to shake their heads, so she ran around the lake crying "Angelo, Angelo."

Dolly told Eliza to stay in the buggy and she ran after her mother and tried to hold her in her arms, but Gladys pushed her aside. "He will come up, Dolly, we just have to watch for him. He is a good swimmer. Angelo, Angelo," she kept calling as she ran back and forth. Some men had arrived with a rope, but they knew that if Angelo hadn't surfaced by then, he had drowned. They helped Dolly get Gladys back to the buggy. Then the little girl's mother came up and said, "Your husband was a hero. He grabbed my Gloria and threw her across the ice where we could get to her, then he tried to get out, but the ice wouldn't hold him. He was a hero, a wonderful hero."

Gladys mumbled, "I don't want a hero; I want Angelo."

Chapter 23

"You can't do any good by going back to the lake, Gladys." Iris said, hoping to convince her friend to stay home and wait for the police to bring her the news. The ice on the lake was thawing, and the New York Fire Department had two boats dragging the bottom wherever it had melted. Every day, they were able to cover more of the lake, and every day Gladys went to watch and wait. She took the big quilt from their bed. No one asked her why, as they knew she wanted to wrap Angelo in it when they found him.

"I want to be there for him, Iris. I know I'm neglecting Dolly and Eliza, but I can't help it. Please, will you try to explain it to them? I think they should go back to England. I just can't spend time with them now."

"Don't you worry; my Friedl wants Eliza to spend a few days with her. They get along very well, and now we are living in the mansion, we have ample room. I don't know if you knew, but Victor asked us to move in and look after the place. I guess he felt lost living there by himself after Lottie died. He said he prefers to stay in one of the apartments over the restaurant. Dolly just wants to be with you, and I think you should let her. She loves you so very much, Gladys, and I think you need her now."

Dolly's presence at the lake did help. The headlines in the local newspapers were all about Angelo's act of bravery. Reporters were hounding everyone who had known him, including Iris and Ike. Although they both tried to be brief with their reports, their stories of Otto's rescue and the loss of Angelo's arm in the process was embellished to such an extent that people began showing up at the lake carrying signs proclaiming him a hero, and even a saint.

They crowded around Gladys' buggy. "I wish they would all go away," she cried. "Dolly, can't someone tell them to leave?"

"I shall talk to the police and see what I can do," Dolly replied. Victor and Ike did it for her, and the police put up a barrier to ensure that no one but Gladys and the firemen would be allowed near the search area. On the fifth day it started to rain. Gladys was afraid the men in the boats would stop looking, but they had come prepared. Not long after the rain started, they were all wearing rain hats and coats.

At times, it was difficult to see the boats, and Dolly had to stop Gladys from getting out of the buggy and walking closer to the water. They only searched for Angelo from nine to noon every day, as they could only take the boats where the ice was thin enough to break up. Around eleven o'clock on the fifth day there was a heavy downpour, and a man in one of the boats motioned to the other boat that he was headed to shore. A fellow in the second boat motioned that he would pull in his line and do the same.

"Are they quitting?" Gladys asked Dolly.

"I think so, Mother. The rain must be filling the boats, and I think we should leave, too. This poor horse needs to be in his barn," Dolly took hold of the reins and shook them. The horse had just taken two steps when Gladys cried, "Stop!" All three men in the second vessel were at the back of the boat pulling something aboard. "Oh, Dolly, they found him." Gladys grabbed the quilt, jumped down from the buggy, and ran towards the water's edge.

The men from the first boat had already pulled their craft up. Two of them held a tarp over Gladys as she waited for the others to bring Angelo ashore. They laid him under the canvas, and Gladys knelt down on the wet grass, covered him with the quilt, and kissed him. Dolly stood over her until the police wagon came to take him to the morgue.

Neither Gladys nor Dolly felt the cold until they were almost home. Then they both began to shake. Victor took care of the horse, while Ike and Melissa saw to the women.

Eddy arrived the next day. Just the sight of him did more for Gladys than anything else could have. He was the picture of his father, and it helped erase the shock she had felt when they laid Angelo out under the tarp. His face had been a sickly bluish colour, and he was almost unrecognizable. Still, she had bent down and kissed his cold lips, even though she knew he was no longer in his body. She would always remember him as he was: alive, loving, and warm.

"Thank you for allowing me to be with him these past fifteen years, Mother. I loved him so very much," Eddy said after the funeral and before he left to return to the academy. Gladys was sorry to see him leave, especially as Dolly and Eliza were going back to England a few days later. Dolly had been such a big help, even though she was still suffering with a broken heart.

"I don't think I could have managed without you, my darling," Gladys told her. Dolly and Victor had seen to all the funeral arrangements, and Gladys was content to let them. She and Angelo had talked about where they wanted to be buried, and Angelo had chosen America while she chose England, but for some reason, she didn't object when Victor bought them a family plot beside his and Lottie's.

A huge crowd attended the funeral, and more were at the graveside—people who couldn't find room in the church. Gladys knew a lot of them were just curious, but she appreciated their presence and the lovely flowers that were sent. Ike delivered the eulogy with tears in his eyes. There was talk of putting up a plaque at the lake in Angelo's honour, but the town council decided that if they did it for one, they would have to do it for everyone who saved a life. They presented Gladys with a medal of bravery for Angelo instead.

Although Gladys felt her life would never feel completely whole again, she was determined to maintain a positive attitude for her family's sake. Iris had lost Otto, and Victor had lost Lottie, but they had managed to carry on, so she prayed she could be as brave. As the days went by, she began to realize that the most amazing thing had happened. She didn't feel like Angelo was gone. Having never believed in spirits, she couldn't understand or explain how she felt, but she knew he was with her all the time. It wasn't an eerie feeling. It was wonderful. She also knew she would never want another man. Toughie—Angelo, was, would always be, her true love.

Two months later, Eddy graduated. He managed to get invitations to the ceremonies for her and six more guests, so Gladys invited Dolly, Eliza, James, Percy, Victor, and Ike. Bob Nicholson wasn't able to attend, but he gave Eddy a lovely leather-bound journal along with an invitation to sail with him whenever he chose to. The ceremony was very touching, with all the cadets in their uniform, and they all enjoyed the elaborate banquet and ball. Amelia Benson persuaded her father, Admiral Benson, to bring her to the ceremony, and they joined Gladys and her family for most of the celebration.

Admiral Benson had once been a fine figure of a man, but after he left the sea and taken on the position of port admiral, he had taken advantage of the tempting variety of foods so easily acquired ashore. Although his uniform still fit him, he found it necessary to hire a talented seamstress to let out seams and move buttons. His hair was snow white, and in contrast to his ruddy complexion, it added a notable attractiveness. He was very taken with Gladys, especially when he learned she was now a widow, and he gave her most of his attention.

"You should be very proud of that boy of yours, Gladys—I hope you don't mind if I call you that," he said as they were sitting listening to the band.

"No, I don't mind, Admiral Benson. Yes, I am proud of Eddy. I only wish his father were here to see him graduate. He is so much like him."

"Please, call me George. You know my daughter is rather smitten with Edward, and I like him, too. I am trying to talk him into joining the British Navy. What do you think about that?"

"Whatever Eddy decides will be fine with me, but I hope he doesn't rush into anything. I would like him to spend some time with me before he ventures off in the world."

"I'd like to invite you and your girls to be my guests the next time you're in London. I was stationed at Her Majesty's Naval Base in Devonport after I gave up my ship, but when I retired, I found myself at loose ends, and last year I accepted a job with the St. Katharine's Dock Company at their new Royal Albert Dock in London. Now I have a home there, so you shall find it handy to visit."

"Thank you, Admiral—"

The admiral cut her off, "George, my dear, please call me George."

"Thank you, George, that's very kind of you, but we have a flat in London. Perhaps we can all meet for tea some day when Eddy is with us." Gladys looked around for one of her party. She didn't like the way the admiral was looking at her. Not that she found him unpleasant, but this was the first time she had been flirted with since Angelo drowned, and for some reason, she resented it. Other than that, she enjoyed the graduation, and she liked Amelia, too.

Eddy came back to New York knowing his mother would welcome the company, but he let on that he wanted to rest for a few weeks before making up his mind what he intended to do. "I have to let the academy know in three weeks if I decide to stay in the navy, but until then, I just want to spend time with you, Mom."

Gladys could tell he was in love with Amelia, but he was sensible enough to realize he needed to decide what he wanted to do, career-wise, before becoming engaged. He knew he could go to England where he could, as Admiral Benson had advised, join the British Navy, or he could sail with Captain Bob for a year. In the end, he decided he would stay with the academy for two more years. Unfortunately, it would mean he would be serving aboard a flagship and couldn't attend Eliza's wedding.

Gladys thought it odd that Dolly hadn't written asking her to come to Four Oaks a few weeks early in order to help prepare for the wedding, and when she did receive a letter and they suggested that she not arrive until a week before the event, she was both shocked and hurt. Then, when she finally arrived, she was further annoyed to discover that they hadn't begun to prepare the house for the occasion. "What is going on?" she asked.

"The wedding is not going to be here after all, Mother," Eliza told her. "Benjamin has bought a home for me and we are having the wedding there."

"But shouldn't we be there making the preparations?"

"Dolly and I have done it all. You just have to sit back and enjoy yourself."

Gladys didn't appreciate that one bit. She needed something to occupy her mind. Besides, she had looked forward to taking part in all the decorating. Now they were treating her like a distant aunt. She complained to James and asked him to at least take her to the estate so she could see what they had done. "We don't need to tell them. Let's just say we're going into town. The place is on the way into town, isn't it, James?"

"I haven't the slightest idea. Eliza wants it to be a secret, and we are not to see it until we arrive the day before the wedding, so we shall just have to be patient."

"That's ridiculous! You can at least tell me where it is, can't you?"

Gladys' tone had changed so gradually, that James hadn't noticed until now, and he wasn't sure he liked it. He wondered if her singing voice would have the same harsh tone. She interrupted his thoughts.

"James, answer me. Where is Eliza's new home?"

"Sorry, old girl, my lips are sealed, and so are everyone else's. So, for Eliza's sake, leave it alone. She is looking forward to surprising you almost as much as she is looking forward to being married. For once in your life, let someone else run things." James thought he said it good-naturedly, but Gladys didn't laugh. For the next few days, she pouted.

"I have never seen mother sulk before," Eliza told Dolly. "I simply cannot wait for her to see the house. Do you suppose we could pack up and go the day after tomorrow? That's only one day sooner than we planned, and then she can help with the last-minute arrangements. That will make her happy. You know what she is like."

Dolly hadn't enjoyed seeing her mother so depressed either, so she agreed. The following day, Hilda, and a few more servants, left, loaded down with trunks of wedding apparel and other clothes. Gladys was told that the estate was quite a distance and that they would be leaving early the following morning. "This way, Hilda shall have a nice dinner ready for us when we arrive," James explained.

As soon as they left the driveway the next morning, Gladys could see they were travelling away from Sandwich, which surprised her. By midmorning she knew they were travelling toward Dover. Then, when they stopped at a small station, she recognized it as the same station where she and Dolly had stopped when they first came to Four Oaks. "My goodness, it is quite far away," she said to Dolly. She was riding in one coach with Dolly and Eliza, and James and Percy were behind in another.

"It's not far now, Mother. I think you shall like the place, and there is a small station nearby where we can take the train and be in Dover, or Sandwich, in a half an hour," Dolly remarked cheerfully.

It surprised Gladys how happy Dolly seemed that morning. It was as though it was her new home they were going to and not Eliza's.

Not long after, they turned off on another road that Gladys recognized. *Oh, no,* she thought. *This is the road that runs past Lord and Lady Sorenson's estate—and Oaken Arms!* She must have made a sound of distress, because Eliza inquired if she was all right. Determined not to upset everyone, Gladys made up her mind to ignore the two places as they went by and answered that she just had a tickle in her throat.

They came to Oaken Arms first, and as they were approaching, Gladys looked out the other side of the coach, not wanting to see the home she had once thought would be hers. Then, when the horses turned into the gateway, she cried out, "Why are we stopping here?"

"Don't you recognize it, Mother? It is Oaken Arms. See, that is Daddy's regiment crest you and Gamby had put on the gate," Dolly said.

"You mean this is now Ben and Eliza's home? They own Oaken Arms?"

"Yes, Mother. Ben bought it, and with Dolly's help, he restored it as close to what it looked like when she last saw it," Eliza said proudly.

"I know there are probably some things I may have forgotten, Mother, but one thing I did remember was how you intended to plant daffodils up both sides of the driveway, and look, there they are all in bloom," Dolly said, smiling. Gladys could hardly believe what she was seeing. The place looked just as beautiful as she recalled. "I only wish Gamby was here with us, Mother. Are you surprised?"

"I am so surprised I hardly know what to say. I never thought I would ever set foot on this land again."

Dolly had done an amazing job, and all of the mansion's décor could not have been more to Gladys' taste if she had decorated it herself. After they took her through the house on an inspection tour, Eliza and Dolly showed her to her suite. It was the same one she and her father-in-law had planned for Millie, and although she appreciated it when Eliza said that it would now be hers, she wasn't as thrilled with the idea as she pretended to be.

When they were building the mansion, Gladys could picture herself as the mistress, and now she realized that was what made Oaken Arms so magical for her. It was Eliza's mansion now, and Gladys couldn't be happier for her daughter, but she wanted to be head of her own household. It didn't matter how small and humble a home she had, as long as she owned it.

During the two years it took to build the mansion, Gladys could hardly wait to move in, and for a few years after she was forced to leave Dover, she continued to dream about it, but that dream had faded long ago. She was a different person now, and she knew that if she moved to England, she wanted her own home. She decided that sometime after the wedding she would talk to Ben about buying a little of his property, and having a small house built on it, but right now she intended to enjoy the last-minute preparations for her daughter's wedding.

The next day, Ben's family arrived. Two of his married brothers, who lived in Scotland, came with their wives and children, but the other married brother lived in Germany and couldn't attend. Gladys moved in with Dolly, and let Rodney and Ida White have her suite. As promised, Ida brought baskets filled with an assortment of flowers from her garden, and Gladys made beautiful arrangements to put in the grand hall and throughout the house, adding a pleasing fragrance.

Ida had made the wedding cake and decorated it with marzipan and icing. The cake itself was made with honey and fruit, and everyone said it was the best wedding cake they had ever eaten. Ida's response was a curt, "Nonsense," but she blushed with pleasure. Victor, Iris, and her daughter, Friedl, had come for the wedding, and somehow, Ben and Eliza managed to accommodate them all.

Eliza looked like an angel in her wedding gown, and Ben had tears in his eyes when he saw her. They made a handsome couple, and James hired his friend to take pictures of them and all the family. Gladys had done Dolly's hair in soft ringlets that hung down her back and complemented the green dress she wore. Ben's brother Ernest seemed quite taken with her, but Dolly did little to encourage him. Compared to Ben, Ernest seemed dull-witted and boring, and Gladys could understand why Dolly wasn't attracted to him, but she hoped in time, a man would come along that could mend her daughter's broken heart.

Chapter 24

Ben and Eliza left the next day for a honeymoon in France. Hilda and James' other servants returned to Four Oaks the following day. That same day, the Whites took their leave, but Gladys talked Victor, Iris, her daughter, Friedl, James, and Percy into staying on for two more days. "Life isn't going to be same from now on, James, especially for you," Gladys said one afternoon when they were all sitting in the garden.

James' face showed his sorrow as he replied, "I don't think I shall like it, even though I knew it would happen one day. Not only am I losing Eliza and Dolly, but now you shall have another place to visit when you come to England, and I shan't have you and Edward to brighten up the place now and then. Do you think you could manage to spend a few days at Four Oaks every time you are here? It would mean a lot to us old codgers."

"Certainly! Visiting Four Oaks will always be something I look forward to, but I doubt Eddy will have time to visit anyone but a certain young lady in London whenever she's there."

"Where else would she be, Mother?" Dolly asked.

"In Eddy's last letter, he said she may go to Germany to study. She wants to be a nurse."

"How wonderful of her; I think I shall like Miss Benson."

"Well, it sounds like they're not going to rush into a hasty marriage, Gladys. I imagine that is a relief to you," Percy added.

"Yes, it is. I think he's too young. Dolly, why don't you take Friedl for a ride and show her the creek? It's warm enough today to enjoy a paddle, and the horses would probably enjoy it, too." Friedl said she had never ridden before, so Dolly suggested they take a picnic basket and go by buggy. Friedl was delighted and they left laughing.

Iris sensed that Gladys wanted to talk to James alone, so she suggested that Victor join her for a little stroll around the property. Gladys surprised her, saying, "I wish you would both stay and hear what I have to say. You see, I'm trying to make up my mind about something, and I value all your opinions."

"Uh-oh, now what sort of a business are you thinking of getting us involved in?" Victor asked, good-naturedly.

"Don't worry, Vic, this has nothing to do with international enterprises; I intend on doing this on my own. At first, I thought of either buying a home in England or purchasing a small piece of land from you, James, or from Ben, and having a house built. Not a large place, but one I can call my own."

"I hope that doesn't mean you intend to leave New York and live in England," Iris cried.

"I am afraid so, Iris, but I'll visit you often. You see, ever since I lost Angelo, I've felt the need to do something in his honour and, goodness knows, I can afford it."

"I feel the same way, but I couldn't think of what to do," Victor remarked. "I thought of donating some money to our museum in his name, but I wanted to ask you before I did. What do you think?"

"I know you're all going to think I'm crazy, but I was thinking of something much more suitable to Angelo himself. He was a real hero—not once, but twice. And what I have in mind would allow him to continue being one. I want to start a home for orphans, and staff it with some of the poor folks from Old Nichol."

No one said anything, and Gladys could tell they thought it was an impossible dream. She let them think about it for a while, then she continued, "That's where Toughie, or Angelo, and I grew up, and it's where we saw some of our best friends die of starvation or sickness. Unless you have lived in such filth, you can't possibly have any idea how horrific it was, and from what I hear, still is. I know I can't save them all, but even if I save as many as ten children from such a fate, I know Angelo will rest easier."

"That's very noble of you, my dear, but do you have any idea how much money it takes to run an orphanage?" Percy asked.

"I don't want an orphanage, Percy. I've heard how they are run, at least many of them. I want to give these children a home with people who'll love them and nurture them. As for money, I do have a large share in the business, and I'm prepared to sell it. Perhaps to you, Victor, and maybe Ike as well. I don't need much to live on, and that way I should have enough to buy a place, or build it, and get started."

"But you've worked so hard to accomplish what you have, Glad. You've earned the right to sit back and enjoy your life," Iris said.

"Besides, you don't just begin a thing like this, at least not with children. It has to continue, or you might do more harm than good. A place like you are envisioning will take a great deal of money to run year after year. I don't think you have that kind of money. In fact, I'd wager none of us has," Percy advised.

"Then I shall raise money by talking rich folks into pledging yearly donations toward it." Without realizing it, Gladys had risen and nervously begun pacing back and forth as she talked. "I really feel like Angelo is telling me to do this." Suddenly she felt spent and sank down into one of the wooden garden chairs. Again, the silence lasted for what seemed an eternity, except for the odd clearing of throats.

Victor was first to respond with the surprising remark, "The Angelo Matthews' Orphanage—I can see it, Gladys, but it will be a huge undertaking."

"I'd rather call it something other than an orphanage, but I'm not sure what. I want it to be like a real home, with folks looking after it who are more like parents than wardens. Do you know what I mean?"

"I think I do," James replied. "You could call it Angelo Matthews' Private School, then the children would be brought up with some dignity."

"That is brilliant, James; and we could hire nannies and teachers."

"Where are you intending to have this school, Gladys?"

"Why not have it in New York?" Victor wanted to know. "After all, Angelo is an American hero, not a British hero, and I think there are a lot of wealthy New Yorkers you could persuade to back your project. You know we have almost as many starving children in our slums as there are here."

"I know, Victor, but let me try to explain. I guess the reason I want it here is because he and I were lucky enough to escape from Old Nichol, where I'm sure we would have died of starvation along with our folks if we hadn't. I just think we should do something to honour those we left behind, like our friends, Billy and Mick, my ma and pa, and Toughie's mother and father. His father was hero too you know."

Victor didn't argue, instead he asked, "Were you thinking of having this home in London then?"

"I would prefer to find something in the country, if possible."

Percy, who seemed to be Gladys' most enthusiastic supporter, spoke up and said, "Well, I for one will do what I can to make it happen, but we do have a lot to think about. Right now, I think we should all go into that beautiful conservatory and see if there are any of those fancy cakes left to have with our tea. What say?"

They all agreed but Gladys, who said she would stay in the garden for a while. It was the first time she had been alone since she arrived, and except for the wedding, all she could think of was her plans for Angelo's memorial. Now she wanted to savour the memory of the carefree times she, Dolly, and her father-in-law, Andrew, had sitting under the same oak tree she was sitting under now.

She tried to imagine what that life would have been like if Andrew had lived and they had moved into Oaken Arms, but she couldn't. All she could think of was Angelo. Getting up, she looked up at the sky, and said, "Always be with me, my darling. Don't ever leave me." Then she smiled and walked into the house.

Dolly was disappointed when Gladys told her she didn't intend to live at Oaken Arms. However, she relaxed when she heard what her mother intended to do, thinking it was probably just a passing whim and she would change her mind eventually, especially if Eliza gave her as many grandchildren as she intended to.

Gladys' first grandchild, a boy, arrived fifteen months later, on September 5, 1876. They named him Sidney. Gladys had arrived at Oaken Arms a month before the event and remained there for a month after. She would have stayed longer, but Dolly was as possessive of the child as she was of Eliza, and they had a most proficient nanny as well.

Eliza was proud of her accomplishment. It was the first independent achievement she had ever undertaken, and the result amazed her. Baby Sidney was perfect in every way, and Ben's delight and praise gave her a feeling of satisfaction she had never felt before. She was content to let Dolly nurture the child, except for suckling, which she did more out of duty than enjoyment, but the business of becoming impregnated and birthing was hers and hers alone. Eliza had found her calling.

Eddy had decided to return to the academy and was promoted to ensign after spending a year aboard a flagship. He had kept in touch with Amelia, and he visited her every time he had the opportunity, but that wasn't often. She was busy with her studies in Germany and only returned to England on holidays. Gladys did her best to be in London at the same time they were, so she could visit them both. She was becoming very fond of Amelia, and Amelia felt the same way toward her. She had also become better acquainted with Amelia's father, Admiral George Benson, but she had let him know that they would never be more than good friends.

Amelia thought Gladys' plans to build a home for underprivileged children was a brilliant idea, and she even offered to work at the establishment when she graduated from nursing school. Gladys hadn't found any suitable property, but she and Percy had seen to all the legal angles so that, when they did find a place, there would be no delays. Meantime, she was spending more and more time in England, which pleased Dolly and Eliza.

In the spring of 1877, James and Percy wired Gladys to come to Four Oaks as soon as possible. They didn't say why, but she had an idea it had to do with property, and she wasn't mistaken. James had let it be known that a friend of his was looking for an estate, and one of his friends said he had heard there was a small one for sale near Worth, a small village not far from Sandwich. Because it was only a short distance from Four Oaks, he and Percy went to look at it, then they sent for Gladys. She was on the next boat.

On their way to view the estate, Percy leaned over and said, "I'm afraid the whole place is terribly run down, Gladys, but if you can purchase it for a reasonable price, you may be able to repair it, and I'm fairly certain that it is large enough to suit your needs."

James and Gladys were riding on the front seat of James' wagon, and Percy and Richard Ellison, James' handyman, were on the seat behind them. Richard had proved invaluable around James' estate, and they brought him along to get his opinion on the soundness of the building.

There was a sign nailed to a post announcing they had arrived at The Three Cribbs Estate. Both the post and the sign showed signs of rot, and the metal gate was just hanging by one hinge on one side—the opposite side being held up by a wire wrapped around a spike in a tree. James looked at his watch, "Mr. Stewart, the realtor, said he would be here at one sharp. We are a few minutes early, but if he doesn't show up in ten minutes, I think we shall go in." They couldn't see the house from the road.

They waited ten minutes then opened the gate and drove in. The driveway had once been cobbled, but grass had grown over most of the stones, and many were missing, leaving large holes in their place. As they neared the house they noticed the grounds had been thoroughly neglected as well, and all the ornamental shrubs were now wild bushes. It seemed no one had used the main doors at the front of the house for years, so they drove around to the back of the house, where they were surprised to find the realtor waiting for them.

Percy explained how they had waited at the gate and the realtor apologized, "I left the gate open so you would know I was here. The watchman must have come in and closed it. I am sorry, but now that you are here, shall we proceed?" He explained that the original owners hadn't wanted a great deal of land and only purchased enough so they could call it an estate.

"Mind you," he continued, "there is enough land to raise feed for livestock, and there are four cottages to house workers. One is now being used for the watchman and his family."

"I'd like to have a look at them after we've seen the house," Gladys announced. She could picture housing some of the neediest families from Old Nichol in them—families with men who could do the farming and raise enough vegetables and animals to supply the home with food, and wives who could help with the household chores.

The interior of the building appeared every bit as run-down as the exterior. Most of the rooms hadn't been used for many years, and there were dust-laden cobwebs hanging from every piece of the well-used furniture and drapery. Gladys' face showed disdain, but in her mind, she was picturing it completely different. Most of the trouble was merely cosmetic, but the men couldn't see that, and she prayed that all of the previous prospective buyers had been men. She knew that a thorough cleaning, fresh wallpaper, and new drapery would make the world of difference.

Of course, the kitchen would have to be modernized, and she intended to see about installing indoor plumbing, if possible. She thought the place large enough to house at least fifteen orphans and enough staff to look after them. The grand ballroom could be used for both schooling and a gymnasium in the winter months. It was all she could do not to smile, but she knew she would get a better deal if she continued pretending she was disappointed with the place.

When they finished looking at the house, they went out to examine the barn and the cottages. Gladys asked Richard to wait for them at the house. He instinctively understood that she wanted him to examine what wood structure there was for rot. When they were ready to leave, Stewart, ignoring Gladys, addressed James. "It has been neglected as you can see, Mr. Hornsby, but the land itself is worth the price the seller is asking. What do you think?"

James shook his head, and answered, "I personally wouldn't buy it, but it is Mrs. Matthews here you should talk to. She is the one who was interested."

"Oh, I had no idea. I apologize, Mrs. Matthews, I should have been addressing you when we were looking around. Are you interested in negotiating?"

"It is not really what I was looking for, Mr. Stewart. You see, I live in America most of the time and this place would require so much work. Maybe the house will have to be torn down and a new place built, and that would cost me far more than I had planned on spending. However, I will make you an offer. It's not what you are asking for, but I'm afraid with all the work that is needed on the place, it's the best I can do."

Gladys shocked them all by offering two-thirds the asking price. Mr. Stewart had showed the house to quite a few but there wasn't enough property with the estate to suit a true aristocrat, and although the mansion was large, it wasn't grand enough. Stewart also knew the seller was an addicted gambler who was deeply in debt, so he surprised them all and said he would take the offer to his client.

Once they were back on the wagon and on the way home, James said, "Well, if he accepts that offer, I shall have to hire you to negotiate any deals I have in the future, Gladys. I thought you were not the least bit interested in the place."

"I think it is just what I am looking for, James, but, Richard, did you have a good look at it?" she asked.

"There are some banisters that need repairing, but as near as I could tell, the beams in the cellar are good. Of course, we shall be able to tell more when some of the dirt is gone."

"Then I think I've found Angelo's Private School."

"The seller has to agree to your offer first," Percy warned.

"I just know he will. I felt it was ours as soon as I saw it. Oh, I can hardly wait to get started. First, I have to hire a crew to clean up the cottages. Then, when they are ready, I want to bring some families out of Old Nichol to start working on the grounds. I won't bring any children though until I have the house finished. I know it's a lot to ask, but I'd like you and Percy to come to Old Nichol with me to find the families when I'm ready, and then later, to find the children. Could you do that?"

"But I thought you said you could never go back there," Percy replied.

"If I am going to help these folks, I have to."

"Well, if you can do it, I'm sure we can. What do you think, James?"

James agreed, but he reminded them that they should also be trying to raise money for the foundation. Gladys said she would ask Ben if she could hold a charity ball at Oaken Arms and invite Dover's most influential members of society, and James said he would throw one at Four Oaks if she would host it. Percy said he would talk to a lord he knew and see if he and his wife would throw a charity ball.

Chapter 25

There was so much for her to do in England, Gladys had little time to spend in New York, but she knew she had to return and settle things there soon. Eddy had earned his promotion and Gladys was anxious to find out what his plans for the future were. Bob Nicholson hadn't retired and was still in business, so Gladys decided to book passage with him and sail to New York while she was waiting to hear if her offer on the property was accepted.

She had only sailed with Bob once since Angelo's death, so she was surprised when he said he knew she had a grandson and that Eddy had graduated. "But how did you find out?" she wanted to know.

"I've kept in touch with Eddy. Didn't he tell you?"

"No, I'm afraid not. All he ever writes about is Amelia."

"Ah, yes, the lovely Amelia. I met her and her father, the admiral. They sailed with me. He was a captain for quite a few years, so we had quite a talk. It seems he would like Eddy to join the British Navy."

"Has Eddy written to you about his plans?"

"As a matter of fact, he has, but I think I should let him tell you."

Gladys would have liked him to tell her more, but she thought Eddy might want to do it himself. She told Bob what she planned on doing for Angelo, and he wanted to know if she had talked it over with Eddy. When she said she hadn't, he looked sceptical and remarked, "I think you should before you make up your mind." This puzzled Gladys, but she couldn't get him to say any more.

Iris met her at the dock with her buggy and took her to Lottie and Victor's house. "I know Lottie would have wanted you to stay here rather your place, at least for tonight."

"Thanks, Iris. Eddy will be here tomorrow, so I'll go home in the morning and prepare the house. You know it amazes me how your presence here doesn't feel the least bit out of place. It's as though Lottie asked you to be here, not Victor."

"May I tell you something I haven't told anyone before, Gladys?"

"Of course."

"One of the times when I spelled you and Victor off and sat with Lottie, she asked me if I would look after Victor when she was gone. That's why I agreed to move in here. Besides, I think Victor needs me. If he asks me to marry him, I feel I can say yes and have both Lottie and Otto's blessings."

"Oh, Iris, that would be wonderful!"

Eddy arrived the next day with all his belongings. He said that as much as he loved the academy, he had decided to leave. "Then you've decided to join the British Navy?"

"No, I've had enough of the military life. I am going to sail with Captain Bob for a year. Then, if I prove myself worthy, he intends to hand the ship over to me and he'll retire. Most of the profits will go to him, and what I earn, will go toward buying the ship.

"Of course, I'll have to give him a sizeable down payment. I hope I can borrow that from you. I'll pay it back with interest, but it may take a few years. It's what I've dreamt of all my life, Mother." Gladys' face fell. "You don't look pleased. Are you disappointed in me for asking?"

"I could never be disappointed in you, Eddy. You've done wonders, and I know your father would be as proud of you as I am. It's just that I had no idea what you intended to do when you graduated, and I've made other plans." When she told him about the home for orphans, Eddy thought it was a great idea, and he did his best to hide his disappointment, saying that he could work with Bob for a year then find another ship. Gladys wasn't fooled, and she could tell he was heart-broken.

"Let's not give up that easy, darling. I'm going to sell the house, and by the sounds of it, prices have risen considerably. We can get together with Bob tomorrow and talk terms. Perhaps we can manage to achieve both our goals."

They invited Bob to dinner the next night, and when they were sitting on the front porch, enjoying a drink of sherry, Gladys asked him how much he would need as a down payment for the Delaney.

"Gladys, you know I wouldn't even ask for a cent if I could help it, but I've promised Asta a new home, and I can't disappoint her again. You see, I was going to sell the Delaney and retire last year, but I put it off to wait for Eddy to leave the academy. Sorry, but I really do need the amount I stated."

"I understand. You've been so very kind, Bob. We shall just have to work it out. You never know; Eddy just might be able to raise enough money in time. When do you and Eddy intend to leave?" When Bob said he was leaving in a fortnight, Gladys said she would try to be ready to sail with them. The next day, she received a wire from James saying that her offer on the estate was accepted. Now she had to figure a way to pay for it besides putting a down payment on the SS Delaney.

It was a busy two weeks. First, she found a realtor to look after the sale of her house, then she called a meeting with the International Enterprise Company partners, so she could tell them that she intended to sell her share of the company.

"As you own fifty percent of our import/export company, Norman, I thought I would offer to sell to Victor and Ike first, so as to even up the shares. If they aren't interested in buying it, then you might want it. If not, I shall have to put it on the market," she told them. Then she explained what she wanted to do with the money. She also mentioned that she wanted to give Eddy a down payment on Bob Nicholson's ship.

"I'd be very interested in buying your share, Gladys, but if I do that, it will mean I won't have as much left to give you for your project, and I want to do my share for Angelo, too," Victor said.

"Ah, but if we buy her share together, Vic, it will only cost us half as much each. That way we can both afford to give Gladys a large donation. When Angelo lost his arm, I promised I would look after him, and I've never felt I have kept that promise. Now I have a very lucrative practice, and so has Melissa. We don't need all the money we have, and I know Angelo would want me to help Eddy. You tell him he has his down payment, and he doesn't have to worry about paying it back," Ike declared.

"That's far too generous, Ike," Gladys replied.

"I insist, but if you want to argue about it, how about if I don't give you a donation toward Angelo's school and I make a yearly pledge instead? That way it will be coming in steady. As for Eddy's down payment, he's going to have enough of a job just paying the rest of what he owes Bob without having to pay anyone else, so please allow me to do this. You have no idea how much it will mean to me."

Norman said he would have bought Gladys' shares if he had the chance, but he was glad she didn't sell to strangers. He also made a sizeable donation and a pledge toward Angelo's school. Victor gave her a donation and pledged as well, so Gladys was ready to return to England with some substantial cheques to add to the Angelo Matthews' Private School foundation. Now she hoped Percy and

James would be able to provide her with the names of some reliable officials to run it.

Gladys spent most of her last day in New York with Iris. She missed Lottie a great deal, but she was very fond of Iris, too, and found she could talk to her almost as freely as she could to Lottie. Iris was worried that Gladys had taken on too much, and she asked her if she had enough help in England. "Greta graduated from medical school last year and she hasn't found a job yet, so if you need a doctor over there, I'm sure she would be glad to offer her services for a time."

Gladys was thrilled with the offer. "That would be wonderful. God knows what condition the ones I bring from Old Nichol will be in. It's bound to take time to build up their strength, and I am sure they'll need medical treatment as well, but it is a lot to ask of her."

"I think she'll welcome the challenge, and perhaps she'll find a doctor over there broad minded enough to hire her. That way I can come and visit you both. She'll be home soon. She often goes over to Melissa's office to see if she can be of help. Forgive me, Gladys, I hope you don't mind me asking, but James and his friend—what's his name?"

"Percy."

"Percy, that's it. Well, I couldn't help but notice that they seemed to be more than just friends. Am I right?"

"Would that bother you?"

"I thought it would, but after meeting them, I can't see why it would bother anyone."

"It bothers more people than you can imagine, and it has to be kept a secret, here as well as over there, so please don't say anything to anyone about it. As far as anyone is concerned, they are just very good friends, which, in fact, they are."

"I'd never say a word to anyone. Now, would I be able to help you clean that mansion if I came over with you for a month?"

"I can use all the help I can get, but I'm leaving tomorrow."

"I can throw a few things in a trunk tonight, and if the captain will allow me to share your cabin, I'll be ready to go." Gladys was happy to have the company on the boat, and she knew she would be glad to have Iris' help once she started cleaning the mansion.

After they had been at sea for two days, Gladys decided she couldn't wait any longer to take Iris up to the bridge and see if Eddy was steering the ship, but when they arrived, Bob said that Eddy was down below in the boiler room working with the Black Gang. The ladies had no idea what the Black Gang was, so Bob explained, "It's just a term we use for the men who work in the fire room—the stokers or firemen. They're called the Black Gang because their sweaty bodies and clothes get so soiled with soot and coal dust as they shovel coal into the boiler's firebox."

"But, with all the training Eddy has, surely he doesn't have to do that sort of work," Gladys protested.

"No, he doesn't, and I have told him that, but he's determined to get to know every man on board and thinks the best way to do that is to work alongside them. He intends to work a while with every one of them during this next year. You know, I think he's right. He's quite a bit younger than most of the men on the ship, and they could resent taking orders from him when he takes over as captain. This way he's earning their respect. He's one fine sailor and a damn fine lad, if you don't mind me saying."

Gladys only saw Eddy once on that voyage, but he told her he was going to ask Amelia if she would marry him when he became captain of the SS Delaney. When Gladys gave him her blessing, he said, "You know, I miss Father a lot, but I have Uncle Victor, James, Ike, and Bob, and they've all been great. I hope I never let them down, but no one has been there for me as much as you have. I love you, Mom, and if you ever need me, I'll come, no matter what part of the world I am in."

It was odd, but Gladys and Bob's relationship changed after Angelo died. The attraction they felt toward each other was gone, and they were far more relaxed in each other's company. Gladys thought it was as though Bob could sense that Angelo was always with her, and she enjoyed the voyage more than ever.

As soon as she received the wire informing her that her offer on the property was accepted, Gladys had wired James and asked him to hire a gardener and some men to clear the brush and tidy the property around the house. She also asked him to see that one of the cottages was cleaned and made ready. When she and Iris arrived at Four Oaks, they just stayed the one night, then went to the estate, stopping on the way for necessities.

As soon as they drove through the gate of the property, Gladys was amazed at the difference in the grounds. The gardener was still working there, so she had a chance to talk to him, or rather, he had a chance to talk to her. He said his name was Fred, but he didn't offer a surname, and that he lived in Worth. "It only takes me five minutes to walk here, Mrs. Matthews, so I have been arriving at six and leaving at five.

"The mister who hired me said he didn't rightly know if you would be wanting me to stay on, but if you do, I shall need to talk to you about the lilac bushes. They've grown out of control, and I think we should take some of them out and cut back the others. You have some of the best soil in Worth here, and if you'll pardon me for saying it, the ones who been living here hardly turned a sod these last five years. It's a bloomin' shame, that's what it is."

"Well, I can assure you that I intend to change that, but it might take time," Gladys replied. Then she told him about her plans and asked him if he would stay on as head gardener. "Perhaps you can teach some of the poor fellows how to grow enough food to feed us all." Fred was so pleased he didn't even ask what his wages would be.

The cottage that had been cleaned needed fresh bedding; therefore, Gladys and Iris decided to stay with James at Four Oaks and travel back and forth every day. Iris stayed for three weeks, and except for the odd times when they walked into the village to pick up supplies, she didn't stop cleaning. They cleaned all the cottages, except for the watchman's, and Gladys bought new mattresses, bedding, and utensils, then she made curtains for each cabin. Fred cleaned the yards and cut the grass. Gladys was very pleased with the results and told Iris, "Now they look far more inviting than they did, and I think whoever we find to bring here is going to be happy with them, don't you?"

Iris laughed and answered, "I wouldn't mind living in one of them myself, but now we'd better get busy on the big house. I only have one more week before I have to leave."

"I think we should take a few days off and let you rest before you go home, or you will never want to come here again."

"I'll have plenty of time to rest on the ship, and when I get home, but if you insist we take some time off, I would really like to see that grandson of yours."

"Splendid! We shall go on the train tomorrow. I was hoping you'd want to see him."

Gladys had planned on going to Oaken Arms in two weeks to celebrate Sidney's first birthday. She had bought him a reddish-brown teddy bear with movable legs and arms. It had shiny black button eyes that the saleslady swore were securely attached to his head and a black embroidered nose. Gladys also made Sidney a soft flannel quilt with appliquéd puppies on it. As Ben was home the same week that Gladys and Iris were there, Dolly and Eliza decided they would have Sidney's birthday party two weeks early.

Gladys hadn't seen her grandson for a few months, and she was amazed at how big he was. He was trying to walk with the help of whoever would take hold of his hands, and because he was teething, he was drooling and chewing on anything he could get in his mouth, including the cat's tail. But, in spite of his discomfort, he was easily pacified, and everyone thought he was a darling boy.

Gladys thought that as soon as she had the cottages ready, they would bring some families out to work the land, but she hadn't the patience to wait to get the mansion in shape, so she hired some local women to work with her. Iris came back the following year for two months, and between them, they managed to have it ready as soon as the grounds were all in shape.

Besides working on the estate, Gladys had to talk at different fund-raising events as well, and to impress the sort of people who could afford to make an annual pledge, she had to dress accordingly. A board of directors had been chosen from the list of donors, and Gladys was pleased with all but one—a woman named Nonie Simms. Nonie was a very practical woman, who was always reminding the others that the only sensible way to run a school like Angelo's was not to let sentiment override expediency.

Gladys didn't argue with her. Instead, she found subtle ways to praise her for giving the orphans love and kindness, as well as food and clothing. James was amazed at how far a little flattery went and said, "You are quite a diplomat, Gladys, but I wonder how long it will last."

"I don't know. I think it's more like blackmail, but I shall keep it up as long as it's needed." Living in New York for such a long time, Gladys had adopted an American dialect, and now she had to try to remember to use what many aristocrats considered proper English in order convince them to pledge money.

Chapter 26

In spring of 1878, the school was just about ready to accommodate some of the families and orphans from Old Nichol, but Eliza, who wasn't supposed to give birth to her second child for two months, went into labour and Gladys had to leave everything to be with her. The baby, a little girl they named Gladys, was born prematurely and only weighed four pounds. Although she survived, she had a weak heart and had trouble breathing. Eliza was sure her mother could cure her, even though Gladys and the doctor tried to tell her there wasn't much hope. "But, Mama, every time we were sick, you always made us better," Eliza cried.

Baby Gladys only lived for two months. Eliza was devastated, and for a while she allowed her emotions to rule her mind and blamed Gladys, but after the funeral, she apologized and wanted Gladys to stay with her until she recovered. Gladys had appointments she couldn't ignore, but she made Oaken Arms her home base until Eliza no longer needed her.

The biggest event she had to organize was the school's grand opening. Now that it was ready to receive the children, all the people who had donated and pledged monetary support were sent invitations. Invitations were also sent out to donors in New York, including Iris, her daughter, Greta, Victor, Norman, Ike and Melissa.

Lottie's uncle Peter Rutten had passed away, and Theresa Rutten was living in Sandwich with her son Mitchell and daughter-in-law Mary. They had all given generously to the school, so would be there as well. The opening was on May the 20th, and Fred had done wonders with the flower garden. The sun was shining, and the people who came were extremely impressed. Once that was over, it was time to fill the place with orphans and families.

Gladys knew that the only way to find the families for the cottages, and the orphans for the school, was to go to Old Nichol herself—a task she dreaded. Fortunately, James and Percy agreed to go with her. Knowing that cab drivers often refused to enter Old Nichol, when they arrived in London, they rented a horse and buggy.

As soon as they came to Warehouse Corner, Gladys wished she had thought of another way to save the orphans. The stench was even worse than she remembered. Holding her scarf over her face, she gave Percy the directions. First, they passed the junk yard that Bob Tweedhope had left to Toughie. Now that she was back in Old Nichol, it seemed more fitting to think of Angelo as Toughie. The old shed he had tried to make into a home for Gladys and her parents hadn't changed, and she could see that the present owner hadn't been able to add any more boards to the structure.

She pointed it out to Percy and James as they were riding by. Next, they passed O'Brian's place. "That's the barn that Toughie lived in, when his mother died," she said. "He lived there from the time he was five until he was fourteen." There were no signs of any of the O'Brian family, and Gladys hoped that they had all joined Rod, the oldest boy, after she had found him a job on Lord Sorenson's estate.

James' face had turned pale, and fearful of the germs he might inhale if he opened his mouth too wide, he mumbled, "I find it difficult to believe you and Angelo managed to stay alive in this hell-hole for all those years, Gladys. I don't think I shall be able to come back here. We shall have to find another way to select the children."

"Don't worry, you shan't have to, my dear," Percy said. It was the first time Gladys had heard either of them use a term of endearment toward each other and she realized how terribly restrained their relationship had to be. "I'll come alone with her next time."

Gladys didn't say anything—she was beginning to doubt if even she could return. It was then she noticed the sign. It had faded and was barely recognizable, but she could still make out the name "Goodrich." "We have to go in there," she said to the men, pointing toward one of the stores. "But when we get out of the buggy, make sure you keep your hands on your purses and your watch. The people here just have to bump up against you and your valuables are gone. I know, because Toughie and I were as quick as any of them."

"My heavens, girl, I find it unbelievable that you were once a poor little ragged urchin like these children," Percy declared as they stepped down from the buggy.

"I can hardly believe it myself anymore, but now you can see why I want to save as many as I can."

When they entered the building, James could see it was supposed to be a grocery store, but it had very little stock. A man was standing behind the counter and showed his surprise when he looked up and saw them. "Yes," he said. "Are you looking for someone?" He knew such finely clad folk wouldn't be looking for groceries. Gladys drew closer while studying him intently. She thought he resembled Toughie's old friend, Mick, but he appeared far too old. "'Ow can I 'elp you, Missus?" The man said, obviously uneasy over her scrutiny.

"It's you! Mick, it is you! It's me, Gladys. Gladys Tunner. Toughie's Gladys. Remember me?"

Mick's mouth fell open. He gaped at her for a second, then he reached over the counter and touched her hair. "Gladys, Toughie's

Gladys," he repeated. "I must be dreamin'. Gladys Tunner, is it really you?"

"Yes, Mick, it really is me. How are you? Toughie told me that you married Mr. Goodrich's daughter, Maud."

"I did, and Maud is just out back. I'll call her." Mick went to an open door at the back of the store and called. Maud entered almost immediately, followed by two children: a tall boy who looked to be in his teens and a girl Gladys thought must be around ten. They were all very thin and poorly dressed, but they were fairly clean. Maud, like her husband, appeared older than her age, but Gladys would have recognized her anywhere by her walk. She still used a crutch that she swung out with each step as though sweeping the floor as she went along.

She didn't remember Gladys, but then she had parents to look after her when they were children and didn't spend her time begging in the streets with Toughie, Gladys, and the rest of the pack. After introductions were over, Mick put a closed sign on the door and insisted they go back into the living quarters and have tea. The house was fairly clean and the street odours less pungent, so James was able to breathe a little easier, but he couldn't force himself to accept the tea.

When Mick heard what had happened to Toughie, he said he was sorry but that he was glad to hear that he had a good life before he died. "And so shall you and your family, Mick," Gladys promised him. Then she told him about Angelo Matthews' Private School. She explained that Toughie's real name was Angelo Matthews and that the school and the estate was his memorial.

"I know he'd want to help you and others from Old Nichol, especially orphans like you three were. Now, besides the big mansion, we have five nice cottages, and I would like you and your family to have one of those. Toughie would have wanted it too. You won't have to pay rent, but everyone will be expected to do what they can to keep the place going. You and your boy might want to help with the gardening, or the animals, and your daughter can help in the dormitories when she's not going to school. You'll be given enough money to buy your own clothing and food, and with hope, we will eventually raise enough produce and animals to allow you a wage.

"Do you think you would like to live in the country?" she asked the four of them. Surprisingly, their response wasn't as enthusiastic as she had anticipated. Ever since she had thought of the idea, Gladys had pictured the people from Old Nichol jumping for joy when she told them she was going to give them a chance to live a good life on the outside, but neither Mick, nor his family, showed any signs of gratitude.

She couldn't hide her disappointment, and when Mick noticed it, he apologized. "It's not that we don't appreciate your offer, Gladys, but we 'as ta think about what we'd 'ave to give up 'ere."

Gladys looked around at the room they were in. Granted it was a large room, but most of it was filled with crates—most empty except for a few containing some tired looking vegetables. There was a stove, sink, table, and four chairs, and the rest of the room was divided into two rooms with the help of some old canvases as partitions. Gladys surmised that was to curtain off the bedrooms. She had to admit it was far better than any other house she had been in when she lived there, but it was still very shabby. She shook her head and said, "I don't understand."

"You see, we 'as seen some who 'as gone out and found it were just as bad there. Now maybe things at this place you 'as will be good for a year or two, but what if the money runs out. What'll 'appen to us then? I knows we goes 'ungry like everyone else round 'ere at times, but at least with the store, we're a lot better off than most, an' if I lets me store go, I shall 'ave nought to come back to. It's a lot to consider, if you sees what I mean."

Suddenly, Gladys understood. Besides losing the store, the thought of moving to a strange and unfamiliar part of the world was frightening for them all. "Mick, I have an idea. Why don't you and Maud, or one of your children, come back with me and have a look at the place. As for the estate running out of money, you needn't worry. There's enough money in the bank, plus enough pledges to keep it running until your children are through school, married, and have children of their own.

"I think if you see the place, you'll feel differently. And if you tell others about it when you return, we may hire you to choose the rest of the people who need help. Will you come?" Mick said he would talk it over with Maud and let her know. Gladys said she, Percy, and James would wait in the store for him to decide. She was looking out the store window when a little girl put her face up to the glass and stuck out her tongue.

Laughing, Gladys said, "Oh, you cheeky little monkey," even though she knew the child couldn't hear her. Then, reaching into her purse, she brought out a shiny coin, held it up, and motioned to the child that it was for her. The girl tried to open the door but couldn't, so Gladys opened it for her. Although she didn't enter, the girl reached her hand in. Gladys said, "Not until you tell me your name."

The child looked as though she was about to stick out her tongue again but then looked back at the coin once more. "Hits Bitsy. Gimme money."

"What do you say?"

"Pulease, an' thank you. Now, you gimme more?"

The child's hair was a mass of tangled curls and she reminded Gladys of herself at that age. She remembered looking in the bakery shop window at Toughie as he was eating a scone. She was about four, the same age as this little one, and although Toughie was only three years older, and just as poor, he motioned for her to come in and share his treat. From then on, he took it upon himself to look after her. "Will you give it to your mother?" she asked the child. Bitsy shook her head negatively. "Well, who will you share it with? I want to know before I give you more."

"Joey. I always give to Joey," she said.

"Who is Joey?" Before the child could answer, Mick came in and said, "Joey is her brother. He looks after her. They're orphans." Gladys gave the little girl two coins and she ran off, while Mick explained, "Jack Roman let's 'em stay in the shed that your pa 'ad his junk in 'long with three other orphan boys. Jack 'as the boys workin' for him as chimney sweeps."

Gladys was shocked. "But I thought using children to sweep chimneys was no longer allowed," she said.

"You forgets, Gladys, this is Old Nichol. Anyways, Jack's a good bloke. 'E an' 'is wife lives in your old 'ouse with their kiddies an' 'e hires a lotta boys so's they don't 'ave to work too hard. 'Is missus, she feeds them all when she 'as enough to."

"But that little girl, Bitsy—how old is this Joey?"

"'E's around seven or so. Their ma died a year ago. She called the girl 'Itsy Bitsy' 'cause she was such a little mite. But now everybody just calls her Bitsy."

"Well if you decide to take the job I offered you, I want you to bring Jack, his family, all the boys who work for him, and Bitsy, to live at the school. Did you decide what you are going to do?"

"Maud and me, we'd like to go with you, if you still want us to, but 'ow long would we 'ave to be gone? I 'as to leave young Bill in charge while I'm gone, you see, an' although 'e's a good lad, 'e's only a lad."

"We can pick you up at Warehouse Corner in the morning and catch the morning train, then we can bring you back the next day. How is that?" Percy asked.

"Blimey! I thought we would 'ave to be gone fer days. An' you say we's goin' by train?"

"Is that all right?" Gladys asked.

"An' if we decides to move, will we all be getting a ride on the train?"

When Gladys said they would, Mick called the rest of his family in and told them. For the first time since she met them, the children smiled. After they said goodbye, Gladys, Percy, and James left, but as much as they all wanted to leave the slums, Gladys persuaded them to drive past her old home. Strangely, it hadn't changed, except there were more old boards around the shed where her father kept his junk. Gladys thought they must have been put there to keep the cold out. She didn't say a word, and her expression didn't change, but tears were running down her cheeks as they left Old Nichol Street.

The feelings of nostalgia, regret, and sadness she experienced as she looked at the house she had been born in surprised her. She always knew she loved Sally, the woman who took her under her wing and taught her to read and write, but she had no idea that she loved her ma and da even more. When she had looked at the junk yard, she could picture her mother with her flaming red hair going through the trash while, every once in a while, breaking out in a lively song and a dance.

In the winter that red hair always seemed to add warmth and light to whatever room she was in. And how she had loved being picked up in her father's big hairy arms for a bear hug. That is what Gladys saw that day, instead of a drunken man, she called pa, who, with soiled trousers, was usually passed out on the floor. Nor did she feel the blows to her face and head delivered in angry outbursts by the drunken woman she called ma. That night, as they were dining, she said, "I did love them, you know." Percy and James knew she was talking about her mother and father and they just nodded.

Mick and Maud were thrilled with the train ride, and after seeing the cosy little cottage they would be living in when they came to the estate, they could hardly wait to get back home to tell the children.

They spent a night at Four Oaks before leaving for London, and after they left, Little Ines told Gladys that they hadn't slept under the covers and she couldn't understand why, but Gladys knew it was because they were afraid of dirtying the sheets.

Gladys gave Mick some money with instructions to choose the neediest families and orphans, then she told him to let her know when they were ready to come, and she would have someone pick them up. She even promised to bring them to Sandwich on the train so the journey wouldn't be too long. She also made him promise to try to persuade Joey, Bitsy, Mr. Roman, his family, and the rest of the boys he hired as chimney sweeps to come. Mick kept his promise, and she, James, and Percy didn't have to go back to Old Nichol. Inside of six months, the cottages were full, and they had twenty orphans in the mansion. Gladys' dream had come true.

Most of the ones who came were thrilled with their new surroundings, but there were a few adults who didn't care for work of any kind and just wanted free food and shelter. They were given three choices: do their share of the work, leave the school and make their own way in the world, or return to Old Nichol. Only one couple left. Most of the children and the adults were undernourished and sickly, so Iris' daughter, Dr. Greta, had her hands full looking after them.

After a year went by, the local people had witnessed the good work Greta Goebel was doing, and some of them asked if she would take them as patients. Before long, she had enough patients to open an office in Worth. She loved the people who lived in the little town, and two years after coming to the school, she married a local dentist. Now Iris had another reason for visiting Gladys, who seldom went to New York now that she had the school to keep her busy.

Because she reminded her of herself, Gladys was especially fond of the little girl, Bitsy, who was now, by her own sanction, called Betsy. At first, Betsy wasn't going to let strangers near her. No one but her brother was allowed to brush her hair, and, afraid she would fall out of it during the night, Betsy refused to sleep in a bed, so was given a pallet on the floor.

When Greta tried to examine her, she received a kick in the stomach, but then, when she allowed the child to listen to her heartbeat with the stethoscope, Dr. Greta became Betsy's idol. From then on, she would do whatever Greta asked her to, and followed the doctor around like a shadow whenever she had the chance. Betsy told everyone she was going to be a doctor just like Dr. Greta when she grew up, and Gladys believed she would be. There were many interesting stories concerning the orphans who came to the school. Gladys kept a journal that she read from time to time, and it gave her a great deal of satisfaction.

In 1880, Eliza gave birth to her third child, a girl they named Dorothy. The pregnancy and the birth went very well, and Eliza gained back her confidence. The same year, Eddy married Amelia Benson. Amelia wanted a small wedding at her father's home, with just the families attending, which suited Eddy as he hadn't as yet finished paying for the SS Delaney. Amelia had finished her nurses' training, but instead of volunteering at Angelo's school, she decided to go with Eddy on his ship. "You never know when a nurse will be needed," she told him. He was delighted.

As a wedding present, George Benson bought them a home in London, so they would have a place of their own when they were in port and a place to raise a family. "I intend to be there for my grandchildren, Gladys," he mentioned at the wedding. "I wasn't a very attentive father, as you know, and I shan't make that mistake with my grandchildren. I don't know how you get time to spoil yours like you do." Then he asked her if she would stay for a drink of brandy after the guests had left. She had an idea what he had in mind, but she didn't say no.

They were sitting in front of the fireplace sipping their brandy and Gladys thought how cosy it felt. It reminded her of the times she and James had sat in front of the fireplace in his library. "That was a very generous gift you gave the children, George. I'm afraid you are spoiling them," she said.

"No more than you, my dear, but they are both very special, don't you think?"

"Yes, I am very proud of them. They've worked hard for what they have and that is all one can ask. This is lovely, George, but I am tired and I should be getting back to the flat."

"Gladys, I asked you to stay for a reason. Now I shan't get down on one knee—I'm a little old for that sort of thing, but I am very fond of you, my dear, and I've wanted to ask you this for a long time now. Gladys Matthews, will you marry me?"

Although Gladys had expected it, the proposal still came as a shock. She was thinking of what to say, and George was afraid it was going to be a refusal, so he continued, "We are both alone, and I know how busy you are with the school. Perhaps I could help with that, but I want you to know that I wouldn't ask you to give any of it up for me. I think I shall make a good husband. What do you say?"

Gladys was touched by his proposal. She had grown fond of George these past few years, but she knew she could never marry again. Ever since he died, Gladys had felt Angelo's presence with her. Perhaps if she married again and slept with another man it would disappear and she didn't want that to happen. Angelo was the only man she would ever need. She reached out and took hold of George's hand as she gave him her answer. Looking into her eyes, he could understand how she felt and didn't feel offended. They ended their evening with a promise to remain good friends, and George said he would still like to help with the school, which Gladys gladly accepted.

Chapter 27

Eliza and Ben kept Gladys supplied with a new grandchild every second or third year until there were twelve: Sidney in 1876, little Gladys, who only lived for two months, in 1878, Dorothy in 1880, Major in 1884, Ernest in 1886, Hubert and Sybil (twins) in 1888, Christopher in 1890, Donald in 1893, Elizabeth in 1895, Madeline in 1898, and Nicholas in 1900.

Eddy and Amelia had four children: Gladys in 1880, Gloria in 1884, Carol in 1888, and Angela in 1890. Eddy had hoped to have a son to carry on his father's name, but when the last girl was born, and he and Amelia were told they couldn't have any more, he named her Angela. The admiral had meant it when he said he intended to be a good grandparent, and doted on each one of his granddaughters.

Gladys had begun to hand over some of her duties she was doing for the school, but she still felt the need to supervise all the departments to make sure the school didn't become too regimental. The following years were good years, but they slipped by far too quickly. Percy and James were both in their mid-eighties and both were plagued with what Percy referred to as, "This damnable rheumatism." Percy had rented out his London flat and moved in with James at Four Oaks, and since then, neither had left the estate unless they had to visit their doctors. James was thoughtful enough to keep his flat for Gladys and the family to use whenever they were in London.

In 1900, Percy suffered a fatal fall as he was coming downstairs for his breakfast. Gladys was surprised at how well James took his partner's death. All the family came for the funeral, except for Ben, who was away on business. James' oldest son, Horace, his wife, Sarah, and their son, Isaiah, came from Antwerp, but their daughter, Rachael, wasn't able to leave her husband, who had suffered a broken leg. Isaiah was a now a rabbi, and James was surprised to find his kind remarks very comforting. After the funeral, James asked Gladys, Eddy, Horace, Eliza, and Dolly if they would meet with him in the library.

Gladys protested, saying that she, Dolly, and Eddy were not part of the immediate family, but James laughed and said that, as he had never been able to get rid of them, that as far as he was concerned, they were all three adopted. James liked Eliza's husband, Ben, but he thought he was far too reckless and erratic. Unbeknownst to Eliza or Ben, he had made inquiries into his son-in-law's finances, and as a result, he knew it might not be long until his beloved Eliza and his eleven grandchildren would need his help. Therefore, he had made out a new will and he wanted to read it to them all.

"I have left all my shares in the shipping business to you, Horace, because I know now that you will never want to leave Antwerp and the Jewish community where you reside." Horace went to speak, but James stopped him, saying, "Wait until I've finished, son. Now, I have left Four Oaks to Eliza and Dolly, along with a monthly allowance for each of them as long as they both shall live. When they pass away, whatever is left is to be divided between the grandchildren."

When Dolly protested, he went on to say, "Dolly you have devoted your life to Eliza and her children, and you deserve to be treated as one of my own. Now, there is one stipulation I have added, and that is this: Gladys shall always have a home here. Gladys, you can forget about building your own place, because as long as you live, this is your home, and as you are practically right next door to the Angelo's school, you can keep active in the project.

"Edward, I shall give you your inheritance right now," James said as he held out a cheque. "I think this shall cover the down payment on that new steamship you have been looking at."

Eddy could not contain himself and cried out. "Oh, my God!"

James laughed. "You certainly never learned that from me. Percy and I had a joint bank account that we agreed should be used for a needy cause, and you, my boy, are our needy cause. So, Percy deserves as much credit as I do, bless his heart. Well, that is all I have to say. Now, is it acceptable to everyone?"

Horace was the first to reply, "I think you have been exceedingly fair, Father, and when the time comes, which I hope is not for years, I'll do my best to run your business as efficiently as you have."

Gladys cried when she thanked James. "You know, James, we could write a book about our lives, starting from the day Dolly and I first arrived at Four Oaks. How fortunate I was when you decided to hire me, and we didn't have to end up in the poor house."

"I almost didn't. If Dolly hadn't spotted that picture over the fireplace and said you had a picture like that of her father, we would not have been standing here together now."

"That's true, and after all these years, you're still making sure I have a roof over my head. I love you, James Hornsby."

"Yes, it would make quite a story, but I doubt anyone would believe it. Perhaps one of our grandchildren will turn out to be a writer and attempt to tell it," James replied.

After Percy died, James' health began to fail, and he passed away peacefully in his sleep six months later.

That following year, Eliza suffered a miscarriage and had to have a major operation, which meant she couldn't have any more children. It broke her spirit and ended her sexual desires. Ben was most understanding and doted on her as much as ever, which Gladys thought was a mistake. Eliza grew very fond of gin and gained a good deal of weight during the following years. She spent most of her days being waited on in her bedroom, leaving Dolly and Ben to raise the children, which they seemed to enjoy. Dolly looked happier than she had in years.

Ben enjoyed living extravagantly, and when his business was doing well, his boys attended the best schools, dressed in high collars and high hats. During those times, there would be at least three different cuts of meat on the table at every meal, along with as many desserts. Ben was always a jolly father and never scolded the children, who fortunately, were all well behaved, thanks to Dolly. They all attended church regularly, except Eliza, who often had a headache on Sundays, and when they were old enough, they all sang in the choir.

Unfortunately, Ben wasn't a keen businessman. He was too trusting and settled many of his dealings with nothing but a handshake. He was impulsive and often made hasty decisions that didn't always prove to be profitable. As a result, there were times when there was scarcely enough food on the table to go around, but even during those lean times, he always managed to take a tray up to Eliza, loaded with her favourite desserts.

Ben was also eccentric, and in 1888, when his twins were born, he was so thrilled and proud that he had a special little coach made to resemble the royal coach used for the queen on special occasions. The little coach was pulled by two well-groomed white goats, and Ben hired a man dressed as a groomsman to lead them. Hubert and Sybil were then coached to smile and wave at the spectators as they rode by. When they outgrew the coach, Ben gave it away.

All the boys were mechanically inclined, and after learning the machining trade, Sidney started a machine shop on the estate and proved to be an excellent teacher to the other boys.

Gladys loved each one of her grandchildren. They each had their own uniqueness, and she found them fascinating. Sidney loved to invent things but had no interest in selling his inventions. He loved animals, and as soon as he could afford to, he bought a horse. However, he wouldn't ride the beast, or allow anybody else to ride it, because he thought it was a cruel thing to do. Instead, he took it for long walks and to visit neighbouring horses.

Sybil insisted on wearing the same kind of clothing that Hubert, her twin brother, wore. She was very feminine in every other way and loved to play with dolls like her sisters, but as soon as she was old enough to express her opinions, she began wearing boys' clothes, insisting that they were far more comfortable and sensible.

Dolly and Ben allowed them their idiosyncrasies as long as they were mannerly and kind which they all were. Gladys was always amazed at the way they accepted each other's quirks without criticism, but her favourite was Hubert (Bert), one of the twins. Bert, the most musical of them all, was like Gladys and only had to hear a song once and he could sing it. By the time he was twenty, he could play both the piano and the violin. He was fine featured and had a good head of wavy black hair—a handsome young man blessed with a quick wit and a pleasing personality. Bert was also very popular among the church's young people, but it was his younger brother, Christopher (Chris) who looked up to him the most.

Actually, he didn't have to look up to him as Bert was only five foot nine. Nevertheless, he admired his older brother to such an extent that he was always ready to run his errands, shine his shoes, or do whatever necessary to be near him. Chris was a little slow compared to the rest of the boys, and although they never bullied him, they often ignored him. That is, everyone except Bert. Perhaps that was why Chris loved him so much, and because of Chris' kind nature, he was Gladys' second-favourite grandchild.

Gladys had been so busy with her grandchildren and the school that she only visited New York on special occasions, one of which was Victor and Iris' wedding. It was a small affair but a happy one, and Gladys was happy for them both. They took a trip out to the west coast for their honeymoon, and Iris said they had a marvellous time. Ten months later, Victor had a heart attack and died. It was a shock to them all. Victor had always been the steady one in the family, and Gladys missed him almost as much as Iris. Lottie's aunt Theresa died the same year.

Iris' boys were both married and living in California; her daughter Friedl and her husband were so busy with the bakery that she seldom saw them. She missed Victor so much that she decided she and her youngest daughter, Emma, should move to Worth so they could be near Greta and Gladys. Victor and Lottie's twin boys were both married and living in France. That meant Ike and Melissa were the only ones Gladys had to visit when she went to New York, and they came to Sandwich every time they had a chance, so she seldom left England.

James had been very perceptive when he willed Four Oaks to Eliza and Dolly, because five years later, Ben went bankrupt, lost Oaken Arms, and had to move his family into Four Oaks. Nevertheless, everyone took it good-naturedly and life continued as usual.

In 1909, the year of Gladys' eightieth birthday, Dolly and Eliza threw a surprise party and invited all her friends. It was a wonderful party, and Gladys sang a few songs, but because her fingers were afflicted with arthritis, she had Bert play for her. The thing she enjoyed most at the party was listening to him sing and play. After the guests had departed and Eliza and Ben had retired, Dolly brought a tray with two mugs of hot chocolate up to Gladys' suite and she lay on the bed beside her.

"Mother, we have to talk," she demanded. "You haven't looked well for months now. What are you keeping from me? And please, don't say you are just tired."

Gladys knew there was no sense keeping it from her. "You're right, darling, I'm not well, but I didn't see the sense in burdening you with my troubles. There's nothing you could do, and thanks to Greta, I am able to dull the pain with medication."

"So you have been seeing Greta. What did she say it is?"

"It's nothing that can be cured, but I've lived to see another century, and I've had a wonderful life, so please, don't feel sad."

"Oh, Mama, I'm so sorry, but I'm so glad you are here with us. Did Greta say how long you have?"

"She said it could be months or even a year, if I'm lucky. The school is doing well, and they don't need me anymore. Whatever time I have, I am going to enjoy just with you and my family, but I want you to do something for me, dear. I want to be cremated and some of my ashes taken to New York and spread over Angelo's grave. You can ask Eddy to do that; I know he will want to. The rest I want spread at his school. Will you see to that when the time comes?"

"Are you sure you want to be cremated?" Dolly shivered. "I don't even like to think of it."

"I've read a lot about it, dear, and I think it is a far more civilized method of disposing of bodies than burying them. Please, promise you will do it." Dolly promised she would. "Now I want to know how you are. You seem so content lately, and it makes me feel that way too. Do you still love him?"

"Yes, but not passionately—it is more like we are the best of friends. We have done so much together that I sometimes feel I've been married to him all these years, and I think, in his own way, Ben loves me too. I wouldn't change a thing, even if I could."

The following year, Gladys' grandson Ernest (Ernie) was working on a job in Dover for the government and he fell and landed on his head. Thereafter, every full moon, he suffered with severe headaches. On one such occasion, Ben called in a doctor, who, he told the family, was employed by the queen herself. Everyone was anxiously waiting in the parlour when the doctor came in after he finished his examination. The prognosis was that Ernie needed a change of atmosphere and it was suggested he go abroad. Although he had a fiancée at the time, he was thrilled with the idea, and promised to return in two years to marry her.

Because Canada was a British colony, it was the destination chosen. Ben wasn't about to allow one of his boys to go to such an untamed world by himself, and he decided Bert should accompany him. This was exactly what Bert had always dreamed of. Ben insisted the boys have first-class accommodations, but he didn't have money to give them to spend when they landed. Gladys wanted to give them some, but they refused, determined to support themselves. "Don't you worry about us, Gran," Bert assured her, "We shall be on the ship for two Sundays, and Ernie can preach while I play my violin or sing, then we shall pass the collection plate around.

"I shall take a pair of shears and offer to cut hair for a fee, and there are other things we can do to raise money. Anyway, I am certain we shall have jobs the day after we arrive. Oh, Gran, how I wish you were coming. We would have such an adventure!"

"You shall never know how very much I'd love that, my darling," Gladys said, and she meant it.

Christopher was upset that he couldn't go along, but as usual, he didn't complain. He did, however, promise himself that he would follow as soon as Bert was settled. Although Bert and Sybil were twins, they were never that close—Bert preferring to chum with his male siblings and Sybil with the girls, so it wasn't such a heart-breaking parting for them as one might think. Ernie's fiancée, a very trusting and devoted young lady, was content to wait for two years, and didn't burden him with a lot of tears.

Although Gladys wasn't feeling well, she did manage the trip to London with the rest of the family to see the boys off, and as she stood on the pier and watched the boat sail away, she remembered the first time she went to America. She kissed her glove then blew the kiss out to sea with a message, "The adventures are all yours, now, Bert, my darling boy. Oh, how I wish I could still be here to hear about them."

Acknowledgements

To my wonderful family and friends who always go the extra mile to ensure I have a successful book launch.

To FriesenPress for making my book presentable.

About the Author

Betty Annand lives in Courtenay, British Columbia. As a writer, she is often inspired by the stories told to her by her "interesting and eccentric" English father about growing up in the old country.

The Lady from New York is the third novel in her successful historical-fiction trilogy, featuring her 19th-century protagonist, Gladys. The other two books in the series, *The Girl from Old Nichol* (2016) and *The Woman from Dover* (2017), were published by Amberjack publishing. Betty has also penned many comedy plays, crediting her experiences and what she calls "the most important credible source—a lively imagination."

Along with her trilogy, Betty has published other books, including *Growing up in the White House* (1999), *Voices from Bevan* (2002), and *Voices from Courtenay Past* (2004).